SUCKER PUNCH

E. M. STOWERS

SILVERSMITH
PRESS

Published by Silversmith Press–Houston, Texas
www.silversmithpress.com

Copyright © 2025 E. M. Stowers

All rights reserved.

ISBN 978-1-961093-97-3 (Softcover Book)
ISBN 978-1-961093-98-0 (eBook)

To those who have served in uniform past,
present, and future.

And to Chris Harrison.

"The most likely sneak attack you will encounter is the sucker punch. This is a lowdown jarhead tactic that requires the element of surprise. By staying aware, you eliminate this element. No surprise, no ambush. Beware of the sucker punch."
—PO1 "Mugs" Brenton, U.S.N.
"A Sailor's Guide to Brawling on Liberty"

LIST OF TERMS & ACRONYMS

AI	Artificial Intelligence
APU	Auxiliary Power Unit
ASAP	As Soon As Possible
BATDIV	Battleship Division
BB	Battleship
CA	Heavy Cruiser
CL	Light Cruiser
CHOP	Change of Operational Procedure
CIC	Combat Information Center
CINC2FLT	Commander-IN-Chief, Second Fleet
CO	Commanding Officer
CPO	Chief Petty Officer
CT	Corvette
CTU	Commander, Task Unit
DCD	Damage Control Department
DCP	Damage Control Party
DD	Destroyer
DSM	Drive-Seeking Missile
ECM	Electronic Counter-Measures

EMCON	Emission Control
EMP	Electro-Magnetic Pulse
FF	Frigate
GNP	Gross National Product
GQ	General Quarters
HUD	Heads up display
ID	Identification
IG	Imperial Guard
IKN	Imperial Karsian Navy
IFF	Identification, Friend or Foe
ITF	Imperial Task Force
LED	Light-Emitting Diode
NCS	Network Control Station (data link)
NIS	Naval Investigation Service
NCO	Non-Commissioned Officer
OB-GYN	Obstetrician-Gynecologist
OCS	Officer Candidate School
ODS	Orbital Defense Station
KPS	Kilometers Per Second
MIF	Missile In Flight
PB	Particle Beam
PBM	Planetary Bombardment Missile
PD	Point Defense
PDM	Point Defense Missile
PO	Petty Officer
RCN	Rigelian Confederation Navy
Rmax	Maximum Range
ROE	Rules Of Engagement
SAR	Search And Rescue

LIST OF TERMS & ACRONYMS

SITREP	Situation Report
SM-1	Standard Missile Type 1
SRAM	Short Range Attack Missile
SSBM	Stealthship, Bombardment Missile
TAC-O	Tactical Officer
TF	Task Force
TU	Task Unit
UCMJ	Uniform Code of Military Justice
WEZ	Weapon Employment Zone
XO	Executive Officer

RCN TERMS

Bladeship	Karsian Stealthship
Bird	Friendly Anti-ship Missile
Bogey	Unknown Contact
Chick	Point Defense Missile (PDM)
Darter	A Class Of Karsian Corvette
Flasher	Energy Torpedo
Klick	Kilometer
Laroussi Field	Cold Plasma Cloaking Field
Lidar	Light Detection and Ranging
Mike	Minute
Omega Code	A code transmitted by a dying ship
Podkletnov Field	Electro-Gravitic Shield
Spoofer	Fake individual or decoy on a frequency
Squawk	IFF code
Tin Can	Slang term for destroyer

| Vampire | Enemy Anti-ship Missile |
| Whiffer | Karsian WF-320 Fighter |

KARSIAN WORDS

Blik	A lactating Karsian domestic beast
Bor'barhg	Over-General (Army)
Bor'klar	Captain (Navy)
Ceyon	Dihexagonal quartz
Darhk'lar	Imperial Army
In'thork	Imperial Guard
Kahthrung	Council of Elders
Kahduhn	Imperial Military
Korguhn	Grand Admiral
K'jir	Conquered people
K'Leesh	A class of midget bladeship
K'toor	Slaves
Ong	Three seconds
Peshai	Toxic or poisonous
Por'tahk	Unbalancing (a tactic)
Shan'lar	Imperial Navy
Shikahn	Emperor
Shiguhn	High Admiral
Shi-thrung	Imperial Court
Sho-ya	Three-ship formation of fighters
Talik	Curdled *blik* milk
Thrung	House (clan)
Thrung-tahli	Clan brother
Thrung'tohk	Thrung chief

LIST OF TERMS & ACRONYMS

Torguhn	Admiral
T'yoni'akar	The star Gulliver
Yihak	Ambassador
Yi'rhang	Over-Lieutenant
Yi'rhork	Over-Commander

PROLOGUE

At first there was Old Terra and her colonies, but as humanity expanded, distance isolated groups of humans among the stars, leaving colonies alone and out of contact. Isolated groups had created new nations and cultures. Such differences brought humans into conflict many times. The greatest was the Interstellar War of 2441 in which the *Rigelian* colonies, allied with a small number of alien worlds, seceded from Old Earth and the United Terran League.

The Rigelian Confederation was a series of star states linked, like all interstellar societies, via "stargates," the hyperspace wormholes allowing ships to jump from one star to another.

The Rigelian Confederation Navy defended Confederation worlds and trade routes with other nations. The Periphery of the Confederation, called the Rim, faced the Empire of Kars, an aggressive and hostile collection of alien star systems. Though contact between the Empire and the Confederation was a T-century old, peace remained fragile and uneasy.

To provide early warning, the RCN saturated the Rim with remote sensors and warship patrols. Theoretically such efforts would prevent *Karsian* ships from entering Confederation space unannounced.

But every theory has its flaws . . .

CHAPTER 1

"Torpedoes inbound!"

The call from the sensor station grabbed Harl Comforti's attention instantly. Comforti commanded RNSS *Gant*, a Brave-class destroyer in the service of the Rigelian Confederation Navy.

Well, what did you expect? Comforti chastised himself as he turned to face the tactical holographic display bubble on Gant's bridge. *Especially after playing cat and mouse with a sensor ghost for the last six hours.*

"Sound general quarters—" Comforti spoke calmly as he turned to pull the pressure suit from the back of his acceleration couch, nodding in approval as other bridge crew reacted in similar manner. "Raise shields. Sensors, bearing and range to those torpedoes."

Petty Officer Peterson replied without missing a beat

even as he donned his own vacuum suit. "Torpedoes bear zero-four-five mark one-zero-eight, Sir."

Comforti grimaced and pulled on his gloves. "Heading?"

"Two-two-five mark zero-eight-two, Skipper."

"Give me a range, Joey."

"Sorry, Sir. Thirteen-point-five light-seconds."

Comforti pulled the pressure helmet over his head, locking it into the neck rings of his vacuum suit. Getting the green light of a good seal, he sat back in his g-couch and began strapping in. "Petty Officer Jackson, bring us starboard one-three-zero mark zero-niner-zero and increase acceleration 3,000 KPS."

Ronald Jackson, Gant's helmsman, responded instantly. "Starboard one-three-zero mark zero-niner zero, increasing acceleration three thousand klicks per second, aye, Sir."

The torpedoes are off our port beam. Comforti tightened his couch straps. *That should optimize our later sensors and weapon arcs.*

Gant had detected the sensor ghost six hours earlier while patrolling the Pan'vu test range, an area of Rim space reserved for the purpose of testing new weapons. The test range faced the border of the Empire of Kars, which meant the RCN was always on alert for unknown vessels entering the range from the border. Relations with the Empire were sketchy at best, and currently tense due to trade negotiations happening at Rigel 2. To prevent unknown entries, the RCN had placed sensors along the Rim. Starship drives and emitters were easily detected by passive sensors.

CHAPTER 1

There had been no ships on the sensor grid when Peterson had picked up the random drive signal six hours ago. The source had appeared and faded, as if *Gant* had crossed through the wake of a passing ship, though no obvious drives readings had been noted. Comforti had ordered a wall of sensor remotes deployed to sniff for more indications. At first there'd been nothing, making Comforti feel the contact might have been spurious, but three of the sensor remotes had detected the same source. Peterson had triangulated bearings from the remotes and narrowed the area of probability to a small triangle of space, which became the search datum. Comforti had ordered *Gant* to the search datum to conduct a detailed localization of the source.

The fact no drive emissions had been detected on passive sensors indicted the bogey was stealthed. A ship crossing the border from Imperial space required clearance from the RCN in advance. That meant known transponder IFF codes and open communications with the RCN on arrival. The sensor ghost had done none of those things. It was trying to sneak in unobserved. The fact it was cloaked was a sign of hostile intent.

Under interstellar rules of engagement, warship captains could engage ships committing hostile acts or demonstrating sufficient hostile intent. Hostile acts meant launching weapons, active jamming, deploying mines or inserting troops or machines of war into Confederation space. Hostile intent was more subtle, and included things like disguising a ship's identity, cloaking, laying chaff corridors, or maneuvering into recognized weapons launch parameters. Captains had a right to defend their ship from attack and could attack any vessel committing a hostile act.

Comforti tapped the intercom on his armrest. "You suited up in CIC, Bobby Joe?"

"Yes, Sir."

The irritation in the voice of Lieutenant Commander Robert Laird was evident across the intercom. RCN regulations required skippers and executive officers to locate to different compartments when a ship went to any alert level higher than Condition Two. They had gone to Condition Two almost two hours ago, when Peterson's sensor AI had identified the ghost ship drive as a Cosmon-C, a type of fusion drive associated with Karsian bladeships. Laird had reported to the Combat Information Center at that time. The procedure prevented the likelihood of commander and executive officer being taken out by a single hit to the bridge.

Laird, *Gant's* executive officer, hailed from the Core Worlds and considered himself Cosmopolitan. Comforti and most of *Gant's* crew were from the Skosian Sector, a group of stars populated mainly by humans of Anglo-Saxon heritage who'd adopted Old South culture centuries ago. Comforti knew Laird considered Skosians to be frontier hicks and privately considered himself more sophisticated. First-and-middle name combinations were common on Skosian worlds, and they irked his executive officer to no end. Which was precisely why Comforti needled him with the name "Bobby Joe." It irritated his XO but was a curmudgeonly form of affection.

CHAPTER 1

Comforti studied the tactical plot. "The ROE's been tripped, XO. Weapons Officer, arm all missile launchers. Set the birds for dispersed volley, proximity detonation, and staggered interval. Power up all beam batteries."

Comforti leaned back in his couch and took a deep breath.

It's strange how normal this all seems, how relaxed and calm we sound, considering we're about to fire actual weapons at people. This feels like simulator training . . . which I suppose is precisely how's it's supposed to feel.

Comforti took a slow breath and steeled himself. "Standby to flush external missile racks one and two. Peterson, where are those torpedoes?"

"Zero-three-six mark one-niner-eight, Skipper. Range is nine light-seconds."

Peterson sounds calm too, considering the enemy's fired real torpedoes at us.

"Bearing and mark on the hostile."

Peterson bent forward to study his displays. "Hostile bears zero-four-zero mark one-one-zero, Sir, range 11.04 light-seconds. She's making for the Pan'vu stargate."

Laird's voice spoke softly in Comforti's helmet headset. "Skipper, I know the ROE's tripped, and we can legally engage but if we do you know what it means."

Comforti felt perspiration trickle down his spine inside the pressure suit. It was odd he could sweat in a temperature-controlled vac-suit. Laird's comment irritated him. "We're in combat now, XO. It started the moment they launched torpedoes at us. The ROE's been met, and we're engaging."

"There might be other options, Sir. Perhaps we should—"

"Negative, Mr. Laird. We're engaging."

Laird hesitated. "Aye, Sir."

Peterson pointed at the tactical display. "Torpedoes changing course, Skipper; new heading's one-five-zero mark zero-eight-six and accelerating."

Comforti glanced at the display and compressed his lips. *The torpedoes changed course due to our turn. They're tracking us. Their onboard AIs have calculated the isosceles lead geometry needed to intercept us.*

Lieutenant Osborne's voice interrupted his thoughts. "Birds powered, Sir."

Gant's SM-1 anti-ship missiles had a powered flight time of ninety seconds. Coilgun-launched, they would accelerate at 50,000 g's until drive burnout. In a minute and a half the missiles would travel nearly two million kilometers before going ballistic with a terminal velocity of 14 percent cee, making the SM-1's maximum effective range six light-seconds against maneuvering targets.

Comforti nodded. "How long until the hostile's in range, Peterson?"

"At present closure, three mike, Sir."

Three minutes? That's forever in combat.

"Shield status?"

The voice of Lieutenant David Harrison, *Gant's* engineering officer, answered in Comforti's headset. Harrison was in CIC with Laird. "Podkletnov fields at 100 percent, Skipper."

6

Okay, shields are up, structural integrity fields are energized. What's next?

"Weapons status?"

Osborne's soprano voice answered. "Birds powered, Sir. Beam capacitors at 94 percent."

Osborne sounds calm too.

Comforti nodded. "Very well. Go active with all lidars. Activate jamming and point defense arrays. Helm, bring us port to zero-five-eight, mark zero-niner zero."

Osborne turned at her console, her green eyes meeting his through their face plates. "R-max, Captain."

Maximum missile range.

"Flush racks one and two."

"Flushing racks one and two, aye." Osborne whirled back to her weapons' console. "Rack one firing. Birds away."

Gant lurched as a pair of missiles ejected from her number one external launcher and zipped away pulling fifty thousand gravities of acceleration.

Osborne spoke again. "Rack two firing. Birds away, Skipper."

Four hair-like strings of light appeared in the tactical display moving away from the green icon representing *Gant* at the center of the bubble. They moved toward the red icon of the bladeship. Comforti's eyes drifted to the flashing red lines of the torpedoes closing on Gant's port side, pulling lead to intercept. "We'll follow our birds in, folks, and finish off what's left with beams."

Laird spoke again in his ear. "Sir, I can take down those torpedoes right now with energy weapons."

Comforti studied the display. Gant's main beam batteries consisted of two 75 centimeter particle beam projectors and a pair of 70 centimeter lasers. The torpedoes were still too far away for point defenses to engage but were within main beam range.

"Negative, Mr. Laird. No need to waste capacitor energy on torpedoes at this range. We'll need those beams if we have to reengage after our birds detonate. Let point defenses handle them."

Laird's reply was muted. "Aye, Sir."

Comforti watched with rapt attention as Gant's missiles closed on the red icon of the hostile. Tabular displays indicated the missiles' vectors, velocities and remaining time to detonation. The missiles would soon achieve their terminal velocity of forty-four thousand kilometers per second.

Comforti grinned at his crew. "Our birds will reach him before his torps can reach us." Everyone knew missiles and beams were faster than torpedoes. A torpedo's primary advantage was its longer range and greater warhead. "They've shot their bolt, folks . . . the last act of desperate men."

Comforti wasn't sure who, but someone quietly corrected him on the intercom.

"You mean Karsians, Sir."

CHAPTER 1

IKS *YAHK'TAH*

"Missile launch detected," Thrung Warrior First Class Mangtoh announced as he activated Yahk'tah's structural containment fields. "The enemy has fired on us."

Yahk'tah was a K'Leesh-class bladeship of the Imperial Karsian Navy carrying a crew of two. Activating structural containment fields was standard procedure for bladeships under attack. The fields were internal and would not emit beyond the bladeship's hull. As with all stealthship designs, *Yahk'tah* minimized emissions while operating under stealth. Unlike RCN stealthships, bladeships did not use cloaking fields to hide them from sensors. Instead, angled hull facets and lidar-absorbent coatings were used to minimize enemy lidar. Only two emissions came from a bladeship. One was a short-range navigation deflector to keep dust and micro-meteors from hitting the bow. The other was a focused tube of energy from the ship's drive field, which projected due aft of the ship in a narrow cone. Unless an enemy stumbled directly into one of them, a bladeship under stealth could not be detected.

The other warrior aboard was the bladeship's commander, Over-Lieutenant Torgh, who had launched torpedoes at an RCN destroyer that had been dogging Yahk'tah's course for some time.

It was understandable, of course. The enemy destroyer had been trailing them for some time and the young commander of Yahk'tah had felt threatened. *Yahk'tah* had a strict rendezvous schedule to meet if the planned

9

operations were to be executed on the briefed timetable. Somehow the enemy had detected Yahk'tah's presence and had closed in. Torgh had decided to destroy it with torpedoes rather than let it send word to the RCN a bladeship was in the test range. Two torpedoes had been launched at the destroyer before Torgh had ordered Mangtoh to make for the Pan'vu jump gate.

The launch of torpedoes had allowed the enemy ship to pinpoint Yahk'tah's azimuth. Now active lidars were pinging from multiple directions, providing both bearing and range data to each lidar. The enemy had them pinpointed, and now missiles were headed their way. Without shields, Yahk'tah stood little chance of survival. The structural containment fields were a forlorn hope.

"De-stealth, Mangtoh." Torgh leaned forward in his battle couch, his dark eyes glittering under bushy brows as he stared at the tactical display. "Full power to the drive. Get us to that jump gate. Our one chance is to jump before those missiles reach us."

"We are receiving lidar scans from multiple axis, Yi'rhang." Unlike the officer, Mangtoh referred to Torgh only by his rank, not his name.

Torgh frowned. "How many Rigelian vessels are out there?"

"I do not know, Yi'rhang. Our lidar is secured for stealth."

"Well, activate it, fool!"

"If I activate the lidar, they will know exactly where we are, Yi'rhang."

CHAPTER 1

"They already know that. They've fired missiles at us."

Chagrined, Mangtoh activated Yahk'tah's single lidar scanner. "Only one enemy ship detected, Yi'rhang, the destroyer that fired the missiles at us."

"Where are those other scans coming from?" Torgh leaned forward, studying his displays. Mangtoh noted the officer's face was a mixture of anger and fear. "Ah, the enemy has deployed sensor buoys, Mangtoh. Some of them are active and scanning us. That's where those other lidars are coming from. We cannot hide under this kind of sensor scrutiny. Accelerate to maximum speed and deploy chaff canisters. Release the decoy, as well. That might distract a missile or two."

Torgh watched the twin cluster of RCN missiles close on Yahk'tah in the display. He realized they would not reach the jump gate before the RCN missiles reached them. Without shields, Yahk'tah was doomed. "We have failed the Shikahn, Mangtoh."

Mangtoh let his eyes drift to the face of his commanding officer. The young officer appeared both defeated and resigned, but he was all warrior and refused to flinch in the face of duty. Mangtoh admired that. Torgh was young, but a fighter to the last. He glanced at his weapons display. "Our torpedoes are closing on the destroyer, Yi'rhang."

"Good. I hope they are the nasty surprises I intended them to be." Torgh ran a three-digit hand across his face and sighed. "Either way, you and I are dead."

Mangtoh saluted him, fist over heart. "We die with honor, Yi'rhang."

Torgh's face hardened as he returned the salute. "For the Shikahn."

Two RCN missiles detonated a split-second later, fusing the hydrogen and lithium in their warheads. Their detonations joined in a massive explosion. A new sun appeared, vaporizing *Yahk'tah* in a searing nova of light.

RNSS *GANT*

"Yes!" Comforti pounded his fist against his armrest. "Nailed him! Helm, bring us ninety degrees to port. Mister Laird, take down those torpedoes."

Laird was on the ball. "*PDMs, you're weapons free.*"

"*PDMs Weapons Free, aye. Chicks away, bridge.*"

Four point defense missiles spat from *Gant* and arced to intercept the torpedoes as onboard targeting AIs calculated intercept courses. The torpedoes were still an eighth of a light-second away when the first PDM reached them. The first torpedo vanished in an explosion. The detonation of the first torpedo transmitted a destruct code to the second torpedo at the speed of light, far faster than any PDM could travel. Upon receiving the first torpedo's Omega code, the second torpedo released sub-munitions: six independently-targeted missiles. Less than two seconds later, another of Gant's point defense missiles destroyed the second torpedo's empty shell.

The damage was done, however. The genies were

out of the bottle. Six missiles boosted toward *Gant* at high acceleration.

Laird's voice rose over the intercom. "*All point defenses, fire!*"

Only a single point defense crew was keeping close track of the torpedoes and managed to target the submunitions in time. Most defense crews had been confident the torpedoes would be destroyed by the PDMs. As a result, only *Gant*'s forward battery of point defense lasers fired, stabbing out at the incoming submunitions. The battery shot well, destroying four of the missiles a second before the surviving pair slammed into *Gant*'s shields.

The deck lurched wildly. Comforti, who had unstrapped, was thrown upward, even as shield generators throughout the ship short-circuited and plasma flared across *Gant*'s shields. At each failure point, tiny holes appeared in the shields, allowing terajoules of energy to burn through. Hull armor melted and fused. Some bulkheads buckled.

Gant rolled with the impact, vibrating like a ringing bell as she slewed to one side. Dozens of tiny ruptures pierced her hull as damage control alarms screamed amid the chaos and loss of internal atmospheric pressure.

In CIC, Laird felt the artificial gravity go offline. The ship began a slow spin, tumbling end-over-end. Lateral g-forces crushed Laird against the side of his seat. Pressure alarms screamed in his headset as *Gant* lost internal atmosphere. On the CIC relays, he saw Comforti ricochet off the bridge overhead and bounce along the deck.

Laird released his own straps and hurled himself across CIC in zero-g. Opening the overhead hatch, he took the emergency tube to the bridge to assist his stricken captain. The CIC hatch closed behind him as he sailed through the tube in zero-g toward the bridge several decks above. The monitors at the top said the bridge still had some atmospheric pressure, so he used the airlock to pressurize before opening the inner hatch and pulling himself inside.

Peterson was hovering over the skipper. Laird pulled himself forward across the bridge by hand. He turned Comforti onto his back, quickly checking the pressure seal on his commander's vac-suit in case the bridge vented to space. Seeing a green light, indicating a good seal, he relaxed somewhat.

As personnel recovered on the bridge, Laird struggled to take command. "Damage Control, report. Helm, cease all acceleration."

"Helm, aye, ceasing acceleration. Going dead in space."

The term was anachronistic. There was no such thing as a true stop in space. It only indicated helm had chopped power to the drive and the ship was coasting ballistically.

Laird felt relief when Comforti's eyes fluttered. Almost as quickly, he felt anger. The skipper had made a tactical error by not using beams to take out the torpedoes at long range. Energy weapons traveled at the speed of light, faster than fusion motors could ever accelerate a PDM. Lasers would have destroyed both torpedoes early enough to give the point defenses a better chance of picking off secondary munitions.

CHAPTER 1

Even Middies at the Academy know you kill seeking weapons as far away as possible, preferably at maximum range, because there's no telling what's inside the damned things.

A skipper didn't ignore the soundness of a tactic to save a few terawatts of capacitor energy, not when he had a full set of operating fusion reactors at his disposal. It had been a bad tactical decision, the type even newbie ensigns didn't make. It was why the RCN required line officers to train in battle tactics from the Academy onward. Comforti was only human, however. He'd killed the enemy vessel, but he'd gotten overconfident, and it had cost his own ship dearly.

Comforti floated an inch over the deck, holding his right arm gingerly. From the expression in his eyes, Laird knew the skipper had realized his mistake too. Nothing good would come from pointing it out, however, at least not at the moment.

"You okay, Skipper?"

"My arm's broken—" Comforti spoke through clenched teeth. "I've got a good seal, though. No leaks in the suit. Thanks, Bobby Joe."

"I'll get a corpsman to the bridge, Sir."

"No, see to my ship, Mr. Laird. Get things under control first. Launch a comm drone to Pan'vu and inform the Fleet we've engaged and destroyed a Karsian bladeship in the test range. After that, get a damage control assessment of the ship. When that's accomplished, then maybe we'll take a look at my arm."

"Yes, Sir."

Laird gave an order to the communications petty officer, and a single long-endurance drone launched from *Gant*. The hypervelocity communications drone quickly adjusted course and accelerated toward the Pan'vu stargate at high speed.

"Comm drone's away, Skipper." Laird helped Comforti orient into a more upright position. "It'll terminate at 0.97 cee, Sir, but that'll still take it fourteen minutes to reach the stargate and wormhole. Pan'vu should have word within a quarter of an hour."

"Let me know when it jumps. Damage report?"

"We've got several holes in the hull, Skipper, but we've stabilized pressure and we're sealing the leaks. I've ordered helm to idle, so we're currently ballistic. We're still leaking atmosphere, but not badly. No major structural damage reported."

"Casualties?"

Laird glanced at the damage control monitors. "Two dead, seventeen wounded, Sir."

Comforti closed his eyes. "My God."

"You did what you could, Skipper."

"The hell I did. I screwed up, and you know it. Two crewmen dead, a dozen and a half injured, and my ship damaged. All because I got overconfident going into battle."

"We were lucky, Sir. If point defenses hadn't stopped most of those warheads..."

"We'd be a shattered hulk . . . or a ball of ionized gas. I *know*, XO."

The helmsman's voice spoke over their helmet intercoms. "Drive field neutral, Sir. We're ballistic."

After a minute, the helmsman put a slow rolling spin on the ship about its longitudinal axis to induce centrifugal force as simulated gravity. It would have to do until artificial gravity systems were working again. As apparent gravity returned, Laird helped Comforti to his feet.

"Take charge of the damage control efforts, Bobby Joe. Let me know when the mains are back online. Get corpsmen to the wounded ASAP. I'll be in the Ready Room."

Laird blinked. It was an odd time for the captain to desire privacy. He should be on the bridge, commanding. "The Ready Room, Sir?"

"Yes, logging this incident." Comforti turned to move away. "And my resignation."

Laird watched him go, speechless.

Minutes later and far away, the communications drone reached a gravitational vortex between stars and began broadcasting its warning on Fleet Common frequency.

A moment later it entered the stargate and jumped, vanishing from the test range.

ZION'S WASTE
RIGELIAN CONFEDERATION SPACE

One by one starships appeared from the wormhole terminus and aligned into battle formation as they angled toward the next stargate in the void.

Thirteen super dreadnoughts came through first,

forming a protective vanguard as they searched for threats with active and passive sensors. Detecting nothing, the battle wall moved away from the stargate to make room for the eighteen battleships that followed. Behind those came cruisers and destroyers, followed by dozens of frigates and corvettes. Behind those came the heavy carriers. Only after all ships had arrived did the carriers make transition, lagging well behind the battle wall for protection.

The fleet numbered over three hundred warships. It was a battle fleet at war and went about its business with deadly purpose. The fleet assumed a fighting formation providing overlapping fields of fire as it moved out across the starless nexus.

Behind and well to one side of the stargate terminus, a massive saucer shape flickered momentarily into view before fading from the visible spectrum. Inside the stealthed craft, alien eyes observed the fleet with silent intensity.

The *Reticulan* turned from the viewing port and moved among the *dumong*, careful to avoid the small, blue-hued creatures lest they trip him and damage his body. The Reticulan was not used to the high gravity levels *Yahntai* preferred, so it moved slowly to avoid strain. Halting before a looming Yahntai, the Reticulan waited, its bug-like black eyes unblinking.

<*Are we secure from detection?*>

The question arrived as thought, for Yahntai were telepaths like all advanced species.

<*Yes.*> The Reticulan gave a mental shrug to color the

thought. *<We have completed shift and are out-of-phase with this dimension. Their sensors cannot detect us.>*

The Yahntai rippled, apparently satisfied. *<How do you evaluate this new batch of strains?>*

<As foreseen.> The Reticulan moved to stand beside the Yahntai and stare out of the viewing port. *<The experiment proceeds according to plan. The cultures have achieved the desired technology levels. Now they must be polished to improve effectiveness.>*

<It seems a shame.> The Yahntai inclined its massive head, a sign of regret. *<So much raw material going to waste.>*

<Materials are always lost during refinement. It is the way of this dimension.> The Reticulan didn't blink, but its eyes rippled subtly. *<The cultures must be improved to be of use. We have an endless supply of cultures, but these strains have proven most promising. Our mandate requires we obtain the most effective strain possible. In this case, that means survival-of-the-fittest.>*

<Have all contingencies been anticipated?> The Yahntai's disapproval was evident by its tone. *<What if they do not perform as expected, or annihilate each other?>*

The Reticulan stared out of the viewport a long moment before answering. It turned its large head slowly, making it appear doll-like. *<Phage is required to improve the strains. Transduction is possible, but controls were embedded in each strain during its creation. All fail-safes are in place. Both cultures progress according to plan.>*

<And what will you do if they advance too fast and change

the plan? What are our options if the randomness built into them becomes unpredictable and they become a threat to us?>

<Then we shall start over, as we have before.>

<Is there still time?>

<Time is relative.> The Reticulan tilted its head, its thoughts pensive. *<Perhaps.>*

In the viewport the warships accelerated, racing away against the backdrop of stars.

Moments later they were lost from view.

CHAPTER 2

Talara Kibbleman tightened her space-black tunic and gazed at her sleeves in the mirror of her quarters. Only yesterday, when her promotion to lieutenant had become official, had she dared add the second set of sleeve rings. The braided rings glowed gold against the black of her sleeve, with twin rows of silver planets and stars etched into the golden bands.

"Those look good on you," a male voice spoke from behind her. Startled, she turned to find Egon watching.

"Oh, it's you." She turned back to the mirror.

Feigning a look of hurt, Egon Storm wrapped an arm around her waist. "Of course it's me. You sound disappointed. You expecting someone else?"

Talara gave him a kiss on the cheek. "No, silly, I thought the Skipper, or the XO may've dropped by. I can't believe this day has finally arrived."

21

"Well, it has, Tilly." He smiled, using his private nickname for her as he pulled her close. "Believe it."

They'd only recently become lovers, though she and Egon had been friends for three years. She stared into his hazel eyes, marveling about all that had changed in that time.

Egon continued speaking, oblivious to her thoughts. "You've done pretty well. You're a full lieutenant now and the new chief engineer of *Kuroshima*. You should be proud, Talara."

She snuggled against him, enjoying his warmth.

Egon was seven years her senior in age and time-in-grade. A senior lieutenant, he was due for promotion to lieutenant commander, but for the moment they were of equal rank.

She had met him at the Academy when he'd guest lectured there on battle wall tactics. At the time, Egon had been assigned to the cruiser *El Jaffa* as a new graduate of the prestigious Navy Weapons School. He had served his first tour as an enlisted rating in the sensor department of a warship before applying to Officer Candidate School. So far he'd served aboard *Custer*, *El Jaffa*, *Kuroshima*, and *Shiva*.

She paused, reflecting on that time. After the lecture, she'd approached to ask him questions about the energy management of beam weapons from an engineering perspective. Egon had seemed friendly, and they'd struck up a pen-pal relationship, later exchanging regular communications via v-mail.

Talara had completed her engineering degree at the

Academy and was a commissioned ensign in the RCN before she saw him again. Her first assignment had been to the destroyer *Kuroshima*, where she'd been posted as junior engineering officer. There she'd been pleasantly surprised to find Egon was the ship's new tactical officer. On *Kuroshima* they'd renewed their acquaintance.

Early on it had been strictly professional. At the time she hadn't seen Egon as an object of desire because she'd been hopelessly involved with another officer. Soon after her assignment to *Kuroshima*, however, that relationship had deteriorated.

Lieutenant Gary Göering, a self-centered fighter jock, had been more interested in his conquests at the O-Club bar than he'd ever been in her needs. Gary had been adamantly against her assignment to a destroyer, despite being too preoccupied with his own career to pay hers much attention. His lack of interest had hurt, and his objection to her assignment had created resentment. The relationship had come crashing down when she'd received a text-only message from him. The "Dear Jane" letter, arriving coldly over Fleet text, had broken her heart.

Looking back, Talara knew she hadn't truly been surprised. She'd known Gary was a bad boy when she'd met him. It was what had attracted her to him in the first place. He'd seemed so reckless and dashing, with the devil-may-care attitude of a fighter jock, a complete opposite of her own personality. Unfortunately, Gary had also been a notorious womanizer. At the time, winning the attentions of a ladies' man had seemed an accomplishment. She should have known better, she reflected wryly. No woman held Gary's attention for long. Getting dumped—while not exactly unexpected, considering their rocky relationship—had nonetheless hurt her badly.

One evening, feeling lonely and abandoned, she'd wandered to *Kuroshima's* observation lounge, seeking solitude while star-gazing. She'd found Egon there, silently observing a brilliant nebula. Talara had entered soundlessly and watched him outlined against the stars. That had been the moment she'd realized she knew little about him.

Egon was a loner. A quiet man respected for his skill at his job, he kept to himself in his off time, almost as if he found socializing uncomfortable. He was considered a competent officer, but a loner. Egon had been an *enigma*.

He'd detected her presence and had turned. She'd jumped at his sudden reaction. Remembering the moment still made Talara blush, especially when she remembered how she'd *squeaked* like a mouse.

She smiled, her vision flashing back in time . . .

"Oh, sorry." Egon smiled awkwardly. "I didn't realize someone wanted to use the lounge." He turned to leave.

Talara, needing to be around someone, grabbed his arm. "No, please stay, Lieutenant. I imposed on you."

Egon shrugged. "I come here to get away from the crowd sometimes, Ensign. I need solitude at times, just to think straight. I'm done, however. The lounge is yours."

CHAPTER 2

"No, Sir. Please, I didn't mean to run you out. It's just that . . ."

He lifted an eyebrow. It felt like it was the first time he truly saw her. No, that wasn't quite right. It felt like he saw into her soul, and she felt naked under his gaze.

Naked yet somehow . . . comfortable.

Egon's eyes narrowed. "Are you okay?"

She'd been unaware her feelings were obvious on her face. An emotional dam burst, and she started confessing her hurt in a most unprofessional manner.

She smiled as she came out of her revelry, remembering the moment. Egon had stood quietly, listening as she got her problems off her chest. It was something she'd always hoped Gary would do, but never had.

Egon had shown no irritation, only concern. They'd been the only two people in the lounge, providing some degree of privacy, and she'd found herself wondering why she'd never noticed Egon as a man before. There'd been no reason to do so, of course. They were professional officers working aboard the same ship. Egon was a quiet sort, a man who rarely called attention to himself, so it made sense she'd only perceived him as a friend.

She'd resolved to correct that error immediately.

Talara had discovered, to her surprise, Egon was a back-to-the-wilderness romantic. He loved being dirt-side on planets, camping in the mountains and forests, preferring the untamed wilderness of nature to the sane life of a metropolis. She'd also found that while extremely reserved in public, in private Egon possessed perhaps the *corniest* sense of humor in the Fleet; a trait he managed to conceal most of the time. In fact, few of his coworkers realized what a true cornball Egon could be.

Egon delighted in atrocious jokes and bad puns. While she'd never found that particularly appealing, she'd found herself starting to appreciate the difficult—if somewhat sick—genius it took to create truly bad puns. Some of Egon's were real *groaners.*

One evening, after a tough day in engineering, he'd been sitting in her quarters, listening to her bitch and trying to brighten her mood, when for some reason—she still didn't know why—their eyes had locked. Egon had stopped in the middle of a punch line, and they'd simply stared at each other in silence.

She remembered seeing her black eyes reflected in the hazel green of his. Something had passed between them. Without warning, Egon had taken her in his arms and kissed her. Caught off-guard, she'd found herself responding enthusiastically. They'd been lovers from that moment on.

Egon's assignment to *Shiva* had interrupted their romance, however. Though they saw each other less frequently than she liked, Egon remained hers. She hoped after Kuroshima's upcoming deployment cruise, she might wrangle an assignment to *Shiva* herself. Her new job title would likely aid her in getting such an assignment to the battleship's engineering section, and Egon had recommended her to Shiva's commanding officer, Captain Kruger.

Joint assignments weren't a sure thing, however, and usually reserved for married personnel. Egon had told her that if they couldn't manage to arrange that, he'd pull a few strings and get them a follow-on assignment to one of the orbital defense stations in the Rim together.

She pulled him closer, admiring his eyes. Their hazel color fascinated her, being nothing like the brown eyes that dominated in her family and unlike the glittering black of her own. "Can you at least come down to the reception?"

"Sorry, I can't, Tilly. Shiva's departing soon and I've got to get back aboard. We're off for a tactical exercise in the Wonder Nebula."

"Oh." Disappointment dripped in her voice.

"I'm sorry, hon. I wish there was a way I could make it up to you."

"Well." An impish smile crossed her face. "Last night will hold me for a while, but you'd better write."

Egon pushed a bang back behind her ear. His hand slowly traced the edge of her face, moving gently to her chin as he tilted her face upward.

She giggled. "Admiring my big schnoz again?"

"I *will* write, Tilly. You'd better write, too. When is *Kuroshima* scheduled to depart?"

"Next week, after we finish upgrading our primary drives."

"Sounds like you're going to be awfully busy, *Chief*

Engineer Kibbleman. I don't know if you're going to have time for anything as mundane as sending v-mails."

"I said I'd write."

"Well, you better . . . or else."

"Or else what?"

"Or else I'll have you arrested, hauled to my quarters in irons, and administer more of that special punishment you're so fond of." He wrapped his arms around her and kissed her forehead.

"Mm, I could use more of *that* punishment." She closed her eyes and rested her head in the hollow of his shoulder, listening to his heartbeat.

Egon chuckled. "I'll just bet you could."

She pushed him away with a look of false shock. "Why, Lieutenant Storm, you're a dirty old man."

Egon kissed her forehead again. "Yeah, and you're a naughty girl."

Talara pulled away reluctantly. Today was promotion day and the skipper was having an officer's call for the crew of *Kuroshima* to celebrate. She needed to be going, too, for the crew was waiting at the club, but it would feel like forever before she and Egon were together again. It always did.

She took in his broad shoulders, trying to drink him in. She wanted to cuddle with him in front of a fire somewhere and celebrate in an intimate way. Shiva's patrol would last two months, and she wanted to impress a kinesthetic image of him on her senses that would hold her through the long days and nights alone. No amount of holding or touching ever adequately covered such periods of separation.

What the hell.

"We're alone, you know." Her eyes twinkled mischievously, the corners of her mouth curling in an impish grin.

Egon blinked in shock. "You've got to be kidding. In an hour, Commander O'Brady's giving you a reception dirtside at the officer's club, and I have to be aboard *Shiva* in forty-five minutes. We don't have time for *that.*"

"Make time darling." She gave him a wicked smile. "Live a little wild. Don't be so . . . proper."

"My God, you *are* a naughty girl." Egon laughed, shaking his head in mock disgust.

"Only for you, sweetheart, but there's only one thing to do for it."

Egon's face sobered. "What's that?"

Smiling, she took his hand and led him to the bedroom.

CHAPTER 3

COMMUNICATIONS ROOM, ORBITAL DEFENSE STATION PAN'VU STAR SYSTEM

Gray Bulkheads and dim lighting made Petty Officer Laura Hernandez feel bored as she sat at her console in the ODS communications room.

How is it I have to pull duty when everyone else is off? Sighing, she took another sip of coffee and scanned the communications panel. An alarm light flashed on the console, indicating a priority message. Its scarlet color indicated an encrypted communication.

"Great." She leaned over the console to punch in the proper authentication keys. "Just what I need when I'm alone on watch."

Pan'vu was home to the RCN's Weapons Test Center. Currently it was experiencing a little-known, seldom-experienced holiday the Navy called a "Down Day." The commander of Turin's World had decided that since all budgetary

CHAPTER 3

goals for the fiscal quarter had been met, local installations could have a day off. As a result, Pan'vu's facilities had shifted to minimum manning status for the weekend. Fleet vessels parked in Pan'vu's orbital docking berths had sent most crews dirtside on liberty, along with most of the personnel assigned to the planet's single orbital defense station. Only skeleton crews remained aboard the ships and the ODS.

Hernandez wanted to be dirtside with everyone else, relaxing or attending a party, but she'd had the bad luck of drawing duty for the weekend. Lieutenant Commander Pickering was the only other person aboard the ODS at the moment. Everyone else was dirtside on Turin's World having a blast. Pickering wasn't exactly working work, however. He was off taking a nap somewhere.

The scarlet light began flashing and Hernandez's eyes widened in surprise. The incoming message was a Priority One Fleet alert.

So much for a quiet day at the office.

Hernandez punched in the decryption software and password. The TEXT-ONLY message had arrived via a communications drone that had popped into the Pan'vu system through the nearby stargate. She downloaded the transmission burst and stared at the text on her screen, gasping as its importance registered.

Hernandez's eyes opened wide. The destroyer *Gant* had destroyed a Karsian vessel in the test range some eighty billion kilometers away, fifteen days travel time through n-space, but vessels from the test range could wormhole into Pan'vu via the stargate in only a few hours.

The message required immediate attention from someone with a higher pay grade than hers. An officer needed to see this. Likely, the message could have repercussions all the way to the president.

Unfortunately, only one officer was on duty.

She hesitated, not wanting to disturb Pickering, and almost rejected the idea out of hand. Hernandez hated dealing with Pickering, who verbally abused enlisted ratings. Pickering could be a bear when disturbed from one of his frequent "naps." On the other hand, he might be tougher on her if she left him out of the loop on such an important matter. It was a no-win situation. No matter what, it was her duty to report the message to him.

She punched the intercom call button and blanched as Pickering's gruff voice answered. From his tone, she knew he was in a surly mood. "Pickering. What?"

"Commander, this is Petty Officer Hernandez."

"I know that, for God's sake, Hernandez. Nobody else is on duty. What do you want?"

Hernandez swallowed. Pickering was *not* in a good mood. "We just received a Priority One message via comm drone, Sir. It's being broadcast on Fleet Common."

"So? Handle it."

"Sir, it's a *Priority One* message."

"I don't care, Hernandez. I told you I'd be asleep in my quarters until 15:00, and I told you *not* to disturb me for any reason until that time. I put you on the duty schedule so you could handle communications, not keep me awake talking about them. Handle it and leave me alone."

"Commander, this is serious." Hernandez tried to keep the pleading out of her voice, not wanting to incur the commander's wrath, but she felt duty-bound to point out the importance of the message. "The destroyer *Gant* attacked a vessel in the test range, a Karsian bladeship. She's taken damage, Sir, and she's inbound with casualties."

"What?"

Hernandez sighed. Pickering came from a wealthy and influential family on Rigel Two, something he'd made sure everyone around him was acutely aware of. He was the "ring-knocker" type of Academy graduate who played politics to enhance his career. Pickering believed no one below his rank had any credibility about anything that he considered himself an expert on, which was practically everything. Pickering believed enlisted personnel were from a social class below him, incapable of having working brains and of little importance.

"*Gant*, Sir. That Skosian Guard destroyer that sends us comm traffic every two or three days. Apparently, she's destroyed a Karsian bladeship in the test range. She's headed here with casualties aboard, ETA 1400 hours. Her commander asks us to warn the Fleet ASAP. He's experienced an act of war. Request permission to relay the message to Fleet Headquarters at Centauri Seven."

"Oh, no you don't." Pickering shouted over the intercom. "That's all I fucking need, Hernandez. You have to validate this shit before you plaster it across the Fleet network and get admirals involved. You've no idea what you're actually dealing with. Likely you intercepted an exercise message from a war game somewhere."

Hernandez's jaw tightened. Pickering wouldn't rock the boat if doing so threatened his chances of promotion. Pickering was a bureaucrat in the uniform of a warrior. Hernandez expected more from a commissioned officer.

Warriors act, she thought angrily. *Bureaucrats pass the buck.*

It was clear Pickering wasn't going to do anything that might cause him scrutiny from the Admiralty.

"Sir, we've got to do *something*. This is time-sensitive information. I believe it's real, Sir, and—"

"And how the hell would *you* know that?" Pickering was working himself into one of his tantrums. "Do you work in naval intelligence now? I'm a field-grade officer, and even *I'm* not sure what you've received. You're a *petty* officer, not a real one. You also happen to work for me, *Petty Officer* Hernandez. I do not work for you. Got that? When I want you to presume you're sentient, I'll tell you what to think and when to think it. I give the orders here; you simply obey them. Savvy? Quit trying to tell me my business."

Hernandez flushed with anger but held her tongue. Discipline had been ingrained in her at boot camp, and that discipline included showing respect for superiors. That discipline allowed her to control her mouth. If she said what she was thinking, it would only cause her more grief. "Aye, aye . . . *Sir*."

She spoke through clenched teeth, trying not to make

the last word sound like she was biting through a nail, but she failed. Any disrespect was lost on Pickering.

"Download the message and forward it to my console. I'll deal with it when I wake up. If I determine it's real, I'll pass it on to the Fleet. Meanwhile, man your post and leave me alone. If you can't handle that simple chore, then paint your nails or something. But whatever you do, stop waking me up."

"Sir, Navy regulations specifically forbid dumping classified information onto an unclassified computer."

"So now you're a security expert? Question me again, Hernandez, and I'll have your ass hauled to Captain's Mast and have you busted back to recruit. Then I'll have you assigned to the dirtiest garbage scow I can find in this quadrant, where you'll spend the rest of your career chipping paint. I don't need you quoting naval regulations to *me*. Do I make myself clear, you pernicious twit?"

"Sir—"

"I said forget about it." Pickering's voice dropped to a dangerous growl. "I'm giving you a direct order. Transfer that message to my computer and shut the hell up. Carry out your orders before I end your career once and for all."

Humiliated and furious, Hernandez heard her teeth grinding. "Yes, Sir."

"Pickering out."

Hernandez turned the intercom off by smashing her fist against the button. After a minute of angry fuming, she punched in commands to transfer the data to Pickering's computer as ordered. The computer would log the transfer automatically, but Pickering's order was clearly illegal under naval regulations. She decided to make it clear the transfer was done under protest and on the direct orders of Lieutenant Commander Pickering. She'd be damned if she was going to take the blame when a Board of Inquiry looked into the violation.

She accessed the duty log and typed in Pickering's orders, verbatim.

The pompousness of the officer infuriated her. He was an elitist snob at the best of times and an egotistical ass the rest.

Worse, he's incompetent, she thought angrily, *more worried about his career than doing his job.*

It wasn't the first time he'd threatened her with wrongful disciplinary action either. Hernandez was junior in rank, but she did her job to the best of her ability. Pickering's insufferable arrogance infuriated her.

I may have to follow the orders of the lords and officers appointed over me, but I'll make damned sure those orders leave electronic breadcrumbs.

Angrily, she finished typing on her log screen and punched the transfer button.

COMMANDING OFFICER'S QUARTERS, PAN'VU ORBITAL DEFENSE STATION

Pickering snapped the intercom off and lay back on the bed, angry beyond reason. He'd left standing orders not to be disturbed, and Hernandez had blatantly ignored those orders. It would damn well be reflected on her next efficiency report too. She could kiss her promotion to second class goodbye.

A voice spoke softly beside him. "Is something wrong?"

"Yeah, Hernandez. I ought to bust her back to slick-sleeve."

The blonde beside him moved closer, placing a manicured palm on his bare chest. Pickering glanced at her, admiring her beauty as he congratulated himself on his latest conquest.

Yeoman Apprentice Kimberly Yeager was a beautiful girl, indeed. Well-muscled and graceful, with dark-brown eyes and platinum hair that hung below her shoulders.

She traced a fingernail over his chest. "Who?"

"Hernandez."

"Laura? She's probably just lonely being up there on the comm deck by herself."

"What about you?" Pickering nuzzled at the blonde's neck. "You lonely too?"

"No, it just scared me when that intercom went off. I thought somebody had caught us."

"Relax. Nobody's going to catch us. I'm in command here, remember? Like I told you, you scratch my back, and I'll scratch yours. I've taken all of the necessary precautions, so don't worry about it. Let's concentrate on us."

Yeager smiled, revealing perfect teeth. She closed her eyes as he moved atop her, his tongue working like a lathe. She began to breathe harder.

Pickering had hand-picked Yeager from a pool of

girls recently assigned to the ODS, earmarking her for special attention. He'd told her she was an important, highly-talented yeoman who would go far in the Navy. He'd informed her he could get her promoted quickly if she performed certain favors in return.

Pickering almost laughed, remembering how easily she'd fallen for it. He felt her pulse quicken as her breath came in ragged gasps.

He constantly scanned the psychological profiles of females assigned to the Pan'vu ODS looking for candidates like Yeager. He'd singled her out as the most exploitable of three potential candidates.

Yeager was ambitious, beautiful, and naïve. Unlike Hernandez and Garcia, the other pair, Yeager had Nordic genes, a look Pickering preferred. He'd always had a thing for blondes, and he harbored a dislike of brunettes, who tended to remind him of his mother. That had quickly ruled out the other two.

Recruits like Yeager were susceptible to power games, and he'd been circumspect in assigning her as his personal yeoman. Then he'd wooed her with gifts and promises of special favors until she'd agreed to join him in bed.

He was careful to keep the rendezvous secret. The Navy had strict regulations concerning fraternization between officers and enlisted, and severe penalties for the sexual harassment of subordinates.

Fortunately, Yeager could keep secrets. She would let him have his way with her as long as he kept the prospect of promotion dangling before her eyes.

As soon as Yeager got wise to his scam, he'd write her up on some made-up infraction and transfer her somewhere else where she couldn't cause trouble, along with a bad personnel jacket that would deny her future promotion. After all, she was a slut and deserved no better. With a bad personnel file, Navy investigators would likely ignore any sexual harassment complaints she might try to file. The brass would consider such charges sour grapes on her part; an attempt to smear his good name and reputation as an officer.

It was an ironic form of justice perhaps, but why should a dumb bimbo be promoted over people who actually did their jobs? Yeager was too stupid to be a petty officer, anyway. The only talents she had lay between her lips and her legs. He'd never allow a whore to threaten his career.

Power was the drug that made him seduce pretty girls out of boot camp on their first assignment. Such harlots believed they could earn rank on their backs, and he reinforced those beliefs at every opportunity.

On his desk, a light flickered on his computer, blinking in alternating green and red pulses, indicating a file had been downloaded. Hernandez's message transfer was complete.

Yeager's breath quickened as Pickering kissed his way down to her navel. She reached up, lifting his head from her stomach.

"The message arrived." Her voice was husky as he caressed her in delicate places with his tongue. "Aren't you going to look at it?"

"Later." He moved to position himself atop her. "First things first."

KARSIAN BLADESHIP *ANG'TAHK*
PAN'VU STAR SYSTEM

Three bladeships exited the stargate at low speed to avoid detection by enemy sensors. Hidden by angular lidar-absorbent hulls, they jumped in unnoticed, like deadly minnows, and angled toward the Pan'vu Fleet facilities over Turin's World.

In the lead bladeship, Over-Lieutenant Toborahnk stared at the back of his pilot's head and smiled, rubbing a bearded face with a three-digit hand. The approach appeared to be perfect. The Rigelians seemed unaware they had entered the system.

He had been worried his ships might be detected while crossing Pan'vu's military test range, particularly when passive sensors had detected the unmistakable flare of nuclear detonations and distant drive sources. The Rigelians must have been conducting a weapons test of some kind, for the orbital facilities at Pan'vu remained calm and not on alert. No warships patrolled the jump gate terminus, which would not have been the case had his force been detected.

The energy pulse from nuclear detonations in the test range would not arrive through n-space for several hours. If the drone that had surged past his ships from the terminus had been sent to warn Pan'vu of attack, it was not readily apparent. More likely it was transmitting the results of the weapons test to the RCN base.

That drone drifted before *Ang'tahk* now, coasting without a drive field and chattering away with encrypted transmissions directed at the orbital defense station. It would continue to do so until its batteries expired or the ODS ordered it to shut up. Judging from the lack of Rigelian reaction, nothing seemed amiss.

Toborahnk's squadron of four bladeships had been dispatched along divergent paths intended to come together in the test range. Four was an unusual number in Karsian culture, which based most things on the number three. Four seemed an unlucky number to Toborahnk.

They had been ordered to insert into Pan'vu undetected and conduct a preemptive strike on the Rigelian facilities there. Dispersion had minimized the chances of detection by limiting the number of bladeships in any one area of the test range. They had evaded Rigelian patrols using widely separated courses and had successfully rejoined to insert into Pan'vu through the jump gate together. Now they were in formation to attack.

Toborahnk leaned back in his chair and nodded. "Signal the others, Moterk."

Moterk bowed slightly in response and touched his communications panel. On the hull of the bladeship, a directional whisker antenna extended, radiating two directional small bursts of electro-magnetic energy at low power. The weak signal was deliberate. If Rigelian sensors detected the bursts, they would see only electronic noise.

The two bursts were answered quickly by a pair of single burst replies, from positions less than a quarter of a light-second away.

Toborahnk frowned, letting the nictitating membranes half-close over his eyes. Only two ships had replied. The fourth bladeship was missing.

Why?

In front of him, Moterk watched his passive displays for any signs the stargate sensor network had detected them. Toborahnk brought up his tactical display and reviewed his mission orders a final time.

The orders required him to insert into Pan'vu, stealth up and close on the Rigelian fleet base. At a predetermined time, they were to destroy the Rigelian orbital facilities, then bottleneck the jump gate to cut off the test range.

K'Leesh-class bladeships carried two crewmen, an officer captain and a pilot/sensor operator. Internal space aboard a midget bladeship was limited, due to the small size of the vessel and the unique angles built into its hull for stealth. Large torpedo bays and the space needed for electronics and drives took up most of the remaining space.

Each bladeship had been assigned specific targets. *Ang'tahk* would take out the ODS, the brain of the Rigelian orbital defenses over Turin's World. His second in command, Under-Lieutenant Torgh, would strike at the orbital missile sites. The remaining bladeships, under Commanders Yort and Dahk, would bombard Turin's

CHAPTER 3

World from orbit. Yort would silence the planet's missile defense complex while Dahk simultaneously rained destruction upon the enemy shipyards dirtside, destroying all combat vessels on the planet's surface. If all went as planned, the destruction of Pan'vu's defenses would allow the Imperial Fleet to surge into Rigelian space unopposed.

Toborahnk rubbed his chin. Only three bladeships had made it to Pan'vu. Four were required to service all targets, but it was obvious the fourth bladeship had run into some kind of trouble and would not arrive in time.

Most likely a broken drive. These bladeships have cranky systems. No doubt the commander of the missing bladeship is frantic as he struggles to make rendezvous by attack time. Unfortunately, we cannot wait for him. The operation requires precise timing, and the Rigelian ODS must be destroyed on schedule.

"We are in the target window, Yi'rhang." Moterk turned and pointed to the ship's chronometer for emphasis. "Shall we proceed?"

Toborahnk squeezed his eyes into thin slits. He needed his entire squadron, but only three ships were present. If the attack were to match the Imperial Fleet's movement timetable, however, he must attack on time. There was no time left. He was out of options.

"Send the signal."

Moterk transmitted another blast of static in three distinct pulses, then retracted the whisker antenna and moved the bladeship ahead. It crawled toward the ODS slowly, hidden, silent and deadly, as the Rigelians went about their daily business oblivious to the threat. They would have no chance at defense.

Toborahnk smiled as the range decreased. If the enemy was listening for intelligent patterns in the ambient static, the ceaseless chattering of the communications drone would keep them from detecting the pulses of his low-power transmissions.

It was time.

Toborahnk leaned forward. "Power weapons and prepare to fire. As our human enemies are fond of saying on one of their strange holidays: '*we are three wise men from the east, each bearing gifts.*' Those gifts will soon be on their way."

CHAPTER 4

KARSIAN EMBASSY
RIGEL TWO

Shafts of blue sunlight speared through the drapes, illuminating the cups on the mat in the center of the luxurious room. *Yihak* Takoom smiled as he brought the cup of curdled *blik* milk to his lips. *Talik* was a bitter drink, but bitterness was an extravagance much admired in the Empire. An old Karsian saying stated one must learn to drink bitterness to become a true warrior.

The human before him gagged on his cup, quickly putting it back on the mat between them. "I say, that's very . . . *different.*" George Clive tried his best not to blanch visibly, dabbing at the corners of his mouth with a napkin.

"You are the only human I know who can drink talik and not become ill, George." Takoom struggled not to chuckle at Clive's efforts to hide his disgust. He had discovered things went smoother if one did not laugh at humans who took themselves too seriously.

Takoom was the emperor's yihak to the Rigelian Confederation. He had lived on Rigel for many years, and Clive was one of the few humans he felt truly comfortable with. Clive came from a proud clan that called itself *English*, a fact Clive made obvious to everyone he met.

Humans called their own yihaki "ambassadors," though Takoom felt the human term failed to grasp the significance of the role. A yihak was a political leader's direct representative to a foreign government and sworn to the allegiance of the leader he represented. In that regard, Takoom and Clive served similar functions for their respective governments. Each ensured peace existed between the Empire and the Confederation, a peace that rested on respect, diplomacy and trust.

The Englishman eyed his cup distastefully. "I understand talik is a lactate; a secretion from an animal your people call a blik."

Takoom watched Clive's attempt at facial control with relish, stifling an urge to grin. "Quite true, George. The blik is a domestic beast, a livestock common on Kars Prime. Humans would classify it as something between a mammal and a giant arachnid, though the genetics of the two species are totally unrelated."

Clive almost vomited, which pleased Takoom to no end. The most wonderful thing about humans was how easily their emotions could be read on their faces. Any thought entering a human's mind was immediately apparent in their facial expressions and body language. Few humans were as adept at concealing inner thoughts as a Karsian. Of all the Confederation's intelligent species, humans were by far the most fun to observe because of that.

Takoom kept his own expression unreadable as he considered these things. Not all Rigelian species were enjoyable. The Zeta Reticulans, in particular, were a species that fascinated him while at the same time filling him with dread. The frail gray Reticulans were reclusive but seemed to have a fondness for humans, the reasons for which were lost in antiquity. With small bodies and over-sized skulls, Reticulans were physically repulsive, but they were the only race of Rigelian beings Takoom truly feared. Their plant-like skin was distasteful, and their huge, black, insect-like eyes terrifying.

The Reticulans never blink. Imperial intelligence has speculated their large black eyes might be lenses that cover their actual eyes to protect them from their native suns, or perhaps to aid with night vision. No one knows. I am happy that, as yihak to the Confederation, I have only predictable old George Clive to deal with.

"Spiders." Clive shivered and his mouth moved as he struggled to prevent regurgitation. "Spiders that make spoiled milk, no less. And I'm fool enough to drink it."

"Oh, it is not spoiled, George." Takoom leaned forward to emphasize the point with the long fingernails of a three-digit hand. The three-inch nails were the status symbols of yihaki. "We ferment talik after milking, then beat it until it curdles."

"Why, for heaven's sake?"

"Until it ferments, blik milk is *peshai*; what your people

call 'poisonous.' I do not know the chemical breakdown, and even if I did, I would probably be unable to translate it into your language. Suffice to say that blik milk contains deadly neurotoxins until it has curdled."

"I see." Clive sobered, his eyes widening perceptively. Takoom noted he made no further effort to drink from the cup, though he knew the Englishman meant no insult. Talik was a Karsian drink, molecularly compatible with Karsian digestive physiology. It tended to have unfortunate gastrointestinal effects on non-Karsians. Clive had paid Takoom a huge compliment by even *attempting* to drink it. Most humans were unable to keep it down. The fact Clive had tried indicated the high regard he had for Takoom.

"Perhaps you do." Takoom folded his hands before him, fingers intertwined. "Yet, I doubt you came here merely to drink my excellent talik. So, tell me, Ambassador, why are you here?"

Clive opened a courier case. Removing an electronic pad, he glanced at it for a moment. Takoom had the impression Clive wanted to be precise with his wording and was checking his phrasing carefully.

"Ambassador Takoom, as High Yihak between the Rigelian Confederation and the Empire of Kars, you know that tomorrow we shall open negotiations on free trade agreements before the Assembly. To be blunt, I would like clear assurances going in that those negotiations will be conducted in good faith on the part of the Empire."

"What do you mean?"

CHAPTER 4

"I want to know the intentions of your government regarding my nation and its sovereign territories."

Takoom waved his hand dismissively. "Certainly, this can wait until tomorrow. Our position has been clear all along, Ambassador. I hope this is not about those ridiculous *human rights* violations again. As we have pointed out numerous times, none of the Empire's peoples are human."

Clive gave the Karsian yihak a frosty stare. "Yihak Takoom, I must inform you that we've received disturbing reports of late from our intelligence agencies."

Takoom suddenly felt uneasy, his eyes widening in surprise. "Oh?"

"Yes, it seems we've recently detected massive deployments of Karsian military fleets away from the Imperial home worlds. They're being moved toward the periphery of the Empire in the direction of the Confederation."

"Really? It is probably a military exercise, George. I have not been notified of any such event personally, but deployment exercises are hardly unheard of even among your own military forces. Rarely do military commanders inform ambassadors before conducting exercises."

"Based on the number of ships, this must be an extraordinarily *large* exercise, Yihak."

"Perhaps." Takoom shrugged. "Anything is possible, George. Why does this trouble you?"

Clive took a deep breath. "We're on the eve of negotiating serious trade agreements, Yihak; treaties that will have far-reaching economic consequences for both our nations."

"I am well aware of this, Ambassador. Surely you are also aware we Karsians have a central government and—like your own—we maintain large military forces. But you must also realize that, compared to the Confederation, we are a poor nation with large economic disadvantages. Our natural resources are limited compared to yours. Our military budget consumes a large portion of the resources we do possess. We are always short of high-grade ores like diluminum, copper, and tritanium, metals needed to build starships and military facilities. Our navy utilizes two-thirds of all high-grade ore we do produce, as well as 80 percent of *ceyon* production."

Clive nodded. Dihexagonal quartz was the crystalline mineral Karsians called ceyon, used to focus energy in starship fusion drives. The Confederation possessed vast quantities of it, particularly in its numerous gas giant systems like Bantar and Wewak, where mineral refineries had been constructed, making the Confederation one of the richest star nations around. Rigel's fuel production for a month exceeded what the Empire could produce in a human T-year.

Takoom shrugged again. "We desire access to new economic resources, George. Establishing trade agreements will provide the Empire with access to great wealth. Open trade between our nations will lower tensions between our governments. In fact, both nations shall benefit. The Empire will acquire new sources of raw material, and the Confederation will gain access to new trade markets."

"I concede those points, certainly." Clive leaned back

against a column to rest his back. "What I cannot understand, old man, is the logic involved. If the Empire is so strapped for resources that it must open trade with the Confederation to acquire them, how then can it afford to expend a disproportionate amount of those same resources conducting a training exercise of this scope?"

Takoom signaled his servant to bring more talik. The servant shuffled forward and replenished Takoom's cup, then retired unobtrusively into the shadows of a far corner. Takoom sipped a moment as he considered his reply, then spread a three-fingered hand in a gesture of dismissal.

"I am yihaki, Ambassador. I do not comprehend the workings of the military mind, nor the rationale of the warrior caste. Warriors are best left to explain martial matters. A yihak's expertise is diplomacy, not battle. The question you ask is more a subject for admirals and generals than ambassadors."

"True enough, old boy, but it's often admirals and generals who must step in and fix things when ambassadors muck them up. Certainly you can understand why my government might be a tad bit . . . worried."

"Of course. Please understand, George, the military is all that stands between Imperial rule and anarchy in the Empire. The fact we are an empire instead of a confederation of worlds means we must impose order upon our citizens for the good of the Empire. Left to free will, many systems would secede from the Empire, as you yourselves seceded from the Terran League long ago. Were that to happen, our resources would diminish rapidly as each seceding world carved another gas giant or asteroid belt from our coffers.

"The Shikahn, our Emperor, will not allow that to happen. The Empire must maintain a strong military to crush any rebellion as well as to handle external threats. It is why the Empire created the Imperial Guard in addition to the Imperial Army and Navy. Security is a constant concern for the Shikahn, for the Imperial Court is awash in plots and intrigue. Without strong internal security, coup attempts would soon place the Empire at risk. Without a powerful military, the Empire would cease to exist."

Clive nodded. "Certainly, Yihak. I understand, and—from your point of view—it makes sense. But you must realize how disturbing massive military deployments are to *my* nation, particularly on the eve of serious treaty negotiations, exercise or not. The timing is inauspicious."

Takoom nodded and sipped from his cup. There was a long silence before he spoke again. "As I have said, Ambassador, I am not an admiral, nor am I privy to military plans or exercise schedules. I assure you, however, the Empire has no hostile intentions toward your government or its worlds. If such were the case, my government would inform me, and I would be instructed to cease diplomatic relations with the Confederation immediately. I have received no such instructions."

"You may not be an admiral, Yihak, but you're the Empire's highest representative to my government. Such relationship between nations depends upon trust, and I know you to be an honorable man."

"Thank you, Ambassador. Honor is first in a Karsian house."

Clive leaned forward. "I know *that*, too, and I respect that tradition. I also know how important honor is to you personally. Based on that, I'd like to ask for a personal assurance, Yihak."

Takoom's eyes narrowed. Honor was a serious matter. He placed his talik mug on the mat and studied the human through slit eyes. "What type of personal assurance, Ambassador?"

"Your *word*, sir. I'd like your word of honor as Karsian yihak that the Empire intends no military aggression toward the Rigelian Confederation, its people, its military, its planets, or its sovereign interests."

"Of course." Takoom smiled broadly and stood. Opening the wide sleeve of his purple robe, he extended a long-nailed hand toward the Englishman in what humans called a handshake. "I give my word of honor as Yihak, Ambassador. My government has no hidden agenda here. We do not attack foreign governments who negotiate with us in good faith. We are a people of honor."

Clive nodded, stood and accepted the Karsian's hand . . . noting how easy it was for a Karsian three-digit hand to emulate a human grip.

Takoom knew Clive recognized Yihaki were special Karsians. A caste of scholars selected in childhood from the warrior caste and trained in academics and negotiation. What a yihaki said was gospel, for they were sworn to the truth.

"Good enough for me, Sir." Clive sighed, relieved. Takoom knew he had worked hard to establish treaty negotiations with the Empire. "That being the case, Yihak, I shall bid you good evening and take my leave. I'll see you at the assembly hall in the morning."

"Of course. Mernacht will show you out, Ambassador."

"Quite all right, old boy. I know the way. Good night, Yihak."

Clive headed for the door. He had nearly reached it when Takoom's voice stopped him. "We have a saying in the Empire I believe appropriate to adjourn our meeting, George."

Clive turned at the door, staring back at the tall, balding Karsian in the purple robes. "Oh? What might that be, Takoom?"

"Peace."

CHAPTER 5

Six multiple-warhead torpedoes spewed from three blade-ships toward the Rigelian facilities, their launches undetected. There was no countering fire from RCN ships or facilities. Fleet sensors, minimized for holiday routine and trained on the stargate to detect capital ships, failed to detect the small stealthed torpedo drives. No shields rose. No point defenses challenged the deadly barrage until too late.

In the communications center of the ODS, Hernandez stared in shock as the torpedo spread appeared suddenly on her sensor console. The platform's sensors had detected the ejecta plumes as the warheads separated from their torpedo shells.

Instinctively, she activated lidar scanners. AIs instantly noted the velocities and trajectories of the incoming weapons. Hernandez hit the defense alarm and attempted to

55

raise the station's shields, but there wasn't time. The torpedoes, launched at short-range, were accelerating too rapidly. Only a single structural integrity field had energized before the first warhead struck the ODS, vaporizing Laura Hernandez and a huge chunk of the station. The succeeding blast ripped the ODS apart in a blinding storm of fire.

Hernandez's efforts weren't totally in vain, however. The single structural integrity field protected one small section of interior compartments from radiation flash, allowing two ODS personnel to live. Everyone else was killed instantly. The ODS tumbled away, descending planetward in a decaying orbit toward the atmosphere of Turin's World.

On the surface of Turin's World thousands more died as two dozen nuclear warheads burst above planetary defense facilities. At the same instant, half a dozen starships exploded on the tarmac of the RCN facilities dirtside. The detonations added to the collective firestorm, and Turin's World boiled in nuclear fire.

It was over in seconds. The Empire's execution had been perfect. Not a single warning escaped the system. The Pan'vu Fleet Test Range facility had ceased to exist.

Aboard his bladeship, Toborahnk watched as the firestorm of destruction killed a world and quietly reflected on his part in it.

A new war has begun, and I have started it.

He watched what remained of the ODS tumble away in a slow spin, disappearing in the distance over Turin's horizon.

CHAPTER 5

"Well done."

Moterk grinned.

Near the stargate, the lone communications drone drifted ballistically, chattering its warning to a dead audience.

IKS MURGAHH
ZION'S WASTE SYSTEM

Fleet Admiral Tork lay in his bunk and squeezed the point between his eyes with his fingers. It was time to join the others on the flag bridge, but he wanted a few moments of quiet; a few precious *ongs* of time in which to contemplate what they were about to do and the monster it might unleash.

"If we are to take on the Rigelians, we must first destroy their forward fleet at Centauri Seven." Those had been the words he had used, almost jokingly, to High Admiral Borok of the Karsian Border Fleet ten months earlier. "If we do not, the Rigelians will mobilize their massive fleet and doom us."

Borok had commissioned staff to investigate the feasibility of such an undertaking. He had called upon a brilliant tactician and attack pilot, Over-Commander Gorak. Within a week, the daring officer had devised a detailed attack plan. It had been a difficult and risky plan that depended upon precise timing, but a plan not impossible to accomplish.

Tork had examined the plan in great detail before downloading it and shuttling it to Admiral Magish's office at the *Kahduhn*. He had walked in unannounced and dropped the data chip on Magish's desk.

"Read it," he had said, and he had waited patiently as Magish complied.

Magish had read the plan without expression, but Tork knew Magish had found it shocking. Rigelian naval capabilities were impressive. The Rigelian system at Centauri Seven was light-years from the periphery of Imperial space. There were Rigelian bases scattered around all the jump gates between Kars and Centauri Seven, including bases at Gallagher's World, Foster's Star, Pan'vu, New Baghdad, and Tzu. Centauri Seven had a small habitable planet in a highly elliptical orbit around its sun, easily defended and difficult to approach undetected. There were only certain times of the year when its orbit brought it within easy strike range of the Zion's Waste jump gate. In addition to such geometric difficulties, Admiral Varnok, the commandant of Imperial Fleet Two's carrier task force, had stalled the process in his usual bureaucratic manner.

"Do not tell me how difficult it is," Tork had raged at him over several mugs of talik. "We are warriors! Tell me how to accomplish it. The *Kahthrung* has decided the Empire must expand. The Shikahn has personally commanded we find a way, and the most likely way is to expand into Confederation space."

Varnok had stared at him with worried eyes. "Why are you so anxious to fight the Rigelians? You spent time on their worlds and know them personally. I thought you had a fondness for them."

Tork had nodded at that meeting. "Yes, I was an exchange officer to the Confederation and studied at their naval academy. That does not mean I will shirk my duty. I have no personal desire for war with Rigel. I have friends on both sides, and many may die, but the Shikahn has spoken. The Kahthrung has convened, and they have decided that without access to new resources the Empire is doomed. The Imperial gullet is hungry once again. I have my duty, as do you. The Centauri Seven strike is my plan, Admiral, but I will require your support to pull it off."

With that Varnok had stopped stalling and gone to work. Gorak's plan had determined the most direct route into the Confederation was through the Nangtashgu star system on the Empire's periphery. It jumped into the Rigelian system of Gulliver's Hold, and from there into the Rigelian systems of Bantar and Centauri Seven. This direct route—while geometrically the shortest distance through n-space—-was also the most dangerous. It required detailed intelligence on Rigelian defenses and pushed through the heavily-defended Rigelian system of Gulliver. Varnok had determined a slightly more complex, but significantly safer, route.

Pan'vu possessed three wormhole jump gates. One connected to Zion's Waste, a starless void deep within Rigelian space, which the Rigelians used as a test range. Zion's Waste had four of its own wormhole junctions, two of which were exit termini. One exit led to a dead end in another starless nexus. Any ship taking that jump gate ended up a long way from anywhere. The other jumped directly into Centauri Seven, the heart of the Rigelian Navy's Seventh Fleet, bypassing the need to push through the heavily defended Bantar and Gulliver systems.

The Rigelians had never chosen to fortify this back door, knowing any intruder attempting to penetrate would have to cross Pan'vu first, and that system was heavily fortified with sensors. The Rigelians maintained a small fleet in Pan'vu at Turin's World, and the jump gates there were heavily covered by sensor networks.

Over-Commander Gorak had found a key to the Pan'vu attack problem: stealthed bladeships. With them the door to Centauri Seven could be opened. While Gorak had discovered the key, Pan'vu remained a tough nut to crack. The base had to be silenced quickly by bladeships if the Imperial Fleet was to enter Confederation space undetected and catch the Rigelians by surprise.

Therein lay the problem. The RCN had saturated the jump gate terminii with sophisticated sensor networks on their side of the wormhole, and throughout the space along their so-called Rim. The RCN fleet, including BATDIV-1, stood ready to react at a moment's notice. Worse, to even get to the jump gate one had to cross the vastness of Pan'vu's test range. Though Imperial ships could easily wormhole from the test range into Pan'vu, it was impossible to approach using conventional warships without being detected. As soon as warships wormholed

CHAPTER 5

into Pan'vu, the Rigelian sensors would detect their drives and warn the Confederation Fleet.

Bladeships could insert undetected and execute a successful attack on Pan'vu. Using specially-angled hull surfaces, baffled drive wedges, sensor-absorbing hull coatings, and sophisticated electronics, bladeships were the Imperial Navy's solution to the problem.

One difficulty was the limited number of bladeships available, for the Empire had produced only a precious few they were willing to expose to RCN capture. The production of bladeships was expensive in terms of both budget and technology. Their drives were also notoriously unreliable, often leaving crews stranded at low speeds deep in space.

The solution had been a hand-picked and well-trained bladeship squadron that would stealth on entrance to the Confederation Test Range and avoid sensors by crossing at slow speed. The squadron would proceed under stealth to the Pan'vu wormhole, a long and tedious trip at n-space velocities. Once there, it would jump into Pan'vu under stealth, reform and destroy the orbital defense station and its interstellar communications relays.

At the same moment, the warships of Imperial Task Force Two-Two would surge through the test range at high speed, wormhole into Pan'vu behind the bladeships and finish off any Rigelian units remaining in the system. ITF Two-Two's carrier force would then wormhole back into Zion's Waste, reform, and launch a following attack through the jump gate into Centauri Seven. The execution of the plan required skill, luck and adherence to a strict timetable.

So far, the operation seemed to be working brilliantly. The penetration of Bladeship Squadron 114 had been successful. Only a single bladeship had failed to make the rendezvous on time and the Rigelians in Pan'vu had been taken by surprise.

Upon entering the Rigelian Test Range, ITF Two-Two had encountered a single RCN destroyer, which had redlined its drives and fled, streaking away from the Pan'vu jump gate into open space. Tork didn't blame the Rigelian commander. A single destroyer stood no chance against an Imperial Task Force. Knowing he controlled the jump gate, Tork had been content to let it go. There was nothing in the test range except space all the way to the edge of the galactic arm. Without a jump gate to escape or send communications through, a lone enemy destroyer presented no threat. It had been cut off from its fleet and trapped in the n-space of the test range.

Tork had ordered ITF Two-Two through the jump gate and across the system to the next jump gate. There, the task force had wormholed into Zion's Waste. Now that force floated before another jump gate as it assumed battle formation, ready to attack Centauri Seven.

Other bladeship squadrons were inserting through other Rigelian wormholes, attempting to interdict RCN supply lines by ambush. They were to prey mainly on merchant vessels, as well as unsuspecting combatants they encountered. If the bladeships could cut the Rigelian lines

CHAPTER 5

of communication between the Rim and the Confederation Core Worlds, the Empire could wreak havoc across the entire frontier, grabbing the resource-rich star systems the Shikahn coveted. By the time the Rigelians recovered enough to organize a defense, the Empire would be in possession of the captured star systems.

The Imperial Staff assumed that rather than fight a costly war to reclaim a few border systems it had little real interest in, the Confederation would seek to end hostilities quickly via diplomacy rather than fight a protracted war, leaving the Empire richer in resources and providing many warriors the opportunity for glory. The Kahduhn felt the Rigelians would negotiate rather than lose the vast number of lives needed to regain the sparsely-populated Rim, especially since such undeveloped systems were of limited value to the Confederation.

Tork harbored private doubts on the Imperial Staff's reading of Rigelian psychology, however. He had studied and worked with Rigelians, most of whom were humans from a culture that had seceded from Earth's United Terran League. They were more capable and dangerous than the Kahduhn suspected. The negotiation belief seemed a bit optimistic to Tork, but it was his duty to carry out their wishes. As usual, the Kahduhn had assigned an Imperial Guard "advisor" to his ship—a spy—to ensure he did just that.

The attack plan was bold, and the Shikahn had authorized its execution, but Tork felt worried. The Confederation was a formidable opponent. While it was true humans were usually open and direct in their intentions, they could be strangely unpredictable, and even harbor bitter grudges when provoked. Human worlds, especially those along the Rim, were ruggedly individualistic, unlike the conformist fiefs of the Empire. This made the Rigelians a dangerous enemy. One never knew what humans might do when angered.

Tork understood Rigelians well enough to know that some human worlds would indeed scream for peace at any cost. Others, particularly the rugged, individualistic frontier systems, would fight. He also knew many states in the Confederation Core Worlds, particularly the professional warrior corps that made up the RCN fleet, would fight to the bitter end if ordered to do so by their government.

It was this latter group worrying him most. Whatever their importance in peacetime, once fighting began, civilians ceased to matter much in the conduct of war. Capable fighters determined the outcome of battles, and the RCN had plenty of them. He had studied beside them at their own naval academy.

Ten months of intense planning stood at the point of fruition. Pan'vu lay decimated, destroyed a short time ago. Imperial Task Force Two-Two now hovered in Zion's Waste, marshaling as carriers took up the front of the wall. Assault fighters would wormhole through the jump gate to make the first strike, followed by the heavy combatants, waiting only long enough to let the fighters complete their initial strikes before jumping in. Tork would not risk his carriers to direct enemy fire. The valuable carriers would stay safely in Zion's Waste, awaiting the return of their squadrons, while Karsian warships finished off whatever was left in Centauri Seven.

CHAPTER 5

Tork wondered what had happened to the missing bladeship commanded by Under-Lieutenant Torgh. It had vanished somewhere between the insertion point in the test range and the squadron's join-up near the Pan'vu jump gate. There had been no word concerning its whereabouts or its fate. Perhaps an accident, he decided. Such things were common enough in deep space. The disappearance of the *Yahk'tah* remained a mystery, however, and Tork did *not* like mysteries.

He sighed and rubbed his eyes again.

He was a warrior. Whatever the reservations in his heart, he was duty-bound to execute his orders and conduct the Shikahn's attack to the best of his ability. He must not show hesitancy before other warriors. The Imperial Guard was paranoid and remained zealous in their quest to root out any hint of treason. His Imperial Guard "advisor" would ensure that. If the Empire must attack the Confederation navy, then that attack must succeed, and to succeed it must be carried out swiftly, powerfully, and decisively. It would require all of his talents to accomplish that.

Tork rose and left his quarters. He took a lift to the flag bridge. As he entered the hatch, a sentry snapped to attention and announced the arrival of a fleet admiral. Admiral Moph and Over-Captain Gutahr glanced over from where they stood huddled over the tactical console, questions in their eyes.

Tork's eyes were shards of black ice as he sat on his command couch.

"Execute the attack."

CHAPTER 6

IMPERIAL ATTACK FORCE TWO-TWO-TWO, ZION'S WASTE NEXUS

Karsian fighters launched from their carriers and accelerated rapidly toward the Centauri stargate. The first wave was ninety-nine WF-320 heavy attack fighters and forty-five WF-130 torpedo bombers. An additional seventy-two Type 00 light fighters provided escort. The second wave boasted similar numbers: ninety-nine heavy attack fighters, forty-five torpedo bombers, and seventy-two escorts. The carrier force maintained a defensive screen of twenty-seven fighters on the near side of the jump gate to fend off any attacks that might emerge from the terminus and threaten the carriers.

The fighters formed quickly, aligned themselves with the wormhole jump gate, fifteen degrees above its entrance vector. In groups of threes, each fighter *sho-ya* circled, forming into squadrons. On sensors they appeared as a cloud of dots, like angry insects circling a disturbed hive. There were only two mechanical aborts in the first wave.

CHAPTER 6

The first wave raced toward the stargate three light-seconds away at nine hundred gravities of acceleration. The carriers' defense fighters patrolled a half light-second from the carriers, making a protective screen between the jump gate and carriers. It took twenty minutes for the first wave to reach the jump gate. By then the second attack force had completed marshaling. The first wave transitioned as a single formation traveling eight thousand kilometers per second. Two hundred and sixteen fighters vanished from one star system and instantly appeared in another 52.6 light-years away, hurtling toward the RCN space docks over Centauri Seven at 3 percent the speed of light.

In the lead fighter of the first wave, Over-Commander Mertahk transmitted the attack signal as he led the attack in.

RIGELIAN FLEET ORBITAL YARDS
CENTAURI SEVEN

The first wave struck the orbital docks as Karsian pilots quickly detected enemy vessels, assessed priorities, and selected targets.

Eight Rigelian battleships and sixteen cruisers hung motionless 899,000 kilometers away. An additional thirty RCN destroyers, forty frigates, and a multitude of smaller craft maintained station-keeping orbits above the mottled blue planet. Most of the RCN vessels were minimally manned, having disembarked their crews to the planet on liberty. No ship had shields or defensive systems online.

Over-Commander Mertahk turned his fighter to attack the orbital docks. One of the battleships appeared to be getting underway, edging out of its docking berth on maneuvering thrusters. Mertahk grinned. It was too late for the Rigelian. He quickly armed his weapons and led his squadron into the attack.

Surely, the Rigelians' scanners have picked us up by now.

The Rigelians would be analyzing the mass of drives appearing from the Zion jump gate terminus. The number and type of emissions would confuse them momentarily, as sensor operators and AIs scrambled, desperately trying to identify the unknown craft locking fire control on them. Only a few of the enemy, the true professionals, would instinctively understand what was happening. Mertahk's attack wave would destroy them before those few could react.

Activating fire control scanners, he put a targeting cursor on the nearest battleship. It hung dormant in its berth, a solid contact despite the lag time of his scanner at the current distance, a massive beast asleep in its nest. The cursor in his heads-up display pulsed, changing from yellow to red, indicating a solid lock. His weapon AI analyzed his lidar returns from the battleship, calculating range, aspect-angle, and closure. It fed data to the fighter's anti-ship missiles even as small, low-power targeting lasers targeted specific points on the hull of the ship. The

68

HUD showed a shrinking red circle as Mertahk closed into launch range.

On his rails, two anti-ship missiles awakened from electronic slumber, their warheads tracking the reflections of his targeting laser's energy with rapt attention. When the collapsing red circle became a dot, he would be in range.

The attack appeared to be perfect; the RCN had been caught off-guard. Their warships were lined up in neat rows, laid out in easily targetable packages. The Rigelians would have no time to react.

The HUD circle became a dot, and Mertahk pressed the launch button. The missiles accelerated away from their rails. G-forces induced by acceleration instantly released the arming safeties in their warheads.

Mertahk watched as each missile activated onboard homing lidars and boosted to forty thousand gravities. Against fighters, such weapons would have been of little use. Fighters were maneuverable enough to avoid anti-ship missiles once they accelerated to cruise speed. Even frigates and destroyers could sometimes avoid them if maneuvering hard, but stationary battleships were another matter. The size of the dreadnoughts made them easy targets that attracted missile swarms, and their great masses made them difficult to maneuver or accelerate since the battleships were stationary. It would take time to activate drives, bring up shields, and start moving their megaton masses. It was time they did not have.

It was impossible to strafe at such velocities. Mertahk's

force slammed on crash deceleration to slow closure rate to a more appropriate velocity for visual targeting and strafing at the time of intercept. As the attacking fighters decelerated, Mertahk's missiles raced ahead. They were just boosting past 11,700 kilometers per second when they slammed into the unshielded battleship *Horatio* thirty seconds later. Microseconds before impact, sensors in the missiles' warheads detected the magnetic field of the target and switched off internal magnetic bottles containing antimatter packages in their warheads. Deuterium fused with antimatter and two superheated suns of plasma eviscerated *Horatio* in a brilliant explosion as she took both hits amidships. Other missiles fired by his wingmen detonated in rapid succession on other ships in the docks an instant later.

Mertahk's steadily slowing fighter force, controlled by onboard AI, brought its short-range weapons to bear as the base came into energy range. Having slowed to strafing speed, Mertahk rolled his fighter away from the orbital docks as his wingmen fired missiles and beams into other targets. Some struck battleships. Others hit cruisers, destroyers, and frigates. Still more bore down upon the orbital docking facilities. Every target the fighters could find was targeted. Flights peeled away, slowing more as they dropped down into the planet's atmosphere.

Rigelian communications activity increased wildly as hundreds of RCN units at Centauri Seven began transmitting warnings and screaming for information across tactical nets.

CHAPTER 6

Mertahk's canopy polarized as a nearby battleship's fusion bottle failed and it died in a massive, searing nova.

RNSS *SHIVA*
CENTAURI SEVEN ORBIT

"Steady as she goes, helm."

"Steady as she goes, aye, Sir."

Captain Peter Kruger nodded as he watched the bridge monitors. The battleship *Shiva* fired maneuvering thrusters to clear the mooring tractors of the orbital docks. Liberty dirtside on Centauri Seven had been one of the best he'd experienced in his twenty T-years of service, and though he was a by-the-book captain, he'd been privately amused at the number of returnees who'd barely made it back in time for departure, including one of his tactical officers, who'd appeared rather disheveled and exhausted on arrival. It was time to leave Centauri Seven. He was anxious to patrol the Wonder Nebula, a vast region of gas and dust. The nebula was beautiful to the eye and had inspired generations of poets, and Kruger knew it would be no less moving despite having seen it many times before.

A flash lashed across the monitors, causing everyone on the bridge to wince. The screens blanked to static as an EMP blotted out the ship's sensors. Moments later, the screens snapped back into operation, and Kruger stared with his bridge crew in silent horror as the monitors showed *Horatio* explode in her docks.

Kruger glanced around. Everyone had the same shocked expression he knew he had on his own face. "What the hell?"

He stepped toward his sensor operator, as if that would somehow improve the sensors' abilities to sort information from chaos and confusion on the displays.

"Fighters!"

The cry came from a sensor rating at the lidar console. "Fighters are spilling out of the Zion stargate and attacking the base!"

"Sensors, ID those bogeys." Kruger strapped himself into his acceleration couch, realizing instinctively that time was critical. The stargate terminus from Zion's Waste was only three light-seconds from Centauri Seven.

Commander Saburo Yamashita, *Shiva's* executive officer, moved up beside him, surprise written on his own face.

The sensor tech, Chief Johann Kanaka, turned to glance back at them. "Negative IFF, Captain. Whoever they are, they're not squawking, and they're using active scanners and jamming."

Active scans? Jamming? Kruger's eyes widened in shock.

The chief continued speaking, staring at his displays. "Fire control lock-ons detected, Sir. We're spiked. CIC identifies the emitters as Cosmon-Alphas."

Kruger's jaw hardened. *Karsian fighters.*

He had no idea how Karsian fighters could have penetrated the plethora of sensor networks in Zion's Waste undetected, but he wasn't about to waste time worrying about it. What mattered was they were here and attacking the base.

"Helm, all ahead flank! Sound general quarters. All hands to battle stations."

Shiva accelerated as her main drives kicked in with a surge of power, shoving her forward with sudden velocity. The acceleration momentarily overcame the inertial dampeners, jerking everyone sternward before the system corrected. Yamashita braced against the back of a couch, his eyes wide as he watched the tactical display, then he leaped for the access tube ladder, sliding from sight as the bridge airlocks began to close.

Throughout *Shiva*, men and women dashed to battle stations rapidly donning vacuum suits. Pressure hatches hissed shut, preparing the battleship for combat.

"The fighters are launching missiles, Skipper. We have Vampires inbound."

Kruger stared at the speaker; a petty officer named Kormanski. "Vampire" was the naval term for enemy anti-ship missiles.

"Raise shields. Active jamming protocols. Guns, get all weapons online ASAP."

"Aye, aye, Sir." Lieutenant Commander Stefan Wade, *Shiva's* gunnery officer, was the link between life and death at the moment. Wade worked his weapons console even as he donned his pressure suit, staring at the displays with intense scrutiny.

Kruger watched the battle holo-tank illuminate as it kicked into a 3-D representation of Centauri Seven's battlespace. Surveillance teams were struggling to establish data link with Port Control even as detonations flashed across the displays and Karsian weapons slammed into orbital docks. Multiple red lines were arcing toward *Shiva* in the holo-tank, telltale signs of incoming missiles. *Shiva's* sensors blinked as a nearby battleship's reactor core detonated, ripping it to atoms.

Wade stared at the explosion in shock. "Holy mother of God."

There was a moment of silence on the bridge as the crew stared in horror. Even the GQ alarms ceased their eerie wailing as the ship assumed general quarters.

Kormanski was the first to regain composure. "There's a wall of vampires headed our way with a wave of fighters behind them, Skipper."

"Helm, hard to port. Roll out two-four-zero mark one-one-two. Guns, bring starboard batteries to bear. Target all hostiles, priority on the vampires. Engineering, maintain flank speed. All hands brace for acceleration and high-g maneuvers. Mister Wade, fire at will. You're Weapons Free." Kruger spat the orders with staccato precision, as if he'd practiced them for years.

Which he had.

G-forces squeezed the crew as *Shiva* rapidly accelerated, overwhelming the struggling inertia dampers again. The battleship's frame groaned as g-force increased to four gravities in a matter of seconds.

A trio of fighters turned toward *Shiva*, attracted by her movement.

CHAPTER 6

Wade turned from his console. "Point Defense Missile racks online, Captain."

"Target primary PDM racks on the vampires. Target secondaries on the fighters. Do it now, before they launch more missiles."

"Aye, Sir, targeting vampires primary and fighters secondary."

Kormanski's voice sounded in his earpiece as Kruger locked his helmet into place on his vacuum suit. "Shields initializing, Skipper."

Wade cut in. "PDM racks one, two and three firing. Chicks away, Sir, good MIF bars, solid locks."

Kruger turned back to the holo-tank. "Tell the beam batteries we need them yesterday."

More red lines raced toward *Shiva* in the display, opposed by thin blue lines moving away from *Shiva's* hull, PBMs intercepting the sparkling red dots of enemy fighters. Explosions danced in the display and the heavens around *Shiva* erupted in strobe-like nuclear detonations.

Shiva shuddered as missiles hit her rising shields, their antimatter warheads jarring her but failing to penetrate her Podkletnov fields. Shiva's point defenses answered in kind as gunners engaged fighters and missiles.

Lieutenant Commander Wade grinned as a PDM took out a fighter in the attacking wave. PDMs were finding multiple targets, each stopping a fighter or missile, but there were too many threats to stop them all. Centauri Seven's space docks were exploding behind *Shiva* in a shamble of torn girders, burning starships, flying shrapnel, and whirling debris. Kruger grimaced as a nearby ODS exploded and tumbled away, ejecting a mass of super-heated viscera.

Shiva lurched again as three fighter missiles struck her flank shields. The shields remained intact, but no shield generator could handle that much energy at once. A cloud of glowing neon-blue plasma swirled around the battle-ship inside the shields, arcing and flashing as it short-circuited external shield generator nodes. Some overloaded and failed, collapsing sections of the shield bubble and opening holes in *Shiva's* defenses.

Another missile smashed into the damaged shield. The ship shook violently as X-ray lasers from its war-head stabbed through gaps in the shield, knifing through her hull like hot bullets through butter. Pressure alarms screamed as the hull was breached. Automatic airlocks began slamming shut and structural fields energized, pre-venting explosive decompression, but *Shiva* was hurt. She was streaming atmosphere like frozen blood through tears in her hull.

Kormanski sounded desperate over the intercom in Kruger's helmet. *"We've lost airtight integrity, Skipper. Whiffers rolling in dead ahead."*

More fighter missiles knocked down Shiva's front shield. As it collapsed a long line of fighters rolled in through the gap to strafe her hull with lasers.

Wade spoke again. "Point defenses, fire at will."

Frequency-modulated lasers and point defense coil-guns erupted along the length of Shiva's hull, lashing out with talons of energy and kinetic projectiles to swat down the angry swarm of hornets stinging her. Fighters began to explode as point defenses found the range, even as laser fire from the fighters sliced through armored plates on the battleship's skin, creating molten slag.

A tremendous lurch rocked *Shiva.*

A new voice yelled on the intercom in Kruger's helmet. "Bridge, Engineering. We just took a hit to our main intercoupler. If it fails now, we'll go ballistic. We can hold this acceleration for a while, but we need to get out of here if we expect to survive this party."

Kruger glanced at the tactical displays. Data link was offline. His chief engineer's warning was all the incentive he needed. If *Shiva* was to have a fighting chance, she had to gain maneuvering room. He had to get her into open space where she could activate drives, gain separation, and achieve maneuvering acceleration. With enough distance and speed *Shiva* could give as well as she got. Trapped in the limited confines of the Fleet orbital yards, she was just a big target.

Centauri Seven was already a shambles. Ships were exploding everywhere. Remaining to die with the rest wouldn't help anyone. Getting some separation might save one of the division's few remaining battleships. The Gallagher stargate lay in the opposite direction but almost as close as the Zion's Waste stargate from which enemy fighters were pouring.

"A second wave of fighters emerging at the Zion stargate, Sir, headed for the Centauri complex." Kormanski pointed at the sensor display.

Kruger had seen enough. "We can't survive in this chaos. Helm, make for the Gallagher stargate, flank speed. All hands, rig for heavy acceleration."

"Aye, Sir."

More scarlet contacts appeared at the Zion stargate icon. The new icons were large and triangular, indicating heavy warships emerging to follow the fighters into the attack.

Kruger resisted an urge to curse. "Sensors, ID those heavies. Those look like capital ships coming in."

Even as he spoke, a WF-320 strafed *Shiva* nose-on, its sponson-mounted lasers shearing molten divets in *Shiva's* ablative armor. Point defense clusters responded in kind and a laser scored a direct hit. The Karsian pilot died instantly, sliced in half by the beams, but his WF-320 fighter lost control, flipping end-over-end as it tumbled toward *Shiva's* superstructure.

Kormanski jabbed a hand at the red triangles in the display. "Positive ID on the heavies at the 'gate, Sir. They *are* capital ships. They're ignoring us and going for the planet."

Kruger cursed. He had no choice now. A battleship, even one as vastly outnumbered as *Shiva*, couldn't run in the face of a Karsian capital ship attack, not with a populated planet in the path of destruction. Fleeing attacking fighters was one thing. Running from enemy warships was another thing entirely. The RCN had been founded to protect citizens, and *Shiva* was the only working warship between the planet and the attacking Karsian force.

CHAPTER 6

He had to fight.

"All hands, prepare to engage enemy warships. Guns, all batteries are cleared to fire."

The tumbling WF-320 slammed into *Shiva* at that moment. Its wreckage, tumbling through the vacuum at extreme speed, smashed through the battleship's armor into the bridge. It became molten in an instant, punching deeper, burning a hole deep into Shiva's bowels.

Kruger and his bridge crew died instantly as the impact vaporized Shiva's bridge. Debris spewed from Shiva's hull. Explosive decompression alarms screamed their fading warnings in the waning atmosphere, even as molten metal tore deep into the battleship's core. *Shiva* belched atmosphere that froze and trailed behind her like blood. Shuddering under the impact, she rolled to port, the destruction of her bridge locking her drive controls at full acceleration.

Out of control, *Shiva* continued straight ahead pulling four hundred gravities of acceleration.

CHAPTER 7

IKS *MURGAHH*
CENTAURI SEVEN

"Launch capital missiles at the remaining orbitals." Tork's voice was grim as he gave the orders. The enemy facilities were now within range of his capital ships.

The fighters had accomplished their task. The Confederation fleet had been caught unaware. The orbital facilities had been smashed beyond repair. Eight Rigelian battleships had been destroyed or gutted. What remained of their charred hulls was tumbling away in decaying orbits. Seventeen enemy cruisers had died as well, allowing Tork's fleet free reign in attacking surviving targets. Only the Rigelian destroyers had managed to respond, valiantly returning fire as they attempted to get underway.

Otarg, Murgahh's senior sensor officer, pointed at an icon in the tactical display. "Enemy battleship bearing zero-two-one, sixteen degrees up-angle and accelerating."

Tork frowned. "Closure?"

"Negative frequency shift, *Korguhn*. It appears to be running away and is increasing acceleration."

"Any sign of the Rigelian carriers?"

"None detected, Korguhn. Shall we pursue the battleship?"

"No. Destroy the remaining orbitals and put capital missiles on all combatants within range."

Captain Gutahr turned in his command chair. "What about vessels on the planet, Korguhn? We can destroy them with PBMs. They are helpless bliks sitting on the planet's surface."

Any Rigelian vessel on the planet's surface was a legitimate target under the rules of war. It was Tork's duty to destroy them as threats to the Empire. A planetary bombardment missile strike, however, was an option he preferred not to use. "No. Send the cruisers into low orbit and bombard them with conventional weaponry."

Gutahr looked incredulous. "*Conventional* weaponry? From low orbit? Why get so close, Korguhn? We can launch PBMs at extended range and smash their planet to rubble without exposing ourselves to planetary defenses. Skimming the atmosphere and taking potshots at targets of opportunity increases our risk. Conventional missiles and beams require precise targeting, and our beams will have difficulty penetrating the atmosphere."

Tork shook his head. "We do not desire needless civilian deaths, *Bor'klar*. Planet-busters will not be required. Use precision weapons, beams and missiles. Surgically remove military targets but keep collateral civilian damage to a minimum. No random targeting of civil population centers unless they are legitimate military targets under the rules of war."

"But why, Korguhn? We have taken them by surprise. They are at our mercy and helpless. Moving so close to the planet will expose our ships to planetary defenses. We have them on their knees, Korguhn. We can finish them now with one blow and make a clean sweep. Dead enemies cannot fight us later."

Tork felt his anger building. *Does this fool understand nothing about his enemy? No, he has never had the opportunity to serve with humans.*

"I intend to finish the job, Bor'klar. Our task is the destruction of the military facilities at Centauri Seven. Nothing in my orders implies extermination of Rigelian noncombatants. This is a military campaign, not genocide. If we slaughter civilians, it will create an emotional backlash throughout the Confederation. What we hope to achieve here by surprise might well then become unattainable. There is no advantage in adding fury to our enemy's psyche. Military strikes they will understand; genocide they will not. There is no reason to supply our enemy with martyrs. That will only make them fight harder, and our task is difficult enough.

"Such an attack would make diplomacy—which the yihaki will require to negotiate an end that will keep the resource worlds we desire—impossible to accomplish. The enemy will not seek terms if we slaughter millions of civilians, and no one could blame them. We want Rigelians disorganized and confused, not united in righteous anger. Besides, we may need the planet for our own purposes later. Using PBMs would leave it uninhabitable, and we do not have time to remain here reducing the planet to rubble, even if we wanted to."

"Why?" Gutahr did not understand. "We have destroyed their fleet. We have them where we want them."

"Do you think this is the entire Confederation Fleet?" Tork shook his head. "We have secured Centauri Seven, but we have failed to destroy Centauri's carrier force. We have destroyed, at best, a battleship division and its support units. That opens a hole into the Confederation, but this was a small fraction of their fleet, and we have many battles yet to fight."

"But Korguhn—"

"We only brought a single battle squadron into this system, Gutahr. It is conceivable the Rigelians may have intelligence of our plans and are even now preparing to counterattack. We will complete our assigned mission and depart this system quickly. If the RCN cuts us off in Zion's Waste, the entire campaign will be at risk. Now stop questioning my orders or I will have you relieved, Bor'klar."

"Yes, Korguhn!" Gutahr's obedience was instant. He pointed at the data link display. Fighters were exiting the jump gate, returning to their carriers in Zion's Waste, where they would rearm to meet any Rigelian counterattack.

Tork turned to the sensor station. "Where is that fleeing Rigelian battleship, Otarg?"

"Headed toward the other jump gate, Korguhn." Otarg

pointed a hand at a blip in the display. "It is beyond weapons range and accelerating rapidly."

"Let it go. One battleship will not change the tactical situation here. We will be gone before it can return. Launch capital missiles at the orbitals, then have the cruisers and destroyers bombard military facilities on the surface with precision fire. When they are done, they shall withdraw to Zion's Waste. Leave a destroyer screen behind to cover our egress."

"But the battleship, Korguhn. We should—"

"Does everyone on this ship question my orders?" Tork's voice became a growl as he rose to his feet. Fear creased the faces of the Karsians near him. "I said *let it go*, Otarg. It is one ship. We have achieved our objectives here. Carry out your orders."

"Yes, Korguhn!"

Tork sighed and sank into his command couch. In many ways, the attack on Centauri Seven had gone too easily. It had worked as planned, except for the failure of destroying Seventh Fleet's carrier force. Imperial Intelligence had believed the carriers to be in port at Centauri Seven, but they had been wrong on that point.

Tork regretted the destruction of Turin's World in Pan'vu, but he had little choice in that case. The RCN facilities there had been deep underground. In order for the preemptive strike to succeed, he had been forced to destroy the planet to keep communications from warning the RCN fleet at Centauri Seven.

The attack on Turin's World had killed thousands of

Rigelians, but all had been military personnel. Centauri Seven had millions of civilians. Using PBMs against it would slaughter those millions and shatter the planet, creating an interstellar atrocity and a military complication the Empire did not need.

The data link pulsed as Karsian ships launched missile salvos at the remaining orbitals. Rigelian destroyers, frigates, dockyards, and ODS platforms died in brilliant flashes that momentarily eclipsed the brightness of the local sun. Rigelians on the planet's surface returned fire weakly. Karsian cruisers moved into low orbit, pinpointing enemy defense sites on the surface and concentrating kinetic and beam fire on them. All military resistance was quickly silenced as cruisers and destroyers circled in low orbit, smashing dirtside facilities.

"The docks and ODS platforms are destroyed, Korguhn." Gutahr continued to stare at Tork after making his report.

Tork realized he had lost his sense of time, his mind wandering around in gloomy corridors. He nodded to Gutahr. "Retrograde the squadron, Bor'klar. All ships will proceed back into Zion's Waste. Destroyer Squadron One-Five-One-Eight will cover our withdrawal."

"Yes, Korguhn."

Tork stood. His presence was no longer required on the flag bridge. The war had begun, and the Confederation had been dealt a serious blow.

If the Empire could maintain the initiative, it might defeat the great industrial power of the Confederation long enough to negotiate for possession of the star systems it had captured. The trick would be maintaining the initiative long enough for it to work.

Otherwise, the Confederation would bring its massive industrial might to bear, producing starships at a rate the Empire could never hope to match. If the war could be won quickly, there was good chance of victory. If Tork's fleets could run the enemy ragged and keep the enemy off balance long enough, yihaki would be able to conclude an end to hostilities before the tide of battle turned. With any luck, the new star systems would remain within the Empire's grasp when the war ended.

Then why do I feel so uneasy? Is it because I know humans too well? I know what they are capable of when driven to desperation and fueled by hate.

Ultimately, the universe was a study in balance. The premeditated attack on Centauri Seven had been too easy, and Fate had a nasty way of balancing great victories with equally great disasters. Everything, it seemed, came with a price.

When the price for the war was paid, Tork hoped it would be worth the number of lives taken.

RNSS *SHIVA,*
CENTAURI SEVEN STAR SYSTEM

Yamashita grimaced as the g-forces increased to six gravities. He was barely able to force his fingers across the control panel and send text commands to Engineering. Bones creaked in his neck, and the steadily increasing g-forces squashed him hard into his seat in Auxiliary Control.

Shiva was running at full acceleration and out of control. Her drive had been set to flank speed just before the explosion on the bridge. The crashing Karsian fighter that had killed Kruger, the bridge crew, and had damaged the inertia damping system controls and cut off drive access from any source except Engineering. *Shiva* was barreling toward the Gallagher stargate with increasing acceleration, and without the inertia dampers, the g-forces would eventually become fatal.

If he could access the engineering protocols and regain control of reaction thrusters, he could flip the battleship end-for-end. That would orient her drive field in the opposite direction, slowing her, hopefully keeping the g-loads within human tolerance. Of course, if Engineering failed to shut off the drive, *Shiva* would simply slow to a stop and accelerate again in the opposite direction, back towards the battle in Centauri Seven, and the process would repeat. Establishing a few minutes of normal gee would allow Shiva's engineers time to move around long enough to reroute computer control of the drive system.

Yamashita's vision became a tunnel as the g-forces crushed him into his couch. Normally he weighed seventy-two kilos. At the moment, due to the g-forces, his body weight was nearing half a ton, and the ship was continuing to accelerate.

He struggled as he punched in command codes, feeling his face stretch from the induced gee. His body was sweating profusely, and g-forces threatened to break his finger joints and neck. A yellow light pulsed on the control panel, indicating Engineering's response. He'd managed to access maneuvering thrusters. The problem would be getting his hands to work under the ever-increasing g-load. He struggled to move his fingers again on the keypad.

Stern thrusters fired, and the vector of the g-forces shifted. *Shiva* began a slow skid. Bow thrusters added additional injects, creating a slow spin that caused the battleship to tumble in a great arc. The universe seemed to spin wildly around them as the starship swapped ends. A surge of weird lateral, transverse, and negative g's threatened to make Yamashita's stomach heave. The g-force intensity waned as the ship's acceleration slowed.

Now!

Yamashita fired opposite thrusters, stabilizing Shiva's orientation a hundred and eighty degrees from her original vector. The drive field was now oriented opposite to her direction of travel. The drive continued rumbling at full power, slowing the battleship rapidly as it raced backwards through space.

G-forces dissipated steadily, and Shiva's engineers struggled from their couches, staggering toward their control panels on shaking legs, desperate to find a way to regain control.

Yamashita breathed easier as the g-force lessened, and punched commands into the control panel more rapidly. His heartbeat was no longer thundering in his ears and his hearing had returned to normal.

CHAPTER 7

He tapped the intercom. "Engineering, Aux Con. Cut the mains any way you can. Damage report, all stations. Aux Con is now the acting bridge."

"We're streaming atmosphere, XO." The response from DCD. "We can't move around much down here yet. Still too much gee on the deck, but auto-hatches have sealed. We've got a dozen minor hull ruptures, but we're sealing off exits to the outer hull. Structural integrity fields are holding."

"Understood. Navigation, get a fix on how far we are from the Gallagher stargate. Before the spin we were only—"

Yamashita never finished his words. *Shiva* reached a point in space where tremendous gravitational forces between stars had eons ago created a dimensional tunnel, and *Shiva* wormholed.

NAVAL OFFICER'S CLUB
NEW FLORIDA, CENTAURI SEVEN

Talara rose from the mud, stunned at the destruction around her.

The officers' club was rubble, smashed beyond recognition by beams that had rained down from space as Kuroshima's crew partied inside the O-Club. The roof had collapsed as the building exploded in a torrent of shattered steel, glass, and ceramic debris.

The first indication of attack had come when *Ghandi* exploded in her docks across the base at the refit yards. The concussion had shattered the club's windows. Talara had rushed to the holes where windows had been to stare open-mouthed as explosions had walked across the starship apron where *Kuroshima* was berthed.

She'd been unable to tell if *Kuroshima* had been hit before beams had lashed back and flattened the officers club in a searing blast. The explosion had tossed her through the open window, saving her life, but it had also buried her shipmates in rubble. She rose painfully, dusting safety glass from her uniform, then rushing back into dust and smoke to try to assist her shipmates. She found only death and destruction.

Commander O'Brady, her commanding officer, the XO, and all of the ship's staff were dead, crushed by a falling girder where they'd gathered at the punch bowl. Only a pink pulp remained of them, oozing out from under the girder. She saw no signs of life.

Stumbling outside, she collapsed amid broken pipes spewing water into the air, shaking as wet mud soaked through her uniform pants. She watched the intense battle in the night sky above, where successive strobe-like flashes pinpointed nuclear detonations and expanding smudges of light, marking the death of starships in orbit.

Egon is up there, she thought, *fighting for his life in all of that.*

Egon had departed for *Shiva* as soon as they'd finished making love, too short on time to escort her to the officers club dirtside. Fretting on being late for castoff, he'd dashed from Kuroshima's gangway to the shuttle apron, where Shiva's last gig had been readying for lift-off.

Battleships were too massive to enter a planet's atmosphere. *Shiva* had waited in the orbital docks above Centauri Seven for the last of her liberty parties to return. *Shiva* was somewhere up there now, preparing to get underway, and Egon was aboard.

God, she pleaded silently, tears streaming down her cheeks, *please let him be all right.*

Sobs wracked her for a minute.

After a while, the flashes in the sky seemed to wane. She noticed mud on her clothing and realized she sat in a water puddle amid shrubbery. Broken water mains were flooding the garden. She was covered with mud and soaked with water. Spots of blood dripped from her nose, caused by the blast's concussion, speckling onto her tunic. New lieutenant's rings adorned her sleeves, glowing dimly in the starlight with a cheerfulness seeming blasphemous in such disaster.

Tears blinded her as she watched the battle above. She cried for the death and destruction around her, and because of shock. She cried for the fate of world she was on, a world that had been bombarded. She cried from terror and a fear of dying. She cried as the first human had cried, kneeling in the muck and wailing at uncaring stars above. Mostly, however, she cried for Egon, caught in the terrible tumult above.

"Lieutenant Kibbleman?"

The voice in the darkness surprised her. Talara turned reddened eyes toward it as she strained to make out the speaker.

"It's me, Lieutenant. Reggie."

She recognized Lieutenant Junior Grade Reginald Yantali by his unique accent. The young officer hailed from the Eusi Hegemony. He'd signed aboard as *Kuroshima's* junior navigator a week ago. Another man stood beside him; a younger-looking officer Talara didn't recognize.

Reggie hooked a thumb at him. "This is Ensign Harper. He received his assignment to *Kuroshima* last night. I brought him over to see what your orders are."

Talara stared at him, nonplussed, as tears dripped down her angular cheeks. Her brows knitted and her eyes became black ice.

"What?" She realized she was shouting, though whether due to fear or her loudly ringing ears she wasn't certain. Her voice shook and tears blinded her again. "Go away and leave me alone."

Reggie moved closer and knelt, concern on his features in the light of the orange flames coming from the ramp. "Are you all right, Talara? Are you hurt?"

"No, dammit. I'm just . . ."

Sobs wracked her again, violently, as she fought her shock and fear. Unanswered questions tormented her soul.

Is Egon still alive? Is he injured or dead? Am I alone? What just happened? Who attacked us? Why won't these people stop talking at me and leave me alone? What is happening?

She felt Reggie's hand on her shoulder and looked up

at him. "Sorry, Talara. It's just that . . . well, you're senior-ranking officer now."

She glared, anger contorting her face. "We're *lieutenants*, Reggie."

Reggie nodded and stood. "That's true, but as of today, you're a *full* lieutenant. I'm still junior in grade. All the senior officers are dead, Talara. The Skipper, the XO, all of them. Next in line is chief engineer, and that means you."

She closed her eyes, wanting to scream and beat the ground with her fists.

Command? Is he insane? I'm an engineer, not a line officer. He should find someone whose universe hasn't been destroyed in the last few minutes. Someone whose lover isn't up there, dying in that raging hell. Why is Reggie acting like I'm the CO?

After a moment, something made her stand. She remembered an oath taken at the Academy. That oath came before her personal needs or desires. The discipline of the service had been programmed into her. Her training took over, almost with a will of its own.

An officer *led*, regardless of professional specialty. Officers were leaders. She had no idea of what to do, but she'd been taught long ago that if one doubted about how to command, one should pretend like they knew, whether true or not. She must act as Commander O'Brady would have wanted her to act. She'd have to make the up the rest as she went. She must act for her shipmates if no one else, no matter how much she was hurting inside.

"Okay." She sniffled and wiped her nose with a muddy

sleeve. It came away wet with mucous. "Get some corpsmen over here. Maybe we can save someone inside. Ensign, hoof it over to *Kuroshima* and take charge there. Find any chiefs or senior petty officers and have them account for the crew, and make sure they know *you* are in charge until I get there. If the ship's destroyed, let me know. If she's only damaged, begin immediate repair efforts and get a casualty count. If *Kuroshima* is capable of launching, have the crew prepare to get underway. Whoever attacked us might come back, and we can't afford to be caught dirtside again."

"Yes, Ma'am." The men answered in unison. Harper turned and took off, jogging at a fast pace. *No doubt he's in great condition from his recent Academy training. He probably ran varsity track or something.*

It was an absurd thought to have in the middle of a disaster, almost as absurd as the disaster itself. She almost laughed, then closed her eyes as the tears returned, but this time she cried in silence and remained standing.

Reggie touched her arm again. She opened her eyes and saw the concern in his. He indicated the heavens with his eyes. "It's going to be okay, Talara. I know it looks bad up there at the moment, but if anyone can get through that, it's Lieutenant Storm. He's a survivor."

Talara smiled at him through her tears. Reggie's words gave hope, something to clutch onto in the depths of a nightmare. She knew what Egon would expect of her. She gripped Reggie's hand warmly for a moment and released it. "Thanks, Reggie. Let's see what we can do around here."

"Aye, aye, *Ma'am*."

The odd way he said it gave her pause. Reggie had said it with respect.

Reggie dashed into the demolished club to search for survivors. Ambulance shuttles were already arriving, descending from the sky, red and blue emergency strobes flashing. Reggie began waving them down and vectoring them to suitable landing zones.

Talara moved to help him. Tears still blurred her vision, but at least now she could act.

Talara Kibbleman had been many things in her young life: daughter, sister, woman, starship engineer, Naval Academy graduate, and a descendent of immigrant Jews. At the moment she felt like a scared little girl, but there was a job to do. She was *Lieutenant* Kibbleman, acting CO of RNSS *Kuroshima*.

Most of all for Egon, who would expect her to do her duty.

She stepped through debris looking for survivors, quickly waving a corpsman over when she found an arm moving beneath a pile of debris. It was going to be a long night.

CHAPTER 8

RNSS *SHIVA*
GALLAGHER STAR SYSTEM

Shiva groaned as she popped back into n-space. Slowly, sensors came online as navigation AIs identified stars and pinpointed the jump coordinates as the Gallagher stargate terminus.

Yamashita ordered *Shiva* in-system, away from the stargate. Fearing pursuit by Karsian capital ships, he knew he couldn't loiter near the terminus. Centauri Seven was under attack, but taking *Shiva* back into that maelstrom would be suicide. It would accomplish little except give the enemy a chance to destroy another RCN battleship. As far as he could tell, *Shiva* had been the only ship to escape the Centauri Seven attack.

The surprise attack had been devastating, yet even as he hated the Karsians for their treachery and the death and destruction they'd caused, the professional side of his mind grudgingly admitted their tactics had been excellent. The bastards had left Centauri Seven a shambles.

His immediate fear was a Karsian battle force might follow *Shiva* through the stargate. In her present condition, *Shiva* wouldn't stand a chance if they caught her. She could fight, but due to the damage she'd taken to her bridge and her drive controls, she couldn't maneuver, at least for the time being.

Yamashita had remained in his vacuum suit. He'd reentered the bridge as soon as Damage Control had cut a path to it. What was left of the bridge was in hard vacuum. Damage control teams had been forced to cut their way in because the exits had been fused by the fighter's explosion. Sealed in his suit, he'd stared at the once-familiar compartment, amazed it had ever been a bridge. Pieces of charred fighter had fused into the deck and bulkheads. Carbon scoring blackened everything, obscuring shattered tritanium and compartment spars.

There were no bodies. Any organic material that had survived the super-heated destruction of the bridge had been sucked into space during the explosive decompression. What remained was a barren, blackened tomb without deceased, a mute testimony to a lost battle. Yamashita was glad they were gone. Body parts would have only further shocked and numbed the rescue parties. The dead had been his friends and shipmates, but they were gone now, and there was no bringing them back. Fortunately, they had never known what killed them.

The bridge's grav-plates had been destroyed in the

collision, forcing Yamashita to tether himself to the deck as he explored the compartment in mag-boots. When he could stand it no longer, he nodded to the DCP officer who'd accompanied him through the opening. "Seal it off, Lieutenant. Auxiliary Control will act as CIC from here on out."

"Yes, Sir." The lieutenant's radio reply was muted. He motioned to suited DCP personnel as Yamashita worked his way back through the airlock into the atmosphere and artificial gravity of the ship.

My ship, he thought bitterly. Like all line officers, he'd dreamed of commanding a battlewagon one day, but he'd never wanted to earn command of one this way.

Lieutenant Commander Robert Campbell assisted him with unsealing his helmet. "How bad is it, Sir?"

"Bad." Yamashita stared at the deck, unwilling to meet his subordinate's eyes. "It's gone, Bob. All of it. It's just . . . gone."

"The Skipper?"

"Gone. They're all dead. Not a fingernail left of any of them."

Campbell looked away, unable to speak. Like most of the crew, he was still in shock. Kruger had been a much admired and respected captain and a noted master of battle employment.

What are we going to do without him?

Yamashita moved to a bulkhead intercom and thumbed in the code for Engineering. "Vishy?"

"*Yes, Sir.*" Lieutenant Commander Vishniandu

CHAPTER 8

Sivananda, Shiva's chief engineer, was of Indian descent. As always, he sounded polite and calm, his voice edged with a slight British accent.

"Ship status?"

"Not good, Commander. Our primary drive nodes are working, but they're out of sync. We have control of the reactor intermix, but little directional control of the drive train. We can continue straight ahead at low acceleration, but if we push it up, we risk another runaway, and possibly a containment breach."

"How about the auxiliaries?"

"Also working but limited, Sir. We can use them to supplement the mains, but there's a power distribution problem. I can use the engines to make us go, or I can use them to make us stop, but I don't have the distribution to do both and still give you firepower. The trunk lines in the main grid are down."

Yamashita sat on a corridor bench. *What a way to get a command.*

So far, the enemy hadn't wormholed into Gallagher behind them, but that didn't mean they wouldn't. It was never a good idea to assume the ship was safe. He'd have to keep the crew at general quarters until they were safely away from the stargate.

At the slow speed they were restricted to, that would be a long time. At their current velocity of 3 percent cee, it was a week's travel to the next stargate, a long time to remain at GQ. He would un-suit the crew once they were far enough from the stargate that the sensors could give them time to resuit if needed. More importantly, he had to get word to the Fleet about the attack on Centauri Seven.

He glanced up at Campbell. "Bob, prep a comm drone with the attack recording and send it ahead to the Fleet. The Admiralty needs to know what happened in Centauri Seven ASAP. Vishy, you still on the line?"

"*Still here, Sir.*"

"Good. If the mains drop off, use the auxiliaries to keep moving away from the stargate and save battery power for the weapons. We'll adjust our acceleration profile based on our firepower needs as the situation dictates. Match the drive configuration profiles in Engineering with those we have on the mains. If we can get the auxiliaries and the mains synchronized, we can eliminate any asymmetrical stress on the hull. Keep the reactor pressures within tolerable limits and watch the intercoolers. One thing we don't need is a fusion bottle breach."

"*Aye, Sir.*" Sivananda's voice sounded cheerful, despite the grimness of the situation. "One question, Sir: will we be returning to Centauri?"

"I think the Confederation's lost enough battleships today, Vishy. No, we'll stay away from there. I'll need the tactical officer in CIC, though. Where is Commander Oto?"

"*He was . . . on the bridge, Sir.*"

Yamashita sighed and placed his head in his hands. "Who's alternate TAC-O?"

"*Lieutenant Storm, Sir.*"

"Is he alive?"

"*Yes, Sir. He's working with DCP teams on Deck 22.*"

CHAPTER 8

"Get him out of that vac-suit and up to my quarters. He and I are going to have a skull session and figure out how we're going to get to a safe haven in one piece."

"*Aye, Sir.*"

"Yamashita out."

He punched the intercom off and closed his eyes, fighting the waves of fatigue washing over him. *Shiva* was a good ship, but she was in a lot of danger. Her engine controls were jammed. She had wounds and tears in her superstructure. Her bridge was gone, and several weapons batteries were out of commission. There were dead and wounded aboard, and atmosphere still leaked from a dozen tears in her hull. It would be weeks before she could reach a repair yard, and Yamashita knew he would personally suffer every second of that long journey.

Captain Kruger was gone. As executive officer, *Shiva* was now his responsibility.

He looked up, startled at the silence around him. The last DCP rating had left the corridor, and he was alone for the first time in hours. He sighed, realizing his quarters were at the other end of the ship and the transit lifts were out. He'd have to walk or use the crawlways.

The ship's hurt, but she's not dead, not by a long shot. Not Shiva.

She had been named for the Hindu destroyer god that shattered worlds, and sooner or later she would do exactly that, and Yamashita knew exactly whose worlds he intended to shatter.

The Karsians had hurt *Shiva*, but they hadn't killed

her, and that had been a grave mistake. The Karsians, by God, would come to regret it, for *Shiva* would return with a vengeance.

Yamashita began the long walk to his quarters, a slow anger burning in his heart.

The war was far from over. Indeed, it had just begun.

CHAPTER 9

ORBITAL DEFENSE STATION
PAN'VU SYSTEM

Yeager paused to catch her breath as she clung to the handrail on Deck 14 and fought her claustrophobia. The explosion that had hit the station had initially tossed her off the bunk where she'd been sleeping against a bulkhead as atmospheric alarms had screamed shrill warnings at her. Pickering had departed, and she'd been alone in his quarters when the explosion had occurred.

Yeager secretly despised the lecherous officer, but he was essential to her ambitions. Coming from common stock, she had no sponsors in the Navy, and promotion depended upon good reports from seniors on her skills as a yeoman.

She'd decided long ago there was more than one way to succeed in a military career. Pickering made it a practice to rut with every pretty female in his command if possible, provided they were naïve enough to let him get away with it. That usually meant the lower enlisted ratings. Female officers and noncommissioned officers, who had more experience, wouldn't have put up with such things from a lieutenant commander, but junior enlisted sometimes would.

Pickering pressured young girls into *entertaining* him in exchange for promises of doing something "good" for their careers. It violated Navy regulations and was punishable by court martial, but that never seemed to bother Pickering. He'd never had a single harassment charge filed against him in a decade-long career. Yeager knew that was true because as his personal yeoman she'd checked his file.

Two could play that game, however. Early on Yeager had decided she could use Pickering as easily as he planned to use her. For the price of playing *load-the-torpedo* once in a while, she'd obtained enough dirt on Pickering to blackmail him into helping her whenever she chose.

Their sessions together, while often bizarre—and which somehow made her feel dirty—nevertheless left her satisfied. She had no love for the slimeball, but playing with him wasn't *always* unpleasant. If a girl had to screw her way to the top, she might as well enjoy it.

Her current predicament was anything but pleasant, however.

As pressure alarms had screeched in her ears, her basic training had taken over. She'd donned a vacuum suit so quickly she hadn't remembered doing so before finding herself suited up and sealed. Successive explosions had nearly jarred her unconscious before the station's lights had flickered and gone out. What followed had been the loss of all power, including ventilation and artificial gravity.

After minutes of disoriented terror drifting in pitch-blackness, she'd realized her only chance for survival lay in crawling to a place where someone might find her. In darkness and zero-g, she'd gone hand-over-hand on the handrails and opened pressure hatches as she made her way to the control center in total darkness. She'd gasped in horror when she'd reached the connecting corridor, for only stars and open space had greeted her.

Half of the station had been blown away, including the communications section, boat bay, and control center. What remained of the ODS had been vented to space. The stars beyond the opening were spinning slowly, with the dome of Turin's World flickering in and out of view with a steady oscillation.

The ODS was spinning and its orbit decaying as it fell toward the planet. She froze, unable to move as she realized the grimness of her situation. She wished she'd taken a shower after Pickering had left. On the other hand, had she been in the shower when the explosion occurred, she likely wouldn't have survived. There was no telling how long she'd have to remain in the suit now.

Something had struck the ODS. Whatever it was, it had been massive or moving fast. A starship bumping the ODS might cause such damage, or perhaps a large meteor, but had that been the case, rescue teams would have been crawling all over the ODS by now. This seemed like something different.

Yeager had seen no one in the corridors since the attack, not even bodies, and feared everyone had been sucked out into space. It had been too dark in the corridors to see the extent of damage the ODS had suffered, but now she knew the station was doomed. She had to get away from it or burn up when the station struck the atmosphere.

She tried to remember where the escape pods were located on the portion of the station she was in. An escape pod had two days of life support, provided she could find a functioning one. The larger models even allowed safe atmospheric entry, though with a hard landing dirtside.

She didn't have the skills to pilot a pod, but her instructors had taught her to use the AI autopilot, which could manage atmospheric entry and landing. She wished she'd paid more attention to the life-support training she'd gotten when she'd reported aboard.

Cautiously, Yeager eased back into the corridor, looking for a cross-corridor or ladder. It was pitch-black inside the corridor and impossible to see an escape pod. Her vac-suit supplied two hours of oxygen without a tap feed, and she had no idea how long she had before the ODS hit the atmosphere.

The station's spin produced some centrifugally-induced gravity, but not enough to keep her from launching herself down the corridor with ease, but she dared not do so. In the darkness she might bump into a sharp edge or a torn frame panel and puncture the suit. *That* would kill her immediately.

She fought rising panic, thankful for the accompanying

shock that seemed to help keep her terror at bay. She was thinking more clearly now; able to operate on more than reflex and training. Unfortunately, the more she thought about the situation, the more terrified she became.

Think. You know this stuff! Where are the life pods located?

She remembered a pod at the intersection of corridors Bravo and Echo on Deck 14 near Pickering's office but had no idea of which way to go to get there. She considered jumping clear of the station and taking her chances drifting in space. The suit had an emergency beacon, but the beacon had a short transmitter life. She stood a better chance of survival if she could find an escape pod.

Jumping clear wouldn't ensure her survival either. The spinning ODS might smash into her as it spun about its axis. If she were lucky enough to avoid that, she would still be in the same decaying orbit as the station and would burn up when she hit the atmosphere.

After minutes of float-crawling down the corridor, she found the escape pod location and gasped in horror.

It was gone.

It had been ejected, either by survivors abandoning the station or the force of the explosion. Icy fingers gripped her heart as she saw her best chance of survival evaporate. She was alone on what was left of the station, with only ghosts to accompany her, and she'd soon join them if she couldn't find a way off.

Suddenly Yeager remembered the suit's emergency light, and mentally kicked herself for not remembering it sooner. With a quick click of an external button, a small light illuminated on the right forearm of the suit, providing an immediate view of her surroundings. She made her way up a ladder to a sealed hatch and manually released the dog toggles holding it closed. The inner hatch opened easily, and she drifted into the airlock to release the outer hatch.

Her beam illuminated the twin shafts of a metal ladder leading to the exterior hull. She was in Section November of the ODS. On the outside of the hull, there would be an escape pod near her present position. She might yet have a chance, if the pod was still there and still functioning.

Mustering up her courage, Yeager crawled up the ladder through the airlock onto the exterior hull of the ODS. She was terrified of missing a handhold and being tossed into space untethered, but she forced herself to concentrate, using her gloves to grip each handhold carefully. As she crawled, she prayed the escape pod was still there.

She dared not consider her chances if it was gone.

CHAPTER 10

NEW BYZANTIUM
RIGEL TWO

Roderick Benton groaned as he stared at the blood-red numbers on the wall chronometer and willed the annoying buzzer to die, but the irritating chime continued to ping. Sighing, he got up, donned a robe, and moved to his communications terminal.

This had better be important, he thought irritably as he flicked on the desk light. He grimaced as he stubbed a bare toe on the end of the desk support and bit off a curse. Angrily, he thumbed the answer button. The face of Vasilov O'Rourke stared back at him from the screen. "Sir Benton?"

"Good morning, Vasilov." Benton tried to keep the pain of his aching toe from showing on his face. "Or perhaps I should say, good evening. Which is it?"

"It's morning, Rod. Look, I know it's early, but we have a situation here."

Benton sobered. If the Secretary of State personally called a staff advisor at this time of night, it had to be an extraordinary situation. He searched O'Rourke's eyes in the screen. "Oh?"

"I can't say more on a non-secure line, Rod, but we have a developing crisis. His lordship wants you here immediately. That's all I can say at the moment."

"I see." Benton rubbed a hand across his face. "I'll be on the tram within the hour."

"No time for that, Rod. The president wants you here ASAP. I've already dispatched a shuttle to your residence. It should be landing on your pad in about five minutes."

"I see. Very well, I'll dress, shave and be right out."

"Forget the shave. Just get dressed and meet the shuttle. This is a Level One state emergency. I'll see you when you arrive. Out."

The monitor flicked off, replaced by the logo crest of Atwell Communications, and Benton sighed before turning for his closet.

Level One? That means a military emergency or a natural disaster.

Benton moved into the lavatory to rinse out his mouth, then punched in codes to open his wardrobe closet. He could've had the servants lay out apparel, of course, but at this hour of the night there seemed no reason to wake them. Home Security was always awake, of course, and he was certain they'd screened the call before allowing it through. Benton preferred to go about his business with a minimum of fuss and a maximum of efficiency.

Besides, he thought grimly, *the fewer who know the better.*

He was donning his boots when he heard the soft roar of the shuttle descending on its lift fans. He hurried out the back door of the mansion toward the landing pad, spotting the rotating beacons and strobe lights of the shuttle as it flared and touched down with a jolt. Two Home Security guards moved forward to verify the identity of the shuttle occupants. Air seals hissed and a boarding ramp descended.

Benton hurried toward the shuttle, wondering what the emergency was.

He supposed he would find out soon enough.

RNSS *SHIVA*, GALLAGHER STAR SYSTEM

Yamashita grimaced as all of Shiva's CIC displays returned to normal. The disadvantage of jumping through a stargate was that you never knew what was waiting on the other side. Smart enemies would set ambushes by surrounding a terminus with weapons platforms. It was standard doctrine for most navies controlling stargate terminii, which acted as choke points on interstellar traffic. The side controlling a stargate's termini controlled all lines of communication and access to that system.

RCN doctrine called for defense-in-depth near a stargate's terminus, in concentric spheres of layered weapons covering the stargate from all angles. In most cases, these weapons were stationary mines. Their stealth positions were known only to friendly forces, who could pass through them safely.

The second layer of defenses usually consisted of fortresses or ODS platforms, positioned with interlocking fields of fire concentrated on the terminus. Lastly, behind the first two spheres, a navy would position mobile fleets. Theoretically, whatever survived the mines and forts would be finished off by warships.

An attacker jumping through a stargate was always at a tactical disadvantage, particularly if they wormholed without prior reconnaissance. It took several moments for a ship's sensors to readjust after wormholing between stars. Though the jump itself was instantaneous, there was a sensor lag as the ship returned to n-space, making it possible to collide with rocks or mines near the terminus. Any waiting fortresses would immediately open fire on a ship identified as hostile to that system's defenses. Attacking a defended stargate could be expensive for an invader, who'd be forced to fight a battle of attrition as they ran a gauntlet of weapons while trying to gain control of the terminus.

The trouble with all stargate defense plans was they gave the initiative to the enemy. Unless a defending commander had friendly on the far end of the stargate—who could relay information through the terminus about the number and type of incoming attackers—a defending commander had no idea of *what* was coming through the terminus at him.

CHAPTER 10

The tactical problem was *Shiva* had transitioned into another system in a time of war and had no idea what was waiting in Gallagher. It was supposed to be an RCN-controlled system, but since the attack on Centauri Seven, that couldn't be assumed. After the last several days, Yamashita wasn't sure of *anything*, and he wasn't prone to take unnecessary chances.

"Sensors, report." He gave the order as soon as sensor distortion began to clear, instinctively checking the seal on his helmet. The crew had been at general quarters since fleeing Centauri Seven.

"Multiple drives detected, Commander. Bearing three-one-seven, mark zero-two-two. Estimate bogies' base course as one-one-three mark zero-niner-zero."

"Range?"

"Three-point-one light-minutes, Sir."

Damn, who are these guys?

Yamashita had secretly prayed the terminus would be clear of enemies. That had obviously been too much to hope for.

He stared at the tactical plot, his eyes narrowing. Multiple bogies flanked Shiva's path, all within beam range. If they were hostile, *Shiva* was as good as dead, but he'd make damn sure she took as many of them with her as she could before she went down.

A lanky lieutenant in a vac-suit moved to stand beside him. Yamashita glanced over, meeting the eyes of his acting Tactical Officer and noted the hardness in the man's stare.

They're like chips of hazel flint.

The young officer watched the tactical display with cold fury, his eyes intense and dangerous above his prominent cheekbones. Yamashita saw his jaw muscles flex, hinting at the tension the man held back.

Though the lieutenant hadn't mentioned it, Yamashita knew his fiancée was an engineer aboard *Kuroshima*, a destroyer that had been dirtside at Centauri Seven when the system had been attacked. It was possible *Kuroshima* had survived the attack and that Lieutenant Storm's lady was fine, but the lieutenant was a professional and knew the odds of that were poor.

Smoldering hate burned in Storm's eyes as he watched the unknown icons in silence, the coldness of a trained killer radiating from him. Yamashita felt a certain awe mixed with pity as he observed the ferocity in his new TAC-O's demeanor. He'd known Storm for only a few months, and this was the first time he'd ever thought of him as deadly. Yamashita was glad the lieutenant wasn't mad at *him*.

He turned to concentrate on the tactical situation. "Sensors, ID those bogies ASAP. When you do, put the IDs on tactical."

He watched as the horseshoe-shaped yellow icons popped up inside the holo-tank. Their yellow color and "pending" status marked them as unknowns. They flickered to life one by one, glowing steadily as smaller codes of white letters and numbers displayed estimated tonnages, headings and speeds.

The unknown fleet had already closed to 2.86 light-minutes. There were twenty-two unknowns in the formation, most with the mass of destroyers, but at least four were capital ships, probably three cruisers and a battleship.

"Standby weapons and external racks. TAC-O, prepare to target capital missiles and grasers on my command. All point defenses stand ready. We could take incoming fire any moment. All hands rig for acceleration and high-g maneuvering. Egon, no fire control lock-ons from us unless I give the order."

"Aye, Sir," Storm replied through clenched teeth and turned back to his tactical console. If the unknowns were Karsians, Storm would be their worst nightmare, for he was primed and ready to kill. If they were friendlies or neutrals, however, Yamashita didn't want his first combat engagement as a CO to result in fratricide of a friendly vessel. He understood Storm's anger, but he knew to keep the man under control.

Storm's voice spoke in his earpiece. "Range two light-minutes, Skipper."

"Sensors, any IDs?"

"Negative, Sir. They're all running EMCON. They're not squawking IFF."

Yamashita cursed.

Under emission control procedures, warships didn't activate emitters, and that ban included Identification, Friend or Foe transponders. The use of EMCON made rapid identification difficult. Of course, unknown ships being EMCON couldn't stop *Shiva* from scanning them with lidar or identifying their drive signatures passively, but doing so took time, time an adversary could use to close into combat range.

The sensor rating spoke again. "No valid IFF codes or modes, Commander, but the drives appear to be RCN. The AI's classified most of them. The fingerprints match known Fleet signatures. The fingerprints appear steady, so I doubt they're spoofers."

Could they actually be RCN?

Yamashita leaned back in his acceleration couch. "Shields to full power. TAC-O, prepare to fire, a full barrage concentrated on the nearest heavy. Comm, issue standard challenge."

The communications officer activated his panel and transmitted. Yamashita tensed, mentally preparing for an explosion of capital missiles and beams he knew could suddenly erupt in his face. To one side Storm waited stoically, implacable as stone, eyes hard and fingers poised over firing keys.

"Commander?"

Yamashita turned toward the communications officer, Lieutenant Commander Barnes. The man touched his helmet with one hand, as if he could adjust the headset inside his helmet to improve his hearing.

The picture in the tactical display suddenly shifted. One by one, the yellow icons changed color, not to the bloodred color of hostiles but the green of friendly vessels.

"They've acknowledged hail, Sir," a communications specialist said, sounding relieved. "Standard IFF codes now being transmitted and validated. They broke EMCON the moment we transmitted challenge."

"Confirmed, Skipper." Barnes turned away from his communications station and smiled. "They've replied in code and have authenticated. They're friendly, Sir. It's Task Unit 17.1.1."

Yamashita sighed as the tension drained from his body. Task Unit 17.1.1 was part of Task Force Seventeen, a force under the command of Vice Admiral Ivanov Montgomery. He'd known a task unit was assigned to Gallagher, but he'd dared not hope it had survived.

Technically, Task Force 17.1. was the first task unit of the first task group in Montgomery's Task Force Seventeen, but it represented both Montgomery and Seventh Fleet as symbolically as any flag. Relief flowed through Yamashita, and he admitted to himself he'd secretly feared *no* units had survived the Karsian attack.

Barnes' voice spoke again in his earpiece. "They're hailing us, Sir. I have an incoming call from Rear Admiral Yu aboard *Excalibur*. She wants to know if we're damaged or require assistance and if we were pursued into the stargate by hostile forces."

Yamashita opened his mouth to answer when Storm suddenly kicked a bulkhead, powered down his weapons console, and cursed. His TAC-O was frustrated, full of pent-up anger and the need for revenge. Storm wanted to kill Karsians, and he'd just been cheated out of it. The behavior was understandable given Storm's many hours of tension and heartbreak and the adrenaline rush of impending combat. Yamashita understood the man's frustration, and though the display was unprofessional, he decided to ignore it. He'd have to keep a close eye on Storm, however. Uncontrolled bloodlust could result in disaster.

Yamashita pressed the ship's intercom button. "All hands, secure from general quarters."

He watched with concern as Storm removed his pressure helmet and tossed it angrily against a bulkhead.

"Lieutenant," he said, a warning tone crawling into his voice.

Storm looked up, abashed. "Sorry, Skipper."

Satisfied, Yamashita turned to address Rear Admiral Yu as her face popped up on the communications display.

CHAPTER 11

RNSS GANT
PAN'VU STAR SYSTEM

Tactical images flickered on the bridge display screens as *Gant* transitioned into Pan'vu. Comforti leaned back and put his cast-covered limb on the couch's armrest. His arm had a fracture, though not a serious one.

Well, this is it. Sadness washed over him as he looked around the bridge. *Your final voyage as skipper of* Gant.

He'd logged his resignation hours ago, while the ship's medical officer was bandaging his arm in Duroplast. Injected nannites would quickly repair the bone, but it would take a few more days before they completed the job, so a cast had been placed on the arm to keep it secure. A signed letter would be required to make his resignation official, but he hadn't had time to write it. The cast would be on his arm for only a week or two, but the damage to his career was permanent.

Why did I allow myself to be overconfident going into

battle? How did I let get myself in a position where enemy's weapons could penetrate Gant's point defense? It's inexcusable. I should have listened to Laird when he requested to use lasers on the torpedoes. Energy weapons would have taken out the second torpedo instantly. If I had, maybe now I'd have an undamaged ship and no casualties.

There was little point in going over it again. He'd beaten himself up a thousand times over it since the engagement. What mattered now was getting *Gant* to a safe haven and reporting to the installation commander to deliver his resignation in person. Laird would assume command of *Gant* upon his departure, though it would be up to BuPers to decide whether or not Laird kept the command. Despite the younger officer's greenness, Comforti knew Laird would make an excellent skipper. He was tactically sound, had an effective manner with subordinates, and knew the insides of the destroyer like the back of his hand.

Laird stood by the tactical console, glaring at the senor display as transition distortion faded on sensors. "Skipper, we've got a problem."

Comforti faced his executive officer's back. "What now?"

The comm specialist answered for him. "Our communications drone is drifting in front of us and chattering away on Fleet Common, Sir. There's intense static on all bands, and no one's answering our hails. There's also a Fleet distress beacon broadcasting a system-wide emergency notice on the Guard frequency. I'm receiving no recognizable transmissions from Turin's World."

"What about the orbital defense station?"

CHAPTER 11

"The ODS isn't answering either, Sir."

What the hell?

Comforti frowned and rose from the couch. The situation required an immediate sensor scan. He wasn't about to get caught with his pants down again.

He turned abruptly and opened his vac-suit locker. "Sound general quarters."

ORBITAL DEFENSE STATION

Yeager grinned when she spotted the escape pod at the end of the ladder. Giving herself a gentle push, she floated to the airlock, using her wrist-light for illumination. She bumped to a stop and opened the pod's outer hatch. It unsealed effortlessly, and she slid inside the airlock and closed the hatch behind her, then opened the inner airlock hatch before entering and closing it behind her as well.

Basic training had taught her the first thing to do in any emergency was to stay calm and check her survival equipment. She quickly checked her suit's seal integrity, then buckled herself into the pod's jump seat. Tightening the shoulder straps, she scanned the control board looking for the pod's power switch. The main power buses from the ODS were dead, meaning she'd have to start life support systems manually with onboard batteries.

Finding the lever, she read the placard above it and activated emergency power. For a moment she feared the power pack had been damaged, but then the overhead lights flickered on, and she could see clearly for the first time in hours.

There was no time to waste pressurizing the pod. She had no idea how fast the station was falling. She needed to get away from the ODS as quickly as possible, but she had to wait until the gyros stabilized before firing the separation charges. Yeager waited for what seemed like an eternity before a green light finally flickered on, indicating gyroscopic stabilization of the pod's autopilot.

"Here goes." She sighed, hoping she remembered the procedures correctly.

Lifting the manual cover, she twisted the separation handle. Annunciator lights flashed yellow warnings in her face, indicating the thruster system was no longer in a safe configuration. Flipping the attitude thruster switches, she watched the lights change from white to orange. Opening a box-like container on the left armrest, she elevated the ejector handle to its full upright position, sighing in relief when the LED flashed a scarlet warning at her:

WARNING!
EJECTION SYSTEM ARMED

She braced against the cushions and pressed the button on the stick firmly with her thumb. The pod lurched slightly, but there was only silence as ejection charges blew away the containment ring holding the pod to the ODS, and the pod launched into the vacuum.

Yeager stared, mesmerized, as the station shot away

at a startling velocity, the pod's acceleration pushing her against the seat. There was a secondary lurch when the attitude thrusters kicked in and the pod's AI aligned it for entry into the atmosphere. If the pod entered the atmosphere at too steep of an angle, it would burn up. If it entered at too shallow of an angle it would skip back into space.

She caught a glimpse of Turin's World as it flashed past the viewport and gasped in dismay.

Even from orbit she could see the black-and-red mushroom clouds from dozens of nuclear detonations hanging in Turin's atmosphere like bloody entrails from a monstrous, eviscerated creature. Radioactive dust and red haze obscured the oceans and continents from view.

My God, they nuked Turin.

She checked the velocity indicator and descent bar, noting the AI had positioned the pod precisely for atmospheric insertion. She knew she wouldn't burn up in the atmosphere, but there was no joy in her soul. Her escape from a fiery meteoric death had only put her in position to die a slower death from radiation poisoning on the planet's surface.

She leaned forward and grasped her helmeted head with her hands as despair washed over her. Then the tears came.

It's not fair! I followed the escape procedures properly. I'm so close to making it, but I'm doomed anyway.

Her sobs turned to curses as her tears became droplets in zero-g, floating around inside her helmet.

RNSS *GANT*

"Holy Mother of God," Comforti spoke over the intercom as he and his crew stared at the surface of Turin's World. Angry red-and-black smudges of nuclear Armageddon boiled in the atmosphere of the planet as they approached at full combat readiness.

The Pan'vu ODS had been destroyed and Turin's World nuked. The realization made Comforti's blood run cold. There had been four million people on Turin's World, most of them centered around the impact points that had once been Fleet yards and dirtside facilities. By now, most would be dead from nuclear fireballs and shock waves. Those still living would be dying from radiation.

Laird stated the obvious. "She's been nuked, Skipper."

"Maintain GQ." Comforti tightened the harness on his command couch. "Sensors, search for survivors. Scan the ODS debris, the orbital docks, everything."

Peterson turned, staring at him through the faceplate of his helmet. "What about the surface, Sir?"

Comforti closed his eyes. "There's nothing we can do for them. I doubt much would have lived through *that*, and if it did, it wouldn't want to be saved. There might be isolated pockets of survivors, deep in bunkers maybe, or far enough away from the impact zones, but they're on their own for now. Our priority is to rescue the people we can save."

Laird blanched. "Good lord, Skipper, that's—"

"I know, XO. It's harsh, but it's reality. The damage to

our hull negates atmospheric entry, so landing's out of the question. We *might* be able to successfully put down on the planet even with this damage, but I doubt we could navigate through that maelstrom below, and even if we could, it would needlessly risk this vessel."

Laird wasn't happy. "Skipper, our primary duty is to protect the lives of Confederation citizens. Taking risks is our business."

Comforti sighed. Without a headquarters to report to, he would retain command of *Gant* for the time being. The responsibility was his, and he wouldn't shirk it.

"In normal circumstances you'd be right, Mister Laird, but we're obviously at war now, and now our primary duty is to report the attack to Fleet Command and save who we can. The rescue of people poisoned beyond recovery is, unfortunately, a secondary consideration. We must now think in terms of protecting the Confederation, not just the people of Turin's World, who are most assuredly dead or dying by now."

"Skipper, we can't just disregard those people. I don't believe this."

"My primary duty remains the safety and survival of this ship and its crew." Comforti felt anger rise. Laird was challenging his orders in front of the others. "I already have one blemish on my responsibility, Mr. Laird, I won't have another. Our priority is survival and warning. That bladeship we destroyed must've been a straggler from a larger attack force, a task force that somehow slipped past *us*."

"No way. We would have detected that many drives, Skipper, even if they were all bladeships."

"Not if they were transited at minimal power and were stealthed. The force that attacked Turin may still be here, waiting to see who shows up, and we just jumped in here like clueless fools. We could be attacked at any moment. I'm not opposed to conducting SAR operations for orbital survivors, as that has minimal effect on our readiness, but I can't risk landing parties on Turin's World. At best, they'd be ineffective in that nightmare, and radiation would contaminate anyone we sent. If the enemy attacks while we're deploying landing boats . . . no, we'll search for orbital survivors for now, nothing else. Meanwhile, I need to know if any threats remain in this system. I want an active sensor search of the debris field. We need to know if the Karsians are still here."

Laird slumped, accepting his orders, then quickly brought up a display on his terminal. "Hell, Skipper, they could be bedded down in a dozen places. If they're conventional ships, we'd detect their drive signatures even in idle at this range. We can scan for those unless they're hiding in the sensor shadow on the far side of the planet. If that's the case, we can launch sensor remotes and eliminate that possibility. On the other hand, if they're hiding on the far side of the planet, it'll be difficult for them to coordinate an attack on us from such an awkward position."

"I'd really prefer not to engage an entire task force if it can be helped, Bobby Joe."

"Understood, Sir. My point is that if this attack was

made by bladeships, it's possible they could attempt to seal off the stargate behind us and prevent penetration by other vessels."

Comforti's eyes narrowed. "Which means if they're still here, they're already aware of us, and may be positioning to attack."

"Yes, Sir. I recommend baffle clearing turns to check astern. If I were a bladeship commander, that's where I'd want to be. It's an easy kill if they get a torpedo up our stern wedge."

Comforti nodded. A starship's fusion drive created a tremendous wake of gravimetric turbulence behind a warship, vortices that expanded due aft of the stern for some distance. Such "wakes" blinded starship sensors immediately aft of the ship, creating a cone of sensor silence. It was the classic position for stealth vessels to attack a warship from. Inside the so-called "baffles" zone, an enemy stealthship could detect *Gant*, but due to drive interference, *Gant* could not detect, target, or fire upon it.

"I concur. Scan the local asteroid belt as well. Bladeships love to hide in those things. Helm, commence zigzag maneuvers. Sensors, continue scans of the orbitals. Navigation, we need to figure out how to get back to Confederation space in one piece. Start plotting a route."

"Aye, aye, Sir."

Peterson whirled at his station. "Multiple distress beacons detected in low orbit, Skipper."

"Survivors." Comforti sighed. "Very well, continue zigzag and take us to them. Tractor-snag the life pods into the boat bay as soon as they're in range. But hear me clearly, folks; if we're attacked, cease tractor operations and engage the enemy. The rescue of survivors is secondary to the survival of this ship. Is that clear?"

Laird nodded. "Aye, Sir."

Laird turned back to his console, but Comforti knew he was unhappy with the order.

KARSIAN BLADESHIP *ANG'TAHK*

Toborahnk nodded with grim satisfaction as the Rigelian destroyer approached the planet. His satisfaction wasn't from seeing the enemy ship. Indeed, now that he had little ordnance left, the last thing he wanted was to tangle with a destroyer, but the offer the Rigelian presented was too tempting to pass up.

So that is what happened to Torgh's bladeship.

Somehow, Torgh had been found and destroyed, probably by this very RCN destroyer. Toborahnk had no doubt of it. Judging from the visible damage in the long-range viewers trained on the Rigelian, it was obvious Torgh had gotten in a few blows of his own.

Moterk glared at him, questions in his eyes.

Toborahnk grinned. "We will engage this Rigelian. The approach will be tricky, however. Maneuver us into the shadow of the dock debris and minimize reactor power. We will hide and play dead. Hopefully, they will not detect

our power source when they pass. I want this Rigelian to
believe we are debris. Once they pass, insert behind into
their drive wake. That will hide us from their sensors and
allow us to target them."

Moterk nodded. It was a classic stealth attack: emulate
space flotsam and sneak into a ship's stern wedge, then
trail the enemy at close range, undetected. All it required
was moving in close and firing up the enemy's drive
wedge, which provided untold amounts of energy to use
as a targeting source. The victim would be unable to return
fire. Stern wedges were the reason warships traveled in
fleets, so other ships could point sensors and fire into a
sister ship's wake to provide mutual support.

This Rigelian destroyer is alone. It has no one to cover its tail.

Toborahnk had a single torpedo remaining in
Ang'tahk's launch bay, but it would be more than enough
if he could get close. If the enemy captain was foolish
enough to lower his shields, it would be enough to finish
him. At point-blank range, the Rigelian would have no
time to react and be unable to target *Ang'tahk.*

He watched as Moterk carefully positioned the bladeship against a piece of debris from a shattered orbital dock.
He felt a slight bump and nodded in satisfaction as magnetic grapples attached *Ang'tahk* to the metal shard. The
lights dimmed as Moterk lowered the power.

They waited as the destroyer came on with agoniz-
ing slowness.

RNSS *GANT*

"Another emergency pod beacon bearing zero-one-three, mark one-one-four," Peterson said as Comforti entered the bridge. Laird had taken the conn while his skipper was in sickbay checking on the wounded.

"Range?" Comforti resumed his seat as Laird vacated it. "I have the conn, Bobby Joe."

"I stand relieved, Sir."

Peterson pointed at his display. "Six-thousand kilometers, Sir."

"Take us to it."

Laird stared at the plot. "That pod's trajectory indicates it was launched from a section of ODS debris, Sir. I can't believe anyone survived on the station. There's no sign of life support or power on the ODS. She's completely vented to space."

"A lucky survivor." Comforti leaned forward on the couch. "How many rescues does this make, XO?"

"Sixteen so far, Sir. We're not picking up any other beacons, though. This is the last one."

"Well, we've saved fifteen people so far today. Let's move in and save one more. Helm, rig for tractor snag."

"The pod's descending toward the planet fast, Skipper." Laird folded his hands behind his back as he watched the plot. "Recommend we push it up if we want to catch it before it enters the atmosphere."

"Agreed. Helm, cease zigzag and make straight for the pod. Maintain current vee."

CHAPTER 11

"Cease zigzag and make straight for the pod, aye, Sir."
Gant surged toward the descending escape pod.

KARSIAN BLADESHIP *ANG'TAHK*

Toborahnk smiled as the destroyer passed. It had ceased zigzagging and was making for the planet.

It was a perfect setup.

"Release docking grips."

Moterk let *Ang'tahk* drift free of the dock debris and spoke without turning. "Clear of debris, Yi'rhang. We are free to maneuver."

"Ahead one-third, Moterk. Put us directly astern of the destroyer inside her drive wake."

"The destroyer has ceased zigzag, Yi'rhang."

Toborahnk grinned. The Rigelian captain had foolishly assumed he was safe and stopped his baffles clearing turns. It was an incredible stroke of luck the Rigelian commander had chosen that moment to cease defensive maneuvering. Toborahnk could not have asked for a better up-the-stern shot. No one at the Imperial War Academy had ever seen this actually happen in battle. It was a textbook opportunity Toborahnk intended to make the most of.

"Open the weapons bay." He tried not to gloat visibly. It would not do to lose the cool demeanor of a professional warrior, but inside he wanted to cackle with glee.

Moterk responded quietly, "Weapons bay open."

"Target their main drive. We will launch our remaining torpedo inside their wedge and close in to finish off whatever survives with energy fire. If you keep us in their wake, they will be unable to return fire."

"Understood, Yi'rhang."

Toborahnk grinned openly now.

This Rigelians would pay for their carelessness, just as those on Turin's World had paid.

With their lives.

RNSS *GANT*

Peterson stared at the data coming from one of the sensor remotes *Gant* had launched to search for enemies. "Contact astern, one-seven-niner relative, mark zero-niner-zero!"

Comforti and Laird jerked around as Peterson called out the contact, and the battle implications rang home. Suddenly Comforti was glad he'd deployed the passive remotes as soon as *Gant* had entered the system. "It just popped up, Skipper, and it's trying to enter our baffles."

Comforti stared at the yellow icon on the tactical plot and cursed. The bogey was under them and already in position to fire. "Drop tractors and raise shields. Helm, emergency turn, hard aport."

Comforti sat and cinched his harness as tight as he could with his good arm.

Laird did the same at his station. "He's too close for

our missiles, Skipper . . . inside minimum range. We'll have to use point defenses until we can gain some separation."

Comforti started to reply, but Peterson cut him off. "Contact is releasing atmosphere."

Comforti grimaced. "He's venting tubes, preparing to put a torpedo up our ass. Weapons, target all point defenses on that contact and fire. You're weapons free."

"Aye, Sir," the tactical officer replied as crisp as if he were in an Academy simulation. The range was too close for missiles, even for the special Short Range Attack Missiles *Gant* carried. A SRAM could be launched at shorter ranges than the standard anti-ship versions, but the enemy was already inside even a SRAM's minimum-range envelope. A missile wouldn't be able to acquire before overshooting, due to the great velocity imparted at launch by its coilgun launcher. Comforti knew a few sneaky tricks that could buy *Gant* precious seconds, however. Beam weapons worked at the speed-of-light, faster than any missile or torpedo. Unfortunately, they required precise lock-ons, something he didn't have.

"Point defenses, launch a SRAM. Program it to detonate a quarter second after launch."

"Skipper, the target's inside min range." Laird looked over. His eyes were bright behind his faceplate. "Even a SRAM can't cage that fast. It has no chance of hitting."

"Do it anyway."

"Aye, aye, Sir."

Gant rumbled internally as she struggled to turn, but the maneuver was enough to highlight the enemy bladeship against the background of stars as Gant's active lidars localized the contact.

Peterson shouted. "Target acquired!"

"Launch the SRAM. Standby lasers."

"Scanning."

"Lasers ready," Laird said without turning. "SRAM away."

ESCAPE POD

Yeager was still crying when a brilliant neon-blue beam illuminated the pod's viewports. The onset of sudden g-force threw her against her restraint harness. She looked through the ports and continued to sob, but this time in relief. An RCN destroyer was visible in the viewport, growing rapidly against the background of stars.

It had tractored the pod and was pulling her to safety. The destroyer had appeared from nowhere, and for a moment, Yeager was unable to do anything but cry with joy. It was a miracle to be saved so close to death.

Even as the destroyer yanked her pod up and away from the planet, it continued closing. Yeager gasped when she spotted a tiny flash of light behind it. She squinted, staring through the blinding blue of the tractor beam. Sunlight glinted off a small shape trailing the destroyer.

She had no idea what it was. Perhaps a rescue boat launched by the destroyer. It was painted dark, almost black in color, and following the destroyer from close behind. It seemed to be trying to catch up to the destroyer for some reason.

The escape pod lurched violently again, and the blue light vanished. She felt her stomach heave as the escape pod began an end-over-end tumble.

No!

The bastards had let her go! The pod tumbled wildly as it was slung away by the dying tractor beam, headed toward the atmosphere like a rock from a slingshot. The destroyer turned rapidly away, this time violently and with an increasing velocity. Yeager fought to keep the contents of her stomach from climbing her throat and filling her helmet. Nauseated by the heavy g-forces induced on the pod by the release of the tractor beam, she gripped her stomach.

She stared forlornly through the viewport at the rapidly receding destroyer.

Why have they forsaken me?

The viewport suddenly flashed white, blinding her with the brilliance of a star gone nova.

She closed her eyes as the light became overpowering.

KARSIAN BLADESHIP *ANG'TAHK*

Toborahnk screamed when the SRAM detonated near his bladeship, its blast melting away hull plating and scanner-absorbent coatings. *Ang'tahk* flipped out of control as internal atmosphere vented from her hull in explosive decompression.

He turned to order Moterk to launch the torpedo, wanting to jettison the volatile weapon that hung exposed in the weapons bay, or at least discharge onboard lasers at the enemy, but the intercom was dead. Before him, Moterk's arms floated limply above his head in zero gravity. He appeared lifeless. The bladeship's lighting flickered and began to fade.

The Rigelian tricked me. He lured me in by offering me his backside as a target and I was stupid enough to take the bait. Who would have suspected a destroyer could turn so quickly?

One by one, Ang'tahk's systems failed, including the targeting computers. Moterk was unresponsive and likely dead. Toborahnk knew the Rigelian would maneuver to bring his main weapons to bear, and a destroyer carried weapons no bladeship could survive.

He manually targeted the torpedo on the Rigelian destroyer and hammered the launch button. The torpedo failed to launch. The launcher system had died with the loss of power. He had only batteries remaining and a few pressurized maneuvering thrusters.

As anger and fear fought for dominance in his heart, Toborahnk labored to control the bladeship with attitude thrusters. He couldn't fire weapons, but there was still one way he might destroy the Rigelian ship.

The bladeship ceased rolling as its thrusters kicked in and went to full power.

Ang'tahk accelerated toward the RCN destroyer.

CHAPTER 11

RNSS *GANT*

Laird spoke quickly. "Pop-up contact, dead astern."

Comforti grinned. "Lasers, lock target."

"She's streaming atmosphere, Skipper." Peterson turned in his seat to look at Comforti. "Imaging shows massive hull damage from the SRAM detonation."

"Lasers acquired," Laird said so quickly that it echoed Peterson's update.

Peterson pointed at his scanner display. "I've got thrusters firing on the bladeship. She's firing maneuvering thrusters."

"Go active and hammer her."

Gant's powerful lidars washed energy across the bladeship's battered hull, updating the targeting computers instantly.

Peterson spoke. "Target locked, bearing one-five-eight, mark zero-niner-zero relative at twenty kilometers."

Comforti stared at the icon in the display. "Fire."

The bladeship had recovered quickly from the SRAM's detonation. It charged on full thrusters, attempting to extricate itself from the trap. Comforti's eyes narrowed as he studied the bladeship's vector. The Karsian was moving to place himself directly abeam, deliberately exposing himself to Gant's main weapons.

Why?

He realized the answer instantly. "He's going to ram."

SUCKER PUNCH

At that instant, Gant's forward point defenses fired a half-dozen short-range lasers into the bladeship.

KARSIAN BLADESHIP *ANG'TAHK*

Toborahnk screamed again as lasers sliced through the bulkhead, shearing off his right arm. His pressure suit deflated instantly, his vision tunneling as the air was pulled from his lungs in a rush, and he slipped toward unconsciousness. His blood boiled in his veins as nitrogen bubbled up without enough pressure to keep it liquid. He would be dead within moments, but he smiled as he stared at the destroyer in his viewport through his small tunnel of remaining vision. His death would not be in vain. *Ang'tahk* would die, but she would take a Rigelian ship of war with her.

The bladeship's thrusters were locked on full discharge. *Ang'Tahk* would ram this Rigelian, and that would be the end of them both.

Another point-defense laser sliced through the warhead of the torpedo in the weapons bay at that moment. Magnetized electrons, accelerated to lightspeed through a neon dye, intersected the volatile molecules in the torpedo's warhead, superheating its actuator. The warhead detonated. The explosion blasted outward in an expanding sphere of superheated gas and shrapnel. It ripped through the bladeship with such force that it shattered her reactor. *Ang'tahk* died in a blinding flash of light that washed across Gant's shields in a tsunami of super-heated plasma.

Gant flickered blue-white as tons of plasma dissipated around her. The blast continued outward like a bright, mirror-like bubble, dissipating with range, fading as it lost luminescence against the backdrop of space.

Then only the stars and a battered RCN destroyer remained, mute witnesses to the bladeship's destruction.

RNSS *GANT*

Yeager looked up weakly as a rescue team opened the pod's hatch and unbuckled her harness. Her fall toward the planet had been a soul-crushing experience that had over-whelmed her with doom. That nightmare had been punc-tuated by brilliant flashes of light leaving her dizzy and sick, but the blue glow of tractor beam had soon returned to snatch her from the jaws of death.

A handsome corpsman in faded blue medical scrubs stood over her in the pod, examining her with a hand-held scanner as two burly bosun's mates broke the seal on her helmet and removed it.

"She's got a bad dose of radiation poisoning." The corpsman stared at his scanner and frowned. "Probably from the explosion of the bladeship. Get her to sickbay stat. I'll notify them she's on the way." The corpsman leaned closer and looked down at her. She noticed his eyes were cornflower blue.

He's cute, she thought.

"You're aboard RNSS *Gant,* ma'am. You're safe now." The corpsman's voice seemed far away, as if coming through a wall of cotton. "We'll be taking you to sickbay now, but everything's going to be fine. Welcome aboard."

As the bosuns placed her on an anti-grav stretcher, Yeager looked back at the scorched escape pod, then at the corpsman. She slowly closed her eyes and smiled.

A girl can use a corpsman like that . . . especially if he has blue eyes.

CHAPTER 12

Talara waited tensely before the door to Admiral LeMieux's office, checking her appearance in a wall mirror as she tried to look presentable to meet a flag officer. Her long hair had been pinned back in a bun. Despite the conditions she'd been working in for the last day or so, she'd done her best to at least *look* professional. She'd somehow managed to find a clean uniform before reporting. She was nervous, wondering why a mere lieutenant had been summoned to meet a rear admiral.

Navy lieutenants, especially *newly promoted* lieutenants, did not go around rubbing elbows with flag officers. That an admiral had requested her by name wasn't just intimidating, it was downright scary. She mentally reviewed her lists of sins, desperately trying to figure out what *faux pas* she'd committed to be called on the carpet.

She was exhausted from pulling people out of rubble

and assisting medical personnel with injured victims. Several, not to mention the dead she'd helped recover, had been shipmates and friends. Her emotional walls, frayed by loss and shock, were starting to crumble, but anger kept her going, setting unaccustomed hard lines in her face. It was an anger she'd never felt before, directed at those responsible for wreaking havoc on her life, her lover, her crew, and her nation. She wanted to strike back, to inflict pain and suffering on those who had attacked Centauri Seven.

A light pulsed on the yeoman's desk, and he glanced up. "The admiral will see you now, Lieutenant."

Checking her uniform one more time, Talara rapped sharply against the door as she'd been taught at the Academy, her officer's cap tucked under her left arm.

A baritone voice answered. "Enter."

The door whisked open at the admiral's command, and Talara approached his desk, back ramrod straight and eyes focused straight ahead. She stopped two paces in front of his desk and snapped to attention. "Lieutenant Talara Kibbleman, reporting as ordered, Sir."

Rear Admiral James LeMieux stood, extending his hand. "At ease, Lieutenant. It's a pleasure to finally meet you. Glad you could make it."

Talara felt consternation. *When does a lieutenant not "make it" when summoned by a flag officer? How does the admiral even know who I am?*

LeMieux read the confusion in her eyes. "I know who you are, Lieutenant. As a matter of fact, I've a copy of your personnel file on my terminal right now. I was the final endorser on your recent promotion, you know. Please sit and relax. You're not in any trouble."

Relieved, she seated herself. *Did the skipper talk to the admiral about all of his junior officers?* She wasn't sure, so she sat at attention.

LeMieux saw her posture and smiled. "Relax, Talara. Can I offer you coffee? Tea?"

"No, thank you, Sir."

"I hope you don't mind if I have some."

"Not at all, Sir."

LeMieux moved to a coffee urn and poured himself a cup. The odor of fresh coffee filled the office. Talara took the opportunity to glance around, surprised that none of the firepower that had rained down on the base had touched the admiral's office. "You were lucky, Admiral."

He resumed his seat. "How's that?"

"Your office wasn't damaged. You're lucky it wasn't located in one of the buildings by the ramp or near the O-Club."

"Indeed, I was. I'd give it up, though, and thousands more like it, if I could get command of a ship of the wall."

Talara sat in awkward silence, uncertain of what to say and desperate to avoid doing anything stupid in front of an admiral. Admirals were larger than life. They came from a different stratum of society and handled bigger issues than her career or cares. Admirals made history, supervised fleets and protected entire star systems. She was intimidated, despite knowing LeMieux was as human as she.

"I know things have been pretty rough the last few days, Lieutenant. Are you all right?"

"Yes, Sir. I'm tired, but I wasn't physically hurt."

"Commander O'Brady was a good man and a fine officer." LeMieux sighed and sipped coffee. "I'll miss him greatly. I know you will too. He thought very highly of you, you know. I know you've been through hell helping with recovery since the attack."

"Yes, Sir." Talara tried not to fidget.

LeMieux leaned back, staring into his cup a moment before lifting his steel gray eyes. "What's the status of *Kuroshima*?"

Caught off-guard, Talara hesitated. "Only minor damage, Sir. The dock tanks tossed debris over the hull when they exploded, so she looks worse than she is. She suffered some minor damage to the hull, but we were lucky. She's still space-worthy, Admiral. Our drive upgrades were completed ahead of schedule, so we're ready for a new skipper whenever one arrives."

LeMieux stared at her for a long moment. "*She* has arrived, Lieutenant. You handled yourself extremely well after the attack. That was impressive work for a junior officer, considering your superiors were all killed in the attack. *Kuroshima* was lucky to be dirtside. Everything in the orbitals was destroyed."

She blinked, fear welling up inside her. "Admiral, do you know the status of *Shiva*?"

His eyebrows lifted. "No, Lieutenant, I don't. There were a lot of explosions in the orbitals. I don't have a full damage estimate yet, but indications are she was destroyed along with the rest of our battleships."

Talara felt tears brimming the edges of her eyes. Her voice was hoarse. "I see."

LeMieux studied her. "Why do you ask?"

"My . . . fiancé, Sir. Lieutenant Egon Storm. He was assistant tactical officer aboard *Shiva*."

Tears leaked down her cheeks and she wiped at them with a uniform sleeve. LeMieux frowned and handed her a tissue.

"I'm sorry, Admiral. I just—"

"No, I'm the one who should apologize, Lieutenant. I didn't know. You go ahead and cry all you want. Get it out. Lord knows, I've done my share in the last twenty-four hours."

Talara let the tears flow until the edge was taken off her pain. She took the tissue, dabbed her eyes and nodded thanks. She would save the hard grieving for another place and time. She'd been crying a lot lately, and knew it made her appear unprofessional. She was embarrassed breaking down in front of a flag officer, but a shell of loneliness stretched around her like an endless void.

LeMieux's voice softened. "It is possible *Shiva* got away."

She met his eyes. "I know the odds of *that*, Sir."

"You're right. The odds are she's gone, and I'm sorry for that, Lieutenant; sorrier than you know. You should also know, however, that no Omega code was recorded from *Shiva* during the battle, so it's possible she escaped the docks and got away. She was underway when the attack occurred, but if she'd escaped . . ."

"She'd have been back by now," Talara finished the sentence for him, her black eyes blazing.

"Yes, she would. I'm sorry, Lieutenant. I don't mean to be insensitive, but at the moment I have bigger fish to fry. There's a possibility the enemy that attacked this system will return to finish off what's left. I don't have much left to resist with, but I'll be damned if I'll let them take this system without a fight.

"Along with *Kuroshima*, I have some destroyers and a light cruiser that somehow managed to survive the attack. I intend to position them to defend the stargate from further penetration by the enemy. I want all ships mobilized and on-station as soon as possible, preferably no later than 1900 hours hundred this evening. You'll need to have *Kuroshima* underway by then."

Talara blinked. "Aye, Sir, but we're short-handed. We don't have a full crew, only junior officers, the ratings, and myself. Our command staff was killed at the O-Club when—"

"I know that." LeMieux looked her dead in the eye. "Unfortunately, I can't wait for personnel replacements, nor can I operate on peacetime tradition. We're at war, Lieutenant. I need people who can fight now, on a moment's notice, not when everything's 'ready.' Have *Kuroshima* launched by 19:00."

"Sir, we still need a captain, an XO, and a tactical command team."

CHAPTER 12

LeMieux sipped coffee and looked at her over the rim of his mug. Placing the cup on his desk, he regarded her with a frank expression. "I don't *have* any officers to spare, Lieutenant. I want *you* to get *Kuroshima* under way. You'll receive launch instructions, clearance and combat orders shortly."

Talara panicked, knowing what launching a ship from dirtside entailed. Without a command crew on the bridge, it could endanger the safety of the ship and result in a disaster if mistakes occurred. Her voice rose an octave. "Sir, we at least need a commanding officer. Can't you spare someone?"

"No. You have launched a vessel from dirtside before, haven't you?"

Her panic became fear. "Yes Sir, as part of positional qualifications training, but there was an operable chain of command at the time."

"You still have one. Get back to your ship and get her ready, Lieutenant. Good hunting. By the way, you'll need a new cap with red piping."

"But, Sir, who'll—"

Her eyes narrowed in confusion. *A white cap with red piping? Those are reserved for starship captains. Why do I need one?*

"You don't seem to understand, Lieutenant." LeMieux leaned forward, resting his elbows on his desk. "*You* are in command of *Kuroshima* until further notice."

"Me?" She began to shake, despite her best efforts. "Sir, I'm just acting commander, a placeholder. I'm an engineer, not a line officer. I work on drive systems and equipment. I don't know the first thing about starship tactics, other than what they taught at the Academy. I'm not qualified to take a destroyer into combat, Admiral."

"Too bad. You're senior-ranking officer, and therefore you *are* the commanding officer, Lieutenant. Sorry, but you know your ship better than any new officer I could send, and frankly, I don't have any to send. We're in a time-crunch and a personnel shortage here. You're senior-ranking officer. By tradition and regulation you must assume command of *Kuroshima.* I'm cutting written orders to make that official, and I'm giving you a direct verbal order to do so immediately."

She stared, nonplussed.

LeMieux gave her a feral grin. "You *do* want a crack at the bastards that killed your shipmates and your husband-to-be, don't you?"

Talara's mouth snapped shut and her eyes became glittering black ice. She answered through clenched teeth. "Yes, Sir."

LeMieux extended his hand again. "Then get your ship ready to launch, *Captain.* Welcome to command."

CHAPTER 13

Yamashita sat quietly as the cutter made its approach to Agni's boat bay, watching the battleship grow in the windscreen. He glanced at the data chip in his hand. Upon finding the Gallagher system a safe haven, he'd downloaded his logs to the chip, detailing Shiva's repair efforts, maintenance condition, repair time estimates, and battle readiness. Master Chief Johnson had added requests for expendable stores, ordnance, food and spare parts. Lieutenant Storm had provided a detailed tactical analysis of Shiva's engagement during the attack on Centauri Seven.

Yamashita recalled the relief he'd felt when discovering the only thing waiting for him in Gallagher had been Task Group 17.2. He'd feared a Karsian ambush and disaster.

Rear Admiral Terrence Yolowski, Task Group 17.2's commander, had moved his force forward to form a protective screen around *Shiva* before ordering Yamashita to report in person. Which was why Yamashita found himself aboard *Iacocca* as the shuttle maneuvered into Agni's open boat bay.

The shuttle settled as tractor beams maneuvered her into place. Yamashita heard magnetic docking clamps take over from Agni's boat bay tractors, locking her in place. A tubular gangway extended from the bulkhead and made solid contact with *Iacocca*, pressurizing with an audible hiss.

"All secure, Sir," the pilot said over his shoulder before turning back to the cockpit to shut down the cutter's drive. The airlock hissed open, and Yamashita stood, carrying his data chip and the accompanying written report. He entered the gangway and saw a Marine in dress uniform waiting at the far end of the tube. The Marine was at parade rest, eyes locked straight ahead.

Puzzled, Yamashita floated through the zero-g gangway to the grav-strip at the end of tube and stepped over the threshold into Agni's one-g environment. He saluted Agni's lights before turning to address the Marine. "Commander Saburo Yamashita, acting commander of the battleship *Shiva*. Request permission to come aboard."

The Marine snapped to attention and threw a sharp salute, which Yamashita returned, embarrassed his own salute wasn't as spit-and-polish as that of the youth before him.

The Marine lowered his arm and extended a white-gloved hand. "Permission granted, Commander. Admiral

Yolowski sends his compliments, Sir. Welcome aboard *Agni*."

Yamashita shook his hand. "Thank you, Gunnery Sergeant."

As Yamashita passed the guard, the Marine pivoted and touched his gangway console. Electronic chimes sounded with three pairs of bells. He heard the guard's voice amplified over the boat bay's loudspeakers. "Commander, RNSS *Shiva*, arriving."

Yamashita halted, staring at two straight rows of Marines in battle armor, each armed with an M-1 gauss rifle.

"Detail, ah-tenn-shun!"

The armored Marines snapped to attention with parade ground precision and sent a thrum of boots clicking together that echoed in the boat bay.

"Pre-seeent...arms!"

The gauss rifles snapped up and down, held by each Marine in a vertical salute. Yamashita stared at the honor guard in surprise, then raised his arm and returned their salute. A lump formed in his throat as he walked through the gauntlet of Marines, holding his salute as he stared at the grinning flag officer waiting at the end of the gauntlet. Maintaining the salute, he stopped before the taller officer. "Commander Yamashita, reporting as ordered, Sir."

Rear Admiral Terrence Yolowski returned the salute and offered an outstretched hand. "Welcome aboard, Saburo."

"Detail," the honor guard commander yelled at the far

end of the rows. "Order arms!" The gauss rifles snapped down again, butt plates striking the deck as a single sound.

"An honor guard, Sir?" Yamashita lifted an eyebrow. "I don't understand. A simple bosun is customary."

Yolowski smiled, long lines seaming his leathery face as he pumped Yamashita's hand. "It's only appropriate for the only man to bring an intact battleship out of Centauri Seven, Commander."

Yamashita blushed, feeling like a kid caught with his hand in the cookie jar. "We were just lucky, Sir. We barely made it at all, and we're far from intact, as you'll see in my report."

"Later." Yolowski waved a hand dismissively. "There's been little good news in the last several days, Commander. The troops need a hero, and for the moment that happens to be you. Frankly, we're glad *any* ship survived Centauri Seven."

Yolowski led him to a lift. Behind, Yamashita heard the platoon leader dismissing the honor guard and thought about how much the Marines must have hated dressing up in battle armor to greet a Navy commander. He felt guilty they'd been put through the effort. He was merely the XO of a battleship that had barely escaped destruction. *Shiva* had survived by sheer luck, something he'd had no control over. It was hardly deserving of an honor guard.

Yolowski exited the lift and led Yamashita through a series of corridors to Agni's ready room. The admiral moved to the dispenser and poured a steaming mug of coffee before glancing at Yamashita. "You still a tea drinker, Sab?"

"Yes, Sir, but coffee's fine."

CHAPTER 13

"Good. Here you are."

Yolowski handed him the mug and poured himself another. The ceramic mug's thickly glazed side was embossed with Agni's crest. He placed the hard copy and data chip on the table. "My report, Sir."

Yolowski picked up the hardcopy folder and thumbed through it quickly. After a long moment, he shook his head and smiled. "Have a seat, Sab."

Yamashita collapsed in the nearest chair.

The admiral sat beside him. "It's good to see you again, Saburo. What's it been, now? Two years?"

"Yes, Sir, when I was skipper of *Masada* in the Tuskegee system." Yamashita smiled, fondly remembering his old ship and crew. Yolowski had been a commodore then. Many years before that, Yolowski had been a senior instructor at the Naval Academy when a young midshipman named Yamashita had begun his induction into the Navy.

"Damn, we're getting old." Yolowski expelled a breath of pent-up air. "You'll be happy to know *Masada* has been chopped to Task Force Seventeen. She's assigned to Commodore O'Brien's task unit."

"Really?" Yamashita grinned. "It'll be good to see *Masada* again."

Yolowski sipped coffee. "She's not here yet. She's still part of Rear Admiral MacDougal's Task Group 17.3. O'Brien's task unit is part of MacDougal's task group. They're coming in from Yamato. Vice Admiral Montgomery is Task Force Seventeen's CO. His flagship, *Pan-Ku*, is currently in orbit over Gallagher's World. Your appearance here was unexpected, Sab. To be frank, we thought everyone in Centauri was dead. Montgomery will likely come out here to meet you."

Yamashita had long known the grizzled and well-respected Vice Admiral Ivanov Montgomery. As CO of Task Force Seventeen, Montgomery was responsible for all Navy units guarding the *Danchi* sector.

Yamashita smiled. "It'll be good to see him again, too, Sir. So you have two task groups holding here at the Gallagher stargate?"

Yolowski nodded. "The Confederation's been at war with the Empire since the Centauri attack. The Admiralty's decided to fight a delaying action along the Rim until we can marshal enough forces for a counterattack. Montgomery's rendezvousing Seventeen here in Gallagher. I've got twenty-four of his warships out here to blockade the stargate. My own flagship, *Yamamoto*, will arrive shortly, along with MacDougal's Task Group 17.3. Admiral Yu just happened to be leaving New Seoul when the attack occurred, so we immediately rerouted her task unit to Gallagher as well. In a week or so, Seventeen will be fully formed."

Yamashita frowned. "A counterattack, Sir?"

"Yes, but not until we've gathered enough firepower. Montgomery wants a full carrier division on hand before we take the offensive. Thank God our carriers weren't caught in Centauri. NavInt claims the Karsians hit Centauri through the Zion stargate."

The horror of the attack flashed vividly through Yamashita's mind. "They came in from the Zion's Waste

CHAPTER 13

'gate with several squadrons of fighters, Sir. Caught us with our pants down. Who would've thought we'd be attacked from the Zion nexus? As far as anyone knew, there was nothing in Zion that posed a threat."

Yolowski's expression was grim. "What the hell happened out there, Sab?"

"The orbital docks took the brunt of the attack, Sir. Battleship Row was hammered right off the bat. *Shiva* was already underway when the attack occurred, so we were moving when they hit us. That gave us maneuvering speed, allowing us to evade somewhat, unlike those poor bastards in the docks. Our point defenses took out several fighters, but one made a kamikaze attack and hit us pretty hard. Thank God our structural integrity fields were up. Captain Kruger and the bridge crew were killed by the kamikaze. I was in auxiliary control."

Yolowski sipped coffee and considered Yamashita's words, trying to picture the battle in his mind, grateful for the regulations placing COs and XOs in different compartments of a ship during combat. "Kruger was a good man, Saburo, and a fine captain. Not a bad tennis player, either, as I recall. It's a damned shame to lose a man of that caliber, not to mention a team the caliber of Shiva's bridge crew."

"Yes, Sir. I can't help but feel guilty about it."

"Why? You had nothing to do with it. You survived."

"That's precisely the point, Admiral." Yamashita felt the sting of sadness bite his heart, but he kept it in check. Samurai did not cry; no naval officer did in front of a superior. "I was a bridge crew member, Sir. I should've been up there with them when they went. I know it sounds silly, but they were family, and I wasn't there with them when they died. It feels like . . . I abandoned them somehow."

"Well, that *is* silly, Sab," Yolowski said softly and leaned closer. "*Dying* would have been letting them down, not surviving. From what little I know so far, one thing's perfectly clear: *you* kept the faith. The fact you're alive is the only thing that gave *Shiva* a fighting chance. You saved Kruger's ship and his crew. That's what Kruger would've wanted. How can you feel guilty about that?"

"It's cultural, Sir. Are you familiar with the Japanese concept of *giri*?"

"No."

"Giri is obligation. In ancient Japan on Old Earth, obligation was a matter of honor. A samurai was obligated to serve his master. A *daimyo* was obligated to serve the shogun. Children were obligated to serve their parents. It's a debt in our culture to repay obligation. The concept of honor is what held ancient Nipponese society together. Giri remains strong in the Japanese colonies of the *Danchi* sector. I had a debt, Sir. I had giri with Kruger and the bridge team of *Shiva*."

"I understand, Saburo, but you also had an obligation to your ship, your crew, to Admiral Montgomery, the Navy and the Confederation, just as they have to you. How's that any different than this giri you owe to fallen comrades?"

"They're *dead*, Admiral. I can't repay them in this life.

I can only attempt to be worthy of what they died for. I must be worthy of their memory, no matter the price. It's a matter of personal honor, Sir."

Yolowski searched Yamashita's eyes and seemed to find an understanding of Yamashita's torment. After a moment he frowned and changed the subject. "I think you're being too hard on yourself, Sab, but I understand. Montgomery wants to return to Centauri Seven ASAP and take it back from any Karsian forces deployed there. First, however, he wants to sweep Zion's Waste and clean out any Karsian lice still lurking in the nexus. He doesn't want threats at his back when he begins his offensive, and he'll need the additional firepower of your battleship to do that."

Yamashita sighed. "*Shiva's* not ready for combat, Sir, not fully. Her engine controls are damaged, and her hull's ruptured in several places. There are a dozen other problems you'll find in my report. Of course, if you need us, I'll have her there, ready to fight as best we can. We'll do whatever's required."

Yolowski shrugged. "Well, *Shiva* might not go out with us, at least not until she's repaired, but I do have something for you to do, so you might as well get prepared for it."

"You're giving me a ship?"

The admiral smiled. "Yes, I'm giving you a warship, Sab. I'm also frocking you to the rank of captain. We need someone capable of filling Kruger's shoes, and you're the only officer I have available who's qualified. The promotion's premature, being below-the-zone, but if you don't want it or know of a more qualified candidate, I'll be happy to consider him or her in your stead."

Yamashita barely hid his grin. "No, Sir. I'll take the frock promotion. Thank you, Sir. I don't know what to say."

"I took the liberty of promoting you to captain over an hour ago, so you're out of uniform. I expect you to be wearing proper rank the next time I see you, *Captain* Yamashita. Congratulations. Oh, I've also cut orders that you're to be the permanent skipper of *Shiva* once she's battle ready again."

Yamashita blinked, stunned. He'd always hoped to one day get command of a battlewagon. His promotion to executive officer aboard *Shiva* had indicated he was being groomed for such a future O-6 billet, but he'd never expected they would give him *Shiva*.

Suddenly, he wondered if it was acceptable. The assignment was a great honor, but it had come at an awful price. *Shiva* was Kruger's ship. It felt like stealing from his former CO. Too many friends and shipmates had died to provide that opportunity. As much as he wanted command of *Shiva*, it didn't seem worth the price, but there was little point in arguing. "Thank you, Admiral."

Yolowski seemed to read his thoughts as he refilled Yamashita's cup. "You *do* deserve it, Saburo. We're at war, and in war people get killed, sometimes our best people. You know that. In wartime we need *leaders*, men and women who can lead, fight, and win. We need doers, action people, fighters. Politicians and dime-a-dozen staff weenies are out. They're useless in a shooting war, and inevitably head to the rear when the shooting starts. Anyone who did what you did, who got a damaged and runaway battleship out of Centauri Seven and brought her back to the fleet, well, that's a man we want on our side."

Yamashita nodded. In peacetime, many officers attained rank by doing the *right* things. They worked at propping up their own efficiency ratings through public affairs, political connections, and advantages gained through social interaction with leaders who held the reins of power. An old saying claimed that in peacetime it was *who* you knew—and how well they liked you—that got you promoted. Actual fighters, the hardcore warriors, were almost always mavericks who thought in terms of battle, even in peacetime. They focused on the best way to win future wars by defeating enemies. Because their focus was on winning wars instead of being promoted, such fighters were often overlooked for promotion during peacetime.

War wasn't a positive subject among peacetime politicians. New ideas and better ways to devastate enemies during war tended to require high risk and cost tremendous amounts of money. Politicians were risk-averse at the best of times, and money was a resource near and dear to political hearts. Warriors were too pragmatic in their approach and tended to be violent, factors that didn't endear them to politicians jockeying for authority and importance.

The result was as predictable and as old as Mankind: the best fighters were relegated to middle and lower ranks in peacetime, where their embarrassingly brutal ideas were regarded with disdain. Not promoted in peacetime as quickly as power-seekers, such fighters were often forced out long before retirement age.

An old Japanese adage spoke about a nail sticking up out of a floor, and how the nail had to be constantly hammered back into place to keep the surface smooth. Professional fighters were like nails. During peacetime, they were a thorn in politicians' sides, reminding them of things they'd rather forget—like the fact that a military's purpose was to kill and destroy enemies. Politicians didn't like to think about that, so leadership often failed to promote such war-like knuckle-draggers. As with the old Japanese saying, politicians decided it was easier to beat nails into the floor than be tripped up by them.

Now fighters were suddenly needed at the front and the peacetime careerists were scrambling for the rear as fast as they could go. It was a good thing, as it would improve the capabilities of the Navy, which had a sudden need to divest itself of weaklings. The warriors were in charge again, at least until the next peace broke out.

Yolowski interrupted his thoughts. "Of course, your pay's retroactive pending Fleet approval of your promotion, but the Old Man's already endorsed it, so I don't see any reason to worry. When a three-star says do it, it's a done deal. Now that all of *that* is cleared up, are you ready for another blow to your sanity?"

"I'm not sure, Sir." Yamashita gulped his coffee and ran a hand through his thinning hair. Things were happening faster than he'd ever seen in the Navy. It was scary how fast changes were occurring.

CHAPTER 13

Yolowski refilled the cup as Yamashita waited for the next shoe to fall. "Effective immediately, you're also in command of Task Unit 17.2.1."

Yamashita nearly dropped the cup. "Sir?"

It was too much. To be promoted to captain *and* given command of *Shiva* in one day had been incredible enough. Now Yolowski was giving him a task unit as well. Yamashita felt his head spinning.

"You heard correctly." Yolowski handed him a hard copy strip of actual paper. "Your acting XO will take command of *Shiva* and supervise her repair at Gallagher's World. You'll take command of *Agni*, as CO of the task unit. I'll be transferring my flag to *Yamamoto* as soon as she arrives. Meanwhile, here's the list of the ships in your unit."

Yamashita glanced at the hardcopy, noting the ships of Task Unit 17.2.1.

BB-71	*Agni*
CA-116	*Capricornus*
CL-211	*Sekigahara*
DD-581	*Yoshitsune*
FF-625	*Nebula Runner*
FF-628	*Aurigae*
FF-659	*Vaulter*
CT-701	*Copernicus*
CT-706	*Hawking*
CT-713	*Lao Tzu*

"This task unit's short a destroyer, Admiral."

"Yes, you're missing *Gant*. She was patrolling the Pan'vu test ranges before the attack on Centauri. No one's heard from her since, and it's likely she's gone, Saburo. There's not much chance she survived all the Karsian task forces sweeping through the Rim, especially the one that hit Centauri."

"So . . . a battleship, two cruisers, a tin can, three frigates and a trio of corvettes."

"Actually, two battleships. Once Shiva's repaired, you can move your flag lights back to her. Marcus Guerrera has the second task unit in my command. He's aboard *Victorious* now, in this formation. Sally Dell commands our third task unit, but she only has two vessels, *Recluse* and *Stalker*."

"Stealthships?"

"Uh-huh. A boomer and a fast attack. They'll be recon for the sweep into Zion's Waste to let us know if we need to assault the stargate or not."

Yamashita pursed his lips, considering the problem. Stargates had a maximum limit for the tonnage of mass that could jump through their wormholes simultaneously. The limit depended upon multiple factors, but the most prominent was the mass of the stars forming the ends of the wormholes. In most cases, massive stars created wormholes with higher transition limits. Any amount of mass below that limit could wormhole simultaneously, but once that wormhole tonnage threshold was exceeded, strange things tended to happen.

CHAPTER 13

One was that the mass transiting the wormhole might try to occupy the same space inside the wormhole during jump. When that happened, the mysterious forces of metaspace tended to shove the excess mass into an alternate dimension. Doing so prevented the impossible n-space problem of two objects occupying the same physical space at the same time. The dimensional "push-out" remained in effect until a sufficient amount of mass cleared the wormhole, at which time the "pushed out" portion would pop back into the wormhole's metaspace and complete transition normally.

Occasionally, however, the excess mass was pushed into an *opposite* dimension. When that happened, the "pushed-out" mass canceled an equivalent amount of antimatter in the opposite dimension. The resulting quantum cancellation then "leaked" back in both dimensions and into the metaspace of the wormhole. The resulting explosion inevitably destroyed all matter in the wormhole, and often anything immediately around the entrance or termini of the stargates at each end. Nothing survived when that happened, which was why commanders preferred to only transit "surveyed" stargates, whose transition mass limits were known.

A stargate's mass limit imposed tactical restrictions on commanders trying to attack through a stargate into another system. Because of the mass limits imposed, only a certain number of ships could safely jump simultaneously. This tended to stagger attacking forces in trail. All ships that jumped suffered the irritating effects of sensor distortion for almost a full half-minute on exiting the stargate terminus, leaving them blind and helpless to any enemy forces waiting near the exit.

To know what waited on the far side, an attacking commander required real-time reconnaissance. Sending a warship through alerted a waiting enemy, lost the element of surprise, and usually resulted in the destruction of said ship. Stealthships could insert undetected, however, particularly if they transitioned at low velocities. This allowed stealthships to jump in and conduct covert reconnaissance at the far-end prior to sending a fleet through a stargate.

If Sally Dell's stealthships found nothing in Zion's Waste, they would signal the task group to proceed through the wormhole normally. If they found an enemy task force waiting, however, Montgomery would have to conduct a stargate assault based on the known strength of enemy forces, their distance from the terminus, and the transition limits imposed by the wormhole.

If the enemy was far away from the terminus, large capital missile warships like superdreadnoughts and battleships would be sent through first, which could engage opponents at range and survive intense hostile fire. If, however, the enemy force was close to the terminus, warships with beam weapons would go through first, because beams were faster than missiles. In either case, carrier forces, like Yolowski's task group—which included *Yamamoto*, *Victorious* and *Reticulus*—would come through last in order to remain protected as long as possible.

If the assaulting force had sufficient firepower to

overwhelm the enemy force, it would do so immediately. There was no terrain in Zion's Waste, as the nexus had neither a star nor planets. It was an empty space in the middle of nowhere. Yamashita doubted the Karsians had fortified the nexus in the brief period of time they'd had possession of it. Such things required tremendous logistical lines the Empire had yet to form. If, however, they had stationed a task force there, Dell's stealthships would let Yolowski know it.

Yamashita looked up, meeting Yolowski's eyes. "I take it I'll be going along on the sweep?"

"You take it correctly, Captain." Yolowski leaned back in his chair. "You'll command your unit from *Agni*. I'll move to my carrier, and we'll wait for Dell's report. Montgomery will keep *Pan-Ku* in-system to defend Gallagher's World in case of unexpected attack. My orders are to secure Zion's Waste while he forms Task Force Seventeen here. Once that's accomplished, Seventeen will proceed into Zion's Waste and make for Centauri Seven."

Yamashita frowned. "If Montgomery rallies Task Force Seventeen in Gallagher, won't that pull ships away from protecting the Eusi Hegemony?"

"Not many. The Hegemony's protected by Third Fleet, and most of its units are defending Antioch at the moment. It'll leave the center of the Hegemony open, but supposedly that's part of a grand strategy. The Admiralty *wants* the Karsians to move in there, hopefully to overextend their supply and communication lines. There aren't many populated worlds in the Rim, but there are a lot of gas giants there the Karsians want, and we'll have to fight to keep them.

"Once we recover Centauri, Montgomery plans to end-run the Empire, hit their forward bases at Nangtashgu, and cut off any fleets headed for the Gulliver system. Task Force Twelve will strike simultaneously from the far side of the Rim from the Tanzania, New Congo, and Antioch systems. The plan is to envelop and kill whatever the Karsians have in Confederation space. After that, we'll counterattack the Empire's home systems, one by one. If we can buy enough time for our fleets to assemble, we'll win any war of attrition, because our industrial capacity is superior to the Empire's."

Yamashita shifted uncomfortably. Unlike the Rigelian Core worlds, the Rim stars had voluntarily segregated themselves by race and culture. Though members of any world could come and go as they pleased under Confederation law, Rigelians viewed the Rim as being distinct and backward, despite being part of the Confederation. Eusi citizens had formed many planetary societies based on African tribal cultures and were notoriously touchy about anything they perceived as bias against them.

"How do the Eusi view this plan?"

Yolowski grimaced as he placed the mug down with a thump. "Unfortunately, nobody's asked them, Saburo. As you know, their home defense fleet rotates warships in and out of the RCN on a reserve basis. At the moment their worlds just happen to provide the perfect bait for our trap.

We expect the Empire will attack the Antioch, Nambo, New Woodlark, New Congo, and probably the Wewak systems over the next several weeks. They're Hegemony systems between the Empire and the rest of the Confederation. The Hegemony has a large number of merchant cartels in those systems, which the Empire will want to disrupt. They've probably inserted bladeships into those systems already."

Yamashita frowned. "No one consulted Hegemony leadership about this plan?"

"No. Oh, we'll tell them, when we can, and they won't like it one damned bit. How could they? They'll scream it's a Confederation plot to sacrifice segregated worlds to preserve Core world diversity values, or some ridiculous crap like that."

"Is it?"

Yolowski's jaw hardened. "Hell, no. The Admiralty devises strategy based on where the enemy's attacking and where our fleets are positioned, nothing else. Unfortunately, the Eusi are caught between the Empire and the rest of the Confederation, so it only makes sense that the main battle will occur in their backyard. It's simply luck of the draw, Saburo; a matter of stellar geometry. Unfortunately, they're caught in the middle. We didn't plan it that way, and we can't change that fact. But for operational security reasons, we can't inform them either."

Yamashita sighed. "An awful lot of the fallout's going to land in their back yard, Admiral."

"I know, and that sucks, but it is what it is. Third Fleet's marshaling in New Texas to cover the stargates linking New Africa and Tongo, and they'll eventually press forward into New Woodlark. Beyond that, we aren't in position to protect the Eusi center. Once our forces marshal, however, we'll pound the hell out of the Empire and drive it out once and for all. The good thing is the Hegemony systems aren't heavily populated."

Yamashita sighed again and drained his mug. He wasn't a coffee drinker like most Navy personnel, preferring tea, yet he had to admit that for a flag officer, Yolowski brewed a good cup of java.

There were other important things to be considered. The Karsians would certainly be waiting for them somewhere. The Eusi Hegemony would be used as bait to over-extend Karsian lines. Yamashita didn't particularly like the idea of using the Hegemony as bait. It hinted at Core World bigotry, at least on the surface. Likely it was just an unfortunate coincidence. A captain in the RCN didn't have to agree with the strategy or orders handed out by admirals, however. His job was to execute them. Such things were planned by higher pay grades than a commander's.

Captain, he corrected himself, allowing himself a slight thrill over the word. He'd made captain at last. "Well, Admiral, what is it you want me to do?"

"Guerrera and Dell will be aboard in an hour." Yolowski leaned forward in his chair. "We have a battle planning conference to discuss assaulting the Zion stargate and our follow-on tactical options. That will commence at 1400 hours, ship's time. Montgomery will likely be there, as well. The captain of *Agni* is Jeff Neher. Get with him about placing your lights aboard and outfitting your quarters. You're both captains, but he's senior. He has more time in grade, but he's not the task unit commander, you are. I want my task group doing something productive by 0600 hours tomorrow."

"Yes, Sir. I'll need to contact my acting XO on *Shiva*."

"Of course. Might as well make him acting CO of *Shiva*, Saburo. At least until her repairs are completed. Let him know that."

"Thank you, Admiral. I'd also like to requisition my acting tactical officer from *Shiva*, Lieutenant Storm. He's been my TAC-O since the attack in Centauri, and he's proven invaluable from a weapons and tactics standpoint, as you'll see in my report."

"Sure." Yolowski nodded "Captain Neher has his own TAC-O, so make Storm the flag TAC-O for the task unit. Anything else you need, Saburo, just ask. I'll move any personnel here that you believe are necessary and CHOP them directly to your command. Is this Storm fellow up to being TAC-O for a task unit? That's asking a lot of a lieutenant."

Yamashita smiled. "In most cases, I'd agree, but Storm's a senior lieutenant. His wife-to-be was at the Centauri Seven base when it was attacked. She was the engineer of *Kuroshima*. She's presumed lost with her ship, and Storm's spoiling for a fight. He's in the manuals day and night, studying tactics, techniques, and procedures. He's been pulling back-to-back shifts without a hitch. He's good, Sir, very good, and he wants nothing more than to kill Karsians. He deserves a shot."

Yolowski sighed, accepting Yamashita's evaluation. "Okay, just see to it that his anger doesn't get the best of him."

"Yes, Sir."

Yolowski stood. Yamashita followed suit, putting his empty mug on the table.

"Very well, Sab, go see to your command. But before you do, we have a lunch date. I'm afraid I'll have to make that an order. I've got several ships' captains—and not a few admirals—who're not only hungry for lunch but to hear exactly what happened in Centauri Seven and what's happened to *Shiva* since. After lunch, command of Task Unit 17.2.1 is yours. Congratulations on promotion and your new command, and welcome to my task group, Saburo."

"Thank you, Admiral." Yamashita smiled. "Again, I'm not sure what to say. This is all rather . . . incredible."

Yolowski grinned, but the grin didn't meet his eyes. "You don't have to say anything, Captain. Just kill Karsians when you can. Let's eat. I'm starved."

CHAPTER 14

"Don't touch me!"

Sarah Jesse Comforti howled as her brother's leg brushed her knee. She raised an elbow and jabbed him in the ribs. "Mom, Jarrod's touching me!"

Jarrod Comforti shook his head. "Am not."

"Are too!"

"Both of you behave." Susan Comforti snapped the words out irritably as she tried to concentrate on driving the hovercar. The trip to the Officer's Club at the naval base wasn't a long one for the Comforti family lived in base housing, but the incessant squabbling of the children was driving her nuts.

"Stop it!" Sarah's complaint was followed by the sound of hands smacking body parts.

"Ow!"

Jarrod spoke immediately. "Mom, I didn't do anything, honest."

Maybe if I ignore them, they'll shut up. Susan tapped the control pad irritably. *Lord knows what goes through their pubescent little minds. They get along great for the first thirteen years, then suddenly go insane and become monsters.*

It was one more in the long line of bitter pills she'd been forced to swallow over the years, and she wasn't happy. *No, I'm not happy at all.*

First on the list of unhappy things was her husband, Harl.

He'd seemed normal enough when they were in college. In those days life had been filled with potential. Her father's limousine had dropped her at the entrance to Avondale, and she'd spotted Harl standing beside the entrance. He'd been handsome in his ROTC uniform with the rank of cadet lieutenant.

Harl had been so dashing she'd been unable to resist flirting with him. Unfortunately, that had led him to date her, the starting point of a marriage that now seemed to crush her hopes and dreams.

She'd agreed to go out on a lark, and they'd had fun together. Susan's father, a space mining company CEO, hadn't supported the relationship. Her wealthy family meant Susan had no lack of suitors, many of them well-connected. Because of more appropriate suitors, her father hadn't approved of her dating a military cadet.

As an only child, Susan had kept her father's accountants busy by wooing her father to constantly purchase new things for her. Her mother, who'd never held a job in her life, was a social debutante of Old South culture, which

CHAPTER 14

dominated on the planet Biloxi. Because the Estacadoan Worlds had descended from Old Earth's American South culture—with system names like Dixie, Appomattox, and Biloxi—her mother's world had been steeped in the traditions of that culture's sensitivity, a culture that traced its roots to a time before the American Civil War.

"You must always act like a lady, Susanna," her mother had instructed her. "Dress for your station, know the right people and uphold your family's good name and character."

Well, Mother certainly lived by that example. Susan frowned, turning to follow the traffic markers toward the club. *She was always at one social function or another, having tea or hosting some party. She made the "right" contacts while schmoozing Daddy's business partners for the family's prestige.*

Susan's mother had led a rather idyllic life, having never cooked, cleaned, or spent quality time with her lonely daughter. There had been an endless line of butlers, maids, and nannies to stand in for her, leaving her mother free to do what she did best: socialize.

It had been a boring existence for young Susan. As a girl, she'd had everything she wanted except parental attention. Her family's affluence hadn't helped Susan with social skills, however. Rich her family might have been, but Susan had been an ugly duckling as a child, at least by her own standards. The uneven teeth had been horrible enough, but teenage acne had been devastating. She'd needed cosmetic surgery in her opinion, but her

173

parents had adamantly refused her demands to get "fixed" as excessive vanity.

Eventually, makeup and hair styling, combined with the removal of her God-awful braces, had turned Susan into a beauty. She'd been eighteen and good-looking at last, but the psychological scars of her childhood ugliness—combined with emotional the abandonment of her mother—had left a hole in her self-esteem. Her childhood fears of being ugly and inadequate had left deep psychological scars that had never healed. Physically pretty she had become—she could almost accept that now, intellectually—but she'd never *felt* pretty, not in her heart. Her mother had fostered a burden of social obligation on her, while her father had disapproved of anyone she'd tried to date. No suitor had ever seemed to measure up to his standards; no one was good enough to date *his* daughter.

By the time she'd entered college, she'd adopted her mother's need for social popularity. Her mother had trained her that the worst of sins was being unpopular. As a blue-blood aristocrat of Biloxian society, popularity was automatically assumed by her family's wealth, power, and influence.

She'd been rebellious at the time, simultaneously hating her mother's lifestyle while desperately craving her approval. In truth, she'd never felt worthy of any of it.

Perhaps it had been the need to feel worthy, to win her mother's approval, or perhaps her own need to feel *desirable* that had led her to flirt with Harl that fateful afternoon. Her father would have been livid had he seen the way she lifted her skirt slightly to show off her legs as she'd approached the dashing cadet.

"Beauregards do not flirt like common harlots," her mother had been fond of saying. "Especially with those of lesser station."

Harl Comforti had certainly been of lesser station by her parents' standards. He had been middle-class, from a family forced to actually *save* money so Harl could attend college.

He seemed so cute in his uniform that day, she remembered with a wistful smile. She'd wanted to flaunt her newfound freedom in her parents' faces, and Harl had seemed exciting, from a different social class than the one she'd been born to. Harl's family did manual labor for a living, never considering physical work beneath them. It had seemed so new and refreshing at the time.

Her father had disapproved, just as she'd hoped.

"How can you possibly date that—that—*boy?*" His voice had thundered through the mansion on a visit home. "It's bad enough he's working class, but you had to pick a military man as well?"

Her father held the military in great disdain. Susan wasn't sure why, though his staunch progressive politics might have had something to do with it. Her father considered military people to be dullards at best. He'd told her on more than one occasion that soldiers were dreamers blinded by delusions of glory, adventure and concepts of honor.

"Power belongs to the wealthy," he'd told her on many

occasions. "Workers are servants. Anyone with a proton of intelligence knows wealthy civilians run the government, not poor people in silly uniforms.

"Our forefathers were so afraid of the military that they had civilian leadership written into the Confederation Constitution. A military man cannot hold elected office by law. Why? Because they can't be trusted, that's why. Soldiers are a dimwitted lot who waste tax revenues that could be put to better use than shooting at similar idiots in foreign governments also wearing silly uniforms. Soldiers don't generate revenue, and they're stupid enough to put up with tremendous abuse while getting paid almost nothing in wages. What kind of idiot puts themselves in that position? Only dim-witted commoners stupid enough to be pawns in someone else's game.

"I don't even understand why we have a military anyway. Soldiers are an outdated idea; an anachronism that's outlived its usefulness. No one has ever attacked the Confederation. We're the strongest stellar power, next to Old Earth. We literally have no enemies, yet the military spends excessive amounts of our revenue to buy pricey toys to use to against threats that don't exist. I'm sure we can do better than spend huge portions of our national wealth buying toys for dim-witted war-mongers, who only break those toys whenever they get their grubby hands on them."

Susan had once heard her father claim the military accounted for almost 10 percent of the Confederation's GNP. He believed the government had better things to do with tax revenues—like investing it in Beauregard Mining. She'd used his dislike of the military against him, needling him with her new Navy boyfriend. Then she'd found herself drawn to Harl for other reasons.

Harl and his friends had incredible hobbies. They did hang-gliding, hover-jumping, and ancient carpentry. It had been fun to interact with a "lower class." They had been more interesting than her boorish parents, and far more fun than the high-class beaus they'd tried to steer her toward.

They had begun serious courting in her junior year. She'd found a level of suitability in him, especially when she'd learned he would be commissioned as an officer. An officer's commission brought a level of authority and prestige, and it would earn Harl a substantially greater paycheck than what enlisted people made. For Susan, it had offered the chance to escape Biloxi and its smothering society, a world she'd found both stifling and old-fashioned. Dating Harl had allowed her to escape her parents' pervasive control and had given her a freedom she'd deeply craved at the time.

They had married after college, against her parents' wishes. Susan had stood beside Harl at his commissioning ceremony and pinned the black boards with their single golden stripes on his shoulders.

Everything had been wonderful at first. Harl had been assigned to New Texas for primary training, and they'd moved to a base on the planet Odessa within a few months. It had been an exciting time, and Susan had found herself off-world in a new and interesting life. She'd reveled spending in Harl's paychecks, setting up a lavish home to meet the standards expected of an officer's wife. She couldn't remember precisely who had told her what those standards were, but it had been a wonderful period in her life. She'd had friends to socialize with and enough money to buy anything she'd wanted.

Then she'd gotten pregnant.

Strangely, it had been the one thing that had made her father proud enough to take her back into the family and treat her husband with respect.

Susan had never wanted children. She'd had few boyfriends until she'd gone to college, mostly due to her feelings of inadequacy. Harl had been the first man she'd ever gone all the way with.

She'd known how to prevent it, of course. Modern birth control measures were foolproof. Unfortunately, she'd been too lazy to use them. She hadn't been thinking at the time. Even now that fact made her furious. She'd read up on the options in college, when Harl's sexual appetite had been unending, and she'd used contraceptives religiously during school, deeply fearing pregnancy (*after all, what would Daddy have said?*). After marriage, it hadn't seemed like an important issue. She'd slacked off, and one of Harl's genetic warheads had scored a direct hit.

A daughter had been born nine months later. Though Harl had been there for the delivery—and despite the fact the new baby had been his pride and joy—the Navy had given him three days at home before shipping him on a Godforsaken cruise to Malon, leaving her alone with a newborn to care for.

Harl hadn't returned for six months.

And damn if he didn't do it to me again just as soon as he could.

On his first night home they'd celebrated his return, and a month later Susan had discovered, to her dismay, she was pregnant again.

The second birth had been hard physically, and the new baby a boy. After two years of being pregnant—months of morning sickness, bloating, and the peaks and valleys of raging emotions, not to mention physical humiliation before a growing list of medical personnel—she'd finally decided birth control was serious business. She wasn't going to be put through *that* again. Not ever.

Harl had been displeased with the method she'd chosen. He'd laughed when she'd suggested male contraceptives. Harl had wanted more children. Deciding that punishment was in order, she'd opted for the most foolproof contraceptive of all and had cut him off.

It had worked, too, wonderfully at first. With two babies to feed, and without the butlers and nannies she was used to, sex had been the farthest thing from her mind at the time. She'd been too exhausted. Harl had pouted like a bull in heat—which he had been—and had tried every tactic he could think of to get back into her good graces. She'd managed to outwit him on most occasions by claiming she had a headache or needed sleep, which had also given her some respite from the constant demands of crying children, at least when Harl was home.

The physical demands and obligations children had imposed on her had crushed her dreams about life. No longer did life seem leisurely or fun. Despite her dreams, she'd ended up with nothing but crying kids, loads of housework, and Harl being gone for long periods of time.

I'm trapped. Children truly are a twenty-year curse, a prison sentence I can't escape. My only hope of parole is they will finally grow up and go off to college. Provided, of course, I can keep Harl from using me to make more.

She loved her children, of course, but two babies, especially so close in age, were more than she'd bargained for. Those children, now fourteen and thirteen respectively, constantly bickered about everything.

Sometimes my plans work too well.

Eventually Harl had stopped pressuring her for sex, acting brokenhearted about it, and the Navy kept him away at least eight months of the year. It had been a relief at first. Harl, having given up on sex, had become withdrawn. He'd come home less often than before. There always had seemed some new ship for him to worry about, some new assignment or school that needed attention, and promotions had brought him ever-increasing responsibilities.

Susan still wasn't sure how he'd done it. She admitted—privately—that perhaps he'd found female friends in the Navy to relieve the pressure with. She'd no idea if that was true or not, and she didn't particularly want to find out. At first she'd been simply relived the pressure was off. The Navy had a saying that what happened in space stayed in space, and she'd been willing to leave it at that. By the time her oldest child was ten, however, things had changed for Susan Comforti.

Suddenly, she'd found herself craving sex. Seemingly overnight she'd gone from abstinence to lust, but by then Harl had given up. He'd still been friendly, but he'd stopped trying to talk her into the sack and had seemed disinterested in any advances on her part. He'd claimed sex wasn't that important anymore. She had finally realized the damage her denial tactics had done to the marriage. She'd said too many hurtful things over the years to be able to take them all back. She'd made a mistake marrying Harl Comforti. Harl, who'd had such potential in college, had remained in the Navy.

If he loved me and the children as much as he loves the Navy, he'd quit the military and get a real job, a job that would support us in the style we deserve to be accustomed to. What's wrong with him? Doesn't he see what the Navy has done to us? I can't scrape up enough money to hire one nanny or butler, much less return home and see my parents on Biloxi. I can barely refurnish the house or attend cocktail parties. How can he stay in the Navy and leave us so destitute?

Old hurts boiled in her heart. She remembered when Harl had asked her to host a party for his crew. Initially, she'd been excited. It had been something she could do well, considering her training in social graces. She'd catered a lavish dinner, complete with a *maitre'd* and *hours d'vours*, and rented the most expensive ballroom in town. She'd sent out greeting cards requesting RSVPs.

Even now she was furious at how Harl had reacted. The officers and men of his ship had complained the party was too formal and had been irritated at having to wear dress uniforms. Even spouses had complained when Susan had imposed a cover charge for admittance. Ultimately, Harl's CO had gotten involved, telling her husband it had all been "a bit much." He'd criticized her through Harl, without openly crushing her feelings.

Harl, however, had been far less tactful.

He'd shaken one of the gold-embossed greeting cards in her face. "What the hell did you do, Susan?"

"Why, nothing," she'd replied with indignation. "I sent out invitations requesting RSVPs."

"This invitation card costs more than some of my enlisted people's uniforms. You must've broken the wives' club's entire budget."

"We'll make it back, Harl. I put a cover charge on admittance to offset the costs of dinner and the cards."

"Cover charge?" Harl had turned red with anger. "For a party? Look how you addressed my people on these cards."

His fury had raised her own ire. "What are you talking about? I wrote 'to officers and their ladies, and enlisted men and their wives.' What's wrong with that? It's polite, well-worded and proper."

Harl had crushed the card in his fist. "Are you kidding me? In the first place, Susan, not everyone in my crew is male. Secondly, most of my female personnel are married to *men*, not 'wives' or 'ladies,' which you imply are different things. Can you possibly grasp how condescending this is to my enlisted people? You've implied any woman with an officer is a lady, which—-while questionable—*might* be appropriate. If you knew some of the 'ladies' my junior officers date, you might change your mind on that point. But you've insinuated that woman married to enlisted men are mere *wives*, which implies they're *not* ladies. That's sure as hell to piss off my enlisted personnel and their spouses. And what about my enlisted women? Their husbands are not *wives*. There is no similar 'husbands' club' on this planet. I'd pissed if I were enlisted."

"But you're not enlisted, Harl. You're an officer."

"You've insinuated enlisted personnel are lesser people, Susan. Can't you see that?"

She'd huffed up. "I was trying to differentiate by rank the spouses of officer and enlisted, Harl."

"Unless they're in the military *spouses* have no rank, Susan. They're civilians. Do you understand how arrogant this sounds?"

"Enlisted personnel are *not* from the same social class as us, Harl. We went to Avondale, for God's sake."

Harl had become so livid she'd momentarily feared he might strike her. Instead, he'd stormed off. It had been one of the more painful arguments of their long marriage, but one that underscored the differences between them. She was a Beauregard from the upper class of Biloxi, willing to lower herself to the middle class standards for a while, but she'd wanted to return to where she belonged. She was now ready to accept the role and status her parents had intended for her. Harl seemed content to remain with commoners.

While it was true Harl was older now and well-respected by the Navy, he was essentially still the same man she'd met fifteen years ago. Harl *refused* to grow up and become what she and her family thought proper for a man married into the Beauregard family.

"Get away from me!"

Sarah's shrill voice cut through Susan's thoughts like fingers on a chalkboard. She heard Sarah slap her brother on the arm. "Mother, Jarrod's taking up all of the space on the back seat. His knee's touching mine, and if he doesn't stop, I'll just scream."

"So what?" Jarrod gazed out the window as if he could care less. "All you ever do is scream anyway."

It was more than Susan could take.

She stopped the hover car over at the side of the guide-way and shut down the anti-grav with a slam of the lever. The car settled with a thump. Susan whirled in the seat and jabbed a manicured finger in the faces of her children.

"Listen!" She was shouting, and knew it, but she didn't care. "You're both being little shits this morning. Jarrod, keep your hands, knees, fingers, toes, and anything else on your side of the car. Sarah, shut your mouth and stop whining. It's bad enough I have to go to a Wives Club meeting without the two of you making me late. I won't listen to you fight. In fact, get out of the car. You can both walk home. It's only a few blocks, and if you start walking now, I won't be late. Maybe it'll give you time to think about your behavior. I'm tired of listening to you. Both of you get the hell out, now!"

CHAPTER 14

The children stared at her in shock. Their faces resembled their father's when his feelings were hurt, and the look infuriated her even more. Their eyes began to mist, and their lips pouted. She knew she'd hurt them, but she was too angry to care. "I said get out, you rotten brats!"

The children dejectedly opened the doors and climbed from the car. With tears in their eyes, they began trudging home.

Susan watched them go with a trembling lip. Guilt and self-loathing slowly overrode her rage. *I've never talked to the kids like that before,* she thought. *Certainly I've never screamed at them. It's not something a lady does. I shouldn't have used profanity either. What is wrong with me?*

In the distance she heard Sarah snap at her brother, her high-pitched whine carrying down the street. "Don't walk anywhere near me, Jarrod. This is all your fault . . . and stay on your side of the sidewalk!"

Jarrod stuck his tongue out. "Ah, shut up."

For no reason she understood, Susan was suddenly overwhelmed by everything in life. Bitterness seemed to squeeze the very soul from her heart.

Putting her head on the dashboard, she cried like a baby as her children walked home.

CHAPTER 15

Benton stared in shock as he walked into the War Room and saw the president's face. The man looked tired and evidently hadn't slept in some time. The president stood staring at the holographic projections illuminated on the walls. Benton recognized many of the systems displayed as stars located along the Confederation Rim.

Hannarubi Poinard, Lord of Ashton and Duke of Aeron, turned from the wall displays and smiled wanly. As President of the Confederation, Poinard had tremendous responsibilities. Despite his haggard appearance, he greeted Benton warmly with a handshake before indicating an open seat at the briefing table. "Sir Roderick, I'm glad you're here."

"As am I to be of service, my lord."

"Drop the titles, Rod. This isn't the Assembly, there aren't any reporters here and I don't have time for it, so cut the Peerage crap. I need to get a grip on this situation fast, and I need people who'll give it to me straight without fussing with titles and courtesies. I believe you know the other people here."

Benton glanced around as he sat. He knew them, of course. To the president's immediate right was Lord James Pledger, Prime Minister of the Confederation, looking deeply troubled. On the president's left a huge man in Marine green sat with a grimace on his face as he toyed with a handheld data pad. General Raoul Lee was the most senior officer in the Rigelian Confederation Marine Corps, as well as Chairman of the Joint Chiefs of Staff.

Across from Lee, Secretary of Defense Thomas Barkonnas appeared pensive. He sat with arms crossed as he brooded, staring at the displays. Beside him, Admiral Sondra Grayson, Chief of Naval Operations, nodded her acknowledgment as Benton's eyes met hers. He glanced briefly at the others, and nodded to his friend, Vasilov O'Rourke, Secretary of State. General Lin Nguyen, Commandant of the Marine Corps, sat beside him. Last was Daniel McTaggart, Director of Ministry of Intelligence.

"Yes, Mr. President, I do."

"Good." Poinard glanced around the table. "I asked all of you here this morning because I need an intelligence assessment on the military situation in Centauri Seven and along the Rim. Rod, you're here because you're our leading expert on Kars."

Benton nodded. "Perhaps if I understood what is occurring . . ."

"Of course. Danny, give Sir Benton the latest SITREP."

"Of course, Mr. President." McTaggart moved to the center of the curved table and lowered the lights as a holographic display blossomed over the table. "These are the Periphery systems along the Rim, Sir Benton. As of 0100 hours three days ago, we've lost all contact with the following star systems."

Six systems flashed to red as McTaggart highlighted them with a laser pointer. "The first was the Test Range in Pan'vu. We lost communications traffic through the stargate, which—considering the distance—isn't that unusual, but it's of great concern when you consider the message received at 02:30 that morning from the Fleet yards at Centauri Seven."

Benton coughed. "I'm sorry, Mr. McTaggart, but what's going on?"

Poinard sighed. "Centauri Seven's been attacked, Rod."

"By whom?"

"The Empire of Kars." McTaggart crossed his hands behind his back. "Which means they had to enter through a connecting stargate, and Pan'vu is the most likely route. If that is the case, it's likely the base at Turin's World has been destroyed or captured. Stargate links with these systems were also lost at approximately the same time." His pointer flashed to the other systems, turning each of them scarlet.

"Good lord." Benton had been prepared for an emergency, but nothing on this scale. "How bad is it?"

"We received an emergency broadcast from a Fleet

relay station about two hours ago, Sir Benton. That message indicated Imperial warships attacked Centauri Seven, and the damage there is severe. We've been desperately trying to reestablish communication with Centauri Seven since, but so far we've been unsuccessful."

Poinard took a sip of tea. "Secretary Barkonnas briefed me on the message at zero-three-twenty this morning. I immediately called General Lee and Admiral Grayson, and we agreed the situation is likely disastrous, so I issued a Level One alert to all quadrants."

Benton nodded. Centauri Seven was the home of Seventh Fleet, the primary military fleet in the Oriental systems. If Centauri Seven had fallen, a breach in Rigel's outer defense ring would be open, particularly if the Karsians had fleets waiting to rush the gap. Centauri Seven was also home of Battle Squadron One, Rigel's frontline battle wall in that sector. "What about Bat-One?"

There was a moment of silence before Sondra Grayson replied. "We received confirmation of the Centauri attack via a communications drone, Sir Benton. That drone came from a battleship, *Shiva*. Apparently, she survived the initial attack but was forced to flee the system to do so. Based on Shiva's report, we lost BATRON One."

"You mean *Shiva* ran?" Barkonnas looked up angrily, cutting her off. "If one of our battlewagons ran in the face of an enemy attack, I'll have her skipper court-martialed."

"Sir, *Shiva* didn't voluntarily run from battle." Grayson's face darkened, but she faced Barkonnas calmly. "She was rammed by an enemy fighter and her bridge destroyed as she was getting underway. Her engineering controls were fused, and a runaway drive nearly destroyed her. During the resulting runaway, *Shiva* wormholed into the Gallagher, and that's the only reason she survived. *Shiva* reported that the Karsian attack on Centauri Seven was overpowering. We only know this because Shiva's drone arrived in Yamato and was relayed back via grav-comm through New Seoul and Vega Nova. We're currently moving Seventh Fleet task into Gallagher, and the report from *Shiva* is at least two days old. We're fortunate she got away at all, Mr. President. If she'd stayed in Centauri Seven, she'd have been destroyed, and if that had happened we'd still have no idea that the Confederation is under attack."

Benton steepled his fingers. "Was Centauri Seven occupied?"

"Unknown." McTaggart looked up and shrugged. "As I said, we've had no further contact with the system, Sir Benton. We'll be sending Task Force Seventeen into Centauri Seven to confirm the situation there, but it'll be days before we have an accurate assessment of how badly we've been hurt."

"Which brings us to why you're here, Rod." Poinard looked at Benton. "You have the expertise to tell us what the Karsians are most likely thinking and why. I should point out that after the intelligence briefings we received last week concerning the buildup of Karsian forces along the Rim, I sent our top ambassador to the Karsian Embassy to obtain diplomatic assurance that the Empire had no militaristic intentions toward the Confederation. The

Karsian ambassador assured him there were none. He told our ambassador that the buildup was likely a war game."

Benton nodded. "That would be typical of Karsian psychology, Mr. President. There's a term Karsians use that embodies their philosophy regarding deception. The term is *por'tahk*, which is loosely translated as 'unbalancing.' It's mentioned in all of their classic military texts as a base strategy. Por'tahk postulates enemies are most easily defeated when their balance is broken. It's not an uncommon idea, really. I believe the martial art of *judo* is founded on something similar. The diplomatic cover story is likely an example of por'tahk, in this case lying as a deception, since deception is a legitimate means—in their eyes at least—to a desired end."

"Legitimate, hell." General Lee's face hardened. "The bastards lied."

Like most Marines, Lee used expletives rather passionately.

Benton nodded. "To our way of thinking, yes, General, but to them it's simply a tactical option. Deception is their preferred tactic. Karsians always try to deceive opponents before attacking. To them, warning us of an attack would have been stupid. It would give us time to prepare and counter their efforts. Karsians are so paranoid about security that it's possible their ambassador had no idea he was lying."

Barkonnas frowned. "You're saying they used this por'tahk ideology to the point of deceiving their own embassy just to pull off a preemptive strike?"

"Likely, Mr. Secretary."

"Let's clarify a few things, gentlemen." Poinard folded his hands on the table. "First, this was *not* a 'preemptive strike.' That may be the technical military term, but what the Karsians did was conduct a *sneak attack*. It may be one of their martial principles, Sir Benton, but that doesn't matter. We've been attacked; we know the attack came without warning; and we know it occurred after receiving assurances of peace. What we *don't* know is how badly we've been hurt. Military forecasts so far look grim, but military forecasts generally do. Soldiers tend to think in terms of worst-case scenarios.

"As I see it, there are several things that must be done. Your part is to get me accurate information on the situation and what the Karsians are up to. I want to know what they're planning and the best ways to keep them from accomplishing it. I won't be the first president to lose Confederation space to an enemy. We must stop them. In fact, I'm so pissed at this deception—no, this *lie*—that I want plans drawn up for a counteroffensive into the Empire as soon as possible."

There was a silence in the room, broken only when Barkonnas spoke. "A formal declaration of war requires a majority vote by the Assembly and House of Commons, Mr. President."

"I know that, Tom. You leave that to me. The Conservatives will vote for it, and likely the Libertarians too. It's the Progressives who'll resist. They'll want to use diplomacy, even though the Karsian diplomacy has proven itself unreliable. My position is clear: the time for diplomacy ended the moment they fired the first missile. We must fight, and with everything we've got, or they'll be in our backyard before we know it. Would you concur with that estimate, Sir Benton?"

Benton nodded, feeling glares from around the table. Most officers and lords in the room were Conservatives, but their political affiliations mattered little. Benton cared only for truth. "Indeed, Mr. President. Karsian military philosophy is based almost solely on the idea of offense. Direct attack is their primary means of achieving victory. Their weakness, if they have one, is they fail to properly understand the art of defense."

Nguyen nodded. "Maintaining the offensive is one of the primary tenants of our own doctrine, Mr. President. Unlike Karsians, we do study defense in depth. The problem is essentially one of *initiative*, Sir. The enemy has taken the offensive and made the first move. They have the initiative at the moment. They can choose when and where to strike and how deeply to drive into our space. Meanwhile, we struggle to try to determine their next move and reposition forces to counter them. They are *acting* while forcing us to *react*, and reaction is always slower than action. Unfortunately, my Marines are primarily an offensive force. We are not self-sufficient, however, as I depend on the Navy to get my Marines to enemy."

"The Navy will get your Marines to the enemy, General." Grayson looked somber as she twisted the coffee mug in her hands. "I don't believe that's the pressing issue. We must first conserve and concentrate sufficient fleet firepower to effectively attack the enemy at a time and place of our choosing. Until then, Mr. President, we're fighting a defensive battle, whether we like it or not."

Lee nodded. "I concur, Sir. The Karsians have massed their fleets along the Rim. They know their targets, and they expect us to defend them. Our forces in those systems must fight a defensive battle to keep control of the stargates, or the enemy will penetrate to the Core worlds. We may be forced to concede systems we can't effectively defend. I agree with Admiral Grayson. We must preserve our battle fleets until we can strike at a time and place of our choosing."

Benton cleared his throat. "Perhaps we can use the concept of por'tahk to our own advantage, Mr. President."

All eyes turned toward him. The president frowned and leaned back in his chair. "Explain, Sir Benton."

"The Joint Chiefs are correct in their estimation, Mr. President. The Karsians expect us to fight, but only in a limited manner. Karsians believe humans only fight when a clear victory is in sight, a battle with a purpose; a *national interest*, as it were. They see humans as a pragmatic and peaceful species, which, in their eyes, means weak. They'll believe once humans decide the fight is no longer worth the effort, they'll concede the contested systems and negotiate a peace, leaving them in possession of those systems.

"As you can see from the stellar cartography, the contested systems along the Rim are resource-rich, precisely what the Karsians need at this time. Rather than rush our dispersed fleets into battle piecemeal—for the likely unsuccessful defenses of those systems—the wisest strategy may be to pull back and leave them undefended."

Air hissed through several rows of teeth as an emotional wave swept around the War Room.

"Like hell." Nguyen slammed a fist against the glossy surface of the table with a violent thump. "You're suggesting we pull back and concede those systems without a fight, Sir Benton. That would only encourage them to attack us everywhere across the Periphery."

"I must agree with General Nguyen." Barkonnas frowned and put his elbows on the table. "We must deal harshly with the Empire if we're to command its respect. We must fight. What you're suggesting would make us look weak and easily defeated, Sir."

"Precisely, Mr. Secretary." Benton smiled. "I think it best to *reinforce* their preconceived notions of us. We could leave token units that appear to 'defend' some systems, and yes, those units must fight, but we should instruct them to withdraw when all hope of victory is lost. This will confirm to the Empire that we're as weak as they believe we are. If we fall back before their main assault fast enough, they may well decide to go for broke: the total defeat of the Confederation."

Poinard looked at Benton with dismay. "Why the hell would we want that, Sir Benton? The idea is to defeat the enemy, not assist them with our destruction."

"Because, Mr. President, we must get them to commit

everything they have; to bite off a bigger chunk than they can chew. They won't do that unless they're convinced they can win. The Empire doesn't have the resources to accomplish a task of that magnitude. At present, we're in a defensive situation with limited fleet assets along the Rim. Because of that, it's impossible to hold every frontier system. To attempt an all-out defense of the Rim will cost us valuable ships and personnel; assets we can't afford to lose, and which we don't have time to replace. Those assets must survive and be concentrated to be effective.

"If we retreat quickly enough, we'll create an illusion of panic. It'll appear we're in a massive retreat and have lost the will to fight. That illusion will be a carrot they can't resist. They'll charge Rigel itself to capitalize on what they'll see as an irresistible opportunity."

"I still don't understand, Rod. How does that help us?"

"I think I see where Sir Benton's going, Mr. President." Grayson looked up at the display screens. "If we withdraw before the Karsian fleet quickly enough, we can create a vacuum that'll suck them in and overextend their supply and communication lines. Overextension will make them vulnerable along their flanks. A fighting retreat also buys us time to concentrate battle wall fleets and gather assault forces. Once the Karsians are overextended, we can hit them at points and times of *our* choosing, defeat them piecemeal and regain the initiative."

"Precisely, Admiral." Benton stood and waved a hand at the displays on the wall. "We must make the Karsians see exactly what they want to see. We must get them to commit to an all-out offensive. It must appear the Confederation government is about to collapse. As they drive deep into Confederation space to exploit that opportunity, they'll overextend themselves. This is the 'unbalancing' we seek; our own version of *por'tahk*. Once they've committed, we choose when and where to strike. Their forces can then be isolated, surrounded and destroyed, regaining the initiative. If we try to defend every frontier system along the Rim, we'll lose precious ships and personnel that'll cost us dearly later on."

Poinard considered the proposal for several moments then turned to his Chairman. "Your thoughts, Raoul?"

"Sir Benton makes an interesting point, Mr. President. In terms of battlespace, *we* currently hold the high ground. We know our systems and the planetary terrain. We control all the stargates, libration points, and defenses. We can pull out anywhere along the Rim or stand and fight wherever we have the ships to do so. On the other hand, the Karsians must capture each of those chokepoints to protect their rear. Their logistical problems will be a nightmare. It could buy us time that we can't afford to lose. Best of all, it gives the Fleet time to regroup for the counteroffensive you want."

Grayson nodded. "And we *can* conduct that counteroffensive, Mr. President. The Karsians can't afford to fight a long-term battle of attrition, and they know it. They'll have to press their advantage as fast as they can. They must defeat us quickly if they hope to win."

Benton smiled. "Bacon and eggs, Mr. President."

Lee blinked. "What?"

"An old saw about the difference between being committed or involved, General. With bacon and eggs, the chicken is involved, but the pig is committed. We must get the Empire to commit fully and turn themselves into bacon. We must cause them to overextend rapidly, then fry them at a time and place of our choosing."

"They'll take a lot of Confederation territory in the process." Barkonnas shook his head angrily. "I don't like it, Mr. President. I doubt the Commons will, either, not to mention the settlers who live on those frontier worlds. Once the Karsians are entrenched, we'll play hell digging them out again."

"My Marines will dig them out, Mr. Secretary." Nguyen gave the Secretary of State a fierce look. "You can count on that."

Grayson nodded. "As will the Fleet."

"All right." Poinard rubbed his eyes. "It seems we have the outline of a strategy here. Raoul, you and Sondra plan this thing out in detail. I'll leave it to you and your experts to take whatever actions you deem necessary. Military plans are your bailiwick, not mine. Your objective is simple: defeat the Karsian Empire. *How* you do that, I leave in your capable hands.

"My contribution will be mainly political. I'll go before the Assembly and get a formal declaration of war against the Empire. The Secretary of State will assist me with that effort. That's what I'll be planning for the rest of the morning. I'll leave you to handle your respective warfighting responsibilities."

The gathered men and women stood as Poinard rose and left the room.

Benton sat down again and studied the floating holo-charts as a Marine steward brought in several pots of fresh coffee. The President was acting decisively, but he knew the struggle on the Assembly floor would be intense when it came time to vote on war. Without that vote, the Navy and Marine Corps would be hamstrung in their efforts to stop the Karsian onslaught.

The strategy will work, Benton conceded, *provided the Karsians don't do something unexpected. Unfortunately, deceit is something they mastered eons ago. Let's hope they're more predictable than we think.*

Refilling his teacup with hot water, Benton dropped in a fresh teabag and settled into his chair for what looked to be a long day in the War Room.

CHAPTER 16

There was the usual bedlam as the delegates filed into the huge auditorium. The Rigelian Assembly had called an emergency session. Multiple tiers of desks and consoles ringed the amphitheater, and Hank Red Water stood calmly in the center of it without moving.

As Speaker of the Assembly, Red Water acted as referee and guide to move debates through their order of business, yet he was unable to shake an ominous feeling as he awaited the upcoming session.

Around the central dais, the primary actors of the Assembly had already taken their seats. Prime Minister James Pledger and Henri Pasilov, Secretary of State, sat immobile in leather chairs, facing the Assembly quietly. To one side, the Chiefs of Staff under General Lee sat reviewing reports on their consoles.

Red Water took a moment to escape into memories.

Apsáalooke was his home planet. Many Old Earth Amer-Indian tribes, now called "Hatchee Clans," had settled on the sparkling blue planet, but the majority of Apsáalooke's population consisted of *Nez Perce* and *Absaroka* peoples, the latter of which were still collectively called the "Crow."

Red Water belonged to both tribes. His father had been Nez Perce and his mother *Absaroka*. His mother's family name, Gray Bear, had ties to a famous feud with a mountain man centuries before on Old Earth. Red Water knew of no direct relation to Chief Joseph on the *Nez Perce* side of the family but felt certain some of his distant ancestors had been among the brave band of horse warriors that led the American army on a wild chase at the end of Earth's nineteenth century. His background provided him some insight into colonial problems, giving him credibility before the Assembly. Red Water was a man *of the people*, as close to his ancient tribal culture as he was to the technology of star travel. His people were warriors, but that didn't make him look forward to the coming debate. He watched in stony silence as Assembly's political leaders took their seats.

Baron Santos Von Boecklin, patriarch of the House of Boecklin and leader of the Progressive Party, was the first major delegate to arrive. Of Spanish and German ancestry, the baron was an obese man with gray hair, bushy eyebrows and pale blue eyes. A firm believer in the Fairness Doctrine, Von Boecklin had made the goal of social justice his battle cry. Progressives believed government to be the source of all freedom and civil rights in a nation-state, and that it was the duty of the government to assist those needing help, regardless of species, behavior or religion. Von Boecklin had fought many battles to gain support for a variety of causes on many worlds. He was considered a revered hero by some—and a hated opponent by others—within the various political factions of the Assembly.

Lord Alan Latourette was next to take his seat. A retired Navy Admiral, Latourette was the Earl of Duxton and the leader of the Conservative Party. A staunch hawk, Latourette and his cronies opposed anything to do with the Karsian Empire. Their battles with Progressives over proposed trade agreements with the Empire were already legendary.

Conservatives were an anathema to Progressives because they believed in minimal government interference in citizens' lives and in Constitutional rights. Conservatives believed people worked things out best on their own without government interference, and usually achieved better results. The one exception was their view of the Karsian Empire, which they called a totalitarian dictatorship and a threat to freedom in the galaxy. Conservatives believed war with the Empire was inevitable and had long supported the buildup of military strength to deal with it when it finally occurred.

Red Water sighed as Lady Pauline Moore entered through the eastern arch and headed for her seat. Moore was a beautiful auburn-haired aristocrat Red Water thought should have been a ballerina. Tall, lithe, and graceful, she led the Liberty Party. The political position of Liberticians was sometimes unclear. Sometimes they supported Progressive initiatives—such as free trade with Empire—but, like Conservatives, they also eyed the Empire with suspicion. The basic Libertician position was that common sense should prevail. They were adamant that a rational approach was best, yet they were often so indecisive they accomplished little during legislative sessions.

Lastly, Lady Angela Svrcek entered at the head of her party, the Isolationists. Acidly paranoid, the Isolationists had long striven to shut off contact with all influences outside the Confederation, including the Empire and the United Terran League. The Isolationist's xenophobic agenda called for scaling stargates along the Periphery and the halt of all interactions with other star nations. They believed external problems would disappear if the Confederation kept out of other people's business.

Red Water shook his head sadly. Such a position was unrealistic. The Old Earth country of Japan had once closed its connections to the world for two centuries. The ancient United States had done something similar almost a century later, seeking to isolate itself from disturbing external events. Like ostriches with heads buried in the sand, time and predators had taught them both that just because you refused to see an enemy, it didn't mean an enemy didn't see you. That self-imposed blindness had resulted in the collapse of traditional society in Old Japan and a world war for America. Red Water feared Lady Svrcek's party could recreate the same disaster for the Confederation.

In addition to the Senate, the House of Commons had

also been summoned in a joint session. News reports were flying about a sneak attack on the Confederation fleet by the Empire, and the sudden call for joint assembly seemed to lend credence to the rumors.

A light flashed on his console, indicating the arrival of the president. Red Water strode forward on the platform and took a deep breath, then pounded his staff of office against the black marble of the Assembly floor. Microphones transmitted the vibration to House loudspeakers, and the gavel-like pounding of Red Water's staff boomed through the Assembly hall, garnering everyone's attention. "Ladies and gentlemen of the Assembly, please take your seats."

There were muffled rumbles as delegates hurried to their seats and seated members rose to applaud. After several moments, silence reigned. Red Water almost smiled, despite his foreboding, at the sudden quiet. "Lords and Commons, ladies and gentlemen, the Earl of Ashton, Duke of Aeron, and President of the Rigelian Confederation, Lord Hannarubi Poinard."

The Assembly applauded as the president entered in his ceremonial purple robes and strode to the dais at the center of the floor as Red Water vacated the position. For the remainder of the session, Red Water's duty would be to ensure the meeting flowed smoothly and that debate followed Assembly protocol.

"Please be seated." Poinard waited as the Assembly took its seats, his face projected on a thousand screens around the Assembly as cameras transmitted his picture and voice to every console. Those consoles also had cameras and pickups, allowing private and public communication between delegates. For the moment Poinard had the floor and delegates remained silent as they waited to hear what he had to say.

"My fellow Rigelians, I've called this emergency joint session of the Assembly tonight for two reasons. The first is to report a treacherous attack upon our nation by the military forces of a foreign power. Since approximately 2000 hours last night, Standard Time, a state of war has existed between the Rigelian Confederation and the Empire of Kars."

There were gasps. Poinard glanced at Von Boecklin, who stiffened visibly. Von Boecklin's sausage-like fingers gripped the sides of his console in shock. The baron had fought hard for open trade with Kars. Now it seemed the greatest political accomplishment of his career was about to go up in flames.

"The second purpose is to decide the best course of action in responding to this attack. I have conferred with Secretary Barkonnas and General Lee of the Joint Chiefs, and they've drawn up contingency plans at my direction, but execution of those plans require a majority vote by two-thirds of this Assembly, which is why you're here.

"At approximately eight o'clock p.m. three days ago, elements of the Imperial Karsian fleet attacked the Confederation naval base in the Centauri Seven star system. This attack, unprovoked and without warning, destroyed the orbital facilities and ships of Battle Squadron

One, resulting a massive loss of life. At the same time, communication through five different stargates was lost, indicating those star systems may also have come under attack, though we have scant information on those systems at this time.

"It's my duty to protect the interests of the Rigelian Confederation and its people. Because of this treacherous and unprovoked attack, made without warning during diplomatic negotiations for free trade agreements—and in spite of specific diplomatic assurances by the Empire to the contrary—I have ordered the expulsion of the Karsian embassy from Confederation space and have terminated all diplomatic relations with the Empire. I called this joint session tonight to seek a formal declaration of war against the Karsian Empire."

The Assembly erupted in bedlam as dozens of delegates punched panel buttons to be heard. Red Water had to smash his staff against the floor for almost a minute to restore order. Poinard waited patiently until he could again address the Assembly over the din.

"Pursuant to my duties, I've ordered the immediate implementation of wartime contingency plans by Confederation armed forces. Those measures are being implemented as we speak, pending resolution of a declaration of war. With that in mind, I open this Assembly to debate."

Poinard turned and strode to his presidential chair behind the Speaker. Red Water struggled to regain order as the delegates thundered questions from all directions.

After another long minute, he managed to restore some semblance of calm. "The Chair recognizes the honorable Alan Latourette, Lord of New Sussex."

Latourette's grim countenance flashed across Assembly screens. "Lords and Commons, this treachery by the Empire is intolerable." Latourette pounded a fist against his console. "My colleagues and I have warned for years that the Empire is a cesspool of deceit and treachery, existing only for expansionistic conquest and enslavement of conquered races. Now you have ample proof. I cannot—nor can any man or woman with a shred of moral conscience—begin to understand the kind of back-stabbing treachery required to attack another nation while negotiating under a flag of truce. For years my party and I have urged you to protect our way of life from these imperialist villains and their malignant desire for galactic conquest. We will not stand idly by in the face of such infamy. I speak for the entire Conservative Party when I call for an immediate declaration of war against the Empire."

More thunder erupted as delegates reacted to Latourette's bold statement, some in favor, some against. Red Water knew he must act fast to maintain control or the Assembly would degenerate into squabbling factions and sidebar arguments, something he couldn't allow.

"The Chair recognizes the Duchess of Hubbard, the Lady Svrcek."

Svrcek's stern face flashed on the screens. She stared out at the Assembly with cold green eyes, her blonde hair pulled back in a bun. Well past middle age, Svrcek remained pretty in a hard sort of way. There was nothing pretty in her gaze, however, as her face glared out from dozens of monitors.

"Thank you, Mister Speaker. Lord Latourette, I am just as appalled as you and the president at this terrible and treacherous betrayal. I agree there must be reprisals against the perpetrators of this dastardly act, both through sanctions and limited military action. However, I must object to the expulsion of the Karsian embassy. Surely, at a time such as this, we must not forego a possible diplomatic solution to this crisis. In the interests of interstellar peace, the Isolationist Party reminds this Assembly that this terrible tragedy is largely a disaster of our own making."

There was more clamoring, but Red Water's staff stopped it quickly, and after a moment Svrcek continued.

"For years my party has urged this Assembly to close our stargates and refrain from involvement with other nations in places where we have no right to be. The recent trade negotiations with the Empire are a prime example. Had we, as I urged in the last four sessions, closed our borders and cut off contact with the Empire, it is unlikely we would find ourselves in this position now. The Karsians are, as Lord Latourette has rightfully pointed out, expansionistic and violent. We also know they have only limited resources, a situation that periodically forces them to conquer new star systems in order to survive. Rather than set up a situation that forced them to attack us, we should have remained aloof and kept ourselves from any dealings with them.

"The way to have prevented this situation was to have cut ourselves off from it, preventing the Empire from gaining any intelligence on our systems and our resources. Our openness has allowed the Empire to place operatives within our worlds, including many key military installations. This has provided opportunities for the Empire to penetrate our security and study our interstellar operations.

"I agree we must act to protect the lives and property of the people in the Confederation, and that we must do so promptly. However, before voting for a declaration of war, I urge you to consider the very real consequences of giving the president what he's asked for. A declaration of war is irreversible. It commits this government to the gravest of actions. It will bind us to the military defeat of the Empire, an empire that can and will retaliate in any way possible to deny us that victory. I do not believe, nor shall I support, any action that is tragically wasteful of sentient life, and largely our own fault. All-out war is unnecessary.

"Must we regain and safeguard our borders? Yes, without question. My party supports immediate action to drive the Karsians from captured Rigelian space. But not a total war. Not a war that requires the defeat and conquest of star systems that rightfully belong to the Empire. Such a course of action would make *us* expansionistic as well, in which case we would be no better than the Empire.

"The proper thing—the only honorable thing—we *can* do is drive the enemy from Confederation space and blockade all stargates leading into the Confederation. These efforts will require only blockading forces, not war fleets, costing a minimum in lives and capital, and allow us to successfully defend the Confederation from attack."

"I dare to debate!" Latourette's voice thundered across the speakers, his face florid, but Red Water shut him off and instead accessed the leader of the Progressive Party. "The Chair recognizes the honorable Baron von Boecklin."

Von Boecklin's flushed face appeared on the screens. A sheen of perspiration was visible on his face. He mopped a handkerchief across his forehead and took a sip of water before speaking.

"My fellow Rigelians, I urge you to consider the ramifications of these proposals. For centuries the Confederation has been a peaceful and representative government of interstellar commerce and hope. We have, with our diversity of peoples, created a multi-cultural beacon of equity that represents our highest values; a shining example to the galaxy of how a free people govern themselves.

"Our highest values include peace and the precepts of nonviolence. These values were taught by such great men as Jesus of Nazareth, Gandhi of India, Lao Tzu of China and Sutwan of Io. We mustn't discard those precepts for mere revenge against an alien people. The Empire attacked us, yes, and that's a terrible tragedy, but Lady Svrcek is right, at least in one regard: if we declare war and retaliate, we're no better than the Karsians themselves.

"If we cannot, as a free nation, live up to our own principles and values, if we cannot practice the very benevolence we preach, then are we not hypocrites of the worst order? If we cannot, in a time of crises and fear, turn the other cheek, upon what grounds do we call ourselves a free and benevolent people?

"The RCN Fleet exists to defend our citizenry from unwarranted military aggression, not to conduct similar aggression against enemy worlds for the purpose of retaliation and conquest. I submit this attack is born of misunderstanding and a lack of communication. I submit the Empire interpreted our military strength as a threat to its own borders and took what must be—in their eyes—a sensible course of action to eliminate that threat.

"I urge you, Mr. President, to immediately reopen negotiations with the Empire and recall the Karsian ambassador to Rigel so war may be avoided." Von Boecklin mopped his brow with the handkerchief again. "War will decimate our economy, cost us countless lives, destroy families, and damage untold planetary ecologies beyond any hope of near-term recovery. Now is the time to use diplomacy to ensure a continued peace between our respective nations."

"Peace, hell." Latourette shouted his words angrily, and Red Water accessed his console, split-screening him with Von Boecklin. "The time for diplomacy ended when they attacked us, Baron. These aren't peaceful, law-abiding colonists we're talking about. They aren't Reticulans or ecclesiastical sages. These are *Karsians*; a sadistic horde of alien carnivores that train for war from birth. They're alpha predators who live and die at their Emperor's command. We've already shown them how gullible and weak we can be. It was that apparent weakness that created this whole mess, not a lack of kindness, empathy, or communication.

"The Karsians see us as weak, and so they attacked. And why would they not? Their culture isn't like ours. They're an aggressive species, carnivores and apex predators, warlike by both instinct and training. The only thing they respect is strength, and the only way to show them our strength is to counterattack immediately and with full force. We must drive them from our space with such ferocity that they never again dare attack us. We must hit them so hard that they never forget the response. What we must *not* do is have nice little diplomatic meetings conducting mindless debates for some crazy peace-at-all-costs idiocy."

"That is barbaric, my lord." Von Boecklin spluttered on the screen. "We're above such measures, surely. We cannot sink to the level of barbarians merely because we must deal with them. We have our own values and standards of honor. We must conduct ourselves as rational, peaceful beings. Our reaction must be beyond reproach."

Latourette scowled. "Reproach from *whom*, Baron? The Karsians? That sounds so very reasonable, but if you take that kind of approach with this kind of enemy, you'll be the main course for their Emperor within a week . . . provided he likes fat."

Von Boecklin blushed as the Assembly erupted in laughter, but Latourette continued without pause. "But I'm not here to trade *ad hominems*, Baron. I speak from direct experience. I've been an admiral out there and I know this enemy. If you show any weakness, he'll gobble you alive. This isn't the time to spout philosophy. Philosophy is created by the children of tougher generations who fought to provide the safety in which to create it. No, we must counter-attack with everything we have. We must send a message across the galaxy: *mess with the Confederation and it will destroy you.* That's the only message that'll ensure peace with our neighbors. They must fear angering us. That's the only position that'll allow Progressives the safety and comfort in which to sit around and dream up pacifistic moral philosophy and wacko social-engineering models."

"Total war will destroy our economy!" Von Boecklin rose his bulk to the microphone to shout back at Latourette. "It will plunge the Confederation into ruin and gain nothing but chaos and death. We'll end up with destroyed planets on both sides and no good to show for it. No one wins a war, Sir; one side simply loses more than the other. Which means even if we win, we still lose. We cannot do that to the people of the Confederation."

Latourette thundered back. "There won't *be* a Confederation if we don't, Baron. Can't you see that?"

Pauline Moore's face flashed onto the screens, interrupting the argument, and Red Water thumped his staff. "The Chair recognizes the Honorable Lady Moore."

All eyes flashed to a new frame in which appeared the lovely face of the auburn-haired leader of the Liberty Party. Moore was particularly respected as a voice of reason during spirited debates. Her brown eyes surveyed the Assembly calmly before she spoke.

"Lords and Ladies, Assemblymen and Commons, I've listened to this debate quietly for some time now. I have the naval intelligence reports from Admiral Grayson on my screen as we speak. Now is not the time to squabble about philosophical differences or engage in debate to further party agendas. The safety of the Confederation is at stake. Whatever our political differences, it is our sworn duty to protect the Confederation. Whatever caused this situation, or how that might have been prevented, is not germane to the discussion.

"We know the positions of the all the political parties within this Assembly, just as we know where we disagree. The time has come, however, to prioritize our needs as a nation and set aside political differences; to agree upon *something*, if only for once. We're not here to debate what we *might* have done or *should* have done to prevent this atrocity. That debate is for another time and place. It is irrelevant. Here we must focus upon one burning question: *what do we do now?*

"We've been attacked by a foreign power. That attack was both deliberate and premeditated. It wasn't an accident nor was it preventable by diplomacy. This attack was not a case of self-defense on the part of the Empire. It was a carefully planned operation by a foreign power we were openly negotiating with. This isn't a matter of speculation or rumor. It's fact. Therefore, we have only a few choices open to us, and those choices must be made. The president has demanded a vote.

CHAPTER 16

"I abhor war more than most. My own planet and people are in the Rim, in the path of the Karsian juggernaut. My home world is more vulnerable to attack than almost any of yours. Nevertheless, I believe we must act strongly, one way or the other, as a *united* government, and that we must do so immediately. As elected representatives it's our duty to act quickly and vote on this declaration of war. Whatever we decide will determine our future, and my party will support either position wholeheartedly, as long as it's reached fairly by a consensus of the peoples' representatives. That is the position of the Libertician Party. I call for that vote immediately, here and now, to determine whether we sue for peace or fight. Squabbling here in Assembly only wastes precious time."

The Assembly erupted in bedlam again, and though it took Red Water almost five minutes to quell the indignant screams and arguments, he regarded the tall ballerina with a new respect.

As Lady Moore cut off her camera feed and gazed upon the Assembly with disdain, Red Water's admiration for her grew by leaps and bounds.

CHAPTER 17

LeMieux tightened the seals of his vac-suit as the surviving ships of Centauri Seven approached the Zion stargate terminus. *Hastings*, his light cruiser, was flagship for his makeshift force, with four destroyers protecting her flanks.

Oriskany and *Kuroshima* commanded the port side of the formation, with *Yang Chien* and *Joseph Brant* on the starboard side. He'd also managed to scrape up a pair of corvettes, *Saganami* and *Ziglar*, to beef up the Centauri Seven defense force. It wasn't enough to stop a serious attack, but it was the best he could do under the circumstances.

If fate destined him to die, LeMieux decided it would happen while fighting the enemy. He refused to sit helpless through another planetary bombardment. LeMieux believed naval officers belonged in space, not sitting at a desk on a planet's surface.

CHAPTER 17

"Transition at the gate." His sensor operator, a chief petty officer, spoke over the intercom, breaking LeMieux out of his mental reverie.

Well, he chided himself, *you've been expecting the Empire to return. Here they come.*

He knew he shouldn't have been surprised or disappointed by the enemy's arrival, but actually having it occur added an odd mixture of fear and bittersweet resignation.

His best chance to maximize the defensive potential of his formation had been to data link the force so it could fire *en masse* at enemy vessels as they exited the terminus. It was most efficient to destroy enemy ships while they labored under sensor distortion after jumping and smarter than holding too far back and giving the enemy time to recover and return fire.

He'd had no ability to mine the stargate terminus. There had been plenty of mines available but not enough ships to transport and deploy them. He'd opted instead to defend the gate with his small mobile fleet, primarily because his ships could get into position quickly without having to stop and load volatile mines dirtside.

LeMieux spoke into his helmet mike. "Sound general quarters. Signal all ships: *Hastings* will lock the target. All vessels will toggle their fire to *Hastings'* net control and engage on my command."

The first ship through the stargate would likely be a reconnaissance probe sent to scout local defenses around the terminus. LeMieux needed to kill it quickly before it could report back. It would be hit with a gauntlet of forty missiles before its onboard sensors could detect his force's presence. Such a massed volley would destroy any unshielded vessel smaller than a battleship. Technically it was overkill, but it was essential to prevent the enemy scout from reporting back through the stargate. If it survived long enough to return fire, LeMieux's own force would begin to take damage. The numbers were on the Karsians' side, of course, and LeMieux knew he couldn't accept unnecessary losses. Any loss would cut his firepower proportionally.

He'd strike the enemy as hard as he could and try to whittle them down one ship at a time as they came through. After the initial volley of missiles, he'd close in and finish off whatever survived with energy weapons.

LeMieux saw the fire control toggles from his small fleet as they appeared in his display and felt his stomach tighten. This was it; the moment he'd prepared for all his life. "All ships, stand ready to fire."

The second battle of Centauri Seven was about to begin.

And this time, by God, the enemy will suffer losses!

The sensor chief whirled to look at him. "Admiral, I'm receiving friendly IFF emissions off the bogey. It has a valid transponder code and has confirmed authentication."

LeMieux leaned forward against his restraining straps and stared at the sensor icon. A green dot sparkled brightly beside the yellow horseshoe of the unknown symbology. "ID that IFF source, Chief."

"It's the *Gant*, Admiral. One of our own destroyers."

LeMieux broke the seal of his helmet and removed it with a sigh of relief. Tension he hadn't realized he carried flowed from his muscles as he relaxed back into his seat. "Secure from general quarters. Open a secure channel to *Gant*. I want to talk to her skipper."

"Aye, Sir."

Grins were exchanged around the bridge as crewmen relaxed and reported the situation to the various compartments of the ship: *friendly ships were coming through the stargate.*

Obviously, the RCN fleet was arriving to rescue Centauri Seven. Relief washed over LeMieux. Crewman smiled as the dreaded battle they'd steeled themselves for appeared to be over.

The communications officer turned at her station. "I have Gant's CO on the line, Admiral, a Commander Comforti."

"Put him on the main display."

A tired-looking commander in a vac-suit replaced the data-linked picture on the bridge console screen. LeMieux smiled into the video pickup. "Commander Comforti, this is Admiral LeMieux of the Centauri Seven defense force. Welcome to Centauri Seven. We're sure glad to see you. How many ships are transiting with you?"

The commander frowned in confusion, as if he didn't understand what LeMieux was asking. "There're seven ships behind us, Admiral, but . . . how did you know that?"

"An educated guess, Commander. We were hit pretty hard here, and we've been waiting for the Fleet to arrive. It's good to see another Rigelian ship. Tell your CO he or she is cleared to wormhole in."

"Sir?"

"The relief force, Commander. You may clear them in."

"What relief force, Admiral? Where are the rest of *your* ships?"

LeMieux frowned. Comforti seemed rather impertinent, almost insubordinate, but he appeared to be exhausted. Likely it was fatigue making him rude. LeMieux decided to give him the benefit of doubt, as there seemed no harm in explaining. "What you see, Commander, is all that's left of Centauri Seven's battle fleet since the Karsian attack. We're glad to see you leading the cavalry in."

Comforti's eyes grew wide on the screen, then he closed them slowly. "Jesus."

LeMieux frowned, getting impatient. "I understand your shock at how few ships remain here, Commander, but that's no reason to—"

"No, Admiral, you don't understand." Comforti leaned forward, moving his helmet closer to the visual pickup. "We're not leading a relief force. We're a single tin can and we're running for our lives. There's a Karsian task force tail-grabbing my ass, Sir. We jumped in here looking for a safe haven. We've led the hounds right to you."

LeMieux's battle senses snapped to alert. "Karsian task force? How many ships? How far behind you?"

"Seven ships, Sir, two hundred thousand klicks aft when we transitioned." Comforti looked miserable. "I'm sorry, Admiral. I recommend deploying your force into battle formation ASAP. They'll be coming through the 'gate behind us any second now."

CHAPTER 17

"Sound general quarters." LeMieux put his helmet back on and snapped its seals shut as GQ alarms rang throughout the ship. "All hands to battle stations. Commander Comforti, if *Gant* is capable of fighting, assume position in my formation. My sensor chief will coordinate bringing you into our data link. *Hastings* is the network control station. We'll fire as a single data-group on whatever comes through."

"Aye, Sir." Comforti's eyes narrowed, but a tired grin creased his features. "To tell the truth, I'm damned tired of running."

LeMieux turned his attention to the tactical problem. Bringing up the data link display, he nodded with satisfaction as Gant's symbology popped into the network. He watched as his formation oriented their weapons employment zones toward the Zion stargate. *Gant* rotated about her axis and took up position astern of *Joseph Brant*, but somewhat forward of the corvettes, acting as a shield for the more lightly armored vessels.

LeMieux's ships waited, sensors focused on the terminus and looking for the telltale signs of a transiting ship. Aboard each vessel, gloved fingers poised over firing keys, waiting to engage.

The reprieve had been brutally short.

All hell was about to break loose.

SUCKER PUNCH

CONFEDERATION ASSEMBLY
NEW BYZANTIUM, RIGEL TWO

The votes had been counted. Red Water tallied the votes and forwarded them to the president's console. Poinard stared at his screen and nodded stoically, not letting the results show on his face. Red Water turned toward the Assembly and pounded his staff as Poinard's visage flashed up on all screens.

"Ladies and gentlemen, Lords and Commons, the votes have been cast and tallied, and the result is very close. In fact, the Assembly vote was tied until the last moment. It has been decided by a single vote."

He nodded to Red Water. For once there total silence reigned, and Red Water marveled how Poinard had the rapt attention of every delegate in the room, considering the usual rudeness of politicians and the bedlam of the past few hours.

Red Water faced the Assembly. "The vote for a declaration of war has been passed. This Assembly stands adjourned."

Bedlam exploded as delegates rushed from their chairs, some in shock, some in horror, and others with satisfaction. Many were arguing with each other, and most seemed confused or scared. News personnel scrambled in from the outer doors to interview delegates. As a closed Joint Assembly session, news correspondents had been barred, but now that the Assembly was adjourned, correspondents would flash the word across the galaxy.

CHAPTER 17

War.

Red Water turned to look at Poinard, but the president had already departed with his staff, victorious in getting his declaration. He'd be busy in the palace for days to come, with a terrible responsibility upon his shoulders as he commanded a nation at war. Red Water didn't envy him.

A shadow suddenly blocked the lighting. Red Water turned to find the massive bulk of Von Boecklin standing before him, flushed and angry. The Baron wheezed for breath.

He doesn't look well, Red Water thought. It was no wonder. Von Boecklin's plans for a "new economy" and a socialist agenda to get more citizens on the dole was supposed to have been his crowning glory, despite the bitter debate those efforts had fostered in the Assembly. Now, with the declaration of war passed, those efforts were in vain. All taxable resources would go to support the war effort.

The Baron wheezed, barely constraining anger on his florid face as he flushed red. "Mister Speaker, might I speak with you?"

Red Water faced him. The Baron was an immense man, sedentary by nature and obese from a life of easy living. The long hours of debate had taxed him physically. Red Water noticed he was sweating profusely. "Of course, my lord."

"You said the decision was passed by one vote. Who cast that vote? Was it that war-monger Latourette?"

"No, my lord. It was not."

Red Water turned to leave but the baron's sausage-like fingers dug into his shoulder. The baron yanked him around, and Red Water glared at him. "Unhand me, Sir."

Von Boecklin stared with pig-like eyes laced with venom. "Don't you turn away from me. Who cast that final vote?"

"I'm under no obligation to tell you, my lord."

"Who, damn you!"

Red Water lifted an eyebrow. "The Lady Pauline Moore."

"The Libertician whore?" Von Boecklin hissed with fury, grabbing Red Water by the tunic. "That rotten bitch."

"On the contrary, my lord, Senator Moore is a lady, and I must demand you show her the respect due her position."

"Respect?" Von Boecklin glared, his eyes furious. "That harlot's ruined everything I've fought to achieve for the last four years. You're a rotten son of a bitch, too, if you support her."

Red Water's right hand pulled the baron's fingers from his tunic and flung them away. "Good day, my lord."

Red Water turned and walked away.

Von Boecklin's eyes bugged as he watched him go, fury distorting his features. Suddenly, he staggered and sat down abruptly, clutching at his chest.

When medics arrived three minutes later Von Boecklin was unconscious, lying on the Assembly floor amid a throng of concerned delegates.

CHAPTER 18

IKS *MURGAHH,*
NANGTASHGU SYSTEM

"Attack is the first finger of the Shikahn's hand."

Yi'rhork T'lihktu recited slowly, even though every Karsian knew the words by heart. As Imperial Guard advisor, he had insight into all of Task Force Two-Two's operations and served as the In'thork's watchdog on Tork's staff. "Defense is the second finger. Security the third."

Which is nothing less than should be expected from an Imperial Guard spy, Tork thought, fuming silently as he filled a mug of talik and pushed it toward the IG officer. *He watches my every move, ready to report me to his supervisors at the slightest hint of insubordination.*

Nothing slipped past the watchful eyes of the IG, who, as state security, suspected everyone of treachery all the time. The Imperial Guard had been established to watch the Imperial Navy and Imperial Army to keep them in check. The In'thork had its own battle forces, who were positioned to put down any rebellion even by military forces. Security was all-pervasive in the Empire. The Shikahn tolerated no resistance to his rule.

Assigned IG officers had complete authority over generals and admirals, even if they were of lesser rank. Military officers sometimes grew ambitious and posed threats to the emperor's rule. The IG swore personal allegiance to the Shikahn, not the government, minimizing the chances of military coups. In order to nip festering rebellions in the bud, IG "advisors" were assigned to all senior officers, organizations, and vessels to advise on proper implementation of Imperial policy. In truth, they monitored anyone ambitious who might challenge the Emperor. If a military officer became a problem, the In'thork saw to it that he "disappeared." When more direct action was required, the IG would dispatch its own fleet to crush a coup. It was a system of control not lost on any warrior and ensured succession of the Shikahn's House and its right to rule.

Karsian society was based on the Triad, with most things done in groups of three. Scholars claimed it was because Karsian hands and feet had three digits each and thus counting came in threes. Tork had no idea if that was true, but the Triad seemed an all-encompassing concept within the Empire. The Emperor ruled three branches of government with an iron fist: the Executive Branch, the Imperial Court, and the Diplomatic Corps.

The Executive Branch had three subgroups, including the *Shan'lar*, or Imperial Navy; the *Darhk'lar*, the Imperial

Army; and the *In'thork*, the Imperial Guard. Likewise, the Court consisted of three subgroups: the *Shi-thrung*, or Council of Elders; the thrung, the greater and lesser warrior houses; and *K'jir*, the Conquered Peoples. That left a third branch of society called the *Hak*, or Diplomatic Corps, which was comprised of yihaki ambassadors, *Thrunghaki* Council scholars, and individual *Dohaki*, or House scholars.

Society was designed to ensure control from the top down. The K'jir consisted of Karsian females and children and the slaves who worked for them. Children were born in a Brood House and later pledged for service into a named House as warriors or scholars, based on their individual dispositions and tests conducted when they reached oath age.

Slaves were from conquered worlds. Karsians were superior to any species, but especially slaves, who had lost all honor by being captured. Yet even among loyal Karsians, the IG remained vigilant to ensure order. T'lihktu, the IG advisor for Task Force Two-Two, was assigned to Tork's staff.

"That is true, of course." Tork took his cup of talik and settled back into his chair. "And I know all about the advantages of attack and the element of surprise, so you don't have to reiterate each one. The enemy must be thrown off-balance and confused. So stunned, such enemies cannot regain momentum or initiative. Surprise is the key to victory. I know the quotes."

"Indeed, Korguhn, truly you do." T'lihktu shrugged and sipped his drink. "Yet, I am sure that you realize that for an ambush to succeed, surprise must be combined with a sufficient level of overwhelming *violence*."

"This is also well-known." Tork's eyes narrowed. "Why do you mention it, Yi'rhork?"

T'lihktu leaned forward in a conspiratorial manner. It wasn't necessary, of course, since they were alone in Tork's quarters, but it made the IG officer seem sincere. "I was assigned to advise you, Korguhn; to comply with the requirements of my duties I must give you the best advice possible. I am concerned over your lack of overwhelming violence at Centauri Seven. The enemy was on his knees and at our mercy. You could have crushed them, ensuring our complete victory, yet you refused that opportunity. Instead, you allowed civilian noncombatants to survive and remain free. You sent in no occupation forces, captured no slaves, and left some facilities intact. Such mercy may come back to haunt you."

Tork scowled. "Why?"

"The survivors may have collected intelligence that we are unaware of." T'lihktu sipped talik, belched politely, and continued. "By letting those Rigelians live and stay free from capture, you left open a door through which such data could be passed back to the enemy's fleet."

"There were no lidars coming from the civilian population centers. Besides, all communications to the system had been severed."

T'lihktu sighed. "You cannot know that Korguhn. While it is true we detected no active scans during the attack, that does not mean the enemy did not record with passive sensors, nor with orbital platforms and deployed remotes. That collection would be unknown to us but could be passed on, proving dangerous to our plans."

"What could they report?" Tork crossed his arms. "That they were attacked by a Karsian fleet? The RCN knows that. If not then it is obvious to them now. They could report that we destroyed their battleships and orbital docks? They know that by now, too. It is somewhat difficult to hide the obvious, Yi'rhork."

"Granted. So I shall speak to you of my second concern. Bor'klar Gutahr wanted to bombard the planet, as we had done at Turin's World, in accordance with standard Imperial policy."

"I know."

"You stopped him. Why?"

Tork rubbed a hand across his face. "The only people left on the planet were civilians and a few warriors no longer able to access weapons, T'lihktu. Warriors without weapons cannot harm us. There is no honor in slaughtering the helpless."

"You have lived among these Rigelians." T'lihktu's comment was a statement, not a question. "You know how humans think, Korguhn. Have you considered the potential *political* issues that showing them such mercy might cause you?"

"Such as?"

"Rigelian warriors left alive will rejoin their forces if their fleet returns, thereby adding to the numbers we must fight. Such warriors, having battle experience, will be better prepared to fight us. Surviving civilians might also join their military, swelling the enemy's forces and making them more powerful. Other surviving civilians will be able to repair and rebuild docks and orbital fleet yards for those military forces. You might appear weak to have let them live."

"To Rigelian eyes?" Tork leaned back in his chair, the nictitating membrane of his eyes half-closing. "Or do you mean Karsian eyes? You are right, I have lived among them. They do not think like us, Yi'rhork. To humans, mercy is not a weakness but a gesture of decency. Nothing would have been gained by slaughtering helpless civilians at Centauri Seven. In fact, doing so would have caused the Empire bigger problems."

T'lihktu tilted his head in curiosity, his eyes narrowing. "How so?"

"Humans are a social species. Many of them possess pacifistic natures, and among all of them mercy is highly valued. The mercy we demonstrated at Centauri Seven proves that the Empire will fight fairly under the rules of war, as outlined by the Interstellar Accords."

"Fairly? Accords? Ridiculous. This is war, Korguhn."

"I will not stain my honor by slaughtering helpless noncombatants, T'lihktu. Doing so would increase the casualty rate astronomically. Such actions might cow some alien species, but not humans. They will accept defeat in battle, but they will not tolerate genocide. They may look like hairless primates, and may prefer peace to fighting, but make no mistake, they *will* fight if their passions are aroused, particularly if enraged. Nothing enrages humans more than killing their old, their young, and the helpless. So enraged, they think of nothing but destroying their enemies. Hatred consumes them, giving them tremendous strength. Considering the power and size of their fleet, such hatred could prove fatal for us. When oozing raw hate, humans will sacrifice themselves to destroy their enemies. They become obsessed with revenge. In such a state, they will not negotiate. One cannot reason with them at that point. We must not allow our policy to create such rage and strength among them."

"Who cares how the enemy feels, Korguhn?"

"I care." Tork shifted uncomfortably and sipped more talik. "An enraged human is unreasonable, Yi-rorhk. He becomes obsessed with vindictiveness. At some point the Empire must negotiate to secure possession of the star systems we capture from Rigel. Otherwise, we will be forced to defend those systems forever. By not massacring an entire population I demonstrated mercy, which humans hold as a virtue. That puts us in a better light, politically speaking, meaning the humans will not fight as hard as they might otherwise. If they know civilians will survive our attacks without needless slaughter, the Rigelians will be more willing to surrender and less willing to fight to the last man. Acts of mercy will weaken RCN resolve, sewing favor for us in the hearts and minds of their more pacifistic politicians, who are unwilling to fight almost anytime.

"The Confederation has a powerful naval fleet. It seems weak only because it is spread across many stars. Once those fleets gather, they will create a monster the

Empire cannot hope to defeat. Combined, their fleet is larger and more capable than ours. It will be overwhelming, especially once they ramp up their starship construction industry. Any chance for victory means we must strike quickly and grab the star systems we need, then negotiate a prompt end to hostilities, leaving us in possession of those worlds. By showing mercy we seem a more reasonable enemy, not a species of bloodthirsty invaders. That will make Rigelian diplomats willing to negotiate a treaty to secure the *Shikahn's* objectives. If, however, we enrage the enemy with pointless slaughter, they will fight to the end . . . and time is on their side."

"Perhaps." T'lihktu made the admission with a shrug. "You may be correct in how the Rigelians perceive us. I defer to your experience, since I have not lived among them. But it might be wise to worry more about Karsian perceptions, Korguhn. Many in the Imperial Court will see such mercy as weakness, perhaps even treason. Gutahr wanted to destroy them. It may have been wise to have let him do so. If your strategy is perceived as weakness by the Shikahn, you could be recalled and cashiered. At the very least, I am required to report your 'hesitancy' to my superiors at the In'thork."

Tork met T'lihktu's eyes. "Not killing civilians was the proper thing to do. I know these Rigelians. Mercy makes them less hostile and more willing to negotiate. We need them to negotiate, Yi'rhork. In the long view, it is we who must fear the Confederation. My approach minimizes that risk."

"Perhaps, Korguhn, but in the short term you should fear your own people more, particularly the In'thork. Our oaths are to the Shikahn, not the war effort. If you displease the Shikahn, the In'thork will conduct an Inquest. I doubt the Shikahn would be pleased by a perceived 'lack of enthusiasm' for his orders."

"I will not exterminate populated worlds without cause." Tork slammed his talik mug on the table. "Needless slaughter is unnecessary to achieve our objectives. Doing so would hamper the achievement of those goals and come to haunt us if the Confederation gains the upper hand."

T'lihktu blanched and leaned forward even more, speaking in a quiet voice. "Do not say such things out loud, Korguhn. Not even in private meetings between us. If such statements are reported, they could be considered defeatist, possibly even treason."

"They are simply the truth."

"Perhaps, but that is no reason to speak stupidly." T'lihktu drained his mug and sat back in his chair, studying his assigned high admiral. "The Confederation may kill you in battle, Korguhn, or you may survive. Those are simply the fortunes of war, and you have little control over that. But stupidity where state security is concerned *will* be fatal if you cross a line, and you have complete control over that. The In'thork remains watchful, and it has long tentacles."

Tork felt his blood grow cold. The threat to his life and career were clear. There was no other way to interpret T'lihktu's words. "Why are you telling me this,

T'lihktu? As an In'thork advisor, why not simply report my 'weaknesses' to your superiors? They would 'disappear' me and put a more ruthless admiral in command of this operation."

T'lihktu nodded. "I could do that, certainly, Korguhn. In fact, my duty requires it. But I have watched you for some time, and I believe you wise where the Confederation is concerned; wiser than most. You understand Rigelian psychology better than the rest of us. Because of that, I believe you the best admiral to lead this operation. I think you are right, both in the reaction of the Rigelians and in the power of their fleet. Therefore, I support your methods, which I believe a wiser course than what most admirals would choose. I am something of an admirer, Korguhn.

"But as an In'thork officer who admires your dedication to duty and truth, I must warn you not to be foolish. I find your honesty and boldness admirable, but unwise. Guard your words carefully. Nothing you do or say must be interpreted as weakness or lack of enthusiasm. There are those who do not admire you as I do, and even more who covet your command. The In'thork are friends to no one but the Shikahn, and if you lose the Shikahn's favor, they *will* dispose of you."

Tork blinked with surprise, not at what his advisor had said, but that he actually had said it out loud. Tork hadn't become an admiral by being stupid politically, but never had an In'thork advisor spoke so candidly with him. Members of the Imperial Guard were not known to be admirers of naval officers. T'lihktu was trying to protect him, not implicate him. That *was* unusual, especially for a member of the Imperial Guard.

He met his advisor's eyes and nodded. "I appreciate your words, Yi'rhork, and I thank you for the advice. Politics frustrate a commander, especially in time of war. Your candor will not be forgotten."

T'lihktu bowed slightly. "We serve the Empire, Korguhn. I would not want to see the Shikahn's plans ruined by the removal of what I consider to be his best commander. House Lahk'nah should be proud."

"I am humbled by your words, Yi'rhork."

T'lihktu smiled. "The honor is mine, Korguhn. So what have we achieved so far in this campaign, and what are your immediate objectives?"

Tork touched a panel on his desk, throwing up a holographic projection of the star systems along the border. "We have destroyed the closest Rigelian battle fleet at Centauri Seven here."

Tork touched the holo-sphere representing Centauri and its color changed to red. "That fleet has been eliminated as a threat, but we did not take possession of the system, as it has no useful resources. The destruction of the enemy's Centauri fleet was done solely to protect our flank, though we failed to destroy its carrier force."

He touched Centauri again and it changed to gray, indicating a system that was no longer viable, but not in Imperil possession. Centauri Seven displayed as neutralized.

"Our main thrust will be at the gas giants of the Eusi Hegemony, specifically in the Pontif, Tzu, New Woodlark,

Wewak, and Nambo systems. I have dispatched forces to probe the defenses there."

T'lihktu nodded. "With *Kundhor*?"

"Yes. That effort will be a good test for our new mega-dreadnought, an operational trial. Confederation forces in the Hegemony may respond quickly, so I have dispatched Imperial Attack Unit Five-One-Three-One-One to probe the Eusi sector. They will press through and move toward the Rigelian Core Worlds by getting a toe-hold in Galderon. If we can hurt the enemy there, we can pose a threat to Rigel itself. Their politicians will then panic and sue for peace rather than risk having the home worlds bombarded."

"So grabbing Galderon is simply a ploy to get the Rigelians to negotiate?"

"Indeed. We won't have to actually bombard their worlds; we have merely to present a threat of doing so. Taking out the orbitals over Galderon will achieve that. When the Confederation sues for peace, we will negotiate from a position of strength and withdraw to the captured Hegemony systems that remain in our possession. The Confederation is unlikely to continue the war for a few barely populated frontier systems. To Rigelian politicians, a protracted war is not worth the cost of ships and lives."

Tork touched each system as he spoke, making the spheres glow blue.

"Brilliant, Korguhn."

"Brilliant?" Tork shrugged. "Only time will tell, Yi'rhork. We must watch what the RCN does. Humans are unpredictable. No doubt the RCN will attempt to mass someplace, and that is something we cannot allow them to do."

"Can we stop them?"

"Not completely. We can, however, scatter their task forces by presenting threats along multiple fronts, leaving them unsure to our real objectives. The thrust at Galderon will stage from Nangtashgu. I will lead it as the commander of Task Force Two-Two. But we must keep our space lines of communication open for resupply as we extend forward. The Confederation must remain unsure of where our main attack is headed. I have sent two task forces into the Confederation on each side of the frontier. One will threaten their Oriental systems, the other Antioch. This will give the Confederation threats on three axis to deal with, leaving them unsure which arm is the main attack. Hopefully, such spaced attacks will divert enough of the Confederation Fleet to the flanks that our main thrust to Galderon is relatively unopposed."

"What is our immediate objective after we leave this system?"

"To foray into the Confederation's heart, we must first capture the Bantar and Gulliver systems. Those are our immediate objectives. Once Gulliver is in our grasp, we will resupply and attack the Hegemony. I will leave forces behind to blockade Gallagher and Antioch after we take them, but we must find and destroy the Oriental Sector's Task Force Seventeen, which guards this side of the frontier. I expect to capture Bantar quickly. Then we will reform and assault Gulliver. I anticipate we shall meet and destroy the enemy's Seventh Fleet in Gulliver, thus securing the flank of our thrust into the Hegemony."

"The enemy's carriers were missing at Centauri Seven, Korguhn. Where are they?"

"I am unsure, and they remain a threat that worries me. Rigelian carriers are a strong force multiplier, so I have ordered several of our own carrier groups to join our task forces for deep operations."

"So Bantar first and then Gulliver?"

"For the opening phase of the campaign, yes."

T'lihktu grinned, showing his canines. "If you pull this off, you will be awarded Hero of the Empire status, Korguhn."

"Perhaps." Tork looked down at his mug. "In case I am, do you have any counsel regarding your superiors?"

"Yes." T'lihktu faced him squarely. "If you become Hero, apply for immediate retirement, Korguhn. As a Hero of the Empire, it will be your right, and your service to the Shikahn will be acknowledged by all. The House of Lahk'nah will grow greatly in prestige, and the Shikahn will be forced to grant a Hero's retirement upon request. Doing so will allow you to live safely in retirement, provided you stay out of politics. Always remember a Hero of the Empire must not show ambition in any form."

"Why would I retire, Yi'rhork? I would be our greatest admiral."

"That is precisely what you must fear, Korguhn. Yes, be victorious and become a Hero of the Empire, but do not become *too* victorious. Great leaders attract great admirers and equally great enemies. A Hero is a potential threat to the Shikahn. The In'thork will never allow that. Be victorious, but only just so, then retire quickly and avoid all political involvement. That will spare you and your House unfortunate consequences."

"And if I am only partially victorious?"

"Then fight on, as you always have. A failure, even a partial one, is no threat to the Shikahn. A great victor is."

Tork nodded, but inside he seethed. T'lihktu was right. Tork had seen many great leaders sacked by the Imperial Guard, always for good reasons publicly, but everyone knew it was because they had grown too powerful. The IG had always stepped in and neutralized them. Many had retired quietly after "conferences" with the In'thork; others suffered unfortunate "accidents" or had vanished under mysterious circumstances.

The idea of retiring after a major victory galled him. He had hoped to go on to bigger things, but now realized a major victory could make him look like a contender for the throne. The Shikahn could never allow that. T'lihktu's advice was sound even if bitter to hear. The Shikahn would allow him to live as a *retired* Hero, but never as a Hero on active duty.

He took a deep breath and sighed. "If I am victorious, I will do as you suggest."

T'lihktu nodded. "Good, Korguhn. It is the wisest course for you and your House, should you become a Hero of the Empire."

"I shall take your words to heart, Yi-rorhk. Thank you."

"My honor, Korguhn."

"I have much to do. Send *Torguhn* Moph in when you leave. He and I must plan the capture of Bantar. That system will be used to stage the attack on Gulliver's Hold."

"Yes, Korguhn."

T'lihktu rose and left.

Tork watched him go as he considered his advisor's words, his face an unreadable mask.

CHAPTER 19

Susan Comforti straightened her dress as she crossed the parking ramp into the Groesbeck officer's club. She'd gotten a grip on her runaway emotions, but fixing her makeup had taken more time than fixing her composure. It had also made her late for the meeting.

Which is probably just as well. It'll give my red-rimmed eyes time to return to normal.

The officer's club was a beautiful building with a stucco exterior. Built around a natural lake, it had three sections containing posh dining rooms, seminar auditoriums, business and administrative offices. On most evenings, senior officers and their spouses dined there. Younger officers, mostly commanders and below, preferred the more dynamic activities at the bar.

Susan yearned for the day when Harl would dine as a senior officer in the formal mess. The truth of the

241

matter—which irritated her to no end—was that Harl was a CO of a warship, and his commanding officer's status already provided him the prestige to dine with captains and admirals. Yet Harl seemed more content to hang with the younger officers at the bar. She'd often fought with him over it. Harl, who could have been dining with her, enjoying the company of his wife and eating *healthy* cuisine in a tastefully quiet room—and around people who might actually do his career some good—instead preferred to gulp popcorn, hot wings and beer with younger officers at the bar. Harl hung out with single officers who had no real effect on his advancement. Junior officers were loud and obnoxious, not to mention rowdy. They worried more about having a good time than furthering their careers.

Harl seemed oblivious to how his hanging out with them made her feel, even though she'd complained on many occasions. It was true that in years gone by, he *had* asked her to accompany him, wanting her to have some *fun*, but Susan had never found doing so to be enjoyable.

People in bars were drunk and unsophisticated. Susan didn't like beer, considering it a drink for the lower rungs of society, but beer was what Harl drank. She preferred wines and cocktails but felt ridiculous ordering them in the company of loud, beer-swilling boors. The young officers' only ambitions seemed to revolve around their next conquest—in battle or in the bedroom—and they were usually only interested in getting plastered.

Harl had recently seemed more enamored with the bar crowd than usual. The more she'd suggested he rub elbows

CHAPTER 19

with flag officers, the more he'd resisted her suggestions. At least, he'd acted that way on the few occasions when he'd actually been home, which wasn't often.

Susan tried to make all of the teas, brunches, luncheons, and meetings expected of an officer's wife. She didn't like them particularly, but they made her feel special and provided an opportunity to demonstrate her breeding and social skills while influencing her husband's career. Someone had to do something since Harl seemed determined to undermine it himself.

Sighing, she climbed the terraced steps and entered the crystalplast doors. Walking on the plush carpeting she glanced around for the "Dedalian Room" where the meeting was to be held. The conditioned air felt chilly after the heat of the parking lot. The club seemed to radiate quiet. Susan felt a kind of tranquility come over her as she approached the room. She pushed through the heavy wooden doors and entered.

Wives were knotted around a table along the far wall. It was their usual gathering place before meetings. The table held tea and coffee carafes, as well as trays of cookies and snacks the wives prepared for such occasions. Approaching, she recognized two women and made her way over to them.

Terri Hottenschlein was a tall, green-eyed brunette married to the captain of the cruiser *Jutland*, a ship in Third Fleet. As with *Gant*, *Jutland* was home-based at New Texas but currently assigned to another sector's fleet.

Emily Nishizawa was the wife of an engineer on the

cruiser *Bull Run*. Though Fred was only a lieutenant, Emily hung out with the CO wives, childishly hoping the association might advance her husband's career.

Perhaps Emily and I aren't all that different. Isn't that why I'm here?

Unlike her short husband, Emily Nishizawa was anything but Japanese. Of medium height, Emily was a stunning blonde with sparkling blue eyes and distinct Nordic heritage. Taken together, Terri, Emily, and Susan were called the "Tattle Trio" among the gossip-prone wives, who no doubt were jealous of how well they got along. The wives were often jealous of the shopping trips the "Trio" often took together.

Well, none of that matters. Without our husbands being home except for a few months of the year, we're forced to create our own entertainment and pass the long periods of being left home alone.

"Hi, Suse." Terri smiled as she approached. "How are you?"

"Fine, but the kids are driving me crazy." Susan found an open spot on the table and dropped her purse on it. Such contrivances were old-fashioned, of course, as most women no longer carried things as archaic as purses, except in the Estacadoan systems, where they were considered traditional. She picked up a saucer and teacup. "Sorry I'm late. I had to drop the brats off. They were being little shits."

Terri giggled and lifted a cup from her own saucer. "I understand completely. We're just getting started, so you haven't missed anything. The teas are excellent today, and Mrs. Porter made crumpets."

CHAPTER 19

"Goodness. Really?"

Susan took a moment to admire Terri's dress. It was a deep sea-green in color and cut in the sundress style favored on New Texas. Beside her, Emily nodded, as if to confirm Terri's comments. Unlike Terri, Emily wore a black pants suit and a beautiful diamond necklace that must have cost her poor lieutenant husband a small fortune.

"The 'Old Man,' as Fred calls him, isn't here yet." Emily gave a lopsided grin. "Hi, Susie."

"How are you, Emily? You look lovely today."

"Oh, *this*?" Emily demonstrated false modesty as she coyly curled her wrists toward her chest. "It's just something I threw on."

Susan smiled. *Bitch.*

Emily smiled back. "I got it at Sandivar's in Mexia."

"Oh, I love that store." Susan tried to sound interested as she poured tea.

Terri raised an eyebrow. "Are you all right?"

My God. My eyes must still be red.

"I'm fine. Why?"

"You seem, well . . . unusually quiet." Terri gave her an up and down glance. "You don't seem your normal self. Is everything okay?"

"It's the kids. Their bickering's driving me up the wall. I don't know why teenagers can't get along for two minutes. I wish Harl was here to deal with them. I have to rant and yell to get them to clean their rooms. All Harl has to do is look at them, and they shape right up."

Terri laughed. "Harl would tan their hides."

"Probably." Susan gave her a slight smile.

Emily seemed shocked. "Harl actually *spanks* your children?"

Susan nodded. "Sometimes, if they deserve it. They certainly deserved it today."

"Isn't spanking bad for children? Psychologists say it damages a child's self-esteem."

Susan sighed. "Harl's a Navy officer, not a child psychologist."

Terri caught the tone and put an arm on Emily's shoulder. "Emily, sweetie, those child shrinks are full of crap. Most have never raised a child of their own. When kids get out of hand, a good swat on the bottom doesn't hurt them. It's not their self-esteem that gets hurt, it's their *butts*. We're not talking about a beating, mind you, just a spanking. There's a huge difference. Kids need limits. They have to learn there are consequences for actions. When you have kids of your own you'll understand. As for you, Susie dear, you should've figured out by now that as the CO of a Navy destroyer, Harl *is* a child psychologist. He's got a whole crew of children to supervise. Speaking of the old curmudgeon, have you heard from him lately?"

"Not for several weeks now." Susan shook her head sadly. "I'm lucky to get a few pages of e-script now and then. Seldom do I get v-mail anymore. Harl's on patrol and doesn't have a lot of time to write. How's Pete?"

"Fine, last I heard." Terri chuckled. "They were in Tanzania in the last message I got, getting ready for an operation. He has over five hundred people to take care of. I'm lucky he finds time to send me anything at all."

At least he finds time for you. Susan felt bitterness creep into her heart.

Emily blinked but said nothing. Her husband, Fred, was a junior engineer, and beyond a small department, not in charge of anything. She glanced between them. "Did you hear that Vice Admiral Torrance is speaking to us today?"

"Oh?" Susan blinked. "Is that the 'Old Man' you're referring to?"

"Uh-huh."

While many of the women present were wives of ship skippers, most were married to less-privileged officers, men filling positions as engineers, navigators, tactical officers and pilots. Of course, there were female officers with male spouses as well, but the males didn't attend wives club meetings. Today the wives would be visited by a vice admiral. It was exceedingly unusual for the executive officer of Second Fleet to drop by and speak directly to the Wives' Club.

Then again, the Navy had always been screwed up, Susan thought.

Groesbeck was the largest naval base on Odessa, the third planet of the New Texas system. New Texas was an Estacadoan world, in a theater protected by Second Fleet. A huge number of ships home-ported at New Texas were assigned rotating duties with other fleets. It was a tradition based on the Navy's desire for well-rounded crews familiar with all theaters of operation.

Harl's ship was currently assigned to Seventh Fleet in the Oriental systems, while Terri and Emily's husbands were assigned to Third Fleet in the Eusi Hegemony. It was Navy practice that numbered fleets were assigned to theaters, but smaller units and ships could be detached and assigned elsewhere with what was known as a Change of Operational Procedure, or CHOP orders. Individual ships could be temporarily "chopped" from their parent fleet to duty in other theaters.

Susan frowned. *"CHOP" is certainly the right term for it. It chops a unit from one command to another as efficiently as it chops a man from his wife and his true responsibilities, like staying home and doing what needs to be done. But Harl isn't chopped off from anything. He's right where he wants to be, out with his ship playing spaceman in vacuum. I'm the one who's chopped off . . . chopped off from love, chopped off from sex, and chopped off from life.*

Emily was blathering on, oblivious to Susan's thoughts. "Yes. Admiral Torrance is briefing us on the war that was just declared and what the Navy's doing to support families for the duration."

Terri sipped at her tea. "Hmm."

Susan moved around the room briefly, talking to other wives and making inane chitchat, as the group waited for the illustrious guest speaker to appear. As she moved to refill her cup, she saw Laura Demning sitting in a corner looking like a lost child.

Laura's husband was an ensign on his first deployment. Laura was naïve and easily intimidated by the other wives. Her boyish husband outranked no one's husband in the group, and Laura hesitated to talk with other women present. On the few occasions where she'd done so, she'd proven herself not only young but ignorant.

Of course, her ensign husband hadn't helped by briefing his new bride on the proper "image" expected of a Navy officer's wife, lecturing her sternly on the do's and don'ts, taking his guidance from the Navy Officer's Social Guide. In truth, the ensign didn't know any better, having only recently graduated from the Academy. The result of his efforts, however, caused his wife to appear naïve and somewhat childish. Laura seemed to think *she* could make or break her husband's career based on social wheeling and dealing; that *she* was the window dressing that would somehow achieve his ambitions, as if the poor boy had no skills of his own. To make matters worse—

The train of her thoughts suddenly made Susan feel sick.

Am I any different than her? Are any of us?

Unfortunately, ensigns' wives were without status in a club where commodores' wives jockeyed for positions of importance. It was the most senior officer's wife present who ran the Wives' Club. Because so many were married to commodores and admirals, and because the senior officer for Second Fleet was a bachelor, at the moment there was no true leader in the Wive's Club. Laura was at the bottom of a very deep pecking order. Until her husband achieved some rank, she wouldn't be considered important.

That didn't keep her from trying, though. Briefed

sternly on her "duties" by her husband, she'd tried to lead by example, to take charge of weekly meetings. She'd been quickly—and rather viciously—put in her place by older, more experienced wives, who'd spared her no insult while doing so.

Slammed would've been the more appropriate term. Many wives were still slamming her over it. Not to her face anymore, but behind her back. They gossiped and giggled about her naiveté and "cluelessness" at every opportunity, referring to her as "the spoiled child" and, more often than not, "the airhead." Others deliberately set her up in awkward situations just to watch her make a fool of herself. Laura was the butt of most jokes in the Officer's Wives' Club.

You'd better get used to it, honey, Susan thought with a sigh. *That's the way the game's played. You'll get no sympathy from me. If you're going to play with the big girls, you'd better get tough fast. I had to pay my dues too.*

"Hello, Laura," Susan said sweetly, keeping any trace of her thoughts from her voice. "How are you?"

"Fine." Laura brightened; happy someone was actually speaking to her today. "Did you hear Admiral Torrance is coming to see us?"

Of course, you ignorant twit; everyone in this room knows that. Why do you think we're here?

Susan kept such thoughts from her face, amazed that Laura could be so excited by a vice admiral. "I've heard. Have you heard from Todd?"

"No." Laura's face fell, as if the change of subject had

focused her on something that was breaking her heart. "Not for over a month."

Get used to it, babe, Susan thought. *He'll be gone more than he's home if he makes a career of the Navy.*

Susan tried to be witty. "Well, look on the bright side. Maybe he won't come back at all, and you can collect that *wonderful* Navy life insurance."

She meant it as a sarcastic barb at the Navy, implying its benefits were pitiful compared to her family's standard. It was also a general stab at their husbands, who dared to go off and leave their families alone to fend for themselves. The sarcasm was lost on Laura, however. Her eyes began to mist.

"Excuse me." Laura put the back of her hand to her mouth and ran for the ladies' room.

Susan felt a moment of malicious glee at hurting her. It was petty and beneath her and she knew it, but Laura was an airhead who irritated everyone with her constant blathering and sickening enthusiasm about being married to a Navy officer. Her naïve optimism irritated all of the jaded wives. It felt good to dump some pain on the stupid ditz now and then. It was also easy to do since her husband couldn't hurt Harl's career. Besides, the little tart needed a reality check.

She watched Laura enter the ladies' room and close the door behind her.

Best wake up, Laura, or your hurts will be many, Susan thought acidly. *If you want to run with these bitches, you'd better grow some fangs. Your feelings may have been hurt by my joke, but that's nothing compared to what some of these gals will dish out. You'll learn soon enough Darwin was right: it's survival of the fittest with this bunch. Know-it-all wives of low-ranking men don't survive here if they act pretentious. We're a mean bunch. Best learn how to be cruel yourself.*

At that moment, Vice Admiral Truman Nathaniel Torrance walked through the thick, double wooden doors into the Dedalian Room. Of medium height, Torrance's snow-white hair and ice-blue eyes offset a lined, weathered face that one would have expected to see on a favorite uncle. He was in dress uniform, wearing a double-breasted coat of black with a golden starship badge with six stars on his left breast, one star for every ship he'd commanded. Below it were six rows of colored ribbons. On each sleeve was a four-inch-wide band of gold and the accompanying twin half-inch bands of a vice admiral, along with three embroidered stars. Torrance's nickname was TNT because of his initials.

The wives surrounded him, and he chuckled as he exchanged pleasantries. Susan made her way to the end of the reception line.

Torrance was shaking hands and talking with women he obviously knew. He gave Terri Hottenschlein a hearty hug, and Susan got the feeling Terri's husband knew the admiral rather well. Emily Nishizawa hung back; aware an admiral probably wouldn't know her husband at all. Vice admirals didn't cavort with lieutenants. When it was her turn, Susan stepped up and presented her hand. "Good afternoon, Admiral Torrance. It's so nice to see you again."

Torrance regarded her pleasantly, but no light of recognition came into his eyes. Susan felt her face redden. "Susan Comforti, Sir."

"Comforti? Comforti . . . I know that name."

"Yes, Sir. My husband commands *Gant*."

"*Gant?*" Torrance seemed puzzled for a moment. "Oh, yes, the destroyer. Pleased to meet you, madam."

Torrance quickly moved on to the next wife in line. Susan felt as if she'd been slapped. Though his manner had been friendly and courteous, his response left her hollow and empty. Embarrassment washed over her like a waterfall.

The destroyer?

The admiral didn't know Harl. Of course, he knew the names of all naval officers from Odessa, particularly ship COs, since he signed their efficiency reports, but he didn't *personally* know her husband. She'd stupidly assumed he would, as Harl was a commanding officer, responsible for two hundred and fifty personnel. His lack of recognition made her feel foolish. The admiral had sounded like a destroyer skipper wasn't important enough for him to bother knowing.

Torrance moved on, making small talk with the likes of Terri, which only gave Susan a heady brew of emotions ranging from jealousy to fury.

I'm not important enough to know? I'm a Beauregard! Has Harl told everyone I'm so snobby that even vice admirals shun me? Why am I jealous of Terri? Why do I feel like bursting into tears again?

Movement in a corner caught her eye. Laura Demning was emerging from the ladies' room, holding a tissue, her eyes red from crying. Suddenly Susan felt an overwhelming sense of shame.

You did the same thing to her, she told herself silently. *You treated her like crap because she's young and ignorant. I'm outcast because Harl won't do anything to advance his rank, and I've become a favor-seeking opportunist just like Emily. Harl's tried so hard to avoid seeking favor that most flag officers don't know him. Worse, he's made me unimportant, as well.*

She felt her anger building. She wanted to scream and hiss, to tell them what she thought of their precious Navy and their stupid Wives' Club. Her face flushed red as she took a seat in the third row of chairs arranged for the meeting. Called "Leper's Row" by the wives, it was at the back of the gallery. She noted with jealousy that Terri got a seat in the front row with the rest of the "anointed." Laura sat in the front row as well, not because she was one of them but because she didn't know any better.

Torrance moved to a dais and smiled at the assembled women as he sipped water from a small glass. "Good morning, ladies. I want to say what a pleasure it is to meet all of you here today. I was just talking with Admiral Luna just this morning, and he told me to pass along his greetings."

There was an appreciative murmur. Fleet Admiral Fontaine Luna was CO of Second Fleet, responsible for the entire Estacadoan Sector. As CINC2FLT, Luna was the boss of every officer stationed in New Texas. It was nice to hear they'd received the attention of the top Navy officer in theater.

Torrance waited for the murmurs to die. "As you know, many Second Fleet personnel are assigned to other Fleets in the Navy. Since the disaster at Centauri Seven, the Navy's struggling to recover as it tries to stop enemy incursions into our frontier along the Rim. Let me assure you the Navy's doing everything in its power to stop the Empire and win this war. While I can't go into operational details for security reasons, you've all seen the news, and I'm sure you're here today because you're concerned about your husbands. You're probably wondering what type of support you can expect from the Navy while your men are at war.

"At the moment, Seventh, Third, and First Fleets are engaged in combat operations. For the moment, Second Fleet has yet to be tasked, but I expect this to change in the near future. Second Fleet's primary job so far has been to assign ships and personnel to the under-strength fleets doing the fighting. Many of you have loved ones in those fleets, and I know you're worried about them.

"Ladies, I won't lie to you. War's a deadly business. People die in war—people on both sides. If one side is victorious, the casualties are usually relegated to its military components. The losing side, however, tends to share casualty rates between military and civilian populations. At the moment, the Eusi Hegemony and the Oriental systems are in the line of the Imperial attack, and it's only because of people like your husbands that those systems haven't fallen. It is they who stand between freedom and tyrannical subjugation. But know this: if we don't stop the Karsians on the frontier, they'll soon be at our door. There's a price for freedom; a cost to be paid whenever we stand up to atrocity and aggression. That price is paid in blood and lives. Make no mistake: we *will* take casualties. Mathematically, the odds are some of those casualties will be among personnel from Odessa. I know that's not what you want to hear, but I'd rather be honest than sell you a false bill of goods."

Torrance took another sip of water and continued. "There's nothing you can do for your husbands except love them, support them, keep the family going, and wait for their return. You must handle all family matters until they're back. I know v-mail is slow right now but realize the interstellar channels are full of military communications that, by necessity, take precedence over civil communications. In the meantime, the Navy is here to support you.

"To that end, I intend to conduct weekly briefings with this club and keep you informed on the situation. I've made available to you administrative and legal support, as well as family and personal counseling services. I'll address any specific concerns you have. I've assigned base legal and our benefits administration services to assist this group however needed. I've also contacted Navy Relief, and they've agreed to help, though they're geared more for enlisted families than those of officers. Does anyone have a question you'd like me to address at the moment?"

A hand shot up on the rearmost row, and Torrance nodded. "Yes, ma'am? What's your question?"

A tall redhead stood at the back of the room. "Hello, Admiral. My husband's ship is chopped to Seventh Fleet. He was gone since six months before the war started, and he's still gone, for God knows how long now. When can I expect to see him again?"

Torrance sighed and leaned on the podium. "All military personnel are currently assigned 'for the duration' to their respective commands. That means indefinitely, ma'am. I don't know how long that will be. Neither does the president, for that matter. It depends on strategic and operational circumstances. You might see your husband in as little as two months, or it might be a year or longer. I don't know, but rest assured we *will* get him home to you as soon as we possibly can."

There was a collective frustrated sigh as the wives digested that tidbit. A year was longer than most had bargained for.

Another hand shot up.

"Yes ma'am?"

"Hello, Admiral. Victoria Rivers. My husband's assigned to *Comet*. My children barely know their father. He's been gone for most of six out of the last eight years, and that was in peacetime. What guarantee do I have he'll be back before my children are grown?"

Torrance sighed again. "Unfortunately, there are no guarantees, madam. I'd like to give you an answer, but I can't. War is dangerous and unpredictable. He could become a casualty. If he doesn't, we'll get him home as soon as we can."

"All right." Rivers placed fists on her hips. "Let's assume that—God forbid—he *doesn't* return—that he's lost in action. Where does that leave me and my children?"

"In that unfortunate event, you'd be provided all of the services due to you as a military dependent. You'd have full access to chaplain, legal, and other services. All pay and insurance would be deposited to the account of the beneficiary your husband specified in his benefits forms."

"That's all fine, but what happens to *us*, Admiral?" Rivers wasn't backing down. "I'm from Jed's Star, not Odessa. How do I get home? Does the Navy just throw us out on the street?"

"Madam, the Navy will never 'throw you out on the street.'" Torrance looked at her firmly. "Under naval regulations, you're entitled to a three-month grace period before you have to move off-base."

"What?" Rivers paled as if dashed with cold water. "What do you mean by 'move 'off-base?' You mean . . . we'd be tossed out on the local economy?"

"Once your husband leaves service, you're required to leave Navy housing and live on your own. In that case, you'd be given three extra months' time to look for new accommodations. That's three times longer than normal when someone separates. It's twelve full T-weeks to reset your life."

"But my husband wouldn't have left the Navy!" Rivers turned beet-red with fury. "He'd be dead! How can you throw us off-base after something like that? What kind of gratitude is that for a family that sacrificed its primary breadwinner for your precious Navy? What kind of pay-back is that for a wife who's lost her husband, or children who've lost their father?"

Torrance was still for a long moment, clearly uncom-fortable with Rivers' anger, watching warily as many wives muttered in agreement. The situation wasn't going as he'd hoped. He met Rivers' eyes carefully and tried to explain.

"You would, Mrs. Rivers, receive all pay and benefits stipulated in your husband's will. That should allow you the time and funds to secure off-base housing or to move home, as well as time to find employment. Surely you realize the Navy can't become a boarding house for civilian families that suffer a casualty."

It was more than Susan could stand. Anger over-whelmed her, as it had earlier with the kids. She was furi-ous with the admiral's attitude and mad at the Navy. She was bitter at being snubbed and still mad at her kids. Most of all, she was furious at Harl for putting her in this situa-tion. She stood without waiting for Torrance to acknowl-edge her, and he became the object she vented her fury on.

"*Civilians*? What *civilians*, Admiral? We're Navy fami-lies, for God's sake! We stay at home, tend the fires, and try to lead normal lives while the Navy sends our men off to die in some Godforsaken star system!"

Torrance's eyes widened at her vehemence, but he sensed it coming from the other women as well and coughed politely. "I should point out that *women* are dying as well, madam, not just men. There're husbands in the same boat as you. Almost half of the personnel aboard our ships are female."

Susan felt her voice rise. "I don't give a damn what the personnel ratio is, Admiral. This is a *wives* club. It's *our* men we're concerned about, not your damned Navy. If you're going to stand there and spout equal opportunity bullshit, go find a husband's group, if you can dig one up. We're giving everything we have to the Navy—our men who are fighting and dying in your stupid war—only to hear you intend to turn us out in the cold if they're killed? You intend to abandon women and children without income, without even houses to live in? That's a hell of a thing to do to families of men who sacrifice their lives for you, as well as the dreams of their families, all for a stupid war."

Torrance looked at her with bleak eyes, caught on the ropes in a ring he'd never intended to enter. This wasn't going to be the pleasant wives' briefing he'd anticipated. "I don't write the regulations, ma'am."

"I know *you* don't write them, Admiral. What I want to know is what you're going to *do* about them. Do you think this is just and fair? I mean, you're a vice admiral, for God's sake. You have the power to change things. What are *you* going to do to *correct* this situation?"

Torrance rested his arms on the podium and looked at his hands. It was obvious the wives had him cornered, and he was looking for a way to extricate himself. That he couldn't find one obviously irritated him.

CHAPTER 19

He lifted his glass again and sipped calmly. It was an anchor of self-control, a way to present an image of serenity in the midst of chaos. Setting the glass down, he looked Susan in the eye. "Your point is well taken, Mrs. Comforti."

Caught off-guard, Susan blinked in surprise. "Huh?"

He remembered my name.

"And you're right. I am a vice admiral, not to mention the executive officer of this theater. It's not right to push Navy families out on the local economy. Not when their breadwinners die defending us. While I can't see the Navy ever fully subsidizing casualty families, I agree we must address this issue in a more positive way. We need to help such families transition after such a bitter loss. To that end, I will conduct a review of the current regulations and make proposals to improve this matter. Thank you, madam, for reminding me of my responsibilities."

There was an eruption of applause from the wives. Susan stood still, stunned at her unexpected success. Torrance sipped more water and waited for the applause to die. Though embarrassed by her attack, he seemed pleased with his response.

"Since you have such strong feelings on the matter, Mrs. Comforti—as does, apparently, Mrs. Rivers—I'd like the two of you to submit your recommendations for changes directly to my office for my personal consideration. I want *you* to tell me what *you* think the Navy should do; what is fair and equitable to dependents in such a situation. Of course, as civilians, I can't order you to do anything . . . but seeing as you're Navy dependents and it's in your own self-interest, I can at least give you the opportunity to make a difference. I'm willing to work with you ladies on this. It's the least the Navy can do."

The applause returned, louder this time, and Susan sat, feeling numb inside. Her anger was gone.

Now she was scared.

My God, Susan thought, *what have I done? I just chewed out a vice admiral; went toe to toe with him, looking for blood. He didn't know who I was until I shot off my big mouth, but he certainly knows who I am now. I doubt he'll forget my embarrassing him either. Which means Harl's probably in hot water, too, and he's not even here to defend himself. I think I just killed Harl's career. Heaven help me, now I have to come up with solutions.*

The ball was in her court. In a way, she and Victoria Rivers had won a victory for the Wives' Club. They'd gotten a vice admiral to address their concerns. On the other hand, the admiral had skillfully thrown the gauntlet right back in their faces. He'd conceded the need for change and made *her* and Victoria responsible for initiating them. Good or bad, that responsibility had been laid at their feet, and now there was no way to escape it. It wasn't something Susan was prepared to accept, and certainly not one she desired.

She'd only wanted to vent her anger, to slap at Harl's Navy and its insensitivity about dependents. Now *she* was the one who had to put up or shut up. It was amazing how fast Torrance had turned the tables on her.

It was no wonder the man was a vice admiral.

CHAPTER 19

As the applause died, Torrance glanced at the faces in the room, obviously pleased with his solution. "Are there any other concerns I can address?"

Laura Demning raised her hand in the front row.

Torrance smiled at her. "Yes, ma'am?"

"Laura Demning, Sir. You said our husbands could be gone indefinitely."

"Yes. Do you have a question?"

"Just one, Admiral."

"Shoot."

"Well, what I want to know is, if our husbands are going to be gone for a long time . . ."

"Yes?"

"Who's going to mow the lawn?"

Torrance froze, his mouth open, but no words came. He stared at her, nonplussed.

Susan giggled.

Laura turned angrily toward her. Titters erupted around the room. The laughter proved contagious. After a moment all of the wives were laughing, and a moment later, Torrance joined them.

Laura sat down, frowning. She knew she was the butt of some joke but clearly had no idea what it was.

Which only made everyone laugh harder.

CHAPTER 20

"Here they come."

LeMieux acknowledged the call with a curt nod, tightening his restraint harness as the first enemy ship popped into existence at the diamond icon representing the Zion stargate terminus on Hasting's tactical display.

The Karsians had not hesitated, pressing their pursuit through the stargate as they chased down what they believed to be a single destroyer fleeing into Centauri Seven. LeMieux intended to show them how wrong that assumption was.

He'd drawn his ships back from the stargate to a range where his missiles would be effective. It was far enough away to allow the missiles time to cage and track but close enough that enemy point defenses had minimal time to intercept them. Missiles required time to acquire targets and calculate intercepts. They also needed time,

264

albeit minuscule, for guidance AIs to manipulate their drives during boost phase. Time equated to a considerable distance when missiles were pulling fifty thousand gravities of acceleration. Missiles could reach their target before their warheads could arm if launched too close, which imposed a minimum range on missiles. Missiles were short to long distance weapons but not effective at extremely close-range.

Because of the minimum range requirement, they became useless at close range, making beams the primary weapons in that envelope. Ships using beams as their primary armament, like *Kuroshima* and *Yang Chien*, were essentially knife-fighters, designed to slug it out at close range. At close range energy ships were safe from missiles and their beams became powerful. Of course, the enemy's beams became more powerful at close range, too, so it remained a two-edged sword. One rule remained true in space combat: *the closer you got with beams, the more deadly they were.*

LeMieux had placed his energy shooters close to the stargate terminus, ready to engage the moment an enemy popped through. Laboring under sensor distortion from wormhole transition, the Karsians would be vulnerable to beam fire from his destroyers until their sensors were back online. Lasers and particle beams moved at the speed of light, reducing the time lag between firing and impact to near zero.

The ships in LeMieux's formation had toggled their fire to *Hastings'* data link, allowing *Hastings* to act as the central "brain" for the task unit, effectively linking all vessels into a single battle architecture.

Kuroshima and *Yang Chien* were ahead of *Hastings*, however, and that distance necessitated a second data link network for the rearward ships. With a separation of three light-seconds between the destroyers and *Hastings*, a single data link network imposed time delays that could be problematic. Because of that, the destroyers had set up their own data link network, with *Kuroshima* acting as network control while *Hastings* maintained a second rear-echelon data link for the missile shooters, allowing each formation to fire salvos as separate but coordinated entities.

By concentrating the firepower of each group on a single target as it emerged from the terminus, LeMieux hoped to produce maximum kill rates with each salvo. Two data groups provided a deadly one-two punch that would hopefully shift the odds in favor of the Centauri defense force. Splitting his groups in azimuth also gave the enemy a targeting problem if he somehow managed to clear distortion in time to return fire.

His surveillance officer spoke softly in the earpiece of his helmet. "*Kuroshima* identifies the bogey as a Karsian *Darter*-class corvette, Admiral. Her captain's requesting permission to fire."

LeMieux smiled. *Young lieutenant Kibbleman is proving to be surprisingly aggressive.*

He called up the schematics for a Darter-class vessel on his in-helmet display. Darter-class corvettes were lightly armored, highly maneuverable vessels with four missile tubes each. While not a significant threat to either destroyer, a Darter could launch eight missiles per volley. Fortunately, a corvette was an easy kill for the massed firepower of LeMieux's force.

"Inform Kuroshima's CO she's weapons free. All other ships are cleared to fire as toggled by its command ship's order."

"Weapons free, aye, Sir. Birds away."

Eight missiles lurched from *Hastings'* tubes, accelerated by their coilgun ejectors. Their drives kicked in an instant later, boosting them to 50,000 g's as they joined the swarm of other missiles from the other data group that launched at the same instant.

Oriskany lofted twelve, as did *Joseph Brant*. Behind them, *Gant*, *Saganami* and *Ziglar* each added four of their own. Thirty-two missiles bore down on the hapless and blind corvette at the terminus. Three light-seconds ahead of them, the energy batteries of *Kuroshima* and *Yang Chien* cut loose, their beams punching into the enemy ship instantly.

Six 60 cm lasers crossed the half-light-second of space and knocked down the corvette's shields, melting hull plating and ablative armor in a molten white-hot spray. Two of the corvette's drive nodes, pierced by lasers, exploded, along with the ship's missile magazine. Rocked by internal explosions, the corvette was a dying wreck well before the missile swarm reached her. When it did, she was vaporized by the combined power of nearly three dozen nuclear warheads. Her dying flare was so intense that not even debris escaped the fireball.

Kuroshima and *Yang Chien* veered away, their shields flaring as the energy released by the corvette's explosion glowed on their shields, sending ionized plasma coiling around each vessel. Even for fully shielded destroyers, a half-light second was close range for such a massive explosion.

The destroyers turned back to face the stargate and repositioned, ready for the next ship to appear.

RNSS *STALKER*
ZION'S WASTE NEXUS

Commander Daniel Villafuerte sat in Stalker's control room watching his sensor displays as *Stalker* approached the enemy ships. Hidden by her onboard Laroussi field, Stalker's passive sensors quietly observed the space around her.

Stalker and her sister stealthship, *Recluse,* had entered Zion's Waste days earlier, expecting to emerge in the middle of a Karsian task force that was supposed to be blockading the stargate. Finding none, both stealthships had separated on divergent courses, following a preplanned search pattern to maximize sensor coverage. *Recluse* had launched a communications drone. The drone had waited several minutes for its SSBM mothership to move away from its launch point before activating its drives, so as not to give away the stealthship's position. That drone was surging toward the stargate behind the boomer, carrying the all-clear message that would allow Admiral Yolowski to bring his task group into Zion's Waste. *Recluse* was far away, approaching the stargate into Centauri Seven from another vector.

Stealthships were vulnerable if detected, forcing them to move slowly and use passive scanners and cloaking fields. SSBM stealthships like *Recluse* were no match for conventional warships. They were designed to sneak through enemy sensor networks and lay mine fields and destroy planets. Captain Sally Dell's *Recluse* was such a weapon, a doomsday machine. Because of the cataclysmic power of the black hole generator warheads carried in their planetary bombardment missiles, *Recluse* and her sister SSBMs were called "boomers" by the Navy.

Stalker was a "fast attack" boat, a stealthship designed to seek out and destroy enemy boomers. She could fight a limited number of conventional warships from ambush, but her primary mission remained killing enemy stealthships. Due to that mission, *Stalker* possessed better passive sensors than *Recluse*. She could also travel slightly faster and remain undetected due to a better suite of Laroussi field generators. Stealthships stood no chance if struck by enemy weapons. Because there was zero time to abandon ship, stealthship crews wore no vac-suits while at battle stations.

Villafuerte cursed his Filipino heritage as he ran a

hand over his head. His short, black hair stuck up like the bristles of a horsehair brush. No matter what he did, his hair always gave him a slightly electrocuted appearance. He'd never been able to get it to lie flat, no matter how much he combed, jelled, or cursed it.

His sensor operator's voice interrupted thoughts about his hair. "Contact, bearing two-four-three mark zero-eight-four."

Villafuerte stared at the sensor display over her shoulder. Petty Officer Barbara Banich was technically a kid, but she was a damned good sensor specialist despite her young age. He pointed at a yellow icon in the display. "Source?"

"Multiple drives, Sir." Banich kept her eyes glued to the screen as her manicured fingers fine-tuned the sensors. "I'm picking up multiple convergence lines, almost like drive harmonics."

"Can you fingerprint them, Babs?"

"Trying, Sir."

"Keep at it."

Villafuerte moved to the front of the control room and stopped beside a tray of sandwiches, freshly delivered from the galley. If nothing else, the Invisible Service boasted the best chow in the Navy. He picked up a salami-and-something, took a quick bite and chewed, wondering about the sensor contacts.

If they turned out to be friendly, the task group could delay its transit into Zion's Waste and marshal for an attack elsewhere. If they were enemy, however, Yolowski would have to fight his way into Zion's Waste to reach

Centauri Seven. He needed to identify the bogies holding at the Centauri stargate and get word back to the admiral.

Stalker had a limited supply of comm drones. He could send a tight-beam transmission to *Recluse* and have Dell relay to the Fleet via communications drone the ID of whatever he found. Radio waves couldn't pass through a stargate wormhole without a drone, and Dell's ship was closer to the Gallagher stargate than *Stalker* and carried more drones.

Banich glanced in his direction. "The AI has a probable ID, Captain."

Villafuerte moved beside her and took another bite of sandwich. "What have we got?"

"They match for Karsian drives, Sir." She pointed to colored lines on her cascade display. Spectral analysis had never been Villafuerte's strong point, but Banich was an expert at reading them. "That line's a Karsian fusion reactor, Sir. That dark purple line there matches for tritium, which their reactors use. This line over here is a known Karsian containment field generator."

"How many sources are you tracking?"

"I've got triangulation on multiple sources, Sir. This line here, that's a heavy drive, most likely a cruiser. The others are all lighter, probably destroyers and frigates."

Villafuerte turned toward an officer standing at the far end of the control room. "Navigator, triangulate bearings and plot an intercept for these contacts. I need to know exactly how far away they are."

"They're not far, Sir." Banich pointed to her screen.

"The frequencies have a negative Doppler shift, so they're moving away from us. Based on their trajectory, they're headed for the Centauri Seven stargate."

Villafuerte frowned and took another bite of sandwich. Logically, a Karsian formation should have been holding in ambush at the Gallagher terminus, not the Centauri stargate. Was it possible the Karsians were withdrawing back into Centauri Seven? Did they plan to occupy it?

It seemed unlikely. Zion's Waste was a middle-of-nowhere chokepoint to bottle up arriving RCN task forces, or at least a place where the enemy could place picket ships. Something had drawn the Karsians toward the Centauri stargate. *But what?*

He needed answers, and there was only one way to get them. Finishing his sandwich, he stepped to his command couch. "Nav, put the intercept course on tactical."

The Karsian contacts were moving away at high acceleration. Villafuerte set Stalker's new speed higher than normal, allowing her to trail the Karsians without being detected. Due to the distance between them, the Karsian formation would reach the stargate before *Stalker* would be in position to identify them all. He could push *Stalker* to maximum speed, of course, which would get her there more quickly, but doing so would cause her to be detected. Still, it might be the only way to gather enough intelligence for Yolowski to know what to do.

"Signal *Recluse* on secure tight beam that were tracking a Karsian formation we've detected. Give them the specifics on the contacts' course and speed. Helm, fly the course on tactical and maintain acceleration. Let's go see what these bastards are up to."

The Condition One alarm sounded, bringing Stalker's crew to its highest state of readiness short of GQ.

If Karsian bladeships were shadowing *Stalker*, it was likely she'd be detected and destroyed before anyone on *Stalker* knew they were there, but it was a risk he had to take. If she remained slow enough to remain undetected, *Stalker* would never get into position to develop a firing solution before the enemy jumped. Dell needed to know what *Stalker* was doing. *Recluse* remained his vital recon link to Yolowski's task group. If things went south for *Stalker*, Yolowski would at least know how far he was from the nearest enemy when he wormholed into Zion's Waste.

Villafuerte leaned back into his couch. "Let's go see what you've found, Babs."

Banich grinned as Villafuerte returned to studying the tactical plot.

Stalker was on the hunt.

IKS *D'BAHTZ*
CENTAURI SEVEN WORMHOLE

Under-Commander Orfon braced as *D'Bahtz* prepared for wormhole into Centauri Seven. Only moments earlier the corvette *Tahk'pa*, the first ship to reach the jump point, had transitioned. Now *D'Bahtz* waited at maximum readiness. The wormhole's gravity turbulence would soon be clear after Tahk'pa's passage, and *D'Bahtz* could move to the jump point and follow *Tahk'pa* through in pursuit of the Rigelian destroyer that had fled into Centauri Seven.

While the wormhole could easily handle the masses of both corvettes in a simultaneous jump, Captain Durok had ordered his corvettes to wormhole in sequence. If the Rigelian they pursued had turned to fight inside Centauri, the slight delay would exacerbate the enemy's targeting problem. Both corvettes would prosecute the battle at close range while maneuvering on diverging vectors while Durok's remaining ships jumped through one by one and joined the fight.

Orfon verified all hands were at battle stations and his ship was ready to go. Satisfied, he nodded to his pilot. "Proceed through the jump-gate, *Thrung'tohk.*"

The jump alarm sounded and *D'Bahtz* transitioned instantly, exiting the wormhole's terminus inside Centauri Seven. Orfon had never liked jump-gate transitions. Though it remained a wonder that a ship could disappear from one star system and reappear instantly in another hundreds or thousands of light-years away, the concept still unnerved him, despite his years in space.

No physical sensation was experienced during a jump. One instant you were in one system and the next instant you were in another star system and temporarily blind. There was only an energy pulse on the ship's systems to indicate a jump had occurred, followed by a short period of sensor distortion, but the process left a ship vulnerable until that distortion cleared. Orfon had never liked feeling helpless after a jump. He preferred to get out of such a condition as quickly as possible.

D'Bahtz's consoles flickered as sensor distortion washed across the displays. Suddenly *D'Bahtz* was in Centauri Seven, the mysterious metaspace of the wormhole having worked its ill-understood magic.

Orfon glanced at his bridge monitors to verify power levels and shielding were at stated norms and that his ship was ready for combat the moment sensors cleared.

His ship exploded at that instant.

RNSS *KUROSHIMA*
CENTAURI SEVEN STAR SYSTEM

Talara grimaced as Kuroshima's lasers fired again, dimming the ship's internal lighting as the weapons sucked energy from her capacitors. Twin 60 cm shafts of invisible light stabbed across the vacuum into the newly arrived corvette in conjunction with beams from *Yang Chien*. The corvette flared under the laser barrage. An internal explosion shattered the corvette's spine and broke her in half, even as Data Group One's second missile swarm bore down on the halves of the ship.

Talara had pulled *Kuroshima* back from the terminus after the first corvette's destruction. Even so, LeMieux's second missile salvo lit the heavens with nuclear fire that had flared on Kuroshima's shields as the swarm destroyed the halves of *D'Bahtz*.

Perspiration beaded her face inside her helmet, and her hands shook uncontrollably on her armrests as she gripped them tightly. An irritating bead of sweat at the nape of her neck trickled down her spine to the small of her back.

She was scared.

Despite the hate she felt for Karsians, this was her first time in battle, and combat was a terrifying spectacle. Having been thrust into the captain's chair without training didn't make the job less nerve-racking. She had two hundred and fifty people betting their lives on her skill and judgment, qualities she knew she didn't have. She was competent as an engineer, but she wasn't a line officer. She'd never been a TAC-O, much less a skipper. Fate had put her in command with a cruel twist and the specter of battle terrified her.

Her gloved fingers clutched her armrests in a white-knuckled grip as she prayed for divine guidance to fight the battle LeMieux expected her to fight.

"Transition at the stargate." The voice in her headset was from her sensor petty officer, Tom Kurth. "Another one coming through, Skipper."

She turned toward Yantali. "Capacitor status, Reggie?" Her voice sounded thin and faint in her earpiece.

"Recharging, 73 percent, Ma'am." Yantali was acting as TAC-O, a job he was equally unqualified for. Everyone, it seemed, had been forced to step up. They were learning by the seat of their pants.

"Prepare to fire." Talara tried to sound calm, but she wasn't. Her lips trembled and she fought the urge to urinate.

"Here comes another." Yantali pointed at the tactical display as a new, larger contact appeared in the battle plot. A Karsian destroyer popped into existence where the second corvette had died only moments earlier.

Yantali spoke calmly. "Target locked."

"Another transition." Kurth's tone rose a notch in pitch, as excitement made his voice rise. "A second tin can, Skipper."

Talara froze with indecision. The enemy was sending bigger ships through and much faster. Two destroyers had arrived barely five seconds apart. She had two targets now, not one, which halved her concentration of firepower. She wasn't sure which ship she should shoot first, but she knew she had to shoot one or the other quickly.

"Lock the closest destroyer." *Yang Chien* would automatically target the same vessel as *Kuroshima* on the data link. Hopefully, LeMieux would see their targeting sort and place his missile swarm on the second destroyer. Splitting the fire would give each Karsian a better chance of surviving the initial blows, but it was the best chance to kill both vessels while they still labored under sensor distortion. While few small warships could withstand the firepower of a massed data group, most could survive a single salvo from a pair of laser-armed destroyers.

Kurth interrupted her thoughts. "Third contact at the 'gate, Skipper. This one's a cruiser."

Oh shit.

Talara panicked. There were three enemy warships in her immediate vicinity now, all within beam range, and latest one was a cruiser. The Karsian commander was pressing through at a fantastically bold pace. She had to do something quickly, for the lead destroyer would soon emerge from sensor distortion and commence firing.

Her destroyer group's combined fire could seriously damage any of the three vessels, but the cruiser's powerful beams were the greatest danger to *Kuroshima*. They would tear her apart if she targeted the destroyers. The lead tin can was a Dusky-class destroyer, carrying three energy batteries. It had transitioned before the others. The second destroyer, a Yellowfin-class ship, could loft twelve missiles per salvo, but their effect would minimal as close as they were, well inside 1.5 light-seconds. While the cruiser had the most powerful weapons, it was the beam-armed Dusky that would be able to fire first.

She gritted her teeth and decided. "Target the Dusky and fire."

At least you decided, a part of her mind chided her as Yantali called out the lock-on and trigger relay.

Six lasers from *Kuroshima* and *Yang Chien* lanced across the intervening space in less than a second, smashing down the shields of the destroyer *Talthrung*. At such short range, 60 cm lasers were powerful weapons. The Dusky flashed as her shields collapsed and her hull ruptured in rips and tears.

Yantali yelled at her through her earphones. "*Hastings'* data group is launching, Skipper."

Talara leaned forward to ensure her helmsman understood her orders, forgetting that her commands were automatically relayed by the intercom in her helmet. "Get us away from that cruiser. All ahead flank!"

Behind them, LeMieux's ships launched their missile swarm at the cruiser. In addition to the thirty-two missiles lofted, LeMieux ordered *Oriskany* to flush her external racks, adding six more to the mix.

The destroyer *Morgahntah* exited sensor distortion at that moment and reacted instantly. Ignoring the pair of Rigelian destroyers that had just gutted her sister, *Morgahntah* fired point defenses at the swarm of thirty-eight missiles bearing down on the cruiser *K'Tahgturk*.

The cruiser, unable to fire due to the effects of sensor distortion, was helpless. Heavy jamming from *Morgahntah* and a hastily-launched decoy managed to lure away a few of the missiles, but twenty-two tracked the cruiser unabated. Morgahntah's point defense made a desperate effort to save her but only stopped a few more missiles.

One missile was a dud and missed. The remaining eighteen struck K'Tahgturk's shields in brilliant photoflashes of nuclear light. The cruiser's shields collapsed, and her hull ripped open, but she refused to die. Instead, *K'Tahgturk* exited sensor distortion and turned upon her tormentors.

"We're spiked!" Kurth yelled. "The cruiser has us locked!"

Talara's blood ran cold. Her orders to move *Kuroshima* away had put an additional half-light second between

Kuroshima and *K'Tahgturk*, but that added distance was negligible to a cruiser's weapons. The enemy's batteries were trained on *Kuroshima*.

"Activate jamming." Talara gripped her armrests desperately. "Launch chaff, all tubes. Max power to the shields. Helm, evasive maneuvering, now!"

Yantali responded. "Incoming! Point defenses firing."

Talara stared at the display as acceleration g-forces crushed her into her couch. *Kuroshima* accelerated, her drives rumbling through the deck plates. Three missiles from the cruiser were homing in. The added distance helped, but Talara knew it wasn't enough to spare *Kuroshima*. The enemy's beam weapons were also locking on and no ship moved as fast as light.

A particle beam and three heavy lasers stabbed out from the cruiser, seeking Kuroshima's heart, racing ahead of the missiles as though they were standing still. Bridge lights flickered as the beams hit Kuroshima's shields, dimming dramatically as the hellish energy smashed Kuroshima's shields like wet paper and stabbed through her armor.

Talara's terror and anger battled to control her. "Damage report, all stations." She felt her terror grow. *Her* ship had been hit.

"Shields down." Yantali's voice sounded oddly flat, considering the din raging around him and the fact they were all about to die. "Shield generators offline. We've sustained armor damage, some severe, but we still have airtight integrity. We'd better stop those missiles though, or we're going to have serious problems. They'll gut us without shields."

Talara felt a burning anger seethe through her heart, replacing the terror as it welled up from deep inside. *Dammit, this is my ship,* her mind screamed. *Nobody's going to kill my people, not without a fight.*

"Point defenses, you're weapons free."

She whirled toward the bridge monitors, desperately seeking some way to attack rather than simply defend her ship from missiles.

Point defense lasers fired as targeting AIs calculated trajectories of the incoming missiles. One missile exploded, cut in half. The second missile missed, taking a chaff bloom for its target. It passed too far away for its warhead to detect *Kuroshima* and detonated on the chaff bloom. The third missile struck home, however, detonating under Kuroshima's keel.

Talara's vision blurred. The bridge lights flickered and went out, replaced by dim red emergency lighting. Backup generators came online. Alarms wailed as air pressure on the bridge dropped, and she felt her vac-suit inflate. *Kuroshima* had taken internal damage and was leaking atmosphere through breaches in her hull.

Shaken, she stared for several seconds in confusion, surprised she was still alive, even as Yantali's voice spoke calmly in her headset. "Laser three offline. Hull breaches on decks two, four, and six."

"Long-range sensors also offline," Kurth added. "We've lost the data link, Skipper."

Talara regained control of her breathing as she became furious.

Damn them to hell, she thought, her anger rising. *This is my ship, not some target for them to shoot at.*

Anger made her fight for *her* ship; the ship where she'd learned to fix drive nodes and repair ship systems. The ship where she'd learned to baby power conduits and been made chief engineer on her skills and ability. The ship where she and Egon had last made love. Now the enemies who'd killed him were doing their best to destroy *Kuroshima.* The same bastards that had killed the skipper and the senior officers and forced her into a command she'd never wanted. Now they were trying to kill *Kuroshima* and her crew as well.

The way they killed Egon.

Her anger burst in an explosion of fury. She bared her teeth and shouted orders. "Damage control parties to the outer hull." Her anger became an uncontrollable force, a talisman insulating her against fear. "Helm, continue evasive maneuvering. Full power to weapons. As soon as capacitors reach base charge, we're coming about to attack."

Yantali paused, staring at her in awe. Her transformation startled him, but he answered with a touch of pride. "Aye, aye, Ma'am, full power to weapons."

Talara's fury rose. "Target all weapons on the cruiser. Kill that son of a bitch."

Yang Chien, cut out of the network by *Kuroshima's* loss of data link, fired independently, her lasers lashing the damaged destroyer *Talthrung* again. Smashed into a shattered hulk, *Talthrung* lost directional control as fires raced through her hull. She tumbled, out of control, as her stabilizer drives failed.

"Capacitors at 80 percent, Skipper." Yantali glanced at Talara. "I've pulled power from life support to charge the capacitors faster. Ready to fire in ten seconds, Skipper, but I can't give you shields. They're offline."

Talara's eyes were black ice. "Screw the shields. Bearing and mark on the cruiser."

"Zero-eight-two mark zero-niner-five, range 1.7 light-seconds."

Talara's eyes flashed. Her hair, plastered to her skull inside her helmet, was soaked with sweat. Perspiration trickled down over her lips. She tasted their brine with a bitterness of loss and hatred. "Helm, bring us about. Prepare to fire."

Kuroshima came about, making her battle run at the Karsian cruiser.

IKS *K'TAHGTURK*

Over-Commander Durok's mouth fell open in surprise as he realized he had wormholed into the teeth of a Rigelian blockade.

The preceding corvettes, *Tahk'pa* and *D'Bahtz*, had been vaporized before they could fire a shot in self-defense. Now his own cruiser was under fire from two destroyers at close range. He was pinned against the jump-gate terminus by eight Rigelian warships, not the single destroyer he had been chasing when he'd jumped into the system. *Talthrung*, one of his destroyers, was already dying, gutted as internal fires raced through her hull. Only his cruiser and the destroyer *Morgahntah* retained any ability to fight.

Durok's frigates, *Gurtagh* and *Zorth'pah* were still light-years away in Zion's Waste, still waiting to jump. The Rigelian destroyer he had been chasing had led him into an ambush in Centauri Seven; a system that was supposed to have no surviving Rigelian warships.

His sensor warrior's voice cut into his thoughts. "Incoming missiles, Yi'rhork! Thirty-two of them."

The nearest pair of RCN destroyers were running now, retreating through the enemy missile swarm, but one of them had been damaged by *K'Tahgturk's* weapons.

This is madness. Hogarh sent me to chase a single enemy destroyer, not conduct a jump-gate assault against a defending force.

His force had plenty of firepower for the first mission but was woefully inadequate for the latter. With three ships already destroyed, Durok realized he was outgunned.

"Activate jammers and take evasive action." He turned toward his communications officer. "Order *Morgahntah* to retreat into Zion's Waste."

His executive officer frowned. "Our orders instruct us not to retreat, Yi'rhork—"

"Do as I say, fool! Launch a drone through the jump-gate and warn our frigates in Zion's Waste to maintain their position. They are to delouse us as we return through the jump gate."

Durok was not prone to taking needless chances. When the fates turned, as they sometimes did, withdrawal to safer ground was more prudent rather than suffering needless losses.

"Enemy missiles closing."

"Activate point defenses."

K'Tahgturk's jammers successfully decoyed two of the missiles. Point defenses fired, and *Morgahntah* added her own in an attempt to stop the carnage targeted on Durok's ship. The combined fire was partially effective, stopping a third of the missile swarm, but *K'Tahgturk* wrenched when twenty-two missiles found her. Alarms howled as she was sliced opened by the missiles' laser warheads. Durok snarled as his vac-suit inflated with the loss of pressure. K'Tahgturk's bridge had been breached.

"Damage report, all decks."

"Data link is down, *Do'klar*." The damage control warrior's voice sounded dead as he read the monitors. "Engines one and two destroyed. Long range scanners are down. Particle weapons inoperable, port laser turret offline. The forward missile magazine has been vented to space, and the boat bay is destroyed."

"Weapons?"

"All missile tubes inoperative, Yi'rhork, as well as beams. We have two functional drive nodes still remaining."

"Point defenses?"

"Offline, but they have priority on repairs."

The Rigelian missiles had left his ship helpless. Durok pounded his fist against his armrest, but there was only silence without any air to carry the sound across the bridge. Too many good warriors had died trying to take out a single RCN destroyer. It was time to cut his losses and withdraw. He whirled toward his pilot. "Make directly for the jump-gate, maximum acceleration. Quickly, before the enemy launches more missiles."

K'Tahgturk came around in a steep rolling turn, streaming frozen atmosphere behind her in a comet-like trail as she tried to run for the jump-gate.

Durok permitted himself a small smile as he checked the range to the jump point. The Rigelians could still hit him with beam fire, but *K'Tahgturk* would jump before more missiles could be launched and reach him. His ship would survive.

"Enemy destroyer closing at high acceleration!"

The call brought Durok upright and his is eyes snapped to tactical. The enemy destroyer they'd damaged had come about and was charging. At the current rate of closure it would reach point-blank range just as *K'Tahgturk* reached the jump gate. With only two working drive nodes, *K'Tahgturk* could not outrun it.

"Transition in five *ongs*." As his pilot transmitted the information, Durok fought an impulse to turn and fight, knowing the speed and vector of the Rigelian ship indicated a potential ramming threat. Durok had never suspected a Rigelian would be so bold. Destroyers did not attack cruisers, not alone. Under other circumstances he would have gutted the destroyer with energy fire, but his beam weapons were offline. He was helpless to do anything but watch.

"They are firing beams."

"Evasive action."

Durok's words died as lasers punched through his ship. *K'Tahgturk* flared, her hull plates buckling as frame seams ruptured. A single drive node remained online, furiously burning to get the cruiser to the jump point. Durok glanced at his battle monitors and a slight grin creased his face.

The range to the jump point dropped to almost zero.

K'Tahgturk would make it.

"Crew, prepare for jump."

Durok gasped as energy beams from the charging destroyer struck his ship.

Lasers chewed through the bridge like invisible knives, cleaving his skull in half. The beams punched through several decks into K'Tahgturk's fusion reactor. *K'Tahgturk* died in an explosion of superheated gas just as she reached the jump-gate, a cloud of ionized plasma and molten metal blasting in all directions.

Kuroshima plowed through the fireball and continued into the wormhole.

A moment later she jumped.

SUCKER PUNCH

RNSS *STALKER*
ZION'S WASTE NEXUS

Villafuerte stared at the scarlet icons of the hostile ships holding station off Stalker's bow in the display. Both were Karsian Grayling-class frigates holding station, waiting to transition into Centauri Seven.

Stalker had approached from astern without being detected. Villafuerte wondered what the frigates were doing. They were obviously waiting to enter Centauri but were holding a half light-second from the stargate.

The frigates' drive baffles blinded them to Stalker's approach. Sensor AIs had analyzed the drive fingerprint of one of the frigates, identifying her as *Zorth'pah*. Naval intelligence routinely gathered intel on the drive signatures of ships encountered in space and that data was kept current in the Fleet database. Every ship had a unique drive signature which identified it by class and associated emissions. Some drive signatures were detailed enough that the ships could be identified by name.

He glanced at Banich. "Any change?"

She shook her head. "No, Sir, they're still holding short of the stargate. No indications of scans aft."

"Bearing?"

"Master Zero-One bears two-six-one mark zero-niner-zero, Sir."

"Mark." Villafuerte turned toward his Combat Systems Officer.

"Mark, aye." Lieutenant George Hook typed on his

board. "Bearing to Master Zero-One is two-six-one, mark zero-niner-zero, labeled as *Zorth'pah*, Skipper."

"Range . . . mark."

Hook glanced at his display. "Fifty thousand klicks."

Villafuerte nodded. *Stalker* was in perfect firing position directly astern of *Zorth'pah*, hidden by her drive baffles. The enemy ship would be unable to react before Stalker's torpedoes struck home.

Villafuerte nodded. "Firing point procedures on Master Zero-One."

Hook replied calmly. "Fire Control, aye, firing point procedures on Master Zero-One. Target steady at two-six-one, zero angle, range fifty thousand kilometers."

"Very well. Vent forward tubes one through four."

Four pressure panels on Stalker's bow recessed into her hull as internal atmosphere was pumped out of the launch tubes behind them. The process took less than six seconds.

Torpedoes were seeking-weapons, which, while slower than conventional missiles, carried more powerful anti-matter warheads. Unlike beam weapons, torpedoes didn't lose damage potential with range. Their accuracy tended to drop off at extended ranges, but that was precisely why they were used by stealthships, which could get close enough to prevent such problems. Once launched, the torpedoes would home on their own.

A spread of four would work. Villafuerte would maneuver *Stalker* to bring her stern tubes to bear on the second— as yet unidentified—frigate.

Villafuerte listened as his orders were echoed back to him. He'd practiced this litany hundreds of times in training, but this time it was real. He'd never fired a real weapon at a living foe before. Villafuerte had no personal hatred of Karsians. Likely, the poor fools on the frigates were just doing their jobs, just as he and his crew were doing theirs. Unfortunately, concern for the enemy had little place in combat during a war. He had his duty, just as they had theirs, and while he might loath attacking from ambush, stealthships were bushwhackers by design. War was kill or be killed.

Villafuerte took one last look at the tactical display and paused, realizing these were his last moments as an innocent. Whatever happened, from here on he'd have blood on his hands. It was a sobering thought, but there was no time to waste on it, and even less for pity. He'd made the decision to kill when he joined the Navy. There was a war on, and he had a job to do.

Villafuerte looked at Hook. "Match bearings and shoot, tubes one through four on Master Zero-One."

"Match bearings and shoot tubes one through four on Master Zero-One, aye." Hook hit some switches. "EM surge. Torpedoes away, Sir."

Four torpedoes belched from tubes in Stalker's bow. The tubes' electro-magnetic coilguns adding a stream of superheated particles to each weapon during launch. The torpedoes boosted at speeds slower than conventional missiles. Armed by the inertia of acceleration, their small Laroussi drive fields energized. The torpedoes accelerated, converging on a point in space computed as ground zero for targeted frigate.

"Conn, Sensors," Banich said, reporting the torpedo status formally over the intercom. "Torpedoes from tubes one through four running hot, straight and normal, Sir."

The passive sensors on the second frigate were not masked by the Zorth'pah's baffles, however. The appearance of torpedo drives drew the immediate attention of its crew. Reaction was near-instantaneous, testifying to the skill of the enemy crew. Only two light-seconds away, it fired reaction thrusters and lurched away vertically, accelerating as its captain struggled to localize the launch point of the torpedoes while simultaneously warning its sister of the danger behind her.

Villafuerte's reaction was as quick. "Helm, ahead flank."

The second frigate would be able to extrapolate Stalker's position within seconds if she remained in position, simply by backtracking the torpedoes' ion trails to their point of origin. Unlike *Stalker*, torpedoes weren't full-up stealth designs, and their drives were detectable at close range. Once weapons were launched, speed and maneuverability became more important than stealth, since stealthships had no shields.

Stalker accelerated, nosing down and dropping out of the plane of attack. *Zorth'pah*, too, began to accelerate, her drives coming to life as her sister frigate warned her of torpedoes astern, but it was too late. The first torpedo missed, passing the frigate to detonate 0.4 light-seconds away. The remaining trio homed on *Zorth'pah* and det-onated on her shields. Expanding spheres of antimatter cancellation bracketed the frigate, shattering her spine and her reactors. *Zorth'pah*, less armored than a heavier ship of war, exploded.

Stalker was moving, increasing speed as she tried to put distance between herself and the second frigate, but she couldn't outrun the waves of active lidar the frigate focused on her hull. It quickly detected Stalker's move-ment despite her Laroussi field and came about to pursue. Unlimbering weapons, it fired a drive-seeking missile at the newly-detected contact.

The DSM accelerated, homing on *Stalker*. In response, Villafuerte turned *Stalker* to point her baffles at the mis-sile, putting it astern. Control room computers continued to display the DSM blip, estimating range based on last known speed and closure.

"Launch chaff masker and deploy the decoy." Villafuerte hoped he sounded less scared than he felt. A small drone shot from Stalker's stern ejector and exploded in a cloud of reflective metal dust, even as another tor-pedo—this one a decoy—shot from the number five tube in Stalker's bow. It carried sophisticated equipment that mimicked Stalker's drive signature, but at a stronger amplitude. The decoy also had no Laroussi field, making it more attractive to the enemy than *Stalker* herself.

"Helm, slow to one-third." Villafuerte wiped his brow. He knew he needed to reduce the ship's drive signature quickly and allow *Stalker* to use her Laroussi field to disappear. "Close outer doors. Helm, make our course one-eight-two, mark one-five-five. All hands rig for bombardment."

Villafuerte's orders were terse, but there were no second chances in this game. *Stalker* was no match for a frigate if it had her localized. She had neither shields nor armor, only her cloaking field. Hopefully, the DSM would pursue the decoy while *Stalker* moved quietly away on a perpendicular heading. If the tactic failed, the DSM would home on *Stalker* and that would be the end of her. Even if *Stalker* somehow managed to survive the missile's impact, the explosion would pinpoint her exact location to the frigate's gunners, who would promptly kill her with energy fire.

Stalker turned ninety degrees in two planes of direction and slowed, her drives running smoothly. The DSM continued to close.

Banich glanced up. "Estimated impact in six seconds, Sir." It was the first time Villafuerte had ever seen her scared. The rowdy Banich had a reputation as a tough girl, one known to challenge Marines to fistfights in bars across the spiral arm. The Banich before him looked pale and scared. "Impact in four . . . three . . . two . . . one . . ."

Banich closed her eyes, anticipating an explosion. Slowly, she opened them again, staring at her sensors and then sighed. "Negative Doppler shift on the missile, Sir. Looks like it took the decoy. Yes, it just merged with the decoy and killed it. But I have positive Doppler shift on the frigate, Sir. She's turning to run us down, bearing zero-nine-two, mark zero-eight-four."

Villafuerte nodded. "All drives idle."

"All drives idle, aye."

Stealth was all-important again. Villafuerte had to minimize Stalker's signature as much as possible to hide. With luck, the Laroussi field would make her vanish into the ambient background of space as he brought the stern tubes to bear on the frigate.

Banich jerked upright and her eyes went wide with shock. "New contact, Sir! Bearing two-eight-seven mark zero-seven-eight. It just emerged from the stargate, and it's coming toward us at high acceleration."

"What?" Villafuerte felt his heart skip. "Is it Karsian? ID that bogey. How could they have gotten word through the stargate so fast?"

"I've no idea, Sir, but the frigate's changing course now, turning toward the bogey."

"Are they joining up?"

"No, Sir." Banich's brow furrowed. "The new contact shows a friendly drive source, Skipper. Yes! There's her IFF beacon. She's Rigelian, Sir, a destroyer. The AI identifies her as *Kuroshima*."

"What?" Villafuerte leaned forward. "You said it came *out* of Centauri Seven?"

"Yes, Sir. She's clearing distortion and firing on the frigate."

Villafuerte stared at the tactical display. The picture was built on a layered fusion of passive sensor inputs. It showed a Rigelian destroyer rushing toward the enemy frigate from the stargate. The Karsian was turning, valiantly trying to meet the destroyer's charge like a medieval knight accepting challenge.

Villafuerte sat. "Helm, load flashers aft and bring the stern tubes to bear. Firing point procedures on Master Zero-Two. Sensors, ping for range. CSO, snapshots on my order."

Energy torpedoes weren't physical objects like conventional torpedoes. They were balls of matter and antimatter contained in tightly focused spheres of magnetic plasma launched at lightspeed. They weren't seeking weapons and were completely ballistic. They stood little chance of hitting a maneuvering target fired as snapshots, but they might be enough to distract the Karsian long enough for *Kuroshima* to get an upper hand.

"Stern tubes vented, Sir. Field troughs open. Energy torpedo containment fields stable."

"Very well. Match bearings and shoot tubes seven through ten on Master Zero-Two."

"Match bearings and shoot tubes seven through ten on Master Zero-Two, aye. EM surge. Torpedoes away."

Banich looked up. "Torpedoes away, running straight and normal, Sir."

The Karsian frigate, zigzagging in three dimensions as it attempted to lock weapons on *Kuroshima*, detected the flash of energy torpedoes the instant they left their tubes at c-fractional speeds. The energy balls missed the frigate by thirty thousand kilometers. In response, the frigate turned back toward *Stalker*, desperately searching the weapons' back-trails to locate their hidden opponent.

The turn was a tactical mistake. At that instant, *Kuroshima* cleared sensor distortion and opened fire. Twin 60 cm lasers caught the frigate as it turned, inadvertently exposing its baffles to *Kuroshima*. A new sun flared with dazzling brilliance as *Gurtagh* died in a brilliant nova.

Banich spoke before the crew could cheer the kill. "Second contact at the gate, Skipper."

"ID?"

"*Yang Chien*, Sir. Another friendly tin can."

Shouts of jubilation erupted in Stalker's control room as her crew realized there were surviving RCN warships in Centauri Seven.

"Go idle on all drives and hail *Kuroshima*." Villafuerte ran a hand through his hair and attempted to suppress a face-splitting grin. "Secure from EMCON. Put me through to her captain."

The comm officer activated transmitters and encryption gear and conversed for several moments. He looked surprised as he turned toward Villafuerte. "Kuroshima's skipper's on Channel Two, Sir. I've relayed access to your viewer."

Villafuerte activated the armrest viewer and stared at the screen. It flared to life, and he blinked in surprise.

A woman in a Fleet vac-suit returned his gaze. She had raven hair, pulled back inside her helmet. Black bangs were plastered to her forehead, damp with sweat. She had a pale complexion and black, almond-shaped eyes that glittered like ice. Her face was a study of angles, particularly along the cheekbones. She looked exhausted.

It wasn't Commander Jack O'Brady, whom Villafuerte knew to be skipper of *Kuroshima*; the man he'd expected to converse with. This woman had the rank of a lieutenant on her vac-suit.

"I'd like to speak to your CO, Lieutenant." Villafuerte was peeved that his comm officer hadn't relayed his request to speak to Kuroshima's skipper. Apparently he had connected him to an underling on the bridge. The woman's eyes held his firmly behind dark lashes. Villafuerte thought she had a Semitic or Mediterranean look to her.

She lifted an eyebrow, her voice a soft soprano as she spoke. "Pardon me, but who are you, Sir?"

"Dan Villafuerte, CO of *Stalker*, Lieutenant. To whom am I speaking?"

"Lieutenant Talara Kibbleman, Sir. Skipper of *Kuroshima*."

Villafuerte blinked, surprised. "Where's Commander O'Brady? I thought he commanded *Kuroshima*."

Her eyes softened. "I'm afraid he's dead, Sir. I'm currently acting captain. It's a long story."

Villafuerte felt stunned. If Kibbleman was commanding officer, then Kuroshima's crew must consist of kids, all lieutenants and below. It obviously *was* a long story. He felt a distinct pang of loss for Jack O'Brady, whom he'd known well. He would have to hear that sad tale later, but it didn't make him less glad to see her.

"I see. Let me extend a hearty Bravo Zulu, Lieutenant. That was a hell of an entrance. I've never seen a tin can tear through a stargate, pull off an attack, and kill a frigate that fast. Well done. We're lucky you arrived when you did, as you may have saved our bacon. It's good to see someone's still alive in Centauri."

Kibbleman looked away for a moment and Villafuerte thought he saw tears at the edges of her eyes. After a moment, she sniffed and turned back to the pickup and smiled. Villafuerte was startled at how the smile changed her appearance. Her eyes sparkled as her face came to life. "Thank you, Sir. We feel lucky to be here too."

CHAPTER 21

RNSS *AGNI,*
CENTAURI SEVEN

Egon crushed her with a fierceness that might have broken ribs had she not been hugging him as hard. He reveled in her touch, her smell, the very essence of her as tears glistened in his eyes.

Talara's head barely reached his nose. At just over 177 centimeters she was tall for a woman but shorter than his own 190 centimeters. That didn't stop him from drinking in everything about her. Egon was overwhelmed with her presence, so real and *here* after the long darkness of fear and desperation.

A plethora of scents registered: perfume, the smell of her uniform, a faint hint of soap, and something else, something less defined, a musk that pulled at his soul. It screamed her uniqueness to the universe. Like a pheromone, it called him with an attraction words couldn't match.

A part of his mind tried to sort the scents out. There was a faint odor of *sake*, the rice wine they'd celebrated with during a teary-eyed reunion with Yamashita in his quarters. The release of emotion and the alcohol had been too much, and they'd found themselves emotionally drained. Egon was exhausted from hours of work and worry, Talara from the *sake* because she seldom drank alcohol. The long nightmare was finally over, and it seemed too good to be true. The relief, physical exhaustion, and *sake* had made them giddy.

"God." Egon's hands traced her shoulder blades beneath the back of her uniform. "I thought I'd lost you, Tilly."

She brushed her fingers across his clean-shaven cheeks, circling his jaw with a gentle caress. Talara's fingers were long, but her manicured nails short. She rarely painted them, preferring a natural blush. Delicate yet strong, empowered by constant workouts in Kuroshima's gym, the touch communicated love in ways beyond words.

One of the things Egon loved most was her ability to be beautiful in a natural way, with little augmentation or makeup. Talara had a healthiness about her. She wasn't the classic beauty in war paint some men preferred, but her naturalness had been the first thing that had attracted him. He felt as helpless against its allure as a comet orbiting the Schwarzschild limit of a black hole.

"I can't believe you're alive," she whispered softly, overcome with emotion, her eyes scrunched in curves. "After the attack, I thought I'd never . . ."

"I know." He pulled her face into his shoulder and kissed her forehead. "Me either."

They'd retired to Storm's cabin on *Agni* after the impromptu reunion in Yamashita's quarters. Talara had sent a message from Yamashita's terminal to Yantali informing him she would be "detained" aboard the battleship for an indefinite period of time. If her crew had known the kind of *detention* involved, they'd have been deeply amused.

With the arrival of *Agni* in Zion's Waste Yamashita had contacted *Kuroshima* and ordered Talara to report aboard in person. She'd hurried over by shuttle, pausing only to shower and don a fresh uniform. It wasn't every day a task unit commander summoned a lieutenant to his flagship, and skipper or not, she'd had no intention of being late or looking shoddy.

Yamashita had carefully *not* informed her of the purpose of his summons. Instead, he'd simply ordered her to report.

She'd arrived to find a Marine sentry waiting in the boat bay, who'd promptly saluted before escorting her to Yamashita's quarters. The summons had left her panicked and wondering what transgression she'd committed that had gotten her personally called on the carpet by CTU 17.2.1. At Yamashita's quarters, the sentry had saluted again and stepped away. She'd returned his salute and activated the chime, waiting with trepidation until Yamashita's "enter" had sounded over the intercom.

She had come to attention, entered, and halted before

his desk. She'd begun to recite the traditional reporting-in litany when a sudden gasp had stopped her mid-sentence. Egon had vaulted Yamashita's desk to get to her. Overwhelmed, the words had died in her throat as she and Egon locked eyes, an eerie moment of eternity as he'd rushed her. The realization he was alive had struck her like a lightning bolt, and she'd almost fainted as Egon had grabbed her in a fierce hug.

Yamashita hadn't told Egon why he'd been summoned, either. The surprise had caught him off-guard as well.

Bursting into tears of joy, Talara put her arms around Egon's neck as he struggled and failed to hold his own emotions in check. Yamashita had stood by, quietly grinning like a Cheshire cat, waving off her report-in litany with one hand, obviously pleased with his little "surprise."

Egon had smothered her with kisses. She'd hesitated a moment and responded in kind, and they'd wept in each other's arms for a while, letting hours of anguish, fear, and loss ebb away.

Yamashita had given them a few precious moments in private, turning away and busying himself with opening a *sake* bottle. When their blubbering had died down, Yamashita had given them a sly smile.

"There are few things to celebrate in a war." Yamashita had smiled at them. "This, however, is a moment I'll cherish the rest of my life. It will stay with me long after this conflict is over, and I'm certain it's forever etched into your minds, too. I'm honored to be here and share a small bit of it with you. You've both had more than your fair share of hell in the last few weeks, but that's over. For the sake of lovers everywhere, here's a toast to both of you."

They'd toasted and drank, cried and hugged some more, until Yamashita had found them hugging *him*. He'd noted with mock seriousness that task unit commanders shouldn't be seen being hugged by destroyer COs and staff TAC-Os. He'd been kidding, of course, but Egon had wisely taken it as their cue to leave. He'd snapped to attention and saluted. Yamashita had returned the salute with a grin, and they'd rushed to Egon's quarters.

"I've waited so long." Egon held her tightly, *needing* her embrace. "Without hope. I was dead inside . . . certain you were—"

"I know." Talara hugged him fiercely. "I died a hundred deaths thinking I'd lost you, too; that you were gone. I don't intend to lose you again. Let's get married; now, before the Navy pulls us apart again."

"*Married?*" Egon's eyes widened and he pushed her back gently. "I can't think of anything I want more, but . . . *now?* We're serving on different ships in case you haven't noticed. We're also in a war zone. It seems a little insane to get married now. We could both be dead tomorrow. Besides, how would we arrange the ceremony aboard ship? We're from different religions. I'm Christian and you're Jewish. What kind of ceremony is needed for something like *that?* What would your parents say about you marrying a gentile?"

"Cold feet already?" She smiled. "Now's exactly the time. If we die tomorrow, I want to die knowing I'm your wife. As for my religion and my parents' views, I really don't care. If that had ever been a factor, do you think I'd have dated you? Where there's a will, there's a way, and after what I've been through, I have a lot of will. Besides, my parents would want me happy more than anything. Wouldn't yours? This is what *I* want, sweetheart. My parents aren't the ones who want to marry you . . . assuming, of course, you want to marry *me*. You haven't changed your mind, have you?"

"No, it's just that I didn't expect—"

She kissed him to shut him up, her hands unbuttoning his tunic as she began working on her own. After a moment, she pulled away, her dark eyes glistening with seriousness. "We won't need a preacher or a rabbi, you know. This is a Navy ship. By law, the captain has the authority to marry people. Marriage in space is nondenominational, as stipulated by naval regulation."

"Are you sure?"

"Yes. I'm a skipper now. I've read the command regs thoroughly on that point."

Egon pulled her closer. "Yes . . . skipper of *Kuroshima* and already frocked to lieutenant commander. So much has happened so fast."

"Yes." She put her head on his chest. "We've a lot of catching up to do, but that can wait."

She unbound her raven hair, letting it fall across her shoulders. Straight and jet-black, it reached the center of her back. She brushed her bangs behind her ears and lifted her eyes to his. They were smoky under her dark lashes. She began to unbutton her blouse.

CHAPTER 21

"All right." Egon, defeated by her logic—and loving every moment of it—grinned at her. "Your family might have a few reservations, you know. Did you ever tell them about me?"

"No. Did you tell yours?" She kept working on her shirt fastenings. "No one cares, Egon. Why are you hung up on what our parents think?"

"Some people get hung up on those things. I love *you*, Talara. I don't care what your religion is. I just want to be sure you've considered all of the ramifications of marrying a fool like me."

"Oh, I've considered." She let her blouse fall and Egon's eyes widened. Talara wore no undergarments.

She giggled. "There was little time to dress properly before reporting. I thought I had to get here quickly."

Egon's eyes rose to hers. "How . . . convenient."

Mesmerized, he suddenly wanted her so bad that he could barely speak. Her dark eyes held his, like pools of black liquid.

"Uh . . ." Egon fought for self-control, but it was a losing battle. "Talara . . ."

"We're human, sweetheart." The rest of her uniform fell to the deck. "*That's* what matters. I want you . . . as my husband, my lover and my soul mate. And I want you right now."

Egon opened his mouth to speak and she covered it with her own.

Between kisses, Egon managed to get a few words out. "Hey, I think *I'm* the one who's supposed to propose."

"So old school." She wrapped her hands around the back of his head. "I almost lost you, Egon Storm. I'm not losing you again."

Talara seemed changed, somehow. She was a more *determined* woman than the girl he'd left in Centauri Seven. She'd grown with responsibility.

He gave her a wistful smile. "I don't know what you see in a big oaf like me."

She wrapped her arms around him. "Leave that to me. I was too dumb to realize what I had until I thought I'd lost you. By the way, you *did* propose some time ago, if you recall, and I said yes then. It's still yes, darling."

She turned, took his hand, and pulled him toward the bed and Egon smiled.

For all her shyness, Talara could be amazingly direct when she wanted to be.

RNSS *PAN-KU*
CENTAURI SEVEN

Vice Admiral Ivanov Montgomery leaned back in his chair and glanced at the faces of the task group commanders who had gathered in Pan-Ku's staff conference room, knowing that his next decisions would be critical for the war effort. With the arrival of two of Task Force Seventeen's task groups in Centauri Seven, he'd had to decide how to best deploy his task force to achieve the most effect.

With Centauri Seven effectively back in friendly hands, the Empire had only a few options left to them on this side of the Rim.

The Karsians could retreat back into the Empire, which would be the most preferrable course, but Montgomery doubted they would do that. They could advance from the Nangtashgu system into Zion's Waste and attack Centauri Seven again or jump from there into the Gallagher star system.

"The enemy returning to Centauri Seven at this point does little to advance their campaign," Yolowski said, pointing at the colored balls representing star systems that floated above the table, courtesy of the conference table's holographic projector. "They've pretty much left Centauri a shambles, though they know we have survivors here now. If they jump into Gallagher, however, they can dart across that system and make a direct jump into Yamato."

Rear Admiral Yu nodded. Her black eyes were intense. "Which would give them a straight shot at the Confederation Core Worlds. If they take Yamato, they'll also cut us off here in Centauri Seven."

"If they secure a foothold in Yamato, they'll cut off this whole sector of the Rim." Montgomery sighed, rubbing an index finger against his lower lip as he studied the stellar map. "They don't even have to capture Yamato, just take control of the stargates from there into Gallagher and Centauri Seven."

Yu sipped a cup of tea as she leaned forward, resting both elbows on the table. "Gallagher's a tough system to control, Sir. It lies in a nebula that limits long-range sensors severely. The Karsians could be there already, hiding in all of that dust and gas. If so, just locating them will be an issue."

"True." Montgomery leaned back again, noting that his chair had a slight squeak. "We can't effectively hold Zion's Waste without placing an entire fleet there. The Empire can always jump in there; there's nothing to protect in Zion, just empty space. It's a halfway point, a staging place for somewhere else. To get anything of value, they'll have to go somewhere else. As I see it, they have three options: Pan'vu, Centauri Seven, or Gallagher. It's a twenty-four light-year jump from Zion's Waste to Centauri Seven and a sixty light-year jump to Gallagher."

"And an eighty light-year jump from this system to Gallagher, Admiral." Yu pointed at the systems with a manicured finger.

Montgomery nodded. "How far from Yamato to Gallagher?"

"Seventy-four light-years, Sir."

Montgomery sighed. "Seventh Fleet was destroyed in Centauri Seven during the initial attack, so the Karsians might delay returning here. If they do return, it'll only be to have another staging place to jump into Yamato. I think it most likely they'll head for Gallagher and try to surprise us there."

Yolowski frowned. "Why?"

"There are gas giants in Gallagher and two habitable planets, Terry. They need the resources and a forward

CHAPTER 21

staging base. It'll also give them a back door into Yamato, which they'll believe we won't be expecting. They know we'll reinforce the stargate terminus from Centauri to Yamato, but probably not the one from Gallagher to Yamato, since we consider Gallagher a friendly system. From their point of view, Gallagher's ripe for plucking. They know we have ships here in Centauri Seven now, since LeMieux effectively fought off their mop-up force. If they get behind us into Gallagher, however, they'll cut us off here. I think they have to go for Gallagher."

Yu lifted a laser remote and indicated the balls of light over the table as she spoke. "Gallagher has three stargates, Sir. One leads to Zion's Waste. The other two go here to Centauri Seven and to Yamato. If they jump into Yamato, which is currently minimally protected at the Gallagher terminus, they can come up behind the defenses at the Centauri Seven stargate and destroy them. If they do, we're effectively cut off here in Centauri, as our only options out of here would be Zion's Waste, Gallagher, or Bantar. We'd have to reach Yamato from Gallagher to get behind them."

Montgomery winced as he sipped of coffee from a mug. "I really don't like the idea of them getting into Yamato at all. Once there they'll have a straight shot through New Seoul into the Core Worlds. Yamato's heavily populated, but Gallagher isn't, so any fight we have in Gallagher will minimize collateral damage. I think they'll go for Gallagher and try to end-run us. So, we need to be in Gallagher waiting for them when they try. With the diminished sensor coverage in that system, however, our work's going to be

309

cut out for us, and I want to keep our carriers safe. I'm going to divide the carriers into two divisions. The first will consist of *Drake*, *Midway*, and *Excalibur*. Those will make up the first division under Rear Admiral Al-Zahrani. Terry, you'll take command of the second division from *Yamamoto*. You'll have *Victorious* and *Reticulus* in your division. I'll lead the way into Gallagher aboard *Pan-Ku* along with Task Group 17.1. Yamashita will lead Task Group 17.2 from *Agni*. The carrier divisions will follow us in well back in trail.

"Get back to your ships and get your units ready. We'll depart orbit for Gallagher at 2100 hours. With any luck, we'll be in Gallagher long before the Karsians arrive. Once there, I'll reassess how to deploy our forces."

Yolowski crossed his arms. "You mean *if* they arrive, Sir. If they don't, we'll just be waiting there doing nothing. What if they jump into Zion's Waste and attack Centauri Seven again?"

Montgomery finished his coffee and put the mug on the table. "If they don't enter Gallagher, we'll wait there for Task Group 17.3 to join us from *Yamato*, then marshal for an offensive through Zion's Waste into Nangtashgu. If they move to Centauri again, we should have adequate warning that'll give us time to rush back here and drive them out. LeMieux's force will remain here to guard the Zion terminus. If the Karsians enter, he'll get word to us and make a fighting retreat, which should buy us time to return."

Yolowski's eyes narrowed. "What if they do both?"

CHAPTER 21

Montgomery grinned. "Then we'll be in for a hell of a fight. Get back to your ships and prepare to get underway for Gallagher. The transition sequence will be the two task groups followed by the carrier divisions. Questions?"

The staff shook their heads.

"Good." Montgomery stood. "Get to it."

CHAPTER 22

Captain Sally Dell groaned as she rolled over in her bunk and the desk pager buzzed again. Slapping a hand at the offending unit, she yawned and wiped sleep from her eyes. "Dell."

"Good morning, Captain," a cheerful voice said. She recognized it as that of her overly-enthusiastic executive officer, Commander Mike "Pappy" Schnell. "Hate to wake you, but we're picking up something you need to know about."

How does he sound so darn chipper in the middle of the dog watch?

"Copy, XO. I'll be right out."

Recluse was lead stealthship for Task Group 17.2. Along with Dan Villafuerte's *Stalker*, she had entered Gallagher with Task Force Seventeen, which had departed Centauri Seven and proceeded across the Gallagher system to await the arrival of the final part of the task force, Rear Admiral

McDougal's Task Group 17.3, which was due from the Yamato any day.

Vice Admiral Montgomery planned to assemble Task Force Seventeen in Gallagher and return to Zion's Waste and then raid the Imperial system of Nangtashgu. In preparation, he'd sent *Recluse* to monitor the Zion's Waste stargate. It would be a while before the task force was fully formed, and Montgomery didn't like surprises, so *Recluse* had deployed swarms of cloaked sensor remotes around the Zion terminus before heading in-system to rejoin the task force, which was clustered near the Yamato stargate. Along with *Kraken* and *Vampire* from Task Group 17.1, the stealthships would be Montgomery's recon into Zion's Waste before the task force wormholed. The remotes would provide early warning of any ships entering Gallagher from Zion's Waste.

Dell pulled on her jumpsuit and boots. Pausing to splash water on her face at the cabin's sink, she stared at herself in the mirror. Brown eyes red from a lack of sleep stared back at her. Her brown hair, cut short and parted on the left, was mussed and ruffled. She smiled wryly.

A captain's job is never done, she thought wryly.

Checking herself once more, she exited her cabin. The walk to the control room was short. She spotted Schnell as soon as she entered, conferring with a sensor technician, Petty Officer Mubashir Shirani. Schnell was difficult to miss. He stood 192 centimeters tall and had broad shoulders and a shaven head.

Petty Officer Kay Smith, Recluse's helmsman, was the first to see her enter. "Captain in the control room!"

Crewmen started to come to attention, even though such protocol was unnecessary aboard a stealthship. Dell waved a hand at them. "As you were."

Schnell turned around. His blue eyes were merry despite the concerned look on his rugged face. "Good morning, Captain."

"Morning." Dell wiped her eyes again. "What've we got, Pappy?"

He pointed at the sensor display. "Those remotes we left at the Zion terminus. They're detecting transitions . . . lots of them. Somebody's moving a fleet from Zion into Gallagher."

"Karsians?"

"Yep." Schnell turned back to the display. "They must've entered Zion's Waste from Nangtashgu and came in behind us."

Dell moved forward, studying the icons. "How many?"

"Thirty-two so far, Ma'am," Al-Zahrani answered for Schnell and turned to face her. "They're still coming through according to the remotes. We've detected at least two superdreadnoughts and two battleships, as well as four battlecruisers and four troop transports."

Dell grimaced. "That's more dreadnoughts than an Imperial attack unit normally contains. It's more like a full battle squadron."

Schnell gave her a knowing glance. "And they're inside Gallagher already, Captain. Due to distance, these sensor reports are already five minutes old."

"Prep a comm drone." Dell move to the command

couch in the center of the control room. "I have the conn, Pappy. Get the drone and a laser comm off to Task Force Seventeen ASAP with these readings. Montgomery needs to know about this."

RNSS *PAN-KU*
GALLAGHER SYSTEM

"According to Dell's report, *Recluse* detected over a hundred warships entering Gallagher from Zion terminus headed in-system toward us."

Montgomery stared at his staff intelligence officer with surprise in his blue eyes. "They're already in Gallagher?"

"Yes, Sir." Captain George Gray Hawk pointed at the icons hanging in the holographic display above Pan-ku's staff conference table. "Given the distance between *Recluse* and the Zion 'gate at the time of detection, the data was ten minutes old before the last Karsian transited. It took Dell's message three-and-a-half hours to reach us here at the Yamato stargate. Our own sensors would've picked them up by now if it weren't for the interference from the nebula. You can figure the Karsians are at least ten light-minutes in-system already."

Montgomery sipped coffee as his eyes wandered across the faces of the skippers gathered around the table. Rear Admiral Hong Na Yu, commander of Task Group 17.1, flew her flag from the battleship *Hachiman*. Beside her were her subordinate task unit commanders, Commodores Leroy Sykes and Wilma Coletti. Captain Saburo Yamashita commanded Task Unit 17.2.1 but he also currently commanded Task Group 17.2, since its regular CO, Rear Admiral Yolowski, now commanded Carrier Division Two. Rear Admiral Benjamin Al-Zahrani commanded the other carrier unit, CARDIV-1. Each rear admiral had three carriers under their command.

"So the question is: where are they headed?" Montgomery leaned back in his chair. "The inner system or one of the other stargates?"

Gallagher had a single F-9 class star with eight planets. The outermost, an icy rock called Niskus, orbited 262 light-minutes from the star, farther out than any of the system's stargates. Only the two innermost planets, Lugus and Boann, were habitable. They orbited at eight and ten light-minutes, well inside Gallagher's "Goldilocks" zone. The Zion's Waste stargate lay 104 light-minutes from the inner planets. The other two stargates, one leading to Centauri Seven and the other to Yamato, were 126 light-minutes and 142 light-minutes out respectively.

Task Force Seventeen's first two task groups were gathered at the Yamato stargate awaiting the arrival of Task Group 17.3, the final task group under Rear Admiral Seamus McDougal, who was due to arrive any day from Yamato. Montgomery's original plan had been to assemble Task Force Seventeen in Gallagher, cross the system, and wormhole back into Zion's Waste, then cross that system and conduct his raid on Nangtashgu. That plan was on hold now, having been overcome by recent events. The enemy had beaten Montgomery to the punch, jumping into Gallagher behind him before he had Task Force Seventeen fully assembled.

"It's difficult to say, Sir." Al-Zahrani pulled at his mustache as he examined the star map above the table. "They could go for the inner planets or head to either of the other stargates. They could also attack Centauri Seven again, or press ahead to assault the Yamato stargate."

Wilma Coletti pushed a strand of black hair back from her square face as her blue eyes studied the map. "The inner planets would provide some logical level of gain for them, Sir." She pointed at the two biggest planets in the system, the gas giants Arawn—which orbited at twenty-two light-minutes—and Macha, which orbited at thirty-eight light-minutes. "If they go for the inhabited inner planets, Lugus and Boann, they'll be able to take slaves, but I think the gas giants are what they're really after. Especially if the Empire needs resources."

"Maybe." Yolowski sighed. "Or maybe they don't want to leave Centauri Seven open at their backs. They'll want to secure their rear before pressing into Yamato. I know I wouldn't want any threats from Centauri Seven behind me if I was going into Yamato."

Commodore Sykes ran a hand through his hair. "I doubt they care about slaves, Sir. Slaves are only mouths to feed, and human mouths at that. They'll have to occupy Lugus and Boann, however, if they want processing centers for the materials they mine from the gas giants. That's what I'd do. Once I took the habitable planets, I'd own all the useable real estate in the system. Then I'd blockade Centauri Seven and Yamato until enough forces arrived to attack Yamato."

Yamashita glanced up from a data pad in his hand and squinted at the system display. "The remotes show drive data for at least six *Piktar*-class troop transports, Admiral. That means an invasion force. It's not enough troops to assault Yamato, but plenty enough for Gallagher's inner planets or Centauri Seven. I think they'll try to occupy the habitable planets in this system."

"I agree, Saburo." Montgomery nodded. "They've already wiped out BATRON-One in Centauri, and six transports isn't enough troops to take Yamato, even though Yamato leads straight to our Core Worlds. It's plenty enough troops to assault Gallagher's inner planets, though."

Yu glanced up from the far end of the table. "There are carriers in that invasion force, Admiral. At least nine of them, if these sensor reports are accurate. That's an *offensive* force, Sir. They plan to drop troops on something somewhere."

Montgomery studied the plot for a long moment. "It's possible they'll blockade the Yamato stargate here in Gallagher. Two battle squadrons isn't a big enough force to conduct an effective stargate assault on Yamato, but they could certainly blockade the terminus here and bottleneck friendly forces trying to come out of Yamato. Actually, I think you're all correct. They don't know we're here yet, but they will soon enough. We must assume they'll do all three things: blockade Yamato, invade the inner planets *and* try to secure Centauri Seven.

"So what *we* are going to do is split Task Force Seventeen and take the battle to them. I'll take *Pan-ku* and head for the Zion stargate with Admiral Yu's task group and Ben's carrier division. We'll cut off any forces headed for the inner planets. Terry, take your carrier division with Saburo's task group and make for the Centauri Seven stargate, in case the enemy carrier force is headed there."

Sykes rubbed his chin in thought. "What if the whole kit-and-kaboodle goes straight for Yamato instead?"

Montgomery placed his elbows on the table and sighed. "In that case they'll be coming across the system straight at us. If they do, we'll flank them from both sides. McDougal will likely arrive while we're at it. If he does, his task group will serve as the anvil for our two hammers."

Sykes nodded. "Yes, Sir."

Gray Hawk waved a hand at the star map. "There are unique difficulties we must plan for here, people. Gallagher lies within the Zentari nebula. All of that gas and dust will play hell with our sensors, especially long-range sensors. We won't have the long distance coverage we're used to having. The enemy will use those clouds of gas and dust to hide in. We must stay alert and ready for possible ambush, because we'll be blind for long periods of time. That means scouting will be a necessity."

"Agreed." Montgomery drained his cup and stood. "You'll all need to send out scouts. I'll take Task Group 17.1

to the planets. Terry, take the rest toward Centauri Seven. Let's be about it folks. Get back to your ships. Godspeed to you all."

IKSS *MURGAHH*
GALLAGHER SYSTEM

Tork sat with T'Lihktu in Murgahh's briefing room staring at the faces on the bulkhead monitor. Over-Captain Kahlor commanded Imperial Battle Squadron Two-Two-Two-Two from the escort carrier *Boshar'tahk*. Kahlor commanded from the only carrier in that squadron. The rest of his heavy ships were all superdreadnoughts and battlecruisers.

Over-Captain Mahktoh commanded IBS Two-Two-Two-Three, which had three carrier divisions in addition to three imperial attack units. Each battle squadron represented a third of Imperial Attack Force Two-Two-Two. A third Karsian battle squadron still waited in Zion's Waste, guarding the route home.

Both battle squadrons had entered Gallagher without opposition. Mahktoh's force was especially powerful, containing three heavy carriers, three attack carriers, and three escort carriers in addition to three imperial attack units, with each IAU led by a superdreadnought.

"Execution will proceed as planned," Tork told them. "Kahlor will take his battle squadron to the inner planets and conduct planetary assaults. *Boshar'tahk* will use its fighter squadrons to cover the assault. Kahlor, you will instruct Imperial Attack Unit Two-Two-Two-Two-One to proceed in-system beyond the middle planet's orbit and search for enemy ships, then sweep the inner system. Special Attack Unit Two-Two-Two-Two-Two will take the transports to the planets for the drop, while *K'bishnahr* leads the third IAU as a cover force for the invasion.

"You, Mahktoh, will take your battle squadron to the Centauri Seven jump-gate and sweep from there to the Yamato jump-gate looking for enemies. The Rigelians likely have a fleet deployed somewhere in this nebula-cursed system. Your job will be to find it. If you do, transmit its location and attack immediately. If you find nothing, return to Centauri Seven and use your fighters to clean out any defenders remaining there. Are there any questions?"

"Yes, Korguhn." Mahktoh stared at him from the screen. "Where will *Murgahh* be while we are doing this?"

"I will have my flagship here at the jump-gate to coordinate each attack, *Yi'klar*. Positioning *Murgahh* here will provide centralized coordination and command and control for both efforts. It will also provide a communications link to our ships in Zion's Waste. Why?"

Mahktoh's eyes narrowed, but not enough to be openly insubordinate. "Our forces will be widely scattered here, Korguhn. The enemy could attack from any direction and with little warning. In the event of such an *unfortunate* situation, I wanted to know how far away our quick reaction force is."

"I will coordinate support for you, Yi'klar."

"Considerate, Korguhn, since *Murgahh* will be safe here at the Zion jump-gate."

Tork's eyes narrowed dangerously. "What are you insinuating, Mahktoh?"

"You have been nicknamed 'Blood and Honor' by many in the Fleet, Korguhn." Mahktoh stared without flinching. "Yet it seems it is your honor and *our* blood that are to be spent. We face the most risk, trying to locate an enemy fleet in a system obscured by a nebula, while you sit safely at the rear and 'coordinate.' Why do we need this cursed system anyway? It has only two gas giants, which are hardly worth the blood and treasure required to secure them, much less hold off enemy counterattacks."

"Are you calling me a coward?"

Mahktoh sobered instantly. "Of course not, Korguhn. I am simply saying I would be more comfortable if you were going in-system with us. An admiral should lead from the front, not the rear."

Tork grinned, exposing his canines. "I agree, Yi'klar. Putting me in the lead ship—however inspiring—would also be unwise, since the lead ship is the ship most likely to be destroyed. You must realize that the capture of Gallagher is but one of several operations I am coordinating simultaneously. In fact, Operation: Glah—while on the surface a straight-up invasion of Gallagher—is actually only a decoy operation. If we take this system and hold it, so much the better. But the true purpose of Glah is to draw the enemy's fleet into Gallagher and away from our main thrust at the Eusi Hegemony. An attack on Gulliver's Hold is underway as we speak, though it will not occur for some weeks yet. Your efforts here should draw the enemy into Gallagher and away from Gulliver as well. Hopefully that will include the enemy's carriers, which we have yet to locate. The more we fight the enemy in Gallagher the less we will fight him in Gulliver. As primary commander of the campaign, I cannot remain here and lead what is essentially a feint. That honor belongs to you and Yi'klar Kahlor. I am required elsewhere. You shall have the honor of destroying any enemies you find."

"Understood, Korguhn." Mahktoh bowed slightly in the display. "I meant no insult."

"Good." Tork looked at each commander and grinned. "You, Mahktoh, are to sweep the system from the Centauri jump gate to Yamato. Report, attack, and destroy any enemy ships you encounter, especially carriers, then return to the Centauri jump-gate and hold. You, Kahlor, will capture the inner planets. Are there any other questions?"

There were none.

"Very well. Execute your orders."

RNSS *WILLIAM F. CODY*
GALLAGHER SYSTEM

Lieutenant Commander Lacey Hagen, CO of the scout pinnace *Cody*, yawned as she stepped from the bridge to the galley to refill her coffee mug. She preferred hot cocoa, but no one had thought to stock any before *Cody* had launched from Hachiman's boat bay six hours earlier.

Task Group 17.1, led by Montgomery's super dreadnought *Pan-ku*, was headed in-system for Lugus and Boann. Montgomery had ordered scouts launched ahead of the task group to search for enemies due to sensor interference from the Zentari nebula. *Pan-ku* and *Hachiman* had launched three scouts each. Pan-ku's scouts had the starboard side of the task group's path. *Cody* was Hachiman's port-most scout moving on a 290-degree vector away from the group.

Filling her mug with coffee, she returned to the bridge and walked past her command couch to the starboard side of the bridge, where her executive officer, Lieutenant Tom Bolego, was conferring with Cody's sensor operator, a petty officer of Lakota descent named Vincent Brings Plenty. "What's up, gentlemen?"

Bolego looked at her over his shoulder. "We're trying to work the passive sensors through this nebula clutter, Skipper. Ambient conditions have reduced passive sensor range to about three light-minutes."

Hagen nodded, understanding. Three light-minutes was a tiny fraction of the coverage Cody's sensors would normally have had in open space. The gas, dust, and plasma of the nebula easily hid drive emissions from sensors. Active lidar would have given precise position data on contacts, of course, but lidar was easily reflected by the nebula's clouds, thereby reducing active sensor range to one light-minute. Unfortunately, using lidar would also reveal Cody's location. As a scout she was running EMCON, searching on passive sensors only. Her mission was to locate the Karsian invasion force and report its location to Task Group 17.1. It would be best if *Cody* remained undetected while doing so.

Brings Plenty's cherry-dark eyes narrowed, and he bent forward to study his displays. Brings Plenty had dark hair and angular cheekbones. Hagen noticed his sudden startled reaction. "What are you seeing, Vincent?"

Formalities were notoriously lax aboard scoutships.

"Flickering contacts, Ma'am." Brings Plenty tapped a copper-toned finger against the display. "The nebula's playing hell with our long-range sensors. Contacts are flickering in and out. I'm getting a drive source along a three-zero-five bearing, Ma'am. Relative elevation appears to be zero, but I'm not sure how far away it is. I've got directional bearings only. The contact keeps fading in and out because of the dust clouds and gas."

"Let's see if we can improve the signal strength." Hagen turned toward Monica Fraser, *Cody*'s helmsman. "Petty Officer Fraser, bring us starboard to three-zero-five mark zero-nine-zero, maintain present acceleration."

Fraser repeated the order and brought *Cody* to the new heading.

Oddly enough, it worked.

"Contact." Brings Plenty pointed to a spectral waterfall display on his workstation. "There it is, Skipper, a definite drive line. The AI's analyzing now . . . definitely a Karsian source."

Hagen leaned forward, waiting expectantly as the AI finished its analysis.

Brings Plenty whistled. "The fingerprint matches for a K'leeshar-class escort carrier, Skipper. I'm getting others too . . . there's a super dreadnought, a battleship and several transports."

"Looks like we've found the invasion force." Hagen turned and stepped to her command couch. She could reach *Pan-Ku* in minutes using a laser whisker transmission but doing so risked revealing Cody's position, and the nebula's dust might block the laser comm. "Do you have a base heading for the hostiles, Vincent?"

"Aye, Ma'am. One-one-five mark zero-niner-zero. They're headed for the inner system."

"Well, let's not close on them too fast. We need to stay out of their sensor range. Monica, bring us starboard one-two-five mark zero-niner-one."

"One-one-five mark zero-niner-one, aye, Ma'am."

Hagen nodded. "We'll try to hide in this dust and monitor them. Tom, get a comm drone off to *Pan-Ku* ASAP. Inform Admiral Montgomery that we've found the invasion fleet."

Carrier Division One's fighter squadrons were dispersed among three carriers: *Drake*, *Midway*, and *Excalibur*. The largest, *Drake*, was a heavy carrier with four fighter squadrons aboard. *Midway*, an attack carrier, had three. *Excalibur*, an escort carrier, had only one.

CHAPTER 22

On receiving Cody's report of the invasion force, Montgomery ordered CARDIV-1 to attack. Al-Zahrani responded promptly, launching four fighter squadrons from *Drake* and three more from *Midway*. Each squadron had twelve fighters.

One-by-one, eighty-four fighters launched. There were no aborts. The fighters joined formation and accelerated toward the hostile force, accelerating to a velocity of sixty-nine thousand kilometers per second.

Excalibur held her single fighter squadron in reserve. They would provide protective CAP for CARDIV-1.

Lieutenant Commander Ned Keller clicked the transmit button on the throttle of his FSF-138 Deathcat and radioed his wingmen. "*Talon One*, contact bogey, three-one-eight mark zero-eight-niner, thirty-five light-seconds. Heavy warship."

His wingman, Lieutenant Cheri Aguirre, replied instantly on the squadron fight frequency. "*Two same.*"

The twelve Deathcats of VF-914 were in wall formation, leading Drake's strike wing to attack the escort carrier that Cody had located. In the sweep role, *Talon's* twelve Deathcats were in front of the forty-eight Starhawk strike fighters of VA-221 and VA-638, with another squadron of twelve Deathcats from VF-666 flying close escort. A second wave of twelve Deathcats and two squadrons of Starhawks from Midway's strike group were three minutes behind them.

The other element leader in Keller's division was *Talon Three*, piloted by Lieutenant Dylan Evans, who added additional information. "Talon Three, *contact additional group three-two-two mark zero-eight-eight, twenty-eight light-seconds, small contacts, capping.*"

"*Talon One,* same." The heavy contact was the Karsian carrier. Keller directed his fighter's lidar into the smaller group of contacts. "*Talon One,* hostile, fighters, three contacts. They print as Double Aughts."

His targeting AI had identified the small group as three light fighters, no doubt one of the carrier's defensive combat attack patrols. "Double Aught" referred to the Karsian Type-00 light fighter, a craft of fifty tons that carried two short-range drive-seeking missiles and a pair of lasers. They were no match for Deathcats, which carried six long-range MIM-140 *Impaler* missiles each.

Impalers were the newest anti-fighter missile in the RCN fleet. With a maximum effective range of six light-seconds they were the first missiles in the RCN inventory that were multi-dimensional, being able to transit momentarily into the lowest band of hyperspace. This allowed them to "jump" through n-space, vanishing from their launch point to reappear near their target, giving enemy fighters no way to counter with jamming, decoys, or maneuvers.

Already the enemy carrier was committing its CAPs, having detected the swarm of RCN fighters bearing down on them. Finding the carrier had been difficult due to the intense gas and dust of the nebula. Keller adjusted his scanner sweep and detected another group of three small contacts. "*Talon*

CHAPTER 22

One, hits, additional group, three-two-six mark zero-niner-zero, thirty-one light-seconds, fighters, hot aspect."

Cody had reported the target was a Karsian K'Leeshar-class escort carrier. Such a vessel carried a single fighter squadron, and in this case that squadron was composed of Type-00 fighters. Karsian squadrons typically contained nine fighters. With six deployed fighters in defensive CAPs, that meant three remained aboard the carrier, unless they were hidden in the clouds of dust and gas somewhere.

"*Talon One* targeted port group. *Talon Six-*One target starboard group. *Talon Two-One*, hold shots for backup."

"*Talon Six-One.*"

"*Talon Two-One*, wilco."

"We'll shoot beak-to-beak going in." Keller adjusted his lidar to track mode. "Each shooter division will double-tap each target."

"*Six-One.*"

Six Type-00 fighters against twelve Deathcats was hardly fair, but war wasn't about being fair. It was about survival and winning. At the current rate of closure— nearly 40 percent *cee*—the targets would be in Impaler range in just over two minutes.

"*Talon Six-One sorted, starboard group.*"

"We'll have to slow to engage after the face-shots, folks. After you pickle, dump vee and slow to dogfight speed, then reengage whatever survives."

Speed was life in fighter combat, and slowing drastically to engage enemy fighters was risky, though better than letting enemy Type-00's reach the more vulnerable

329

Starhawks, especially if there were no other enemy fighters in the area. Besides, with only six targets, VF-914 had missiles to spare.

Keller locked the center bandit in the portside group. A flashing cue on his HUD told him the target was in missile range. He launched an *Impaler* with a press of his thumb.

"*Talon One*, Fox Three."

Twelve Impalers from *Talon* squadron launched at six light-second's range. From each flight division two missiles targeted outside bandits and four targeted the center bandit in each group. The *Impalers* jumped into hyperspace three seconds after launch, with positional data calculated between the Deathcats' fire control lidar and the missiles' own AIs. They reappeared in n-space less than a half light-second from their targets. Six Karsian fighters vanished in near simultaneous explosions as the missiles struck home.

In the end, VF-914 didn't have to slow at all, as there were no survivors left to engage. Instead, they pitched up and over to stop closure with the carrier, remaining outside the range of the carrier's point defenses even as their onboard electronic pods began jamming for the Starhawks behind them.

In desperation, Over-Captain Kahlor turned *Boshar'tahk* a hundred and eighty degrees to bring his starboard point defenses to bear and ordered the remaining three Type-00 fighters on ready alert to launch. Other than Boshar'tahk's point defense, there was nothing remaining between the carrier and the incoming attack. Twenty-four Confederation Starhawks launched pairs of anti-ship missiles before breaking away to stay out of Boshar'tahk's point defense range.

Heavy electronic jamming and good shooting by the carrier's point defense teams stopped a third of the forty-eight missile swarm launched by Drake's strike wing, but thirty-two got through.

Their subsequent detonations downed Boshar'tahk's shields. Lasers from ASM warheads stabbed through the carrier's armor into her bowels, knocking her data link offline, destroying six critical drive nodes and half of her hangar bays. Amazingly, the three Type-00 fighters still in the hangar bay survived unscathed, but massive damage was done to the carrier. Fires broke out, snuffed out instantly by the vacuum of space as atmosphere was sucked out through the myriad of holes in her hull. Badly damaged and unable to launch her fighters, Boshar'tahk ran for the protection of the Karsian cover force two light-minutes away as Drake's fighter squadrons pulled off target to return home.

Three minutes later, Midway's fighter wing caught up to Boshar'tahk. Forty-eight more ASMs were launched by two Starhawk squadrons. This time carrier point defenses stopped only eight missiles. Forty struck home, the seventh penetrating her magazine.

Boshar'tahk died in a massive explosion, taking her crew of nine hundred with her.

SUCKER PUNCH

RNSS *VAMPIRE*
GALLAGHER SYSTEM

"Midway's fighters took out the carrier, Captain."
Lieutenant Commander Sharon Willers brushed a strand of
red hair from her face as she turned her green eyes toward
Vampire's CO, Commander Jordan Quaid. "The invasion
force has no remaining fighter cover."

Vampire was one of two stealthships assigned to Task
Group 17.1. She'd been sent to assist *Recluse* with moni-
toring the Zion's Waste terminus before being ordered to
move in-system to provide reconnaissance on the enemy
invasion fleet. *Vampire* was coasting ballistically, hidden by
her cloaking Laroussi Field, her passive sensor array towed
behind her cloak bubble, observing the enemy force as it
approached the planet Boann. The planet's single moon,
Cork, orbited the planet at a range of one light-second.
Vampire was drifting just above the moon's Mercator line.

An imperial attack unit of sixteen warships had broken
away to sweep the inner system looking for threats. The
remaining imperial attack unit had continued toward the
planet. Led by a super dreadnought, the second force also
contained sixteen vessels, but six of them were Piktar-
class troop transports. The enemy intended to land troops
on Boann.

"We can't let the Karsians deploy troops unopposed."
Quaid made the statement in a flat voice as he observed the
tactical monitors. "We have to interfere."

Willers' eyes widened. "They've no idea we're here,

Sir. We might be able to take on a couple of destroyers in a fight, but not cruisers and dreadnoughts, not alone. We can kill any of those ships with a good torpedo spread, even the superdreadnought, but as soon as we do the others will be all over us. We also have strict orders to remain EMCON and report the enemy's position, not engage."

"I know that, XO." Quaid turned away and flopped into his control room command couch. "And that would indeed be the *smart* thing to do, hide and observe. But it's also the wrong thing to do. The attack unit that just went past us contains six troop transports. They intend to land those troops on the planet. The civilian population on Boann is helpless. We can't allow that to happen, orders or no orders. We may not be able to stop this many warships, but we can damn well stop the transports. I intend to do just that before they start launching shuttles toward the planet."

Quaid turned to his Combat Systems Officer, Lieutenant Rodney Rosachi, who sat at the fire control station. "Rodney, put Mark 21s in all forward tubes. Put Mark 18s in the stern tubes. Plan an initial spread for two torpedoes per transport. Right now plan to fire the fore tubes, then swing around and fire the stern tubes in succession."

Willers blinked rapidly. Her expression was worried. "You know what'll happen if we launch torpedoes, Captain. Those warships will be on us like flies on honey. They have plenty of escorts. If they can't find us quickly, they'll call in proximity fire from the dreadnoughts. This is suicide, Sir."

"Yes, it is." Quaid nodded and faced her. "I'd much prefer to sit here, hide and watch, XO. But I can't do that in good conscience while Imperial troops attack civilians and do nothing, orders or no orders. We've a moral obligation to interfere, no matter the cost. We're going to attack. If Montgomery doesn't like that, he can court-martial me later."

Willers voice dropped low. "You mean if there is a later."

Quaid stared at her for a moment, then smiled. "You knew the job was dangerous when you took it, Sharon. Sometimes moral duty exceeds orders. Rig for battle stations, torpedo. Mr. Rosachi, work up attack solutions on all the transports."

"Aye, Sir."

Vampire made her approach from directly behind the transport formation, hiding in its drive baffles. Minutes later Quaid looked at Rosachi. "Fire control, do you have a firing solution on the nearest escort?"

"Aye, Sir." Rosachi nodded without turning, his eyes focused on his displays. "I've got firing solutions on all of the transports and destroyers, but the best are on the nearest escort and the trailing three transports, designated Masters Two-One, Two-Two, and Two-Three. Should I select targets for torpedoes five and six?"

"Negative. Keep those in reserve in case an escort makes a run at us or a bladeship shows up."

"Aye, aye, Sir."

"Has the IAU changed its defense posture?"

Petty Officer Larry Goree responded from Vampire's sensor station. "No, Sir. The escorts, except for the nearest one, are spread in a defensive sphere around the transports at a range of one to three light-seconds. Their lidars are all active and pinging like crazy, but we're still outside their detection range, especially at this angle."

"Very well." Quaid took a breath and looked at Willers across the control room. She was scared but doing her duty—which was, he reflected, the definition of courage. It was time to commit *Vampire* to battle. "Mr. Rosachi, make tubes one through six ready in all respects, including opening the outer doors."

Rosachi parroted Quaid's order verbatim. A moment later Willers looked over from her station. "Tubes one through six are ready in all respects, Captain. Tubes are vented, outer doors open."

Quaid nodded. "Firing point procedures on Master Two-One. New plan, CSO. I'm going to put one torpedo into each transport and observe results, then give follow-on targeting."

Rosachi nodded and bent forward over his firing control panel.

Gorree spoke next. "Master Two-One steady, heading zero-six-three mark zero-niner-two, Captain, speed thirteen thousand, 799 klicks per second, range 10.2 light-seconds."

"Match bearings and shoot, tube one, on Master Two-One."

Rosachi nodded. "Match bearings and shoot, tube one, on Master Two-One, aye." Rosachi touched a button on his panel. "EM surge. Tube one fired, Sir."

Gorree nodded. "Torpedo from tube one running straight, hot and normal, Captain."

"Very well. Standby firing point procedures on Master Two-Two."

The first torpedo went active at close range. The Karsian troop transport *K'hohn Piktar* had no chance to react. It was like having an anti-ship missile suddenly appear at close range without warning, only with a warhead far more powerful than any known ASM. The torpedo went straight up the transport's baffles, unobserved by onboard sensors. It detonated, blowing the transport's stern away in a brilliant explosion that vented most of the ship to vacuum instantly.

Moments later additional torpedoes hit the transports *K'Laiht Piktar* and *K'Bho Piktar* with similar results, except *K'Bho Piktar* exploded, vaporized by the detonation of her failing drive reactors.

Reaction from the Karsian destroyer escort screen was immediate. They circled wildly in all directions, lidars pinging, chasing their tails. By then *Vampire* was ninety degrees out-of-plane and well above them. Quaid launched his fifth and sixth forward torpedoes at the remaining transports.

K'Churj Piktar was destroyed by a direct hit, but the sixth torpedo missed *K'shaka Piktar*.

The nearest Karsian destroyer *P'lahg*, got a solid lidar hit on a stealthed vessel a moment later. She charged the datum, readying missiles and beams, but Quaid put two of

CHAPTER 22

Vampire's stern torpedoes into her face, vaporizing *P'lahg* before she could fire.

The destroyer managed to transmit Vampire's position before dying, however. The battlecruiser *Kah'Borg* launched a swarm of missiles at Vampire's datum. They didn't hit her directly, but proximity explosions from their nuclear warheads highlighted Vampire's Laroussi bubble against a background of gamma radiation. Lasers from the destroyers found her almost instantly, destroying the Rigelian stealthship. Quaid and his crew died with her, but not before Vampire's final torpedo, launched moments before, struck a fifth transport, *K'Durk Piktar*.

With the loss of five troops transports the mission of Karsian Special Attack Unit Two-Two-Two-Two-Two became impossible to accomplish. Only a single transport survived, and it didn't carry enough troops to capture its target.

With the loss of the carrier *Boshar'tahk* and most of his transports, the surviving Karsian commander aboard the super dreadnought *Karh'stahn* panicked. Without fighter cover and with five transports vaporized and a destroyer lost, the invasion was no longer impossible, leaving the force vulnerable to follow-on attacks by fighters and stealthships.

The threat to the planets Boann and Lugus vanished when he ordered Imperial Battle Squadron Two-Two-Two-Two to retreat back to Zion's Waste and await further instructions.

SUCKER PUNCH

JOUST 21 FLIGHT
GALAGHER SYSTEM

Joust division consisted of two CAP fighters from VF-426. They had launched from the RCN attack carrier *Victorious*, one of three carriers in Rear Admiral Yolowski's Carrier Division Two. Unlike the other fighters in CARDIV-2, these were FSF-81 Wasps, smaller than Deathcats or Starhawks. They were one of many CAPs put out to guard Yolowski's carrier division.

Joust 21 was piloted by Lieutenant Rachael "Quag" Mire, one of VF-426's division leads. Her wingman, Lieutenant Junior Grade Akihito Two Persons, was positioned off her starboard side in echelon formation.

His voice spoke in Mire's helmet. "*Joust Two-Two, contact single group, two-eight-six mark zero-eight-four, fourteen light-seconds. Bogey.*"

Mire acknowledged, adjusting her *Wasp's* lidar to search the reported bearing. "*Joust Two-One same.* It's playing hide-and-seek in the dust clouds. Let's go see what it is." She switched to the control frequency to talk to the intercept controllers aboard the cruiser *Capricornus*. "*Corona, Joust* has contact on a bogey at two-eight-six mark zero-eight-four, fourteen light-seconds. We're moving to investigate."

Corona's reply took a few seconds due to the range. "*Corona copies, Joust. Keep us advised.*"

Mire led her wingman toward the bogey, accelerating steadily. At maximum speed a Wasp could cross the distance in seventy seconds, but *Joust* was currently at CAP speed and nowhere near maximum. She calculated that if she accelerated to six percent cee, they would get there in four minutes and twelve seconds, which would appear far less aggressive and give them more time to analyze and ID the contact.

"Joust Two-Two *shows the bogey changing heading. It's dragging and accelerating.*"

"Yeah, they probably picked up our lidar scans." She put a cursor on the contact's lidar blip so the AI would begin analyzing it. "Stay with me, Two-Two. Stay in echelon, but float."

Two Persons widened his spacing as the fighters closed, and Mire's AI analyzed the bogey's drive signature quickly. "She prints as a Karsian N'lahk-class pinnace. Looks like an enemy scout. I'll advise *Corona.*"

It took three minutes for the warning to reach *Capricornus* and three minutes for the response to come back, causing *Joust* to offset to keep some distance. "Corona *copies,* Joust Two-One. *Cleared to engage.*"

"*Joust Two-One* engaging. Two, arm hot." Mire switched on her master arm switch, activating the Wasp's DSM racks and laser pods. They were in a tail-chase now and it took some time to achieve missile range.

It took all four of their missiles to destroy the scout. Mire hit the transmit button to relay the information back to *Capricornus.* "Corona, *Joust Two-One*; splash one scout. We detected no indications the scout transmitted anything. *Joust* is resetting to CAP, weapons red, laser only."

IKSS *TAHK'NAHR*
GALLAGHER SYSTEM

Tahk'nahr was one of six carriers in Carrier Squadron Five and the acting flagship for Imperial Battle Squadron Two-Two-Two-Three. The carrier squadron had three imperial attack units with it as it proceeded from the Centauri Seven jump-gate terminus across Gallagher toward the Yamato jump-gate.

An under-commander approached Mahktoh where he sat drinking talik in Tahk'nahr's staff battle center cursing the dust clouds of the system's nebula.

"One of our scouts, *Duj'nah* Four, has failed to report, Yi'klar."

Mahktoh glanced up at him. "Do you think it suffered a mechanical breakdown or was it destroyed by the enemy, *Do'Rhork?*"

"Unknown, *Yi'klar*. Its captain was Yi' rhang Fargh, one of our best scout captains. He is always prompt."

"Do we know where he was scouting when contact was lost?"

"Yes, Yi'klar."

"Then we have an idea of where the enemy is in this cursed nebula. Inform the squadron and all attack unit commanders that we will proceed to that location. Launch additional scouts and have them search that area."

"Yes, Yi'klar."

CHAPTER 22

RNSS *GEORGE DROUILLARD*
GALLAGHER SYSTEM

Drouillard was a scout pinnace from the carrier *Yamamoto*. She'd launched two hours earlier to search in conjunction with the other scouts. Her sensor operator was Craig Bannon. He turned at his station and looked at his CO.

"Skipper, I'm detecting multiple drives on a two-seven-zero bearing, all headed toward us."

Lieutenant Commander Fred Komack, Drouillard's captain, spun his command couch away from where he'd been conferring with Drouillard's engineer, Lieutenant Mary Stuart. "Give me a mark, Petty Officer Bannon. How far away?"

"Two-seven-zero mark one-zero-two, Skipper, range 45.4 light-seconds. They have a steady acceleration of 27,000 KPS."

Komack's eyes narrowed at the velocity. "What's the AI breaking out?"

"Intermittent at the moment with all of this dust, but it's breaking out definite carriers and dreadnoughts in the mix."

Komack turned toward his executive officer, Lieutenant Oopik Bonanno. "Send a laser comm to *Yamamoto*. Admiral Yolowski needs to know ASAP so he can pass it to Montgomery. Launch a comm drone, too, to back it up. I don't think we need to get any closer to this enemy fleet. Petty Officer Red Bull, turn us away from that battle squadron."

Drouillard's helmsman responded. "Aye, aye, Sir."

Bannon looked at Komack with a raised eyebrow. "I think they've detected us, Skipper. I just picked up several high-velocity drives closing on us from that force. Their speed is 63,000 KPS."

Komack felt a chill run up his spine. "Fighters."

He stood and removed his vac-suit from the back of his command couch. "Red Bull, get us the hell out of here, now! Flank speed! Raise shields. All hands to battle stations."

In the running battle that followed, *Drouillard* destroyed three Karsian Type-00 fighters with her laser turrets before enemy fighters got enough missiles into her to down her shields and damage her drives. The damage to her drives slowed the scout and the fighters caught up. They quickly destroyed *Drouillard* with multiple laser passes, then swung away from her dying nova and returned to their carriers.

Komack and his crew died with *Drouillard*, but the damage was already done.

Yolowski knew where the Karsian carriers were.

A similar event occurred a few minutes later on the starboard side of Yolowski's Task Group, when a Karsian scout also detected and successfully reported CARDIV-2's position to the second imperial battle squadron.

Both sides launched simultaneous fighter strikes on the other.

CHAPTER 22

RNSS *PAN-KU*
GALLAGHER SYSTEM

Montgomery touched the shower's control panel, switching it from sonic depilatory mode to warm water spray. He stood enjoying the hot spray as long as he could stand it, slowly counting to a hundred, then switched it to cold, dropping the spray's temperature to 8 degrees Celsius. He shivered and exhaled as the shock of the cold water knocked the wind out of him.

It was his habit to take a hot shower and a cold rinse each morning before coffee. The warm water relaxed stiff muscles, and the cold water woke him up, closed his pores, and prepped him for the day. He quit shivering after thirty seconds of cold water, counted off another seventy seconds, and turned the shower to air-dry mode. A minute later he stepped from the shower and began donning his uniform.

"Admiral?"

The voice came from the pager on his desk. He stepped over to thumb the answer button. "Montgomery."

"Flag bridge, Sir. The enemy invasion force is retreating. After we destroyed the carrier, *Vampire* attacked several of the transports. It looks like she got several of them. The enemy's called off the assault. All three enemy attack units headed toward the planets have reversed course and are returning to Zion's Waste."

Montgomery's eyes widened. "What's the status of *Vampire?*"

There was a pause. "Contact was lost after her attack, Admiral. We've had no contact since."

Montgomery cursed. If *Vampire* was lost, she had nonetheless stopped an entire invasion. The inhabited planets of Gallagher were safe for the moment.

"Very well. Inform Rear Admiral Yu we'll be turning the task group to rejoin with Yolowski's force."

GALLAGHER SYSTEM
SOUTH HEMISPHERE

While a single Rigelian fighter squadron flew CAP for Carrier Division Two, Yolowski launched sixty Deathcats and ninety-six Starhawk attack fighters at the enemy's Carrier Squadron Five. At almost the same moment, Carrier Squadron Five launched 180 WF-320 attack fighters with 108 Type-00 escorts to attack Carrier Division Two.

There was much confusion induced by the thick clouds of nebula gas and dust. Carrier Division Two changed course to starboard, while Yamashita's Task Group 17.2 continued ahead, making straight for the reported enemy force.

CARDIV-2's strike fighters proceeded to the reported location of the enemy carriers, steering wide of the imperial attack unit leading it. They located the Karsian attack carriers *P'Tahknur* and *Deesh'lar* on the starboard side of the enemy formation, holding well aft of the warship screen for protection. Detecting the incoming Rigelian fighter raid, both Karsian carriers turned a hundred and eighty degrees to escape, but the maneuver pulled them beyond the mutual support range of their warships.

The Karsian CAPs committed nine groups of three fighters each, a twenty-seven-fighter force of Type-00s. They proved no match for sixty Deathcats armed with long-range Impalers. Though they bravely managed to destroy three Deathcats, every Karsian fighter was blown out of space before it could attack a single Starhawk.

Splitting up, the Starhawks attacked both carriers, firing ninety-six anti-ship missiles at each. Without the defensive support of their attack unit, it proved to be a disaster for both of the Karsian carriers. Each took a storm of multiple hits that punched through their shields and armor and ravaged their insides. The blasts left them eviscerated hulks. Their point defenses, overwhelmed by the mass swarms of fighter anti-ship missiles, never had a chance to fire at a single Starhawk.

Though *P'Tahknur* and *Deesh'lar* were not destroyed by the attack, what was left of them was burning junk. Both carriers suffered massive losses of life, with over two thousand Karsians killed along with the twenty-seven fighters destroyed by the Deathcats. The surviving 1,200 crewmen abandoned their ships, relegating their shattered carriers to space. The nearest Karsian attack unit was forced to call off its advance and swing around to rescue life pods. The RCN fighter force steered clear of them on its way home.

The attack resulted in the second and third Karsian carriers lost in the war. It was decidedly an RCN victory: two Karsian attack carriers destroyed for the price of three Deathcat fighters.

Such wasn't the case when the Karsian fighter strike, looking for the RCN's carriers, ran into Yamashita's Task Group 17.2.

RNSS *KUROSHIMA*
GALLAGHER SYSTEM

"Here they come, Skipper." Winston Hosea, *Kuroshima's* sensor operator, turned in his seat and looked at Talara across the bridge through the face plates of his helmet. "Raid count's 135, all high-speed contacts, moving inbound at 17 percent cee."

Talara nodded and stared at the tactical display.

Sixty-five thousand kilometers per second. At that speed they could get from Old Earth to its moon in less than seven seconds. Those things are moving incredibly fast.

Such speeds were beyond human reaction time, requiring AIs to fight the battle. With Task Group 17.2 moving at 9 percent the speed of light, the closure rate was over ninety-six thousand kilometers a second.

Task Group 17.2 had assumed a spherical formation

upon detecting the incoming fighters. The gas and brilliant plasma of the nebula had blinded their sensors for some time so that the fighters hadn't been detected until later than usual. Fortunately, the nebula also hid CARDIV-2, which trailed almost a half-light-minute aft and starboard of the task group.

Agni, Yamashita's battleship, was at the center of the sphere. The heavy cruiser *Capricornus* was on her port side and below, with the light cruiser *Sekigahara* to starboard and above. The task group's four destroyers were spread in a rough diamond formation around them, with *Cochise* on point and *Braddock* in drag position. *Gant* had the port side and *Kuroshima* the starboard. The smaller frigates, four in all, were closer in around *Agni*. The group's six corvettes, being the most vulnerable, were trailing directly aft of *Agni*, shielded by her massive bulk.

Yamashita ordered the task group to assume a tight formation so that Task Force 17.2's sphere had a quarter light-second radius, making the sphere's diameter 172,000 kilometers. It was wide enough to allow tactical maneuvering but close enough to minimize time for weapons employment. Best of all, it minimized lag time for data link, allowing the formation mutual support from all warships.

Talara watched the red dots representing the enemy fighters close on the green icons of the task group in the display. The fighters seemed to be opening in azimuth like a swarm of approaching bees, intending to envelop their victims from all sides.

Normally, Yolowski's fighters would have intercepted

them by now, but most of those fighters were escorting a strike on the enemy carrier force. The CAPs from *Excalibur* and *Reticulus* had committed, but they had only eight Deathcats and four Wasps, hardly enough to stop a raid of this size. With six MIM-140 Impalers each, the Deathcats had forty-eight missiles between them. The smaller Wasps had only eight drive-seeking missiles. If every missile destroyed an enemy fighter, it would reduce the incoming raid by fifty-six fighters, but that would still leave seventy-nine enemy fighters, and that was the *best* case. Intense jamming by the enemy fighters as well as chaff and decoys would reduce the kills to a lower number.

"Half the raid's arcing to starboard, Captain." Hosea pointed at the display. "Seventy-two fighters in all. The other sixty-three are taking the port side of the formation."

Talara nodded again, feeling her stomach crawl up her spine. "*Agni* can't use her capital beams until our own fighters get out of the way. Until our CAPs break off, *Agni*, *Capricornus*, and *Sekigahara* can't shoot."

Agni carried eight 175 cm grasers in addition to three 105 cm capital lasers and a trio of 150 cm particle beam projectors. Such massive weapons were designed for use against warships, not fighters, but any fighter hit by them would be vaporized. It was a lot of energy to waste on something as small as a fighter. Charger-class destroyers like *Kuroshima* had a pair of 60 cm lasers and a single 50 cm particle beam, which could recharge and reengage fighters much more quickly, which was why destroyers were a task force's primary anti-fighter unit, at least at medium range. Inside of 1.5 light-seconds, a warship's point defenses became lethal, which tended to make attacking fighters launch their ASMs before reaching that range.

"Flutter, Mr. Harper."

One of the biggest problems of warships in combat was heat. Increasing drive speed, using active sensors, shields, and firing beams tended to produce tons of thermal energy. Getting rid of excess thermal energy was a problem for every combat skipper. "Flutter" was a command to extend external radiators to help keep *Kuroshima* cool. Space wasn't a good conductor of heat, however, and cooling remained a problem in combat, where ships overheated quickly.

Harper, the acting weapons officer, acknowledged in her headset, "Radiators extended."

The RCN fighter CAPs launched their missiles at the Karsian strike force. The Deathcats shot well, taking out multiple fighters, most of them Type-00's in the leading edge of the formation. The Wasps did poorer, being forced to close inside of 1.5 light-seconds to launch. Drive decoys caused three DSMs to miss, but the Wasps killed five more enemy fighters. Five Wasps died in the same exchange, however, taking multiple missiles in the face.

The Deathcats, now out of missiles, climbed up and over at high speed, never slowing and never getting inside the enemy's missile range. With only lasers remaining and unwilling to reengage missile-armed fighters, they returned to their carriers to rearm.

Hosea pointed at the display. "Vampires inbound, Skipper. Lots of them, targeted among our ships. I show twenty-two targeted on *Cochise*, sixteen on us."

The enemy force had launched its ASM swarm at Task Group 17.2.

"How many are targeted on *Agni*?"

"Thirty-six."

Talara relaxed a bit.

Egon was safe for the moment.

Yamashita's battleship had enough shields and armor to handle that many ASMs and its point defenses would reduce the number of missiles long before they reached her. It was *Kuroshima* she needed to worry about.

At the leading edge of the formation sphere, *Cochise* swatted down seven incoming fighter missiles, but fifteen punched through her point defense. A series of explosions hid her for a moment, followed by a massive explosion as her reactor core breached. She died in a brilliant sun, vanishing from the data link; her final omega code lingering on the tactical display.

Hosea sighed. "*Cochise* is gone."

"Full power to shields." Talara tightened her retraining straps. "Activate all jammers and release chaff. Point defense, you're weapons free. Splash those vampires."

"Point defenses engaged," Yantali reported over the intercom. "Chicks away."

The point defense clusters opened fire. Laser clusters took down three of the missiles targeted on *Kuroshima*. Point defense missiles got two more. Nine missiles got through, closing to a quarter of a light-second before detonating.

Without atmosphere, the detonations created no shock waves or sound in vacuum, but they did create blinding light. Lasers in the AFM warheads stabbed outward in a porcupine spray of deadly needles that downed Kuroshima's shields and stabbed through her light armor like hot knives through butter.

There was a loud *whump,* and the bridge vanished in a thick fog as lasers penetrated the compartment, causing an explosive decompression. Blinded by sudden mist, Talara felt her vac-suit inflate as the bridge lost pressure. In the same instant the lights dimmed to emergency red. The brief spray of sparks on the bridge, caused by lasers punching through metal, vanished as the air was sucked out into space. The fog cleared with it.

Talara glanced around. Everyone seemed to be all right except Ensign Harper, who lay slumped over his console, unmoving. A laser had punched a hole through the back of his suit and out the front of his chest. His vac-suit had deflated.

Talara unstrapped and tried to rush to him, but the ship's artificial gravity failed at that moment. Her run became a leap that disintegrated into an uncontrolled tumble. She bounced off the overhead and back toward her couch before her training kicked in and she stopped her ricochet with her arms and legs. Using gloved hands, she quick-crawled to Harper and pulled him back in his chair. Opening a pouch on his vac-suit's leg pocket, she removed a package, which she ripped open. Taking out two patches, she slapped them over the holes in Harper's suit to reseal it. Hopefully, the suit would repressurize.

She glanced around desperately. "Damage report, all stations."

Yantali's voice spoke in her ear. "Shields are down Skipper. We've got multiple holes in the hull and we're streaming atmosphere. The data link's offline, and all radiators and external racks on the hull are gone. Three drive nodes and one missile launcher are offline as well as one laser battery. The boat bay's damaged, as well as some crew quarters. We've got casualty reports coming in from all over the ship."

"Get a corpsman to the bridge when you can."

"Roger, but it may take a bit. Sickbay's being called by everyone at once."

"Copy." She looked up to see the helmsman, Ian Awbrey, trying to unbuckle himself. "Where are you going, Petty Officer Awbrey?"

"Coming to help you with Ensing Harper, Ma'am."

"Negative. Stay at your station. You're driving the ship."

"Aye, aye."

Talara turned back to Hosea. "Where are those fighters, Hosea."

"They've made their pass, Captain." Hosea leaned over his sensor monitors, some of which had been damaged by the missile lasers. "Sensors are sporadic due to damage. It looks like they hit *Agni* and *Capricornus* pretty good too."

Oh God. Egon!

Hosea continued as he studied his panels. "The shields are down on both ships, but otherwise they appear undamaged, Captain. *Sekigahara* had her shields knocked down, too, and she has some internal damage, but it looks negligible. *Cochise* took the brunt of the attack. She's gone."

"Are the fighters headed away?"

"No, Ma'am. They're decelerating hard and coming back around."

"They're going to strafe." Talara unbuckled Harper and gently pushed him out of his seat. He drifted in zero gravity, unconscious. Oddly, she saw no blood at his station, then realized the laser had cauterized his wound even as it had punched through him. His suit did appear to be inflating again and perhaps he was still alive, but she had no time to spare on him.

The laser that had hit Harper had gone through him into the weapons control console, destroying the missile launch panel. *Kuroshima* still had a working missile launcher, but no way to launch a missile. Anti-ship missiles were useless against fighters, anyway. The fighters would be slowing hard to make strafing passes, spinning and pivoting to rake Kuroshima's hull with their fighter-grade lasers as they zipped past at close range.

"Ian, hard aport, bring our starboard side to bear. Point defenses, you're still weapons free. Splash those fighters."

Two WF-320 attack fighters were coming straight at *Kuroshima*, dumping velocity to make a portside pass. Such an attack would have been suicide against a full-up warship with shields, but with shields and weapons down *Kuroshima* was vulnerable. Even fighter lasers could penetrate her hull with the shields down. But they'd have to get within a half a light-second to do any real damage.

"Come on, come on." Talara struggled with the beam fire control panel, trying to get the AI to lock a fire director on the fighters.

"We're beam-on, Skipper," Awbrey reported. Awbrey had used thrusters to spin the ship sideways. *Kuroshima* was still moving along her original heading but traveling sideways.

The beam fire control panel froze up as the fighters reached two light-seconds' range. She slammed a gloved fist against the panel. Nothing happened.

Cursing, she hammered the panel again with her fist. She felt the impact through her bones, but without air, there was no sound. The display blinked, then unfroze.

She activated her battle comm. "Point defenses, fire!"

Her fire control AI suddenly locked a fighter at one light-second, but the fire button wasn't working.

"Damn it!" She hit the button with her fingers, hammering at it like a machine-gun, trying to get the fire button to activate.

It lit up just as the approaching fighters reached a half light-second's range and opened fire.

Lasers tore through the bridge like slashing knives even as Kuroshima's remaining main 60 cm laser battery fired.

The console exploded before her in molten spray. Talara flinched away, believing she was dead. Two WF-320 fighters, caught by Kuroshima's 60 cm laser, vanished in silent but brilliant explosions.

Smelling blood, more Karsian fighters turned toward *Kuroshima*. Three of them exploded as lasers from *Agni* took them out. The battleship passed above *Kuroshima* at that moment, firing on the fighters. Two more exploded. The rest, who'd been content to kill a badly damaged destroyer, had no intention of taking on a battleship, even if its shields were down. They broke off and accelerated away at maximum speed.

Talara glanced around, amazed she was still alive, then quickly checked her suit to make sure it hadn't been punctured. Artificial gravity returned as engineering got the system back online and she sank into Harper's chair. Harper's floating body sank to the deck. She got up and ran to him, kneeling by his side.

"Corpsman to the bridge," she said, repeating her earlier order. "Harper's hit. Be advised we're in vacuum on the bridge. Comm, open a channel to *Agni*. Thank Captain Yamashita for saving our hide."

Two vac-suited corpsmen opened the bridge hatch and entered. Talara realized Harper was in better hands than hers and moved back to her command couch. "Casualty report, Reggie."

"Seventeen dead, Skipper. Forty-three wounded."

Damn, damn, damn.

It was a 60 percent casualty rate.

"Copy." She closed her eyes in grief and sat down on the couch, feeling numb all over.

The battle was over. Like most space battles, it had been quick, silent, and violent. She knew she needed to contact DCD and supervise the damage control parties working on the ship. She also needed to get to sickbay and check on the wounded, but that could wait. She was suddenly exhausted beyond reason, unable to do much but sit and stare at the deck.

She lowered her head to rest.

Kuroshima had survived . . . barely.

GALLAGHER SYSTEM

Among the 135 Karsian fighters launched by Carrier Squadron Five, casualties had been high. They had launched thirty-six missiles at *Agni* and *Capricornus* each, thirty-four at *Sekigahara* and more at two RCN destroyers. The battleship and cruisers had lost their shields but were otherwise undamaged. One Rigelian destroyer had been vaporized, another badly damaged. Only 107 Karsian fighters had survived the strike. Twenty-eight had been lost, including nineteen Type-00s and twenty-one WF-320s. It was a stiff price to pay for killing a single RCN destroyer.

When the Karsain fighters reached their carriers, they discovered two of their attack carriers had been so badly damaged by an enemy fighter attack that they'd been scuttled.

Karsian Carrier Squadron Five circled as it recovered

fighters, having more fighters to recover than bays to store them in. The fighters circled, waiting in frustration as individual flights were called in to recover and carrier commanders struggled to figure out where to put them.

RNSS *RECLUSE*

"What are they doing?" Dell asked the question as she stepped into the control room.

"They're circling while they recover fighters."

"Is this contact a carrier?" She pointed at a scarlet icon in Al-Zahrani's sensor display.

"Yes, Ma'am. It just passed the popper we deployed."

Conformal Torpedo Pods were called "poppers" by stealthship crews. Each pod carried six torpedoes and its own Laroussi Field, allowing it to hide from sensors. CTPs were dropped to drift silently, creating a sort of torpedo mine. *Recluse* had deployed three in the area, but this was the only popper the Karsians had gotten close to.

Dell bit her lip. "What's the bearing to the carrier?"

"From us, one-four-five mark zero-niner-one at twenty-two light-seconds, Captain. From the popper it bears three-four-zero mark zero-one-two at six light-seconds."

"What type of carrier?"

Al-Zahrani looked at his readouts and tapped the icon with a finger. "According to the AI, the parametrics match for a *Borrahka*-class heavy carrier, Ma'am. The data base identifies her as *Tahk'nahr*."

"And what about this one?" Dell pointed to another contact. "That a carrier too?"

"Affirmative, an escort carrier named *Zorj* with a single fighter squadron. She bears one-six-seven mark zero-eight-two from us at 31.6 light-seconds."

"The heavy's the priority target." Dell nodded and pointed at two smaller scarlet icons. "Are these escorts?"

Al-Zahrani nodded. "Affirmative, one tin can at zero-seven-eight mark zero-niner-zero at twenty-six light-seconds and another bearing one-five-two mark zero-eight-niner at forty light-seconds."

Dell turned toward her Combat Systems Officer, Lieutenant Carol Bolan. "*Tahk'nahr* is the priority target, CSO. I plan to set off the popper to force a reaction and then attack the carrier from the opposite side. Put Mark 21s in all tubes, fore and aft."

"Aye-aye, Ma'am." Bolan had a petite frame and short black hair. She tilted her head, her blue eyes as calm as a mountain lake. "The heavy carrier is designated Master One-One. The port destroyer will be Master One-Two, and the starboard destroyer is Master One-Three. The escort carrier will be Master One-Four."

"Very well." Dell sat in her command couch and strapped in. "Petty Officer Smith, make our heading one-four-zero mark zero-niner-zero, maintain speed."

She saw Smith's blonde head nod. "One-four-zero mark zero-niner-zero, maintaining speed, aye."

"Pappy, set battle stations torpedo."

Schnell nodded as he set *Recluse* to battle stations.

Dell waited until all lights on the status board were green. "All right, then. Petty Officer Al-Zahrani, initiate launch on the popper."

Al-Zahrani touched a button on his console. A thin mast on the towed array pointed a narrow beam whisker laser at the CTP and transmitted a command. It reached the CTP seventeen seconds later. After a minute, Zahrani turned and looked at her from his seat. "The popper's engaged, Captain. Six torpedoes away, all running straight, hot and normal."

"Good. Let's rattle their cages. Have the popper torpedoes drop their Laroussi fields, go active, and accelerate to maximum vee."

Each torpedo would drop its cloaking field, go active with lidar, and home on the heavy carrier as they boosted to maximum acceleration at fifty thousand gravities. The sudden appearance of torpedoes only five light-seconds from the carrier would draw the enemy's attention immediately.

"Torpedoes have gone bulldog, Captain." Zahrani grinned. "All are homing, hot and normal."

The reaction of the Karsians was immediate.

Zahrani reported it. "The heavy carrier's making a hard turn to port, jamming and dropping chaff and decoys, Captain. Both escorts have turned inbound and are accelerating toward the torpedoes' launch point. Their lidars are pinging like crazy."

Dell nodded grimly. At full speed and without their cloaking Laroussi fields, the popper torpedoes were now effectively anti-ship missiles with powerful warheads and Tahk'nahr's point defenses could engage them. The hard turn to port had brought the enemy carrier toward *Recluse*, however, and the same would not be true for her fully-stealthed Mark 21 torpedoes, which would remain cloaked until three seconds before impact.

She took a breath and sighed. "Firing point procedures, Lieutenant Bolan. Make all tubes ready in all respects, including opening the outer doors."

GALLAGHER SYSTEM

Tahk'nahr's point defense stopped four of the CTP's Mark 18 torpedoes with extremely accurate shooting. Her chaff corridors and heavy jamming blinded the remaining two torpedoes, which circled to reacquire, buying time for her point defenses to destroy them as well. With amazing luck, *Tahk'nahr* stopped all six popper torpedoes.

The four Mark 21 torpedoes from *Recluse* remained fully cloaked until they went bulldog a half light-second off Tahk'nahr's bow. Her point defense crews had no time to react. All four torpedoes struck the carrier.

By then *Recluse* was out-of-plane, fully stealthed, eight light-seconds above the carrier. The port destroyer escort came screaming in, its lidar pinging, desperately

CHAPTER 22

trying to locate the stealthship that had launched the torpedoes. Dell put a fifth torpedo into it, blowing it in half.

Turning away and climbing, Dell released four additional Mark 21s from Recluse's stern tubes, all targeted on the shattered wreck of the heavy carrier. Without shields or point defense, *Tahk'nahr* was helpless to stop them.

She died in a supernova-like explosion.

With the loss of its flagship and a destroyer, command of Imperial Battle Squadron Two-Two-Two-Three fell on the captain of the superdreadnought *K'Bork'nahk* in Imperial Attack Unit Two-Two-Two-Three-One, who sent a desperate comm drone to the Zion's Waste stargate to inform Admiral Tork of the losses and to await further instructions. Realizing he had RCN stealthships in his immediate vicinity, and that the invasion force was withdrawing, he turned his battle squadron for the Zion stargate, taking the survivors of Carrier Squadron Five with him.

The battle for Gallagher was over.

CHAPTER 23

KARSIAN EMBASSY, RIGEL TWO

Takoom sighed as he closed the last of his trunks, then stared at the empty room. Once a place of splendor, furnished with the best extravagances the Empire could afford, it was now a barren shell, stripped of its former glories. Even the heavy satin curtains had been packed away. Blue-hued light from Rigel streamed through the room's tall windows. Takoom sighed again as bitter thoughts returned.

Exiled.

He had been ordered to depart the Confederation by delegates from the Confederation government, who had informed him diplomatic relations between the Rigelian Confederation and the Empire of Kars had been terminated.

The Confederation had declared war on the Empire.

In an ironic twist unique to diplomacy, a Karsian liner now waited in orbit, ready to return him to Imperial space, protected by an escort of Confederation warships. Under the protection of diplomatic immunity, the liner would bear Takoom and his staff home under Rigelian protection.

Takoom reflected on the irony, wondering again the question that endlessly swirled through his mind.

How could those fools in the Kahthrung attack the Confederation without informing me, their own ambassador?

The loss of face had humiliated him, not only in the eyes of other yihaki, but more unforgivably, in the eyes of Outworlders, former Rigelian friends who were now officially enemies. Such betrayal by the Imperial Staff— perhaps even the Shikahn himself—implied they feared a security leak from his embassy. His bitterness increased. His own people didn't trust him.

It was an unbearable insult to his honor, his family and the House of Khar.

The insult to his honor hurt the most. He had given the Confederation ambassador his *word* that no such attack would occur. His government had betrayed that word and made him a liar. Yihaki did not lie. His masters had tarnished his honor in front of everyone.

Though a yihak, Takoom was a loyal Karsian and understood war. His people's culture had been built upon it. That the Empire and Confederation would go to war was unfortunate, but inevitable. He could have accepted that had it been handled properly. But the Kahthrung should have informed him in advance so that he might have broken off diplomatic relations with his honor still intact. War was a reality for a race of warriors, and it was obvious the

Empire must expand to survive. That truth was as plain as the three fingers on his hands.

Takoom was not a warrior. His House had removed him from that path in childhood. He was yihaki, and a yihak's word was not something to be questioned.

They could have told me. He ground his canines in fury. *They* should *have warned me. Instead, they hung me out to dry.*

He would never have betrayed the Shikahn's security, but neither would he have betrayed his honor by giving Clive his word had he known such an attack was about to occur. He was now a liar in the eyes of his nation's enemies, and a liar was someone whose word could not be trusted. It was an unbearable insult for a professional yihaki, for whom protocol and trust were considered bedrocks.

Even his staff considered him a liar now.

A yihak without honor.

He had called Clive upon receiving the coded message informing him war was about to begin. Takoom had owed the human that much. Unfortunately, the message had arrived two hours after the attack on Centauri Seven had been reported by Confederation news services. There had been no excuse for such delay. Takoom had been asleep when the news had broken. The delay had been deliberate on the part of the Kahthrung, a ruse to lull the RCN into vulnerability.

The Kahthrung had used him like an expendable pawn, casting his personal honor aside like a handful of dung. It had been deception by the Imperial hand, por'tahk in execution, but it had destroyed all that Takoom had worked to accomplish over the years.

Clive had refused his call. Takoom had wanted to apologize, to assure Clive he too had been duped; that he hadn't broken his word. He had wanted to explain that he had been caught off-guard as much as the Rigelian Fleet. The refusal of the Imperial Staff to inform the Emperor's top *yihak* to the Confederation of such an action was unprecedented and unforgiveable, a clear indication of the kinds of intrigue festering inside the Kahthrung.

His need to restore his honor had been great, even at the unheard of price of asking Clive—an Outworlder—for forgiveness. Takoom had gnashed his teeth as he'd made the call, but Clive had refused to answer it. Clive's servant had replied, rather curtly, that Clive was in session and was not to be disturbed for any reason. Then he had cut the connection.

Takoom's dishonor had been complete. No one trusted him now, not even his old friend. He was just another victim of Imperial treachery.

He closed his eyes, his mind screaming about the injustice of it. He opened them when he heard the shuttle approaching, its landing thrusters roaring as the craft crossed over the mansion and flared, shaking the building. Takoom had been on Rigel for many years and the thought of leaving—of ending this part of his life—disturbed him greatly.

In an odd way, Rigel had become a home. Here, in this place among Terrans, Vegans and the eerie beings called

Reticulans, he had come to admire the complex diversity of Rigelian society. While the Confederation retained the trappings of a monarchy with all of its titles of peerage, it was not a kingdom. There were scores of human star systems that operated independently of direct Rigelian control, yet all remained part of the Confederation. Such systems paid taxes and provided military service to the Confederation but were allowed to keep their own local laws and cultures. They maintained their own governments however they chose, as long as their laws did not violate the Confederation Constitution. Alliance with the Confederation provided star systems access to trade revenue, as well as protection by the RCN. Astonishingly, no system had ever been forced to join the Confederation by conquest.

In the Empire there was only one Way, and it was the Way of the Warrior. On Confederation worlds, people were free to choose their own Way. Rigelians could choose the comforts of modern technocracy or select from a hodgepodge of frontier, secular, or religious societies, each different and unique, with varying political and philosophical views. It was a freedom that was unknown in the Empire. If Confederation citizens found themselves in a system not to their liking, they were free to immigrate somewhere else. Confederation citizens were free to even change their social status through hard work.

Such things were not allowed in the Empire, which maintained a strict caste system. Species not from Kars were K'jir, or "conquered peoples." The Way of the

Warrior dominated everything. Only two major classes existed in Karsian society: warriors—which included the Emperor, Imperial Court and the warrior houses—and K'jir, who were slaves to everyone else. Karsians were born to a thrung, a warrior house, by house breed wives, and they remained members of that house for life. K'jir could be forced into military service, but they were considered lesser beings without the rights of warriors, always subservient to actual Karsians. K'jir were never considered real warriors, having not being born to a warrior house and without Karsian blood.

Of late, Takoom had begun to perceive a different vision, one inspired by his association with Rigelians. The Confederation conquered worlds not by war but with freedom of choice. Confederation worlds joined the collective *willingly*. Rigel induced them to join by offering them a better way of life *together* than such worlds could achieve alone. Rigel pooled resources and produced things for the benefit for all its peoples. There were certainly warriors in the Confederation, but there was nothing resembling K'jir.

The Empire was a thing of hunger, its appetite insatiable and its maw ever open to devour. The Empire took worlds by force, enslaved their peoples, consumed their resources and then moved on to the next objective, the next battle and the next conquest. Or—more precisely—the next victim. The Empire took from conquered worlds and returned little.

Takoom had never questioned the rightness of it, not until recently. It had simply been The Way, and The Way had been with Karsians since time immemorial. His years on Rigel had provided him a new insight, a greater understanding of what could be possible. Takoom had come to see the future of the Empire with stark clarity.

The Empire must change to survive. Any form of government that took from its people without returning made eventual collapse inevitable. The Empire was like a dying star. It expanded outward, constantly starved for fuel and consuming everything in reach. As with hydrogen, resources were eventually depleted by endless consumption. Once hydrogen fuel resources were depleted, red giants inevitably collapsed, starved for fuel still too far away and difficult to reach.

The Empire was dying from gradual starvation. It would inevitably collapse when its consumption exceeded the available resources. To survive, it must learn both conservation and replenishment. It must give something back for all that it took. Something, at least, beyond obligation, duty and the possibility of a glorious death in combat.

It was necessary that the K'jir desire to be part of the Empire. To create such desire, the K'jir needed rights as Imperial citizens. If they *wanted* to be a part of the Empire, if they freely *chose* to join it, they would by definition no longer be "conquered" peoples. They would become invested and no longer K'jir, for only a free people had choices. It was a disturbingly alien thought for a Karsian, yet somehow oddly inspirational.

"Yihak." The voice spoke low and softly. Takoom turned to see his head servant. Mernacht was dressed in formal robes at the doorway. "The shuttle has landed. The pilot awaits departure at your pleasure."

Takoom glanced around the again. His time in this house was at an end. "Have my trunks loaded and have the staff board the shuttle. I will join you shortly."

"Yes, Yihak."

Mernacht withdrew quietly. Takoom walked to the room that had once been his office. His hands found the secret recess in the wall. Pressing his thumbs against it, he waited as scanners analyzed his DNA. Tumblers clicked and the door to the secret safe whisked opened.

He removed the encryption gear, then pulled a classified data chip from it and torched it with a pencil laser. The chip melted into a silicon puddle in the waste basket. Takoom watched the puddle cool and hardened, then destroyed the encryption gear. The device contained secret communication codes, allowing him to decode messages sent to the Embassy by the Empire. His last duty as ambassador was to destroy classified material and equipment before closing the embassy.

Not that there is much point, he thought bitterly. *The Empire no longer trusts you.*

He had lost face, but he would remain true to his people. He had been made a liar and a fool. He was considered untrustworthy by enemies and his own government. He had been ordered to leave Rigel by the Confederation president. He was *a* yihak without honor, and a yihak without honor was nothing, a useless part that served no purpose.

Only darkness seemed to loom in his future.

"Excuse me, old boy."

Startled, Takoom turned, his hand instinctively reaching for the dagger on his belt. He relaxed as he recognized the stiff and somewhat reserved face of George Clive staring at him from the doorway.

Takoom nodded. "Greetings, Ambassador. I am surprised to see you."

Clive gave a curt nod. "Sorry to startle you, old boy, but I thought it best to come in unannounced. I've been sent to assume control of the Embassy grounds upon your departure. I wanted to first wish you a safe voyage and assure you of Confederation diplomatic protection. I'll see to the upkeep of the grounds. After all, it's still sovereign Karsian territory, and we'll take good care of it. I hope it won't be long before we reestablish your embassy here."

"Perhaps we will, but I doubt I shall return, George."

Clive blinked. "In all the years I've known you, Takoom, you've never once called me by my first name. It's not something done in yihaki society, is it?"

"No, it is not."

"You told me once that honor was first in a Karsian house; that your government would never attack while we negotiated in good faith. You promised me we were safe as long as we treated the Empire fairly."

Takoom's gaze dropped to the floor. "That is indeed what I told you."

"You know, old boy, I've always believed yihaki to be unquestionable." Clive let some of his anger and sense of betrayal slip into his tone. Takoom knew Clive had also been made a fool in front of his peers, and perhaps worst of all, in front of his president.

"As did I, George."

Clive blinked. It wasn't the defiant riposte he'd expected. "Then why in heaven's name did you lie to me?"

Takoom looked up, anguish on his face. "I did not know it was a lie. I, too, was deceived, Ambassador."

"Deceived? By your own government? You're a bloody yihaki."

"The attack was done without my knowledge. I was not informed of the attack until after it had already occurred."

Clive scowled, incredulous. "Are you telling me your own government initiated an act of war without giving its top ambassador any warning of its intentions?"

"Yes."

"And you expect me to believe that?"

Takoom met his eyes, and Clive's rage faded as it began making sense. Takoom knew Clive wanted to call him a liar, that he had come in part to humiliate Takoom with righteous anger and indignation, as he himself had been humiliated before his president.

Yet the statement had the ring of truth, and Clive sensed it instinctively. He had never known the Karsian to tell even a white lie.

Pity quickly replaced Clive's anger as he realized he'd come to castigate an ambassador that he now realized was also a victim like himself.

"Why would your government do such a thing, Yihak?"

"Political intrigue within the Empire is tumultuous at

the best of times, George, and often fickle. As a race we Karsians are paranoid by nature. We are a culture dominated by warriors, and an Empire is surrounded by hostile neighbors. Security is always of primary importance. The life of any warrior, even his entire thrung, is expendable in the interests of the Empire. Security is the bedrock of strategic deception, of por'tahk. Any Karsian may be sacrificed for that ideal, even a yihak. Is it surprising that a government that would sacrifice millions of lives to gain a strategic objective would sacrifice a yihaki?

"When one of our subjects, however loyal, has lived too long among Outworlders and is exposed to alien ideas—too much *non-warrior* thinking—his allegiance becomes suspect. Though yihaki, I have become such an individual. I have lived too long among humans for my loyalty to remain unquestioned. Though of royal heritage, I, too, am expendable. From the Shikahn's perspective, it is a cheap price to pay for strategic surprise."

"You're telling me you had no idea your Empire's 'wargames' were a deception for an all-out attack?" Clive stared in disbelief.

Takoom took a deep breath. "George, Imperial leadership made me into a liar. They stole my honor without my choice, without my knowledge. Because of that, I am now ni-yihaki, an ambassador without honor. The Shikahn knows, as do all Karsians, that yihaki do not—cannot—lie. The word of a yihak is unquestioned. Remember, however, not all Karsians are yihaki.

"The Way allows for lying to be an acceptable strategy

if it achieves surprise. Unless bound by a specific honor oath, as yihaki are, warriors are permitted to distort truth to gain advantage in battle. If no specific oath has been taken against it, a warrior has no obligation to be honest with enemies. I, however, am. The Imperial Staff decided *my* honor was expendable as long as it accomplished their objective: the surprise of your fleet at Centauri Seven. To them my reputation was a small sacrifice to achieve such a victory."

"But again, Takoom, *why?*"

"Por'tahk, George. Unbalancing. It is the basis of military doctrine. Move the enemy with a feint until his balance is broken, then strike where he is weakest. So unbalanced, a slight push can win a battle if applied at the right place and time. I was a means to Imperial por'tahk. Unwittingly, I was used to relax your fleet posture. Apparently, the Imperial Staff felt my assurances would be more convincing if I actually believed them. The loss of my honor—indeed, that of my House—was considered a small price to pay."

Clive sighed and shook his head. "I doubt my government will ever buy such a story, Takoom."

Takoom nodded. "No, likely not. I would question such a story myself. It seems implausible to rational minds."

Clive placed a hand on Takoom's shoulder. "If it's any consolation, old boy, I believe you."

Takoom lifted his eyes. "Truly?"

"I've known you a long time, Takoom. In all that time I've never known you to lie about anything. I suppose that's why I felt so betrayed. I thought you'd lied to me intentionally to set me up. I was embarrassed before my superiors, you see; hurt and angry. That's why I refused your call. I thought I'd been duped . . . Now I realize I'm not the only dupe in this game. Sorry for my suspicions, old boy. I apologize for the anger I've harbored against you."

"Apologize?" Takoom shook his head. "Why are you sorry, George? Anger at being told a lie is understandable."

"Why?" Clive chuckled softly. "There's a simple reason, old boy: the word of a yihaki is gospel. I know that, and you know it as well. Between the two of us, that's all that matters. What you told me was indeed *incorrect*, but it wasn't a lie. There was no intentional deception on your part. You told the truth as you knew it. You were simply backstabbed by your superiors. I learned long ago that you are many things, Ambassador, but one thing more than any other: a man of honor."

Takoom's inner eyelids closed, growing wet, and he averted them from Clive's gaze. "No longer. I am ni-yihaki now."

"Not to me, old boy. Not now, not ever."

Takoom turned away, overcome with emotions he dared not let an Outworlder see. His voice was hoarse when he spoke again. "I must go, George."

"Yes, I suppose you must. I'll see you to your shuttle."

They walked in silence through the terraced hedges of the garden past the embassy security fence to the landing apron. A Karsian *Utuam*-class shuttle rested on the pad, its APU screaming, navigation strobes blinking brightly in the fading light.

The sky above was a violet dome. Proto-birds chirped happily in the hedgerows, lending a sense of calm unreality. Clive looked at the shuttle, which seemed to be squatting, waiting for a command to leap into the heavens.

"I must take my leave of you, Sir George." Takoom turned toward Clive. "I thank you for your kind words; they mean much and return an old yihak some shred of honor. Your kindness will not be forgotten."

"I'm not a member of the Peerage, old boy, not even knighted. The title of 'Sir' is improper. It's simply George Clive."

Takoom paused near the stairway of the shuttle, turned back, and yelled to be heard over the roar of the shuttle. "Not to me, Ambassador. To me, you are *Sir* George, a human with honor. Thank you for your friendship, *Sir* George. I am eternally bound to you. Your House and mine are henceforth *thrung-tahli*."

Clive seemed to know the term. It meant clan brother; warriors sworn to a blood oath to defend each other to the last, usually declared just before both were to die in battle. Clive didn't seem sure how to respond. The *thrung-tahl* was an oath of obligation and commitment, not something to be taken lightly.

Clive smiled and bowed. "I am honored, Yihak."

A crew chief appeared in the hatchway, waiting for Takoom to ascend the steps to the passenger compartment. Takoom's bags were already onboard, having been loaded by Mernacht.

Takoom yelled over the APU's roar. "Goodbye, Sir

George. I shall miss our conversations. This will be a long war, I think. If we do not meet again, it has been my honor to know you, Thrung-tahli. Beyond that, I know not what to say. Your Rigelian words fail me."

Clive took Takoom's three-digit hand and shook it, his eyes twinkling in the setting sunlight. "Rigelians have a term I believe most appropriate for such a farewell, Yihak."

Takoom released his hand, moved up the shuttle's ramp and paused at the hatch to look back. "What might that be?"

Clive grinned. "Peace."

Takoom lifted an eyebrow, smiling as his own words came home to him. With a wave he moved into the shuttle. The ramp whisked shut behind him as the pilot powered up the shuttle's drives.

Clive stepped away from the apron, watching as the shuttle lifted off. Tucking its landing gear, it climbed away with a roar, strobes flashing.

He watched until its lights disappeared among the stars beginning to peek through the purple twilight.

CHAPTER 24

MEDICAL EXAMINATION ROOM 14
HOSPITAL, CENTAURI SEVEN

Yeager shivered on the examination table. Sickbays always seemed cold. It didn't seem to matter if they were on starships, ODS platforms or at dirtside hospitals. Sickbays were cold everywhere.

The thin gown they'd given her barely covered anything and remained open at the back, held together with a thin pair of ties. Cold air from the air vents above made her skin pucker with goosebumps.

She'd finished the last round of medication the doctors had prescribed for the radiation dose she'd suffered. She'd lost her hair in the process, but it was finally growing back again and nearly two inches long. Yeager had always been a platinum blonde, and her hair had been her pride and joy before Turin's World. Doctors had assured her it would grow back, so she'd decided to worry about vanity again once she knew she wasn't dying.

Lieutenant Commander Waldo Pickering had also survived the attack. As far as she knew, they were the only survivors from the ODS. Laura Hernandez had been killed, as well as others working on the station. Pickering had received a lethal dose of gamma radiation, too, but doctors had managed to save him. Rumors claimed he would recover physically, but the same couldn't be said for his career. A board of inquiry had been convened to investigate his failure to pass warning of the impending attack to authorities on Turin's World. The destroyer *Gant* had communicated the threat early on. Pickering had not only ignored the threat but also ordered Hernandez to illegally download classified onto an unauthorized computer. The spillage of classified information had been a serious breach of security. The board was to determine why he'd done those things. Naval inspectors were conducting an investigation and had already yanked Pickering's security clearance as a precaution.

Of course, the real question wasn't what Pickering been doing, but *whom*. NIS hadn't put all the pieces together yet, but she intended to tell them all about it when they finally got around to asking, which they most assuredly would.

Pickering was a prick—the term suddenly struck her as hilarious—but he wasn't much different from many men she'd known. Men had always wanted to be around her, primarily for sex.

Not that she'd objected. Men were easy to manipulate, and she'd learned long ago to beat them at that game. Such men thought they were using her, when in reality she'd used them to advance her career.

Such men were arrogant and rarely suspected she had a brain. Only a few had ever figured it out, and always too late. They'd been willing to give her anything she wanted for some hanky-panky. All it took was enough acting skills to convince them she liked it, and then she owned them. In fact, she actually *did* enjoy it with some of them, at least the less abusive ones. She'd had fun, but she'd never considered sex as "making love." That term indicated emotional attachment, something she'd never felt.

Yeager didn't make love to men. She *fucked* them. It was a crude distinction, perhaps, and a vulgar term, but accurately described the *quid pro quo* relationship she had with abusers. They got their jollies and occasionally she got hers, but it was all business, never love.

Men were like deck plates; if you laid them right the first time, you could walk on them forever. They were simple-minded creatures with only enough blood for one head at a time.

A man entered the hatchway, a young doctor. He glanced up from the electronic chart in his hands and smiled. "Good morning, Yeoman Yeager."

The doctor's pale-blue scrubs displayed the rank of a lieutenant. Most Navy doctors she'd encountered were commanders or captains. The doctor's name tag showed the name Bennet.

She smiled at him. "Good morning, Sir."

"Well, Yeoman, I've reviewed your charts with Dr.

Simon, and we agree you won't need any more Raydalon infusions. The nannites we injected have done their job and your blood work looks good. Scans show no remaining cell damage, malignancies, or tumors. We'll still want to check you regularly for the next year or so, and you should avoid spending time in direct sunlight for the immediate future, but otherwise it appears you have a clean bill of health."

"Does that mean I can return to duty?"

"I don't see why not." The doctor frowned as he thought it over. "Of course, you don't have a duty station to report to, since your last one was blown out of the sky. On the other hand, yeomen are pretty easy to assign since all commands need administrative assistants."

"How is Commander Pickering?"

The doctor pursed his lips. "I'm sorry. I can't really discuss another patient's medical information."

"I mean his legal situation." She leaned closer. "I hear he's in a lot of trouble."

Dr. Bennet nodded. "I've heard he's under some kind of investigation by NIS and I know he's under arrest."

"Wow." Yeager leaned forward more, showing as much cleavage as she could. "Any idea why?"

"No, but if I did, I probably couldn't discuss that, either. Admiral LeMieux's supposedly pressing court-martial charges against him, but I don't know the specifics. My business is medicine. I try to stay out of things that concern the brass. I've noticed anytime there's a disaster in the Navy it's usually followed by a witch-hunt. The powers-that-be always want a scapegoat. I don't know the specifics of his case, only that he's been arrested."

And it couldn't have happened to a nicer asshole. Yeager carefully kept her thoughts from her face as she squinted at his nametag. "How long have you been in the Navy, Sir?"

"Not long. I was commissioned a couple months ago, right out of medical school."

"Were you here during the attack?"

"Unfortunately." Bennet sighed. "I was at an orientation briefing when the attack occurred. The space yard and most of the base infrastructure exploded. It knocked out every window in the hospital. That was our first warning. The Karsians devastated the orbitals, the docks, and the landing aprons. I heard they even hit the O-club. It was horrible and . . . excuse me, Yeoman, I'm sorry. I know you were on the ODS at Pan'vu. It's not for me to tell *you* what it was like. I got shoved into a medical response team and ended up doing triage for the next forty-eight hours. It was grim stuff. We had victims arriving all day long, many we could do nothing for. Some died on the operating tables, others before they reached the ER."

Yeager winced. "A lot of people?"

"Yeah. A large number of burn victims, too, some of them terribly." He closed his eyes and shook himself at the memory. "We're supposed to be immune to it as medical professionals, but it was horrible. We lost a lot of good people that day. I had to work double shifts for a week to catch up. It wasn't a good time."

Yeager smiled wistfully. "Mine wasn't either."

"No, I suppose not."

His eyes flickered to her cleavage a moment before looking away, and she felt her interest increase. Bennet was young for a doctor, good-looking, and not much older than herself. She clearly made him uncomfortable, and he was trying to hide it with professional demeanor.

Good, she thought. *That's leverage.*

Regulations forbade personal relationships between officers and enlisted personnel, but she ignored such rules. She wasn't held to the same standards officers were. Besides, rules were made to be broken. She smiled at Bennet sweetly. The lieutenant was a man, and he was reacting like a healthy male.

The cold air from the vents had puckered her nipples. Bennet furtively glanced at the peaks in the fabric of her gown. He quickly looked at his chart and Yeager smiled.

He's a man all right, she thought.

"Can I ask you a question, Sir? About the Navy, I mean."

Surprised, he looked up. "Certainly."

"I've heard there are positions open in Officer Candidate School."

"Yes, there are." Bennet nodded. "That's how I joined the Navy. I signed on right out of med school and went straight into OCS. They commission doctors as lieutenants on graduation because med school takes so long. I should make lieutenant commander in a couple of years. OCS is a great program. Why do you ask?"

Ninety-day wonder.

Yeager gave him an innocent look and tried to appear a little scared. "I was wondering if you knew how a girl might get an OCS slot. I want to make the Navy a career and the officer route seems the best way to go."

"Well, I agree about that." Bennet smiled and sat back on his stool. "Of course, I'm an officer, so I'm biased. I've never been enlisted, so I can't really speak from that perspective. Have you completed any college?"

"Yes, Sir. I have a BS degree."

"Really? In what field?"

"Biology."

Bennet frowned. "Why didn't you choose OCS right off the bat?"

Yeager had no intention of telling him how she'd obtained the diploma from a professor on Turin's World who'd had a particular fetish she'd satisfied for him on a regular basis. She possessed a signed and certified diploma from his university, and that was all that mattered. She'd gotten it for nothing more than time spent on her knees. That professor was dead, killed in the attack on Turin's World at his university. He was gone, along with all of the university's records. Fortunately, after the destruction of Turin's World, no one could prove her degree wasn't legitimate.

"I didn't know about OCS when I joined." Yeager lifted her eyes to his. "I wasn't sure what I wanted to do at first."

"Are you thinking of a medical career?"

"No, Sir, a line officer. I want to command a fleet someday."

His eyes twinkled. "Well, you're certainly ambitious, Yeoman. You'd need a sponsor to get to the Academy, but you can enter OCS with a degree and an officer's recommendation."

"A recommendation?"

"Yes. If you have a degree, a letter of recommendation will get you an appointment to OCS. You can obtain one from your CO or any commissioned officer. You'll need to pass the physical, of course, but since you're already in the Navy and we just gave you a clean bill of health that shouldn't be a problem."

Yeager feigned surprise. As a yeoman, she knew the regulations about OCS by heart. She batted her eyelashes at him. "Really?"

"Sure. Since you already have a degree, it should be pretty easy to get a slot. Your status as a Pan'vu survivor will give you priority over many candidates. There are application forms in admin. Just have your CO sign them, and you'll be put in the OCS que. Your enlisted time will help too."

Yeager pouted. "My CO's under arrest, Sir, and being brought before a board of inquiry. I doubt anyone will take anything he recommends seriously. Besides, he's never been a fan of mine."

"Yeah, I've met him." Bennet shook his head. "He is a rather *unpleasant* man, but he's not your CO anymore. He's been relieved of command. Do you know another officer who might recommend you?"

"Yes, Sir. A local one."

Bennet leaned forward, curious. "Who?"

"Before I answer that, Sir, I have a medical problem we need to discuss."

"Oh." Bennet stood, concern on his face. "What seems to be the problem?"

Yeager's eyes drift to the examination room door. "I'd be more comfortable discussing it privately, Sir. I don't want someone walking in while you're examining me."

"Of course." Bennet hit a button on the bulkhead. The examination room hatch hissed shut and locked, illuminating a flashing "PRIVATE" sign in yellow letters. Bennet moved beside her, looking concerned. "What seems to be the problem?"

"I have an itch, Doctor."

"It could be a reaction to the Raydalon nannites. *Urticaria* is a well-known side effect. Where's the itch exactly?"

"It's in a rather private place, Sir."

"Oh." Bennet stood straighter, assuming a serious and professional expression, and Yeager smiled.

This is way too easy.

Bennet seemed uncomfortable. Beads of sweat were forming on his brow. "I can get an OB-GYN specialist here if you prefer."

"No, Sir, I would *not* prefer. I want you to deal with it." She put her hands on her breasts and lay back on the table.

Bennet swallowed. "Okay . . . where do you itch?"

"There's also something in my eye."

"Your eye?"

He leaned closer to look in her eye. Yeager hooked her heels behind his waist and pulled him closer. Grabbing his wrists, she put his hands on her breasts and gave him the doe-eyed expression of innocence she'd perfected long ago.

Bennet stiffened and tried to pull away. "Yeoman . . . I'm your doctor. This is inappropriate."

She pulled her gown off and tossed it aside. She pulled him closer with her heels as her hands fumbled at his trousers. "I *do* have an itch, Doctor, and you're going to help me scratch it."

She grinned and licked her teeth.

Bennet's breathing became erratic. Getting her hands inside his trousers, she felt his pulse rate increase. Bennet tried to reassert control, straightening up half-heartedly but seemed unable to pull away. "This is wrong, Yeoman. Entirely wrong. This is . . . unacceptable conduct."

He gasped and closed his eyes.

She grabbed his scrubs and pulled his mouth down to hers. "Then write me up, Lieutenant."

Bennet pushed against the table with both palms. "Please . . . you'll cost me my career."

"Shut up and fuck me, Doctor."

She pulled him on top of her. Bennet relented when she thrust her tongue in his mouth.

Her recommendation letter was as good as done.

She hoped they wouldn't make too much noise before they finished.

CHAPTER 25

IKS *MURGAHH*,
NANGTASHGU STAR SYSTEM

Murgahh drifted at the outer edge of the Nangtashgu system, her sensors trained on the jump-gate terminus from Gulliver's Hold, which lay only light-seconds from her hull. Far enough away to allow for coordinated weapons fire but close enough to engage should a Rigelian task force suddenly emerge from the terminus.

Tork watched as Imperial Task Force Two-Two marshaled. He had carefully monitored his back trail as he had led his forces back to Karsian space. The Shikahn had authorized the attack into Confederation space, and—according to the timetable—Tork was supposed to have taken control of Gulliver's Hold by now. In the olden days, the warrior houses of Kars had gazed heavenward at Gulliver's Star and called it *T'yoni'akar*, the Eye of the Beast. Current convention assigned a star's name to whatever power possessed it, which, in this case—unfortunately—was still the Rigelian Confederation.

Gulliver is a strange-sounding name, Tork admitted, *but easier to pronounce than T'yoni'akar.*

Gulliver's Hold held nothing of strategic importance beyond its location, but it contained a plethora of wormholes leading to other Confederation star systems. The original plan had called for ITF Two-Two to secure Gulliver as a forward staging base for Battle Fleet Two. That plan had been made with the assumption lateral operations against the Eusi Hegemony and Centauri Seven were successful. It had turned out that such had not been the case, for the RCN had defeated or pushed back most of the planned invasions. Tork had been forced to withdraw to Karsian space to consider his next move.

His hesitation before the enemy—while tactically sound and strategically necessary—had not set well with his superiors, despite the fact every instinct in Tork's mind screamed Gulliver was a trap.

The unfortunate loss of Imperial Attack Unit Five-One-Three-Two-One in the Hegemony had upset his well-laid plans when it failed to capture the Eusi system of Nambo. Something had gone horribly wrong there, and until he could ascertain exactly what that *something* was, he had no intention of charging into Gulliver blindly. The whole plan needed revising.

His intent had been to secure the Hegemony while simultaneously incapacitating the enemy's Seventh Fleet at Centauri Seven, followed by a massive attack against the heavily defended Rigelian system of Galderon. Each of those efforts had failed disastrously, requiring readjustment of the plan.

Tork had decided to fall back to Nangtashgu while he examined the enemy's weak spots and located vulnerable places to attack. Whatever he ordered, ITF Two-Two would do, but he felt a moral responsibility not to waste his warriors' lives in pointless battles that could not be won.

The attacks on Pan'vu and Centauri Seven had gone extremely well initially, but he'd failed to capitalize on those initial advantages. His forces had held too long in Zion's Waste, anxious to ambush a counterattack. He had not felt—at least at the time—that ITF Two-Two had been strong enough to hold Centauri Seven against the large component of the RCN's Seventh Fleet that had arrived to challenge him. Looking back, he realized he should have pressed his advantage when he had still had the element of surprise.

He should have occupied Centauri Seven and blockaded its jump-gates, but his combat instincts had talked him out of it. He had believed his force had achieved the desired objectives—with the exception of destroying the enemy's carriers—and it had seemed wise to withdraw to the Empire to support a quick thrust at the Eusi Hegemony. With the failure of his forces to capture even a single system in the Hegemony, however, the plan had collapsed.

The Rigelians had fought fiercely and bravely in Centauri Seven, Gallagher, and Nambo. They were fighting just as hard in Antioch. With the enemy bunching on the right and left sides of the *Rim, the center seemed open for the taking.*

No, it is too easy. The enemy has regained strength on both flanks and has opened an obvious weakness up the middle that leads to their heart worlds, which makes no strategic sense. The Rigelians are using their own form of por'tahk against us; they seek to lure us into death ground where they can envelop us from both sides.

Tork had refused to bite and had ordered his forces to reform in Nangtashgu while he reassessed the situation. The withdrawal had angered his superiors. Tork was certain his "advisor" had reported his hesitancy to the Imperial Guard.

Which is why an IG super dreadnought is now holding station off your starboard bow, he thought irritably.

The In'thork ship had arrived in-system hours earlier and approached quietly. Before entering capital missile range, its captain had hailed *Murgahh* to demand an immediate conference with Fleet Admiral Tork on matters of Imperial security.

Tork had had little choice but to comply. Failure to immediately comply with an official demand from the Shikahn's Own would be insubordination and place him under suspicion and arrest by the Imperial Guard.

The IG was the third finger of the Karsian Triad and was known as the "Hand of the Shikahn." To maintain the loyalty of the armed forces, the IG monitored their compliance with the Shikahn's will, ready to crush the slightest hint of rebellion on a moment's notice. Rebellion remained a constant threat in a nation made of subjugated worlds, and preventing rebellions was the Imperial Guard's "official" purpose. Their real job, known by everyone but never publicly acknowledged, was to prevent mutiny by the Karsian military. IG forces remained vigilant to root out and crush treason. The Empire was a hive of intrigue. The Shikahn feared a *coup de' état* more than he feared enemy fleets, and that fear trickled down through all of the Karsian services. Which was why Tork found himself waiting in Murgahh's boat bay as the IG shuttle arrived.

Bay lights flashed from yellow to green as the shuttle's heavy double doors opened with a hiss. The officer that stepped through the hatch wore silver mail beneath a tunic of black leather, offset by a crimson cape and glittering badges of honor. A patch covered one eye, a scar of honor from a life of violence. His rank was intimidating. The shoulder tabs indicated the rank of over-general, one of the top officers of the fanatical IG service Karsians called the In'thork. The three colors of his uniform heightened his dramatic entrance into the boat bay.

Tork remembered their significance. An ominous fear crept up his spine as the over-general glanced about with his good eye and casually waved a pair of black-garbed escorts behind him to stand at ease. The IG's uniform had been designed in antiquity. and the colors were well-known to every Karsian, consisting of black, silver, and red.

Black is the color of the eternal night of space. Tork remembered the recitations from childhood. *Black is the heart of the Imperial Guard. Black is the future of traitors who incur the wrath of the Shikahn.*

Silver is the color of armor that shields the Empire. Silver is the color of loyalty to the Shikahn. Silver is the color of the Knife of Justice that plunges into treasonous hearts with righteous anger.

Red is the blood of the Shikahn's enemies. Red is the fury of the Shikahn's wrath. Red is the purifying fire that destroys the Shikahn's enemies and forges the spirit of the warrior.

Tork bowed slightly and saluted. "Welcome aboard, Bor'barhg. It is an honor to receive you."

The over-general returned the salute brusquely and stepped into the reception area. His minions followed, grim-faced and ominous in their black leather and silver mail. Their eyes darted about suspiciously, looking for threats as they fingered the hilts of their weapons in silence.

"The Kahthrung sends its salutations, Korguhn." The over-general stared at him with his good eye. "I am Bor'bargh Agnahr. The Shikahn sends his regards."

Tork inclined his head. "I am honored."

"Perhaps." Agnahr continued to glance around the boat bay, searching for threats. *Murgahh* was just another battleship to him.

Little love was lost between the IG and the Imperial Navy. The arrival of an IG ship—a super dreadnought no less—was ominous anytime, for it usually meant one of two things. The first was that a security inspection was in progress.

The second was far worse.

"Is there a place where we may confer in private, Korguhn?"

"Of course, Bor'barhg. Follow me."

Tork led them to the flag conference room, where Admiral Moph and Captain Gutahr waited, along with T'lihktu, his IG advisor. He let the In'thork officers seat themselves and offered them warm talik, which they accepted in cold silence.

Agnahr looked at him. "Korguhn Tork, I have asked Yi'lahk T'lihktu to join us to officially record our conversation as we discuss the Shikahn's business."

"Of course, Bor'barhg."

"I shall be direct with you, Korguhn. Your hesitancy in achieving your operational objectives has not pleased the Shikahn."

"There are extenuating circumstances, Bor'bargh." Tork answered carefully, well aware of the minefield he was treading. "The recapture of Centauri Seven by the enemy's fleet, combined with the failure of Imperial Attack Unit Five-One-Three-Two-One to secure the Hegemony worlds we targeted, has made execution of our original plan too risky. I thought it best to pull back and reassess before determining my next course of action."

"That is precisely what T'lihktu told us."

Tork felt a sudden sense of gratitude toward his IG advisor.

Agnahr shrugged. "T'lihktu has much admiration for your tactical abilities, Korguhn. Your reasons for pulling back and reassessing were discussed and evaluated in advance. Unfortunately, they were rejected by the Kahduhn."

"Why would the Imperial Staff reject my actions?" Tork tried not to show his irritation. "I am the one at the tip of the spear, not them. I know the situation here better than they."

Agnahr shrugged again. "There have been political changes at home of late, as well as plots and intrigue within the Shi-thrung. The House of Khar has come into prominence on the Kahthrung. This has resulted in unexpected changes for the Imperial staff, including the In'thork."

Tork's eyes widened slightly. If the House of Khar was now the dominant on the Council of Elders, it made sense there would be leadership changes. Unfortunately, that meant Tork's house, Lahk'nah, had been superseded in power. Such things happened, but to hear of the changes to leadership from Emperor's Own spoke volumes about the size of the political coup. House disputes were not supposed to affect the Imperial Guard.

"I see."

"The new leadership of the In'thork has—after detailed review of your battle actions—noted your failure to achieve even the most basic objectives of the Kahduhn's plan. There is now question of your loyalty to the Shikahn."

"How can they question my loyalty?" Tork felt himself growing angry. "I am a warrior of the thrung; a fleet admiral of the Shahn'lar! The whole battle plan was *my* idea. Who are those rear-echelon *k'toors* to question my loyalty?"

Agnahr locked his good eye on Tork. "There are many questions about your perceived *lack of enthusiasm.*"

"Such as?"

"Bor'klar Gutahr logged your failure to destroy a Rigelian battleship that fled the Centauri Seven attack, as well as your later refusal to bombard the planet and render it unusable to our enemy."

"Bombarding Centauri Seven was never part of the plan."

"Perhaps. But doing so was strategically sound and would have rendered the planet useless to the enemy. Anything that hurts the Confederation aids the Empire. By failing to grasp that opportunity, you showed incompetence before the enemy, allowing them to foil the Kahduhn's plan."

Tork fought to keep insubordination out of his voice, but it was difficult. "Destroying noncombatants would not have helped our mission, only caused needless slaughter. The mission was to destroy Rigelian *military* targets in Centauri Seven, which was accomplished, not to eradicate every Rigelian living there. Doing so would strengthen the enemy's resolve to fight. By not slaughtering civilians I weakened their resolve. The plan was to get the enemy to the bargaining table, Bor'barhg, not make them refuse to negotiate."

"Irrelevant." Agnahr's baleful eye bored into Tork. "That assumption presumes the Rigelians will negotiate at all, which is a political assessment, not a military one. You had within your grasp the ability to ensure Centauri

Seven's complete destruction, and you failed to do so. That choice was made by you, deliberately and intentionally. You also allowed an enemy dreadnought to escape destruction, a battleship that inevitably we will have to fight again at another time, probably at great cost in Karsian lives. By letting that battleship escape, you allowed it to warn the Confederation. The resulting loss of surprise is unforgivable."

Tork felt anger heat his face. "Risking the battle group's mission to pursue a single battleship that was no longer a threat would have been inept. It would have—"

"Silence!" Agnahr's cold eye bored into Tork. "I am not finished. Your errors and lack of enthusiasm were then compounded by the loss of several of our task units, including the loss of the Shikahn's new and most highly-valued flagship in the Eusi Hegemony. Do you think such massive vessels are cheap, Korguhn, or that the Empire has unlimited numbers of them to waste?"

"*Kundhor* was assigned the wrong mission, Bor'barhg. I have argued that from the beginning. Her assigned mission was commerce raiding, but it should have been—"

"*You* allowed the Rigelians to reoccupy Centauri Seven without a fight. Is this true or not?"

"No." Tork felt icy claws of fear wrap their talons around his heart. The discussion was not going well. Officers who garnered IG wrath usually "disappeared." It was unlikely the IG would murder a fleet admiral outright, of course, but stranger things had happened. The current attitude of the IG following the coup at home did not instill

Tork with confidence in his own survival, particularly if the Council of Elders wanted him gone. The Kahduhn was fond of saying it was better to have many dead heroes than one live traitor.

Agnahr was glaring. "Explain."

"Surviving enemy ships strongly resisted the small force I sent to mop up Centauri Seven. That mop-up force was ambushed by Confederation ships that appeared from Zion's Waste, as I feared they might. It was clear the enemy fleet was assembling in Yamato and our occupation force was overly extended and exposed to destruction."

"There would have been no surviving ships in Centauri had you destroyed them properly in the first attack. You contradict yourself, Korguhn."

"There were enemy light combatants that survived our initial strike, Bor'barhg. Such things are inevitable. I sent a force to clean those units out. We assess it was these surviving combatants that ambushed our force in Centauri Seven. That force had discovered an enemy destroyer in Pan'vu and pursued it into Centauri Seven. But another Rigelian force entered Zion's Waste behind it and caught ours by surprise. I suspect they were enemy stealthships, for our vessels saw no enemy drive indications while crossing Zion's Waste. The mop-up force was unaware of them and found itself caught between the defenders of Centauri Seven and the stealth threat near the jump-gate in Zion's Waste. The Rigelian Fleet in Yamato was at the time in no position to launch an offensive, and I had little fear of an immediate attack from Gallagher. Under the circumstances,

I thought it best to avoid prolonged exposure in Centauri Seven, given the needless number of casualties occupation of that system would impose upon us once the enemy in Gallagher and Yamato mobilized. I opted instead to support our main thrust into the Eusi Hegemony, since the gas giants there are, after all, our true objectives."

"Yes, objectives *you* failed to achieve." Agnahr's canines became visible. "You dispatched a single attack unit to capture the entire Nambo system, a target whose very importance demanded a full battle squadron at the least, and likely an Imperial attack force."

"We planned to decoy defending RCN forces out of Nambo into a trap we had set up in New Woodlark." Tork held up his hands to emphasize the point. "IAU Five-One-Three-Two-One's mission was to decimate Eusi sensor outposts and lure defending forces in Nambo through the jump-gate into our trap, where *our* megadreadnought was lying in wait. My own task force was supporting that effort by blocking the jump-gates from Gallagher. Once Nambo was secured, I intended to send battle forces into Tzu and New Woodlark, then blockade the Pontif system while the rest of our fleet supported the attack on Antioch.

"The Hegemony would have been in our hands at that point. We would have had possession of Gallagher, Tzu, Pontif, Wewak, New Woodlark, and Nambo, including every gas giant those systems contain. We would have possessed the Hegemony, which would satisfy the plan and provide every resource the Empire needs. At that point, Bor'barhg, it was to be up to the haki to negotiate a peace with the Confederation. We would have been extended to our limits holding the systems we had managed to capture. I never intended to defeat the RCN in its entirety."

Agnahr's eyes narrowed to slits and his voice grew cold, making Tork fight the urge to fidget. "What are the results of *your* efforts, Korguhn? Tell me, which of these Confederation systems—that *you* commanded our forces to capture—do we now possess? I will tell you. None! Not a single planet for all of the blood and ships lost. It has all been for nothing. You had the enemy helpless, and you hesitated to strike the fatal blow. Indeed, you withdrew. Such actions are incompetent at best and cowardly at worst. *You* failed to exploit the plan to its fullest."

"It would have been insane to attack full-out." Tork was angry now, for while officers of the Imperial Guard fancied themselves military experts, they were in fact only state security. "Had I proceeded into the core Rigelian system of Galderon—which you seem to think was the proper thing to do—without securing my lines of communication and scouting my flanks, the RCN would have enveloped us, cut us off, and destroyed our fleet. If they managed to hold Gallagher, Zion's Waste *and* Pan'vu behind us, we would have been cut off. Our only option then would have been to slug our way through New Woodlark and through the Rigelian-held Antioch system to return to the Empire. Logistical lines must be maintained in a military campaign, as well as lines of communication. Principles still matter, Bor'barhg. Rational thinking is required; will alone does not suffice. Battles are won by tactics, not enthusiasm."

"Offensives fail where there is no spirited attack."
Agnahr leaned back on his cushions and steepled his fingers. "But perhaps you have a point. It may indeed be as you say. Unfortunately, the Shi-thrung does not see it that way, Korguhn. They have given the In'thork instructions as to your disposition. The fact remains that whatever the reason, *you* failed to achieve the objectives assigned you. Do you deny this?"

Tork swallowed and dropped his head. "No."

"You admit you have failed the Shikahn?"

"I admit I failed to achieve the objectives, but I have never failed the Shikahn."

Agnahr put his hands in his lap. His one eye stared at Tork without blinking. "Elementary, Korguhn. Failure to achieve assigned objectives *is* failing the Shikahn. A commander is responsible for the success or failure of his command. Do you deny this?"

Tork closed his eyes. "No."

"I am glad you agree."

Tork agreed in principle, but it seemed unjust. He was honest enough to admit he had failed to achieve his assigned objectives. There was no sharing of that failure. As commanding admiral he had been in charge and the failure was his responsibility alone. One could share authority, but never responsibility.

Tork lifted his head. "Am I to be relieved of command?"

"Yes." Agnahr's voice grew calm. "By the orders of the Shikahn, you are relieved of the command of Imperial Task Force Two-Dash-Two. Torguhn Moph shall assume temporary command until a permanent replacement has arrived."

"And who will that be?"

"*Shiguhn* Borak. The Shikahn feels confident the new high admiral will prosecute the Empire's objectives with proper enthusiasm and achieve his objectives. The Shikahn wants a *fighting* admiral who will accomplish his will."

"Borak?" Tork's face grew dark. Borak was a warrior who advocated fanatical all-out attack as the only method of combat. "If you put Borak in charge of this task force it is as good as lost. He will waste it. He will charge against the biggest enemy fleet he can find. He is utterly predictable. The Rigelians will decoy him, trap his units, cut them off, and destroy them piecemeal. He is reckless. You cannot be serious."

"We are quite serious, Korguhn."

Agnahr made a subtle motion with his hand. The warriors in black leather and silver mail rose and pulled apart, drawing side arms. One pointed his coil pistol at Tork's head, the other at his heart.

Agnahr smiled. "The Shikahn has put a new admiral in charge of this force; one who will fight, not run from Rigelians, and in doing so, will win. He believes Borak to be that admiral. More importantly, Borak is of House Khar. He is enroute as we speak and will arrive in a few days. You are recalled to Kars to face questions about your failure to achieve objectives and explain your lack of enthusiasm. There is also the question of your loyalty which must be resolved."

Of course, and if the questions are answered correctly, I will live to rot somewhere in a staff job. If not, I will be executed. They will declare me an Imperial hero that was 'lost' in some distant battle . . . after they shoot me to save face.

To resist the In'thork was a death sentence that could even result in the death of his family. Worse, it would bring dishonor upon House Lahk'nah and generations of future Lahk'nah warriors. Tork had little choice but to comply, yet the idea of letting a fool like Borak take over the task force he had built was galling.

Tork lowered his head. "I will comply, of course, but the Shikahn is making a grave mistake putting Borak in charge. Mark my words, the Kahduhn will come to regret his assignment."

"Perhaps, but *you* are under arrest, Korguhn."

Agnahr made another motion with his hand. The guards in black stepped forward and took Tork by each arm. He rose and stood silently while they applied the magnetic restraints to his wrists and searched him for weapons.

"The Shikahn is above right or wrong." Agnahr smirked. "He cannot make mistakes. Unfortunately, you are not the Shikahn, and you have made some very serious mistakes. I suspect it is *you* who shall come to regret them, Korguhn. Take him away."

The guards pushed Tork roughly toward the door and out into the corridor.

Agnahr watched them go in silence, then turned back to Moph and Gutahr, who sat unmoving, their eyes wide with fear. "See to your fleet, Torguhn. You are both dismissed."

Both warriors jumped up and happily vacated the conference room. Agnahr waited until they were gone, then turned toward T'Lihktu. "Your loyalty to Korguhn Tork is most admirable, T'lihktu. Loyalty, even when misplaced, is a virtue. Because of that loyalty, you shall be spared Tork's fate."

T'lihktu stood and saluted. "Thank you, Bor'barhg."

Agnahr looked at him coldly. "Do not thank me, T'lihktu. You failed to report Tork's treason until he had already withdrawn from the Gallagher attack. There is no excuse for such a delay. While loyalty to a commander is an admirable trait for a military warrior, it is *not* a desirable trait for the Emperor's Own. Only loyalty to the Shikahn matters. You have confused your priorities, T'lihktu. Your first duty was to the In'thork, not your assigned officer. The In'thork has considered the specifics of this case carefully and has decided. Tork will be questioned, demoted, reprimanded, and likely shot if he fails to satisfy the Inquisitors. I have no idea what his eventual fate will be. It is possible he may even be spared despite failing at his primary job. As a member of the Imperial Guard, however, *you* should be under no such illusion."

T'lihktu's eyes widened as Agnahr removed a hand pulser from under his cloak. "The Shikahn's retribution is swift."

Agnahr fired twice, the cracks of hypersonic darts sharp in the hollow confines of the conference room.

T'lihktu's head snapped back. His body fell and lay unmoving in a widening pool of blood.

Agnahr stood, glanced down at T'lihktu's body, nodding in satisfaction as blood soaked the carpet.

Justice had been administered.

He holstered his pulser, listening to the sound of the guards' footsteps as they receded down the corridor.

CHAPTER 26

COURT ROOM, JAG SYSTEM HEADQUARTERS, CENTAURI SEVEN NAVAL BASE

"The Defendant will rise."

The ominous words, delivered in the monotone peculiar to presiding judges, came from the officer in charge of the RCN general court martial, who cast a baleful eye on the lieutenant commander sitting glumly at the head of the courtroom. Waldo Pickering straightened the tunic of his dress uniform and stood to face the court.

Pickering's hair had grown back some. It had fallen out due to the nannite treatments he'd been given to overcome the radiation dose he'd received aboard the ODS during the Pan'vu attack.

Pickering arrogantly faced the judge and picked imaginary lint from one of his shoulder boards. Beside him, Commander Wayne Ovslovsky, his defense counsel, fought an urge to sigh. Pickering was a conceited, spoiled, and utterly lecherous fool, as Ovslovsky's brief association with him had proven, but he'd never believed Pickering was an idiot until this moment. Assuming a haughty demeanor as a defendant in a general court martial was particularly stupid, especially when facing the number of charges Pickering faced.

Ovslovsky had been assigned as defense counsel by the judge advocate general's office when the Navy had brought charges against the former ODS commander. Ovslovsky's job at building a credible defense had been an unpleasant and difficult task. His client wasn't an easy man to defend.

Pickering had been one of five survivors rescued in escape pods over Turin's World. He'd been taking a shower when the attack had occurred. Surviving the attack had been a miracle. Rescue crews had found him alone and naked when they'd tractored his escape pod aboard. Unfortunately for Pickering, what was left of the ODS hadn't burned up in Turin's atmosphere. Salvage ships had tractored the broken sections and hauled them back into stable orbits, preventing their complete destruction. Those salvaged sections had yielded a treasure trove of incriminating evidence the prosecution had been able to use against his client.

Pickering had been undergoing treatment for radiation poisoning when the Inspector General's office had received a tip from a whistleblower whose name had been withheld for witness protection reasons. It had been another survivor of the Pan'vu attack—Ovslovsky was still unsure who specifically, though he had his suspicions—who'd told the Naval Investigative Service that crimes had been committed by Pickering while in command of the ODS. That whistleblower had also told them precisely where that evidence could be found.

Acting on the tip, NIS agents had sealed off the commander's quarters and forensically recovered data files from Pickering's computer, as well as other ODS logs that had survived the blast. What they had discovered had led to a general court-martial.

In the computer log of a deceased petty officer named Hernandez they'd found evidence Pickering had deliberately ignored a Priority One distress signal and had ordered Hernandez—against her recorded objection—to dump classified information on an unsecure computer in violation of Navy regulations. The compromise of classified data alone would have justified Pickering's court martial, but Hernandez had also logged that when she had objected to the order, Pickering had threatened her with disciplinary action and reassignment.

If that had been all there was to it, Pickering might have gotten off with a hard slap on the wrist, for he was the son of the very wealthy Emerson Pickering, a prominent member of the Progressive Party and a confidant of no less than Baron von Boecklin himself.

Compromised classified was serious enough, but more serious charges had evolved from the NIS investigation.

Pickering's blatant ambivalence about the Priority One message, which had resulted in Turin's World being unprepared for the Karsian attack that followed, made it difficult for Ovslovsky to defend Pickering. The evidence had made it painfully clear to everyone in the courtroom that Pickering had been derelict in his duty when he'd failed to follow the orders issued to him by competent authority. The ODS had been Turin's only orbital defense station. The Prosecution had argued that Pickering's dereliction of duty had caused the deaths of thousands on Turin's World. In addition, they'd argued that had Pickering followed orders regarding the Priority One message, Centauri Seven might have had adequate time to prepare for the attack.

It was a ludicrous assertion, of course, emanating from a fallacy of false cause. Even if Pickering had complied with regulations regarding the disposition of classified material and had promptly passed the warning on, there was nothing to prove it would have done anything to save Turin's World or the fleet yards at Centauri Seven from destruction, much less the civil populace on Turin's World. Ovslovsky had successfully argued such an assertion was non sequitur and clearly speculation, but he remained worried. Just because the prosecution hadn't been able to *prove* those facts beyond reasonable doubt didn't mean his defense had *disproved* them.

Pickering had been arrested by NIS while recovering in a hospital and had been thoroughly questioned. That was when things had gone from bad to worse in Ovslovsky's opinion. One by one, witnesses had appeared, seemingly out of the woodwork, to levy charge after charge of sexual misconduct against his client. Without exception, every witness was enlisted and a female who'd been under Pickering's command. Most were young in age and junior in rank at the time of the alleged offenses, and three had been married personnel. Each had sworn under oath they'd been coerced into a sexual relationship with their commanding officer. The alleged offenses had occurred over a span of years at various locations where Pickering had been the officer in charge. As the witnesses had emerged in a continuous stream, Ovslovsky had begun to wonder what kind of sexual monster he'd been assigned to defend.

NIS had soon realized it had a major case on its hands. The Navy—ever anxious to find scapegoats for the Centauri Seven debacle—had zeroed its witch hunt in on the man they'd been looking for. On orders from Admiral LeMieux, a general court martial had been convened to try Pickering.

The charges against his client were many, starting with the deceased Hernandez's logged accusation of violating security procedures regarding the handling classified information, his orders to force her to participate in an offense and his retaliation threats against her if she failed to comply.

Ovslovsky had been somewhat successful at getting the prosecution to drop several of the weaker charges. The Article 98 charge for noncompliance with procedural orders had been dropped, as had the Article 110 charge for improperly hazarding a vessel or station. Both were conjecture at best, and extremely difficult for the prosecution to prove beyond reasonable doubt. Several Article 133 charges for sodomy had likewise been dropped because the number of physical acts the UCMJ declared to be sodomy were so broad in nature that half the Confederation was probably guilty of them. The prosecution had been more than happy to drop those since they had no desire to open that particular can of worms.

The remaining charges, however, were serious enough. Pickering had been charged with such a plethora of crimes it had become almost impossible for Ovslovsky to defend him. But criminal defense was his job, and Ovslovsky had known from the start he'd have to give it his best shot.

He'd failed, of course. Not that another defense counsel could've done better. Certainly, Pickering's bad manners and insufferable attitude hadn't helped his case, but Ovslovsky still felt he'd let his client down.

Pickering had as much of a chance of acquittal as a snowball had in the heart of a supernova. The essential problem, of course, was Pickering *was* guilty, and the evidence against him was overwhelming. That alone would have made the job hard without also having to suffer Pickering's holier-than-thou demeanor, an attitude that almost certainly would guarantee his punishment. The man was arrogant as only the son of a wealthy family could be, and that arrogance was on full display as he faced the court about to convict him.

Article 125 of the Uniform Code of Military Justice required all jury members to be of equal rank or better than the accused. The officers composing the jury were certainly that, Ovslovsky reflected bitterly. The lowest-ranking was a full commander, and the rest were all captains and commodores. The senior member was a rear admiral. While one could never tell exactly how a jury might vote—Ovslovsky had certainly been surprised in the past—he'd honed an ability over the years to read a jury's general sentiment. The faces of the officers in the jury box contained barely repressed hostility. His client's case was all but lost.

I guess that's only reasonable, Ovslovsky told himself philosophically, *considering how Pickering's behavior has brought discredit upon the Navy in general, and on naval officers in particular. Every member of the jury is or has been a commanding officer. Pickering is more than an embarrassment to his fellow officers. They consider him a predatory criminal.*

Pickering had been given the honor of commanding an RCN space station, only to violate the trust placed in him for the basest of impulses. There was retribution in the eyes of the jury, and Ovslovsky steeled himself for the inevitable storm of justice he knew was about to descend on his client like the blade of a guillotine. Pickering, who'd always been protected by wealth and power, seemed oblivious to that fact.

He still thinks Daddy's going to save him, Ovslovsky thought, fighting an urge to shake his head.

"Has the jury reached a verdict?" The presiding judge, Vice Admiral Fahd Al-Qatani, was from the Jaffai Worlds. He was one of JAG's most eminent justices. His brown eyes were expressionless as the senior officer of the jury, Rear Admiral Bjorn Velasquez, stood to face the court.

"We have, Your Honor."

"Very well." Al-Qatani glanced at the charges on his

desk monitor. "On the Article 92 charge, failure to obey a lawful order or regulation, how has the jury decided?"

"Guilty, Your Honor."

"On the thirteen counts of Article 93, violations for cruelty and mistreatment, how has the jury decided?"

"Guilty, Your Honor."

Ovslovsky felt his guts tighten. The thirteen Article 93 counts were for sexual harassment, charges Ovslovsky had known he would be unable to successfully defend Pickering against. The guilty verdicts on those were no surprise.

Al-Qatani nodded and moved down the list without expression. "On the two Article 107 charges, making false official statements, how has the jury decided?"

"Guilty, Your Honor."

"On the eight counts of Article 133, conduct unbecoming an officer, how has the jury decided?"

"Guilty on all counts."

Ovslovsky detected a slight change in Pickering's demeanor as the guilty verdicts were given. He wasn't sure, but the jerk's shoulders seemed to drop a little with each verdict. Reality was beginning to sink in, even to Pickering's pea brain.

Guilty verdicts continued to drop like hammers, each one slamming nails into Pickering's coffin, all under Article 134, the general, or "catch-all," article of the UCMJ. He was found guilty on three counts of adultery and six counts of wrongful cohabitation. What followed were seventeen guilty verdicts for fraternization, five counts of indecent acts with another person, two counts of requesting commission of an offense, and eighteen counts of pandering. By the time it was over, Pickering had been pronounced guilty on every charge except two fraternization charges and five charges of indecent acts, which Ovslovsky had managed to successfully argue were too vague and ill-defined to be used against his client. Apparently, the jury had bought his arguments on those charges, but the remaining stack of guilty verdicts were more than enough to put his client in prison for decades.

As each guilty verdict was read, Pickering seemed to get smaller, his shoulders drooping, and Ovslovsky felt more and more like a failure. His job had been to defend Pickering. He'd done his best, but he'd failed.

On the other hand, he *had* defended Pickering to the best of his ability. The man's own actions, particularly his cruel treatment of subordinates and his pathological sexual abuse of enlisted females, meant Pickering was not only unfit to wear the uniform he wore but had brought dishonor and discredit upon everyone who did wear that uniform with pride, including Ovslovsky. If Ovslovsky felt bad about his inability to defend his client, he could live with it. There was nothing about this trial he'd lose any sleep over, for justice would be done.

Al-Qatani glanced at Pickering, whose half-lidded eyes now belied some anxiety. Ovslovsky saw sweat forming on Pickering's brow.

"Lieutenant Commander Waldo Pickering," the judge said, his voice booming ominously as his eyes locked on Pickering's face like the barrels of a laser turret. "You have been found guilty on multiple UCMJ charges as stated by the president of the jury of this court martial, and innocent on specific counts as stated by the same. Do you have anything to say on your behalf before I pronounce sentence?"

Pickering smirked and shook his head. Obviously, he regretted nothing and believed his family connections would save him.

"Very well. By the authority vested in me by the Rigelian Confederation Navy, I now pass sentence for the charges you have been found guilty of. While none of the charges against you constitute a capital offense under the UCMJ, your guilt under lesser offenses proves your conduct has not only been grossly negligent but criminal in nature. It is therefore the judgment of this court that you knowingly and willingly committed said offenses with full knowledge of their criminality and awareness of your own culpability in them. You are hereby judged a disgrace to the uniform you wear, and your continued presence in that uniform an affront to the good men and women who have had the privilege to wear it. Men and women, I might add, who are fighting and dying even now to maintain its honor.

"It is the judgment of this court that you be formally stripped of all rank and privileges, reduced to the paygrade of E-1 and dishonorably discharged from further service in the armed forces of the Confederation. In addition, this court orders you to pay a fine of one hundred thousand credits and that your pay and benefits be terminated immediately. You are hereby remanded to correctional

custody until such time as your formal stripping ceremony can be conducted, and all fines, court costs, and
out-processing fees have been paid. Sergeant-at-Arms,
remove this individual from the court."

A burly Marine in green approached Pickering, who
quailed as the sergeant took him by the arm and attached
electronic handcuffs. As the Marine stooped to apply
leg shackles, Pickering's eyes darted about furtively,
his expression that of a trapped rat. The Marine guided
Pickering toward the doors at the back of the courtroom.

A sudden commotion at the jury bench caused them
to stop.

"Your Honor!" Velasquez stood angrily from his seat,
his expression incredulous. "We found this man guilty
of multiple punitive counts that, under naval regulation,
should put him in prison for years. That's *all* the punishment he gets for his crimes? Busted, fined, and a dishon-
orable discharge? The man deserves hard labor!"

Al-Qatani pounded his gavel on his desk, and for the
first time showed anger as he addressed the president of
the jury. "Sit down, Admiral. There will be order in this
court. The jury has given the verdict, and I, as presiding
justice, have passed sentence on the defendant in accordance with the procedures for court martial."

"Your Honor, that's the most lenient sentencing possible, given the subject's—"

"Be quiet, Admiral Velasquez. The jury will not debate
sentencing with the presiding judge. Juries do not have
sentencing power. That is solely the prerogative of the

presiding judge as defined in Article 125. Now sit down or I'll have you held in contempt of court."

Velasquez sat, but Ovslovsky saw he was clearly fuming, as were the other jury members. Pickering had somehow escaped the harshest penalties, arguably the ones he deserved the most.

In a practical sense, some justice had been done, for Waldo Pickering was no longer a naval officer nor a member of the RCN. His name would be stricken, and his record forever tarnished with dishonor. It wasn't quite what the jury or the prosecution wanted, of course, but it would do. It had been the best compromise Al-Qatani had been able to find.

Pickering's father saw to that.

"All rise," the Sergeant of the Guard said as Al-Qatani rose from his bench.

The courtroom stood as the sergeant-at-arms led Pickering through the double doors to the brig. Ovslovsky thought he heard Pickering whimpering as he was dragged away, but he wasn't sure. His eyes moved back to Al-Qatani as the judge pounded his gavel again.

"This court stands adjourned."

CHAPTER 27

Egon pulled at the collar of his dress blues and stared at the people gathered in the boat bay. He felt uncomfortable in dress uniform, even more so with the inconvenience *his* ceremony was imposing on the people gathered in the crowded boat bay.

His deal with Yamashita had been for a quiet *little* ceremony, one within naval regulations and little commotion. *Yamashita agreed far too quickly*, Egon thought, grimacing as he remembered the grin on his captain's face. *Now I know why. If I'd known what he was up to, I'd have forgone the ceremony altogether.*

Over five hundred personnel were gathered on the boat bay deck, including most of Kuroshima's crew and several from the destroyer *Gant*. Many well-wishers were present as well, including Rear Admiral Yolowski of Yamamoto and the captains of the cruisers *Sekigahara* and *Capricornus*.

Most attendees were from *Kuroshima* and *Aurigae*, but virtually every ship in Task Unit 17.2.2 was represented by someone in the audience, and some from the other units in Task Force Seventeen.

News had spread faster than a neutrino surge through Rear Admiral Yu's Task Group 17.1 to Rear Admiral McDougal's newly-arrived Task Group 17.3. Then Vice Admiral Montgomery himself, the Task Force Seventeen CO, had gotten involved, graciously offering the boat bay of his superdreadnought *Pan-Ku* for the ceremony. Egon had declined that offer, preferring a *small* ceremony.

What should have been a quiet ceremony with a few guests had somehow morphed into an event requiring a calculator to handle. He suspected a number of attendees were just looking for some reason to get away from normal shipboard routine, and a wedding provided that. But most were well-wishers. Weddings on warships were practically unheard of in combat zones during a war.

A few skippers had made attendance mandatory, strongly *recommending* personnel attend. Such orders were made as suggestions, but everyone knew they were orders. It was political, of course. The skippers wanted their crews represented in any official ceremony involving the CO of Task Force Seventeen. The theory existed that task force commanders handed out promotions faster to captains whose crews were "team players" at social functions, at least faster than to those who never showed. Failure to attend said functions made some commanders *unhappy*, and more than one rebellious skipper had found himself passed over for promotion over such trivial things. It was something from a peacetime Navy that had nothing to do with a person's competence, but often determined success or failure for promotion. Egon doubted Montgomery would stoop to such a thing, but it had happened with other task force COs. The result was most skippers played it safe. Egon wasn't ignorant of the political manipulations, but they irked him to no end.

Why make people attend if they don't want to be here?

He'd asked himself that question a hundred times even though he knew the answer. Most skippers were bucking for eventual flag rank and dreaded the label "*not a team player.*" Politics always seemed to rear its ugly head, with COs filling the squares in a bid for power.

Regardless of how he loathed such things personally, the situation existed, and there was little he could do about it. If it created resentment among the personnel in the boat bay before him, he couldn't tell by the looks on their faces. Most were acting like the ceremony was the best thing since antigerone therapy. If anyone in the crowd felt half as uncomfortable as he felt in dress uniform, Egon was truly sorry on their behalf.

Agni's crew had nearly nine hundred personnel. A quarter were present in the boat bay. The ceremony would be conducted by Yamashita himself. There were higher-ranking officers present, but it was Yamashita's ship, giving him precedent. Besides, Talara had asked him to conduct the ceremony. Commodores and admirals from other task units were arriving as guests of honor. Egon had met most of them at one time or another as part of Yamashita's staff, but he doubted many had ever heard of Talara.

They knew about her now, of course, based on the battles that had gained her a combat reputation in a startlingly brief amount of time. A newly frocked destroyer CO was rare enough, but the conditions under which she'd been given command—as well as the battle she'd fought with LeMieux's defense force and in Gallagher—had made her something of a new legend in Task Force Seventeen.

Egon shook his head, smiling. For all her sweetness and naiveté, Talara had done well as a reluctant destroyer skipper. She wasn't the type Egon would have thought could command a warship, nor even be assigned to the command line. Talara had always seemed a bit *too sweet* for command, but she'd risen to the occasion with flying colors in the heart of disaster. His girl had steel in her marrow, even if she didn't realize it, and it had served her well. He was damned proud of her.

Talara wore her emotions on her sleeve most of the time. Facing combat hadn't changed that, and it was one of the things he loved about her. She'd become many new things in recent weeks, but she remained the woman he'd fallen in love with. She'd seen shipmates and friends killed in battle and had turned out to be a surprisingly successful CO, despite her youth, inexperience, and the wrong personality for the job. Despite all that had happened, she wasn't jaded, bitter, or hardened like many who suffered such experiences. She still radiated the same sweetness, and the same impish delight was in her eyes when she giggled.

There were times, he admitted--particularly when she flashed a smile that put the dimples in her cheeks—when she looked like a little girl. It made her seem younger than her twenty-six years and hid the inner strength that allowed her to stand among giants when necessary. Egon loved her, and—judging from the number of people present from *Kuroshima*—so did her crew.

Egon felt awkward as he considered the procedure for the ceremony. Naval marriages aboard ship were nondenominational by regulation.

Which is a good thing, Egon thought with a grin. A denominational ceremony would have been a nightmare. Talara was Jewish, and her Semitic origins were obvious in her dark eyes, hair, and features.

She'd been attending both Jewish and Catholic services when he'd met her, and Egon was still unsure what her actual faith was in terms of religion. Egon was descended from Welsh, German, Irish, and Amer-Indian culture. His parents were Christian, and he'd been raised in that faith. Yamashita, who would conduct the ceremony in place of a chaplain, was Shinto as well as a devoted disciple of Buddhism.

Try getting a denominational ceremony out of that, he thought wryly. The humble Yamashita would've had to be rabbi, priest, minister *and* monk at the same time. The mental picture of Yamashita wearing a *yarmulke* while wearing Buddhist robes made Egon chuckle.

Dress uniforms were black and gold. Egon's had the twin golden rings of a lieutenant on its sleeves and a pair of golden-ringed silver planets—the rank of a senior lieutenant—on his collar and shoulder-boards. A golden delta badge embossed with a gunsight glowed prominently above the ribbons on his left breast, identifying him as a tactical officer. A regulation saber hung from a scabbard at his left hip and his hands were encased in gloves of white silk. He rubbed his gloved hands together, fidgeting nervously.

Combat was something he'd trained for. Marriage was not. The idea of marriage made him nervous as hell and bordered on terror. Fighting alien fleets seemed far less frightening than dedicating one's life to another person.

He had no doubts about Talara, however. They hadn't been able to contact their families yet, due to the distances involved and the interstellar communication blackouts, which had understandably log-jammed communications with the war on. Messages had been sent, but they wouldn't arrive for several days. The views of their families were important to Egon and Talara, but they didn't matter that much in the end. They would be married, regardless of what anyone thought. Still, it would've been nice to have had their blessing.

A wedding in a combat zone would have precluded families from attending anyway, and Egon regretted the unfairness of that. On the other hand, if a marriage was to take place, this was the only time it could be done for the near future. Besides, he didn't want their families anywhere near a war zone. He or Talara might be killed in combat on any given day. Life in wartime could be short, and Egon had decided to grasp happiness when and where he found it. Life was too fleeting to put off what one wanted, especially if tomorrow might never come. He supposed that wasn't unusual for people in wartime regardless of the period of history. Their families would understand.

Lieutenant Levi Harrigan, Egon's best man, was standing beside him. Resplendent in dress blues and a white cap, he was grinning like the proverbial Cheshire cat. The expression made Egon wonder if his best friend was happy to see him get married or was merely amused at how uncomfortable Egon felt.

"The Skipper's approaching, Egon." Harrigan seemed relaxed, and Egon felt mild jealousy at his ability to remain so calm. "She'll be ready any moment now on the far side. Do you have the ring?"

Egon blinked. "What?"

"The ring, knucklehead. As in *wedding* ring."

"Oh, yeah. I almost forgot."

Egon dug in the pocket of his uniform and stared at the Rigelian naval crest on Harrigan's cap. Dress uniforms were ridiculous things to wear on modern starships. They were uncomfortable, easily soiled and as archaic as stone knives, not to mention the fact it was impossible to get a vac-suit over them. The Navy loved its traditions, however, including any excuse to play dress-up. His fingers found the ring and he pulled it from his pocket. It was a simple band, white gold rather than yellow. It wasn't the ring he wanted to give her, but it was the best that could be replicated aboard *Agni*. The final ring would have to wait until they were safely home.

If we survive to get home.

He handed it to Harrigan, who deftly placed it on a white-gloved pinkie and assumed a position of parade rest. Harrigan nodded toward the far end of the boat bay. "Here she comes, guy. Make ready."

Egon stared across the boat bay looking for Talara. She exited a hatch on the far side of the bay with her maid of honor, Lieutenant Junior-Grade Prescilla Monet.

In contrast to Egon's black and gold uniform, Talara had chosen dress whites, hoping the contrast would approximate the traditional bridal gown. Unlike everyone else in the boat bay, neither bride nor groom wore caps, though Talara's command cap was attached to her belt as regulations required for a starship captain. Her black tresses were done up in braids and tied behind, with a single braid draping down the nape of her neck that was pinned up to keep it off her collar. Her bangs fell to her eyebrows, and sideburn wisps draped in front of each ear down to her jaw line. A pair of nonregulation crystal earrings dangled in each earlobe. She wore little makeup, but she didn't require much.

Egon felt her dark eyes lock onto his like fire control scanners from across the boat bay. There was no malice in the lock-on, however, only adoration. Her eyes sparkled, though her usually impish face remained serious.

Yamashita had explained the ceremony in advance the

night before. They would be positioned at the top of a large T at opposite ends of the boat bay. Each party would move to the center from those positions, halt and face Yamashita. He would perform the ceremony, after which they'd about-face and march down the long leg of the T through the honor guard and spectators to Montgomery's personal cutter, which waited to whisk them away for a short honeymoon. Task Force Seventeen's commander had graciously given them two days off-duty in Pan-Ku's distinguished visitor quarters before they had to return to their ships.

The sound of a bugle suddenly cut across the boat bay, and formations of people snapped to attention in unison. Shouted commands were given on the far side of the boat bay. Egon watched as a Marine honor guard marched up on either side of the imaginary T leg, trailed by eight naval officers in dress uniform wearing sabers. Both groups halted and faced inward, then assumed positions of parade rest.

A drum roll sounded. Egon snapped to attention in concert with Harrigan, noting with pride that Talara did the same thing with her bride's maid at the opposite end of the bay. The commander of Task Unit 22.1.1, Commodore George Quan, stepped forward and took Talara's arm. She'd chosen him to give her away in her father's stead. Quan was the senior officer of the task unit *Kuroshima* was assigned to. The dignified little commodore from Yamato's resort city of New Saigon had his flag aboard the carrier *Enterprise*. He seemed as pleased as punch to be escorting one of his tin can skippers down the aisle of matrimony.

Though Talara had met the commodore for the first time only two days ago, she'd intuitively known Quan was the right man for the job, and Egon trusted her instincts. Of course, Talara's first choice had been Yamashita, but that was impossible since he was the one performing the ceremony.

The traditional strains of the wedding march blared over the boat bay speakers as Egon and Harrigan walked slowly toward Talara and the commodore at the top of the T. With entourages in tow, they halted a few feet from each other at the apex of the T.

Egon could see Talara's face was glowing. The commodore took a step back and assumed a position of attention. As one, Egon and Levi did a facing movement, ending up with Talara to Egon's immediate left as they faced the dais, where Yamashita stood waiting. The soft strains of the bridal march slowly faded away. The sergeant of the honor guard issued a guttural command, and the honor guard snapped to attention in a single movement.

"Ladies and gentlemen, please stand at ease and be seated." Yamashita's voice reverberated through the boat bay, amplified by the podium's microphone over speakers. People shuffled to comfortable positions and sat in the rows of chairs that had been placed in the boat bay. A soft hubbub filled the air, then quickly faded away. Yamashita put his white-gloved hands on the edges of the podium and stared out across the gathered crowd.

"We assemble today to bring together two people in the holy bond of matrimony. I don't believe this battleship's designers ever envisioned a wedding taking place here when they designed her, but here we are. I find the setting appropriate for this pair of individuals, given the circumstances. I promise not to keep you here long, as we all have work to do, as do these two . . . though I think it's safe to assume their immediate *endeavors* will probably be far more fun than ours, at least for the next forty-eight hours."

The crowd chuckled. Yamashita smiled as the laughter wormed its way across the hangar deck. Talara blushed, causing Yamashita's grin to grow larger. Then his face grew serious.

"It's rare in life that two souls find each other across the gulf of space and time and come together as one. It's rarer still when that bonding occurs in the middle of a war. I'll tell you about these two people and the obstacles they've overcome to be here.

"The crew of *Agni* knows Lieutenant Storm quite well, as he puts them through their drills every other day. Originally assigned to *Shiva*, Egon transferred with me when I took command of *Agni*, and serves as my staff tactical officer, as well as TAC-O for Task Unit 17.2.1. He is a fine officer and a good man, one I'm pleased to call a friend as well as a subordinate.

"Lieutenant Commander Talara Kibbleman is certainly no stranger to the crew of *Kuroshima*, but many of you may not know her, so let me tell you about this beautiful young lady. Talara was junior engineer aboard *Kuroshima* and a newly-promoted lieutenant only a month ago. Within hours of that promotion, she unexpectedly found herself in command when all that vessel's senior officers were killed in the attack on this system.

"Despite being a junior officer and an engineer, she unflinchingly assumed command of *Kuroshima* and got her into space within hours of the attack. She then commanded that vessel in battle under Rear Admiral LeMieux during his defense of this system, taking out an enemy cruiser, then in another battle under my command in Gallagher. Due to her actions commanding *Kuroshima*, she was frocked to lieutenant commander two days ago by Admiral LeMieux himself . . . which has to be the shortest time-in-grade for any lieutenant in naval history. Her efforts and bravery were noticed by the Admiralty. She's a beautiful, charming lady and we're lucky to have her as one of our own."

Yamashita paused. "After the Centauri attack, due to circumstances we all know too well, each believed the other dead, killed in the attack. Egon was with me on *Shiva* when we wormholed out of Centauri during that attack, and we had no time to communicate. Despite overwhelming grief—or perhaps because of it—each continued to lead and fight. Despite their personal hells, they kept doing their jobs to the best of their ability in the finest traditions of the Navy, while believing the other lost.

"A week ago I had the privilege of reuniting them, when I read a roster showing that *Kuroshima* was in Centauri Seven and had survived the battle. You can imagine what a heart-warming reunion that was."

CHAPTER 27

"They decided to marry immediately, before the war could pull them apart again. I can't tell you how humbled, pleased, and honored I am that they asked me to perform their ceremony. I do so with a grateful heart and wish them Godspeed in their future lives together. So let us wait no longer. Lieutenant Storm, front and center."

Egon snapped to attention and stepped to the podium. The sharpness of his movements would have done a Marine proud. Clicking his heels, he faced Yamashita and saluted. "Sir, Lieutenant Storm, reporting as ordered."

Yamashita inspected Egon's uniform with a practiced eye, returned the salute, and assumed a serious expression. "Lieutenant Storm, we gather here to conduct a marriage. Is it your wish to proceed?"

"Yes, Sir. It is."

"Very well. Lieutenant Commander Talara Kibbleman, front and center."

Talara stepped forward, stopped at Egon's left side and saluted.

"Sir, Lieutenant Commander Kibbleman, reporting as ordered."

Yamashita returned her salute. "Lieutenant Commander, you appear here today pursuant to a marriage between yourself and Lieutenant Egon Storm. Is it your wish to proceed?"

Talara's soprano reply was soft. "Yes, Sir."

"Very well. Honor Guard, attend!"

The honor guard leader, a Marine sergeant in dress greens and chrome accoutrements, snapped to attention and faced his troops. "Detail, atten-shun!"

The Marines snapped to attention, the sound echoing across the boat bay. Yamashita faced the adjutant. "Officer of the Deck, are there any objections recorded to the marriage of Lieutenant Storm and Lieutenant Commander Kibbleman?"

The OOD came to attention and faced Yamashita. "No objections have been logged, Sir."

"Are there any present who object to this union?"

The boat bay remained silent.

"Very well." Yamashita faced to the audience and motioned with his right hand. Harrigan subtly slipped the wedding ring into Egon's right hand—no mean feat while wearing silk gloves—and Talara placed her left hand into Egon's left hand.

Yamashita cleared his throat. "Lieutenant Egon Malachai Storm, do you take Lieutenant Commander Talara Rachael Kibbleman as your lawfully wedded wife, pursuant to interstellar law and naval custom; to have and to hold, to protect and to ward, to love and to cherish, in full view of those present?"

Egon smiled as he looked into Talara's eyes. "I do."

"And you, Lieutenant Commander Talara Rachael Kibbleman, do you take Lieutenant Egon Malachai Storm to be your lawfully wedded husband, pursuant to interstellar law and naval custom; to have and to hold, to protect and ward, to love and to cherish, in full view of those present?"

Talara's eyes were liquid pools. "I do."

"Are these oaths made freely of your own volition, without coercion, duress, or the desire for illicit gain?"

"They are," Egon and Talara replied in unison.

Yamashita assumed the position of parade rest. That was the signal for Egon, who carefully removed the white glove from Talara's left hand and placed the gold band on her third finger. Talara's eyes glistened, and Egon would have died a thousand deaths to keep that expression in her eyes. She stared at the ring with a mixture of wonder and joy. Then she produced a similar band, removed Egon's left glove and slipped it on his ring finger.

Yamashita snapped to attention. "The bride and groom have placed the wedding bands, symbolic of marriage, upon each other's fingers. That done, I, Saburo Tadashi Yamashita, Captain, Rigelian Confederation Navy, under the authority vested in me as master of the battleship *Agni*, by naval law and interstellar accord, do hereby legally proclaim these officers to be husband and wife."

Egon drew Talara into his arms and kissed her and was devil enough to slip his tongue into the act. Talara, caught off guard, giggled. The boat bay exploded with laughter and applause.

Yamashita's face was beaming. "That concludes the ceremony. The bride and groom may depart. Congratulations, Mr. and Mrs. Storm. *Bon voyage*."

The honor guard leader shouted. "Detail, present . . . arms!"

The applause continued as the honor guard pivoted inward and presented arms with gauss rifles. In unison, the eight officers behind them drew sabers and crossed them above the path to the cutter.

Egon and Talara performed an about face. Egon moved to her right side and took her right arm in his left, then led his bride between the rows of Marines and under the crossed sabers of the naval officers as he took her to the cutter.

The cheers and applause in the boat bay were still deafening when the cutter's hatch closed behind them.

CHAPTER 28

GROESBECK NAVAL BASE, ODESSA
NEW TEXAS SYSTEM

Comforti grimaced as the shuttle descended through New Texas' cloudy stratosphere and the turbulence threw him against the side of his seat. The motion slammed his recently healed arm into the bulkhead, sending a twinge of pain through the limb. Bio-nannites had repaired the fracture, but the arm still tended to ache.

Descending into atmosphere from space was much like cliff diving into an ocean; one never knew how rough the current was below. The incredible reduction of velocity, the soupy thickness of the atmospheric medium, and induced turbulence were annoying to a man who spent most of his life in space.

After Task Force Seventeen's arrival at Centauri Seven, Comforti had been placed on medical leave and sent home. He'd quickly turned command over to Laird and departed. No doubt his case had been made easier for his superiors by the fact that New Texas was only two stargate jumps from Centauri Seven. Bobby Joe had assumed command, and the Navy had cut Comforti leave orders, signed by Rear Admiral LeMieux himself. Laird would remain as Gant's new CO. Comforti had assured that with the brass before catching a transport to Galderon, where he'd caught a connecting liner to New Texas.

It was good to be back, but Comforti hadn't enjoyed the trip. He'd had too much time to reflect on the carnage he'd seen in Pan'vu and Centauri Seven. The viciousness of the battles and the death toll in people—especially on Turin's World—made it difficult for him to be happy or sleep well. Many people had died, and Comforti couldn't help but feel that some of those deaths were his fault. At least two of the dead had been personnel under his command, kids who'd trusted him to bring them home alive, and he'd failed them.

Worse than his tactical error during the first engagement of the war and the damage *Gant* had suffered was the fact that the warning he'd sent to Pan'vu had never reached Turin's World or Centauri Seven, which likely wouldn't have occurred if he'd made a proper tactical decision during that battle. Had he done so, *Gant* would have not been damaged, and he could've warned Pan'vu in a timely manner. Which meant the whole disaster at Centauri Seven might never have occurred. LeMieux had assured him he was taking too much responsibility for events whose prevention was conjectural at best, but Comforti felt guilty anyway.

CHAPTER 28

His using PDMs to target torpedoes when lasers would have done the job instantly had been stupid. That stupidity had allowed the horrible chain of events to occur, resulting in the deaths of two crewmen aboard *Gant*, thousands on Turin's World, and more at Centauri Seven.

He *had* known better. That's what bothered him most. He was well-trained and had still made the mistake. He could find no excuse, no personal forgiveness for that. On reflection, he suspected he'd grown soft in the peacetime Navy. When combat had finally found him, he hadn't been truly prepared, despite his years of training to be so. The mental leap from peacetime to war had been a bridge too far, but he felt he should've been able to do it.

It was understandable, perhaps, for combat induced grim reality checks on personal worldviews. There'd been no war in Comforti's lifetime beyond the occasional pirate battle, and the likelihood of interstellar war had seemed as remote to him as to everyone else. The Confederation and the Empire had been in the midst of peaceful trade talks. No one had believed the Empire might strike without warning. Nevertheless, it was a military officer's job to be ready for just such surprises. That was his credo, his job description and his task as a Navy professional. That he'd not been as ready as he should have been had taken a toll on his self-esteem, riddling him with guilt.

Comforti had been forced to take a hard look at himself. He'd always demanded much of himself in his personal standards, and because of that he had expected to have performed better than he actually had. His sloppy reaction time and mushy decision-making had gotten two of his people killed. He'd let himself and the crew of *Gant* down terribly.

Comforti had forced himself to write letters to the families of those who'd died, doing so with a hellish intensity. It had been tough to do, for their blood was on his hands, but he'd made himself do it. He owed it to the families of the people who'd died under his command, and he would no more shrink from that responsibility or his culpability in it than he would from anything else. A skipper remained responsible, and that was especially true when bad things happened.

Coming home wasn't an easy, either. V-mail from Sue and the kids had dried up long before the first shots of the war had been fired in Pan'vu. Communications home had been nonexistent since. It was possible there were valid reasons for that, such as the shutdown of civil communications networks to support military traffic, but he didn't believe that was the cause.

He and Sue had been suffering marital difficulties for years. Somehow, he never seemed to live up to her expectations, and her family had never approved of him or his career. To Sue's family, service was something done by *servants*, not the elites of society. His willingness to participate in what they considered "manual labor" put him beneath their contempt.

Sue's unrealistic expectations and haughty demeanor irritated him at the best of times and infuriated him at the worst. Over time, as her disapproval had grown, he'd voluntarily returned to space more often to avoid conflicts. As love had turned to frustration and disgust, he'd hidden in the routine of military life and deployment rather than face the fact they'd grown apart. The relationship had reached a low point before his last cruise, when he'd realized he didn't really know his wife anymore.

Sue feels I've failed her, he thought with overwhelming bitterness. *She's been pulling away for some time, trying to turn me into something I'm not and will never be. I'm proud of who and what I am, yet she's disappointed. The one person who should be most proud of me, the one person who's supposed to be there unconditionally is the one most disappointed by what I am. She knew I was going to be a naval officer when she married me. If it was good enough then, why is it not good enough now? If she didn't love me, why did she marry me?*

Comforti wasn't sure he wanted to know the answer.

The lack of correspondence was a clear indication she'd left him. She'd been disappointed and frustrated too long; too angry about the military and it constantly pulling him away. *She's probably decided to find someone else,* he thought, *someone more presentable to Daddy.*

The thought left a bitter ache in his chest, which loomed before him as inevitable as death.

I feel horrible for the kids. Jarrod's a tough boy but old enough to accept the situation without too much harm, but Sarah Jesse? Can I bear being pushed away and never see my babies grow up?

It suddenly struck him that Sarah was no longer a baby. Jarrod was a teenager. *Where did the time go? When* did the months and years slip by? It seems they were just born yesterday, maybe a year or two ago at most.

Maybe Sue has a point. Perhaps I have been gone too much.

The Navy had taken from him the things that mattered most in life, and he'd gone along willingly. He'd been content to play skipper, distracting himself with duties and responsibilities while the truly important thing in life had passed him by, the family he'd unwittingly abandoned.

Sue's right. All this time I've been in space, doing what I thought was important, when what was truly important was always at home. What's more important than family, a home and raising children? They've been there all along, waiting for my attention and I shoved them away every time they needed me most.

Suddenly the price of service became woefully apparent to Harl Comforti.

He'd come home to resign. His mistakes, in combat and in private life, had proven his ineptitude if nothing else. Despite the accolades LeMieux had showered on him for the rescues in Pan'vu and the fight at the Centauri Seven stargate, he had failed the Navy and his family. It was perhaps too late to fix the family, but if he couldn't serve the Navy better than he had, he had no business being part of it.

He was coming home at last, available for the civilian employment his wife had always begged him to take, but now his wife was likely gone, and she'd have taken the kids with her. He was probably a bachelor again and dreaded facing an empty home. *A divorced bachelor most likely,* he corrected himself. The thought made his feelings of failure almost unbearable. He'd no real home to return to now, no family to greet him. In the end, he'd been left by those that he had himself abandoned. There would be only an empty house and likely custody battles in court.

Who's here when I need them, he wondered. Despite his despair, a part of his mind answered. *Who was there for them when they needed you?*

The shuttle banked as the pilot initiated the approach to Groesbeck's spaceport. Below, aquamarine patterns shimmered in the Saltgrass Sea as the shuttle approached the white beaches of Midland. The craft settled as it descended, calming as it moved into the denser air near the surface.

Comforti looked at the letter in his hand. Only Laird knew what the letter contained. Laird had tried to talk him out of it, of course, but to no avail. Comforti had been careful not to mention his resignation intentions to LeMieux, who would've screamed with indignation. Professional officers did not resign in the middle of a war. Such things were not done. He'd signed the letter the night before, on the transport from Galderon after it had passed through the New Texas stargate. All that was left was to submit it to BuPers through the personnel office at Groesbeck.

Of course, they wouldn't actually let him resign, not with a war going on. The "stop loss" laws would prevent it, especially with the Confederation struggling to call up reserves. His resignation wouldn't get him released from duty, but it would certainly take him off the list of future command opportunities and end his career once the war was over. Promotions would be withheld.

The Navy didn't approve of quitters.

Funny how a piece of paper can hold so much power over a man's life, he thought. *It seems strange that some ink on a piece of paper can destroy me when enemy warships could not.*

The shuttle banked again. He found himself staring through the port, watching the pea-green sea of the *Pampas* grasslands drift past below, splotched here and there with darker patches of mesquite and violet feather-willow, a native plant that surrounded the base.

There was a change in the whine of the drive as the shuttle pilot brought up its Planck field and decelerated, switching to anti-grav. A gentle thump followed as the shuttle's gear touched the landing pad.

For the first time in almost a half a year he was home again. It felt hollow now, with a powerful sense of loss; something he'd never expected to feel coming home. It was both terrible and overwhelming, as if life itself was at an end.

The passengers stood and retrieved their bags from overhead compartments as soon as the seatbelt lights were out. As the crew opened the pressure hatch at the forward entrance, Comforti sighed. He realized it was a subconscious fear of vacuum carried by all humans who spent much time in space. The constant fear of explosive decompression subsided only when back on a planet's surface. A spacer didn't dwell on it, but the fear always lurked in the back of one's mind. Comforti seldom noticed it in space, but it became apparent when he landed dirtside.

He felt the inflow of humidity. The air had the smell of the sea, a salty fragrance that wafted into the compartment. He stood awkwardly amid the mix of passengers as they rushed to depart the shuttle. He was in no hurry. There was nowhere to go; no place to be, no pressure to be anywhere on time.

He lifted his space bag and hoisted it on his good shoulder, holding the resignation letter in the hand of his damaged arm. With a sense of impending doom, he followed the last passenger through the hatch and down the ramp. A crewman said goodbye as he reached landing pad, where he paused to take a deep breath of humid salt air.

A brightly colored buzzdragon hovered before his face, riding the ocean breeze as it hovered, its glass-like wings beating furiously in a blur. It was similar to a Terran dragonfly, especially the transparent wings, but the creature was reptilian more than insect. Mottled in blue and green, it stared at him with strange, strawberry-like eyes before flitting away on the breeze.

He was indeed home.

Comforti turned to walk to the terminal. A uniformed man waited for him a few feet away. The man had white hair, a dark tan, and piercing blue eyes that stared at him through a wreath of crow's feet, but it wasn't the eyes that held his attention. It was the three stars of a vice admiral on the man's collar. It wasn't just any flag officer, either, but Vice Admiral Torrance, executive officer of Second Fleet.

"Welcome home, Commander." Torrance smiled and stepped forward. It wasn't a predatory smile but seemed genuine. "You and I need to talk."

Comforti snapped to attention and saluted. Torrance returned the salute and shook his hand, causing Comforti to shift his space bag to the other arm.

"So you're the CO of *Gant* I've heard so much about. I read Montgomery's report on Centauri Seven and Gallagher and LeMieux's report on the battle at the stargate. You did a hell of a job out there, son. You've done Second Fleet proud."

Comforti blinked his eyes in confusion. "Sir?"

"The engagements in Pan'vu, Centauri Seven and Gallagher. That was truly outstanding work."

Comforti frowned. He certainly knew who Torrance was, for he'd sat in staff meetings with the man on many occasions. Being a destroyer CO, however, placed him pretty low in the pecking order for him to have been taken note of by a vice admiral. In fact, he'd been certain Torrance had no clue who he was. Something had changed, and Comforti wasn't sure if that was a good thing or not. To have a vice admiral—the XO of 2nd Fleet no less—greet a field-grade officer at a shuttle ramp boggled his mind.

"Admiral . . . well, thank you, Sir. I don't know what you've heard about what happened in Pan'vu, but—"

"Indeed I have, and it was outstanding, Commander." Torrance beamed with admiration. "What happened to Turin's World is horrible, of course. We'll pay the bastards back for that, I assure you, but you saved a lot of people in the orbitals there; people who'd be dead if you and your crew hadn't rescued them. More importantly, you detected the Karsian attack before anyone knew it was coming and fired the first shot of the war, successfully destroying an enemy bladeship. The subsequent fights in Pan'vu and Centauri Seven are already famous. No other skipper in the fleet has *two* bladeship kills to his credit."

"Are you *sure* you read the correct reports, Admiral? Perhaps if you'd read this letter—"

"I don't need a letter to know about you, son. I have your superiors' reports on my desk. You're a hero here in New Texas. Nice try attempting to sneak home without any fanfare. The reporters will swarm you if they find out you're here. I only found because I saw your name on the shuttle manifest at base ops. By the way, your wife and children are well, Commander. You have a fine family. You should be proud."

Comforti swallowed, hoping it wasn't audible. "My . . . wife, Sir?"

"Yes. A wonderful lady, the very example of a Navy spouse."

"Are we talking about *my* wife, Sir?"

"We are." Torrance laughed and clapped him on the shoulder. "Have no doubts about her, son. She's the talk of the town here at Groesbeck, and some of the things she's done for Navy families are simply amazing. I know you're eager to get home and start your well-deserved leave, so I won't keep you. I just wanted to drop by, welcome you back personally, and tell you how proud of you we are. I want you to drop by my office tomorrow, however. I want to hear about those battles firsthand, from someone who was actually there. In addition, I have some insight on your next assignment."

"My . . . *next* assignment?"

"You're bound for bigger things than a tin can, son. We need good, capable leaders in the Navy. You've set an example, and it hasn't gone unnoticed. But we'll talk about that tomorrow. Right now, there're some folks anxiously waiting for you. I see no reason to keep them waiting."

Torrance hooked a thumb at the terminal and Comforti stared in disbelief.

Sue stood at the entrance, shielding her eyes from the sun with one hand as she smiled in his direction. She wore a sea-green cotton dress, and her brown hair fluttered in the wind. Beside her, Jarrod and Sarah were jumping up and down with excitement.

Torrance took the space bag from Comforti's hand.

"I'll give this to the purser, Commander, and have it delivered to your house. You have higher priorities to attend to."

"I can carry it, Admiral—"

"No." Torrance patted him gently on the back and smiled. "Go see your family, son. That's an order."

Comforti saluted again, sharply. Torrance returned the salute, watching in amusement as Comforti dashed across the ramp toward his family. They quickly became a knot of people hugging each other tightly. Torrance turned away, smiling as he stared out over the sea.

CHAPTER 28

On the ground behind him, the unopened resignation letter fluttered on the pavement. A passing gust of wind suddenly whipped it off the ground and a rising thermal carried it high into the air.

A moment later a passing breeze carried it out to sea.

EPILOGUE

Liquid eyes stared through the transparent bulkhead at the myriad of stars pinning the velvet of space against the firmament. The larger yellow eyes of the Yahntai bulged as it turned its wide, squat body toward the fragile Reticulan.

<So where was the great clash of fleets?>

<It is yet to come.> The Reticulan moved its black eyes away from the view. <We have observed only the first culling. More of what these species call 'time' will be required, but all proceeds according to our plan. The phages in this dimension are diverse, but these two are the most promising for the transduction that we desire. Only crucible will eliminate weaker elements and create the strand we need. There is no cause for concern.>

<This is dangerous.> The Yahntai shuddered and settled on its foot. <The humans are unpredictable, a random and deadly virus. Using them could induce chaos. They are a vector that makes accurate prediction difficult.>

<We are able to control them.> The Reticulan moved past a pair of blue toad-like dumong, who flushed violet

with irritation. Folding its arms the Reticulan inclined its head toward the viewport. <*Both strains remain unaware of our reality. They have had only limited contact with this dimension. What they know of us comes through their dreams and legends.*>

<*It is their dreams we fear most.*> There was a taste of terror in the Yahntai's thought. <*Both strains have imagination. Imagination cannot be controlled, not like genetics. Imagination is impossible to contain. Overlooking that could be a grave mistake. We must take care with what strains we release into the Continuum.*>

<*Other species with free will have been culled in the past.*> The Reticulan shrugged. <*We have always managed to control them.*>

<*Is your memory so short? What of the Fleahr and the Garoong? Did we keep control of them? We were completely unable to control the El, and the El almost destroyed us. These humans greatly resemble the El.*>

The Reticulan tilted its head. <*We were able to control the El, too . . . in the end.*>

"*We disagree. We do not yet control even the handful of* El *that survive.*> The Yahntai quivered irritably. <*The El lived among these humans once. They may have induced mutations in the species we have not accounted for.*>

<*Humans barely remember the El, only ancient legends and myths. We have monitored their collective thoughts. The El have not dwelt among humans for many of their centuries, and humans no longer believe they are real, only myth. Their lack of belief has sapped the Els' power. Unlike the El, we have*

complete domination of both species in this dimension. They will accomplish whatever task we assign them.>

<*We are not as sure.*> The Yahntai settled its bulk in a depression on the deck and pulsed its displeasure. <*We fear unleashing a vector that cannot be contained; a virus we have no immunity against. They could infect many galaxies in this plane alone. They are dangerous to allow to exist. If they learn of us and their history . . .>*

<*They cannot. Their conscious minds are trapped within this dimension.*>

<*It is their subconscious minds we fear. Already their technology probes alternate dimensions. They have imagination and they dream. If they wake from their dream, we could be placed in great peril; a chain-reaction which cannot be controlled. We would do better to exterminate them and start over.*>

<*Perhaps.*> The Reticulan fixed its eyes on the Yahntai. <*It may be as you fear. We will proceed cautiously with this test before deciding. It is true they pose a potential risk, but they may also be our best hope. To be useful they must be tempered and forged. Note the ships of the Karsian strain gathering near the sixth inter-dimensional tunnel they call 'Nangtashgu.' The clash will continue until transduction occurs. If the humans prove to be what we need, it will be apparent. If not, the test will take other, less interesting turns. In that case, neither strain will exist long enough to become the threat you fear.*>

<*So you believe.*> The Yahntai trembled. <*Have you maintained the proper controls on them?*>

<Of course. Through religion we have always controlled them. By distracting them with images, we keep them from discovering their true nature and blind them to their powers. It has been so since their creation. Both cultures remain trapped within the three-dimensional space-time matrix of their physical senses. With only five senses they are unable to comprehend reality.>

<No, but they imagine.> The Yahntai's tone made its fear evident. <They dream, learn, and evolve. Therein lies the danger. That is how they could destroy us in the end. How long must we risk infection of the Continuum? We must move carefully for we play with great danger.>

The Reticulan moved toward the mind panel that controlled the dimensional craft they were on. <Culling must proceed to determine which strain is worthy to continue. In the interim, we might as well enjoy the drama. The ramifications for both species are most intriguing.>

The Yahntai balked. <Hardly. They may be our greatest creation or become monsters that awaken and devour us all.>

The Reticulan was beyond emotion, yet there was something amusing about the Yahntai's fear of a biological primate. Yahntai were like that, always worrying over every possibility, fearful of everything, despite their vast technology. It was best to let Yahntai believe one agreed with them.

<Those are indeed possibilities.> The Reticulan's admission caused it black eyes to ripple in its teardrop skull. <It keeps the game interesting.>

The Reticulan pressed a palm into a recess on the

EPILOGUE

curved wall and the violet saucer transcended dimensions and vanished, leaving only stars behind to watch the fleet gather at the stargate.

END

www.ingramcontent.com/pod-product-compliance
Lightning Source LLC
Chambersburg PA
CBHW060759030726
47503CB00002B/315